PRAISE FOR THE NOVELS
OF SUSAN DONOVAN

"Ms. Donovan knows how to tell a story that will make
your heart melt."　　　　　　　—Night Owl Reviews

"Impossible to put down. . . . Susan Donovan is an absolute riot."　　　　　　　　　—Romance Junkies

"Goofy comedy, white-hot sex, and ticking-bomb pacing."　　　　　　　　　　　　—*Publishers Weekly*

"Donovan proves that she will have serious star power
in the years to come."　　　—Romance Reader at Heart

Also by Susan Donovan

Sea of Love

THE SWEETEST SUMMER

*A Bayberry Island
Novel*

SUSAN DONOVAN

A SIGNET SELECT BOOK

SIGNET SELECT
Published by the Penguin Group
Penguin Group (USA) LLC, 375 Hudson Street,
New York, New York 10014

USA | Canada | UK | Ireland | Australia | New Zealand | India | South Africa | China
penguin.com
A Penguin Random House Company

First published by Signet Select, an imprint of New American Library,
a division of Penguin Group (USA) LLC

First Printing, August 2014

ISBN 978-0-451-41929-3

Printed in the United States of America
10   9   8   7   6   5   4   3   2   1

In loving memory of my mother,
Beverly J. Flick Lewis, 1928–2013.

All the world is made of faith, and trust, and pixie dust.

—J. M. Barrie, *Peter Pan*

Eighteen years ago . . .

"How's it comin', boys?"

Clancy Flynn ignored the police chief and pretended to focus on his cruel and unusual punishment. Old Pollard didn't really care how much bird shit they'd scraped off the mermaid statue since sunrise. He came to Fountain Square only to snicker and make sure they had suffered enough to "learn their lesson."

Pollard didn't have much else to do. Being a small-town police chief must be kind of lame. It probably got old walking around thinking you're such a badass, protecting the mean streets of Bayberry Island, Massachusetts, from the evil of spray-painted cuss words.

When Clancy grew up, he was going to have a wicked awesome job. A *real* job. The kind you could get on the mainland.

"It's going great, Chief!" Chip Bradford was Clancy's best friend, even though he could be a brown-noser sometimes. "I got dibs on the neck up, including all her hair!"

"We're making progress, sir." Mickey Flaherty put his head down and scrubbed the statue's barely covered boobage, like it was the most fascinating thing in the world.

"Looks like you got the good stuff, Flaherty." Pollard chuckled.

"Yep, I did—everything from the neck to the sweet spot."

"And how about you, Clancy? Did you know there are two thousand, four hundred and twenty-four individual scales in that mermaid tail?"

I do now.

"The mayor asked how you're doing this fine morning."

I just bet he did.

"What should I tell him?"

Clancy held his toothbrush thoughtfully in midair. "You can tell my father that I believe this experience has already made me a better human being."

Pollard let go with a laugh so loud it scared the birds from the bushes. That was the worst part of the situation. All the adults thought it was hilarious. His dad had laughed his ass off when he heard that the three of them were arrested for spray painting the back of Wilbury Drug & Dime and sentenced to a week of prefestival community service. He especially enjoyed hearing that the slave labor would include scrubbing every inch of the mermaid fountain with toothbrushes and a bucket of Ivory soap bubbles.

"Keep up the good work, gentlemen."

They waited until Pollard was beyond hearing range. Mickey was the first to say something. "I hate this island. I can't wait to graduate and get off this stupid fuckin' rock and never come back."

"It's not that bad." Chip always saw the best in everything, which sometimes annoyed the hell out of Clancy. "Besides, you haven't even started tenth grade yet, so you should probably chill out and make the most of the time you have here."

Mickey didn't appreciate the positive crap either.

"Yeah, well, this week has totally sucked balls, in case you weren't paying attention, Chipper Chippity-Chip-Chip."

"Don't call me that or I'll crack you upside your dome."

"I'd like to see you try."

Clancy rolled his eyes. "Cut it out, assholes. The truth is we broke the law and we should pay the consequences."

Mickey laughed. "Oh, yeah? Who are you, the Prince of Bayberry Island?"

"We spray painted Wilbury's back wall, so we had to paint over it. That part makes sense. But you're right. The rest of this has been complete bullshit."

"I guess," Mickey said.

"At least all the stuff we did made the island look nice," Chip said.

"What are you, Martha-Chippin-Stewart?"

"Shut up, Mickey." Chip wasn't giving up on his quest to put a positive spin on their week from hell. "Think about it. All the flower beds are mulched and grass is mowed. The boardwalk is scrubbed and the tourist center is painted and the dune fences are repaired. And this is our last job, right? After we clean the mermaid statue, we'll be done."

"God, I hate this stupid mermaid."

Mickey's and Chip's toothbrushes went quiet. Clancy felt his friends staring at him, so he looked up. "What's the problem?"

"You shouldn't say that."

"Why not?"

"Because!" Chip's eyeballs bugged out. "That could be bad luck. She might hear you."

Clancy cracked up. "You're kidding, right? Because there's no way you actually believe this statue has magic powers to grant true love."

"I just don't think you should risk it," Chip muttered.

"Please tell us you're joking around, dude." Mickey

pointed his toothbrush toward Chip's face. "'Cause if you're being serious, that means you are more of a pussy than I thought you were. You're a pussy who believes in fairy tales."

"Stop it!" Chip looked like he was about to cry. "I don't know what I believe, okay, but the legend is important and it means a lot to a lot of people on this island, and we're, like, climbing all over her right now. I don't think this is the time to piss her off. She could put a curse on us or something."

Clancy laughed so hard he almost knocked the soap bucket off the scaffolding. "You can't piss off a pile of metal, okay?"

"She's made of bronze."

Mickey smacked himself in the forehead. "Bronze *is* a metal, you doof."

Chip's face was turning really red, and it wasn't because the morning sun was heating up. "Actually, Einstein, bronze is an alloy of several metals—most commonly brass, tin, and zinc. What I am saying is that everyone should just stop bad-mouthing her. *Please.*"

Not much cleaning was getting done by that point, so Clancy decided to have some serious fun with this.

"Oh, great mermaid!" He dropped his toothbrush into the calm water of the fountain basin and put a hand over his heart. "I come to you, dear magic maiden, with an open, honest heart. I seek something true and special." Clancy took the mermaid's slippery, smooth hand in both of his, and touched his lips to her cool knuckles.

"If you're not serious, you'd better stop *right now.*"

"Ignore Chip." Mickey smiled. "Go for it."

"Great mermaid, I come to you to ask for my first piece of ass. Please make sure her ta-tas are as nice as yours." Clancy tweaked a strand of the mermaid's long hair in the general nipple area.

"Oh, man. This isn't good." Chip began to climb off the ladder.

Clancy raised his voice and made it even more singsongy and dramatic. "But you can forget the love part, oh beautiful one! I don't believe in love. But I sure would appreciate that piece of ass if you can fit it into your busy schedule!"

Thunder rumbled off in the distance, which was weird because the sky had been clear.

"Uh, hey, dude." Mickey frowned and glanced around nervously. "Maybe Chip is right and you should, you know, shut the fuck up now."

Clancy just laughed, spurred on to greater heights of rudeness. "Oh, chick of the sea, babe of the waves! We can be real with each other, right? You and I know you're a total made-up lie—just a way for people to make a buck around here. You've got nothing to do with love, and all these freaks in costumes who come to celebrate you every summer with their open hearts and open wallets are complete dumbasses!"

A gasp rose from where Chip stood on the brick walkway below. "How can you even say stuff like that? You're a Flynn!"

"I am. So that means you can trust me when I tell you—the whole mermaid legend is a complete load of crap."

"You're on your own, dude." Mickey began climbing down, too. "Later."

"What's the matter?" Clancy howled with laughter. "Oh come on! You guys can't be for real! The mermaid legend has both of you whipped? Are you kidding?"

Thunder growled again, closer this time. Clancy's buddies tossed their toothbrushes onto the brick and bolted. Clancy busted out laughing again. "Gee, was it something I said?"

Since raging against the machine wasn't much fun without an audience, he decided to get down, go home, and grab some breakfast. He noticed that the mermaid's cool and smooth hand was still clutched in his own.

That's when it got weird.

A faint female laugh rose up around him, like a wispy

fog. He definitely heard it, but he also *felt* it. The sound tickled his skin and moved through his muscle and bone like a shiver, which was totally insane, because it was already above eighty.

Clancy raised his eyes to the mermaid's face. She was gazing out to sea, as she'd been doing since 1888 when his nutso great-great-grandfather built the fountain in honor of his wife, who he swore was a mermaid. But if her eyes hadn't moved, then why did it feel like she was staring right through him?

Suddenly, the wind picked up and rain began to pour. Clancy hauled ass down the ladder, got the hell out of there, and promised himself he'd never go back.

Chapter One

The insanity didn't officially begin for another twenty-four hours, but Police Chief Clancy Flynn knew the tourists didn't give a damn about the particulars. The half-dressed throng was already in full-on party mode. There was no avoiding it. This was Bayberry Island on the third Friday of August, and that meant that tomorrow would kick off the annual Mermaid Festival, the Mardi Gras of New England.

For Clancy, it was going to be the longest week of the year.

"Excuse me, Officer."

And here we go. "How can I help you, ma'am?"

"Ooooh, aren't you adorable? I love your little navy blue shorts! Why don't more policemen wear shorts? You have such nice legs from all that walking and frisking you have to do." She wagged an eyebrow. "You can call me Florence."

Clancy glanced down at the bejeweled and age-spotted hand now stroking his bare forearm. After four years as a Boston cop and thirty-two Mermaid Festivals—one for each year of his life—nothing along the spectrum of human behavior shocked him anymore. Not even Florence was particularly disturbing, even with her bottle red hair, neon cat's-eye sunglasses, sequined jumpsuit, and the fairy wings glued to the back of her sneakers.

"Sure, Florence. What can I do for you?"

"We were just wondering where the fountain is. You know, the mermaid statue. The legend. You see"—she gazed over the tops of her cat's-eye shades and fluttered her fake lashes—"we're here to find luuuuuuv." Florence and her entourage of similarly dressed older women giggled and hooted. "So do you know where she is?"

Yeah. He knew. Clancy was a Flynn, and his family would be forever linked to the bronze bimbo in Fountain Square, no matter how much he wished it weren't so.

"Of course, ladies." Clancy pointed down Main Street. "Two blocks that way is Fountain Square. You can't miss it."

Florence popped up on her tippy toes to look down the street and lost her balance, falling against Clancy. He returned her to an upright position.

"Where did you say it was, Officer?"

Clancy closed his eyes for an instant, imagining his happy place, that sweet spot of September, when the weather was still delightful and the pace of life returned to near normal. He smiled politely at the women. "Two blocks thataway. You'll see a big mermaid fountain right smack in the middle of the square, water spraying all over the place. The area is surrounded by banners and balloons. And lots of people. Plus, there's a real big sign."

Florence patted Clancy's chest with the flat of her palm. "You know, hearing you put it like that I feel kinda silly. Would you like to come with us?"

"Thank you, but I'll have to pass."

Florence shrugged. "Let's go, girls!" And off they went.

As Clancy watched the ladies walk arm in arm down the crowded street, he wondered what all these tourists would think if they knew the truth—that for nearly two decades, Police Chief Clancy Flynn hadn't been within twenty feet of the mermaid, which took some effort, since she was the island's only claim to fame, the engine of its entire economy, and the reason he had a twice-monthly paycheck. But his peace of mind was worth it.

Clancy's police radio crackled to life. It was Chip, his second-in-command.

"Flynn, here."

"Chief, we got about a dozen juveniles swimming past the rocks off Moondance Beach, a possible 10-51. Deon and I are taking the boat out. Over."

"Copy," Clancy said. "Any injuries?"

"Unknown. Lena called it in as a trespassing."

"10-4. Keep me posted. Flynn Out."

Underage drinking was always a problem throughout the tourist season, but during festival week it became a crisis. As police chief, Clancy felt personally responsible for the safety of every visitor to his island, especially kids. But sometimes it felt like festival-week tourists were trying awfully hard to get themselves killed. Not only were those kids probably drinking, they'd picked an area designated a no-swim zone because of its wicked riptide. To make matters worse, they were on Adelena Silva's private property, and nobody had to remind Clancy how much Bayberry's only celebrity despised trespassers.

Right on schedule, the long, monotone horn of the Nantucket passenger ferry announced its approach. For Clancy, the sound of the arriving boat was just background noise, part of life on Bayberry Island, like the roar of the sea, the rush of wind, and the cry of seabirds. But the rumble of the engine and bellow of the horn were enough to scare some of the tourists, who clasped hands over their ears as the boardwalk began to vibrate. Clancy made his way through the crowds toward the public dock, where he would perform a duty he'd done three times already that day and would do twice more before night-fall. Clancy made a point of greeting every passenger ferry that arrived during festival week, unless a dire emergency kept him away and his father, Mayor Frasier Flynn, stood in for him. Clancy wanted visitors to know they were welcome, but also that the Bayberry Island Police Department took its duty seriously. As he'd learned walking the beat in Boston, a little eye contact and a firm handshake were the most effective tools in crime prevention.

Clancy leaned his back against the public dock railing, hooking the heel of his shoe on the bottom metal rung. As always, he returned the friendly salute from Old John, the Nantucket Ferry conductor, who stood his post at the aluminum gangway. It took a good five minutes for the captain to complete his docking procedure and for Old John to open the gate for passengers.

Clancy couldn't help but smile as the latest batch of tourists descended. Barbie, his ex-wife, once asked him why he seemed to be in a bad mood during festival week. "Everyone seems so happy just to be here," she'd pointed out. "Can't you be happy for them?"

He was happy for them. He understood that everyone deserved a little time to cut loose and have fun, but it was his job to keep them safe while they were doing it. As it turned out, the foul mood Barbie noted wasn't due to the demands of his job at all—it was from living with her.

Clancy watched the tourists flow single file down the gangway and onto the dock. This was his favorite part of festival week, truth be told. He got a kick out of the kids, how their eyes grew huge at the sight of the colorful banners, balloons, street vendors, and costumes. It never took long before they began to squirm and jump up and down and the boldest ones tried to make a solo run for Main Street.

Though Clancy had been through this cycle every year of his life, it was impossible not to share in the delight he saw in most every visitor's face. For many of them, this was their annual getaway, the event they'd planned and saved for during the other fifty-one weeks of the year. And though there were no prizes awarded for costumes worn by ferry passengers, about half of the new arrivals made their grand entrance already dressed to impress.

Clancy blinked in surprise at a man who wore the purest display of gender confusion he'd ever seen. The dude's left side was all mermaid, with a shell bikini top, smooth skin, fake eyelashes and flowing hair, while his right side was all mer*man*, complete with a hairy chest, tattoos, and one hell of a five-o'clock shadow. Clancy had to give him extra points for self-expression.

"Hello. Welcome to Bayberry Island." Clancy tipped his chin, smiled, and shook hands with the mer*person* and a string of tourists who followed behind. "Hello. Have fun. Welcome."

He chatted with a few people, took pictures with a few more, and recognized many that had been coming to the festival for decades. Among them were Willa and Chet Chester, an older couple who had been regular guests at his family's bed-and-breakfast for decades. They happened to be lifelong nudists as well, founders of a parallel version of festival week for those who preferred to party in the buff. The nudist colony on the far side of the island did it up right. They had an opening ceremony, a parade, reenactments of the mermaid legend, plays, food, music, a craft fair, and a clambake—all of it done sans clothing.

"Chief Flynn!" Willa hugged him tight and delivered a damp kiss near his left ear.

Chet shook his hand firmly. "Nice to see you, son," he said.

"Mr. Chester, always a pleasure."

Willa slapped both her hands on Clancy's upper arms and squeezed tight, smiling up at him. "Now, my dear, when are we going to get you to come out and celebrate with us? Hmm?"

This was Willa's usual routine. Starting the summer Clancy turned eighteen, she began attempting to recruit him into the "lifestyle." It had never much appealed to him. He was the kind of guy who preferred to carefully choose who he wanted to see naked and then do so in a one-on-one kind of format. Hanging out with a hundred or so sunburned nudists draped in mermaid and sea captain accessories wasn't his thing. Never would be.

"Oh, Willa." He grinned at her. "You know I get out to Colony Beach at least a few times every festival week."

She waved her hand to dismiss his teasing reply. "Only when there's a problem. I'm talking about taking some time to come out and see how we do things, just relax and let everything go."

Like his boxers, no doubt.

"Festival week is crazy busy for me, Willa. You know that. But I appreciate the invite, as always."

She wagged her finger. "You don't know what you're missing, Clancy. Well, we should be off. Checking in right away. We can't wait to see all the renovations at the Safe Haven. How excited you all must be with all the changes on the island this year."

"Absolutely. Be safe, now."

Clancy resumed his glad-handing, hearing himself repeat his mantra: "Welcome to Bayberry Island . . . have fun and be safe . . . let me know if there's anything I can assist you with . . . two blocks that way . . . you can't miss it. . . ." All while he mulled over Willa's last comment. She was right. Everything had changed on Bayberry since this time last year. It began when Clancy's sister, Rowan, fell in love with a Boston blue blood with plans to inject loads of cash into the local economy. As good as all that was, seeing how Rowan and Ashton Louis Wallace III made each other happy was even better. In fact, he'd never seen two people more in love.

"Welcome . . . two blocks down . . . great costume . . . have fun. . . ."

Love.

The irony didn't escape Clancy. Day-to-day life on Bayberry Island revolved around the "mystical power of love," as his mother called it. Yet here he was, a naysayer, a nonbeliever. He didn't make a big deal about it, but everyone who knew him knew that he and "love" weren't exactly on speaking terms.

"Hello ... enjoy yourselves ... just two blocks that way ... really? ... all the way from Minnesota?"

It was simply a fact: the mermaid stuck it to him. It happened on the last day of festival week eighteen years ago, when Clancy stood right here on this dock, in tears, watching the most wonderful, funny, smart, and pretty girl he'd ever met board the ferry with her family. She promised to stay in touch but she never wrote. So much time had passed that he'd forgotten her name—Emma or Emily maybe—but he sure remembered how he felt about her. The only thing he had from that week was a Polaroid of the two of them dancing at the Mermaid Ball, but he hadn't looked at it in probably ten years. Maybe his mom stashed it somewhere in the attic.

"Yes, ma'am, the kickoff ceremony and parade is tomorrow ... just two blocks that way ... enjoy yourselves ... welcome...."

Of course, Clancy would never tell another soul that he blamed his bad love juju on a slab of bronze. That was just between him and the stone-cold harpy of Fountain Square.

The afternoon ferry must have been filled to maximum capacity, because the bodies continued to spill from the passenger cabin. In the middle of the throng, one woman sparked Clancy's curiosity. She was tall and slim, wearing hiking shorts, a fitted tee, and big sunglasses, chunks of blond bangs sticking out from under a shapeless canvas sun hat. She held the hand of a fidgety little boy in a pirate costume.

Clancy straightened, squinting into the afternoon sun. Something about her body language didn't sit right with him. Her face was pulled tight in worry. Her smile seemed forced. And she jerked her head from side to side, as if checking the surroundings.

After studying her for a moment longer, Clancy decided the woman didn't pose any physical danger to others, but her energy was most definitely off. Despite her nervousness, he noticed the elegant way she moved. The set of her shoulders was straight and her back was strong. The long and defined muscles of her legs allowed her to progress down the gangway as elegantly as a dancer.

She fascinated him, though he couldn't pinpoint what it was he found so intriguing. One thing was for certain — she wasn't a regular visitor. Clancy would have remembered a woman with such a pretty face, funky hair, and spectacular legs. He studied her as she stepped off the gangway onto the dock.

So strange . . . a gentle wave of awareness lifted him up and set him back down, carried him out, and pulled him back in. The sensation felt like a tap on the shoulder and sounded like a whisper in his ear.

Look closer.

Nope. He didn't know her. But he *wanted* to. Clancy realized he'd already started walking in her direction. The undertow was too strong to resist.

For what felt like the thousandth time that day, Evelyn McGuinness questioned her sanity. She had to be certifiably crazy to attempt something like this. Her niece's welfare was the most important thing in the world, of course, but she wasn't stupid. Evelyn knew it was unlikely she could outsmart a powerful Massachusetts congressman with connections all over the country. No matter how far, how fast, or how carefully she ran, this was one race she could easily lose.

But she had to try. She'd given her word.

Evelyn squeezed Christina's warm and sticky little hand. "You ready to play our game?" She made sure she kept the strain out of her voice as she helped her niece off the ferry.

Christina nodded, looking up with wide brown eyes. "Yep."

"Good. Now, who am I?"

"You're Aunt Cricket, silly." Christina giggled with

delight as she stomped on the metal gangway, making a racket.

"And who are you?"

"I'm a little boy named Chris! I'm four and I'm a pirate boy! I'm Pirate Jellybean!" She stomped again, tugging on the bandanna she wore on top of her close-cropped hair.

"Yes, you are!"

Evelyn pasted on a smile, hoping she could stop the hot rush of fear spreading from her belly into her chest and throat. She reminded herself that she had a strategy, and following it would dramatically improve her chances. She would attack this ordeal the way she'd done with each of the thirty-seven marathons she'd completed, relying on her physical strength and mental clarity to reach the finish line. It was all about pacing. Focus. About taking one step and then another, one breath and then another. And just as in a race, she couldn't afford to be distracted by what others were doing or obsess about how many miles she still had to go.

So what if the whole world thought she was a kidnapper?

"Can I have ice cream?"

"Sure, sweetie. Once we get settled in the motel."

"No! I want it now!"

Evelyn scooped her niece into her arms, kissing her warm cheek just below her eye patch, ignoring the beginning of a temper tantrum. So far during this ordeal, Christina had been surprisingly low-key, taking all the confusion and surprises in stride. Evelyn was immensely grateful that the preschooler hadn't drawn any extra attention to them by throwing a fit, since news of the "abduction" was probably already on TV.

In fact, her niece had sailed through all of it—the unplanned after-school pickup, a strange motel room by the interstate, the drastic change in Evelyn's appearance and her own haircut. Christina was cheerful through much of the car ride from Maine to the Logan Airport parking lot, then slept on the train and bus to the Cape.

And she'd been happy and excited on the ferry to Bayberry. But as of right that moment, Christina had clearly hit the wall. She was heading into full meltdown mode, just minutes from safety.

Evelyn knew distraction was her only hope, and she nearly laughed with relief when a young woman in a sparkly mermaid costume met them at the end of the gangway, handing Christina a purple mermaid-shaped lollipop. "Are pirates allowed to have candy?" the girl asked.

"Of course!" Evelyn smiled. "That was very sweet. Thanks."

"Sure. Have fun!"

Once they were on the dock, Evelyn took a minute to get organized. She lowered Christina to her feet and unwrapped the candy, gave it to her niece, and tossed the cellophane wrapper in a nearby trash can. Then she hoisted the large duffel over her shoulder and grabbed Christina's hand. She began to walk. According to the map of Bayberry Island she'd printed out at the public library computer, the Sand Dollar Motel was four blocks from the dock. It was funny how it had seemed like miles when she'd been here as a kid. Now, if only she could keep Christina calm during the walk through town, then she could get her something to eat and put her to bed early. And then maybe Evelyn could breathe.

Please, please, she thought to herself. *Whoever's looking down on us—God, Amanda, Mama, the Mermaid, or anyone at all—please give us a lucky break.*

Christina began to whine. Then, even with her lips tight around the lollipop, she began to cry, shoulders heaving and body trembling. It wasn't long before Evelyn saw beet red splotches form on her niece's cheeks and throat. It was going to be a bad one, and she couldn't blame her. She felt like having a meltdown, too.

Evelyn scooped Christina into her arms once more and clasped her tight against her left hip. She kept walking.

Pure hell. That's what this exhausted little girl had

been through in the last two months, beginning with the death of her mother. Any healing that had taken place since Amanda died was destroyed the day a Boston lawyer showed up at the farm with his client's petition for paternity and full custody. Since then, life had been a blur of magistrate hearings, lawyers, stress, tears, and heated discussions, all of it baffling to Christina. The poor little kid was even dragged off to play paper dolls with a man she'd never met before.

That's when temper tantrums became the norm.

"It's OK, baby." Evelyn glanced around the crowd to make sure no one looked at them with suspicion. Thank God, nobody seemed to notice them. It was just a stroke of luck—the Mermaid Festival on Bayberry Island was nothing but one long and wild costume party, and she and Christina could mask their appearance any way they wished and still blend right in.

It would buy them time. A week, to be exact. That's how long Evelyn had to figure out their next move.

"I . . . I want . . ." Christina sobbed and hiccupped so hard that the lollipop had become a choking hazard. When Evelyn pulled it from her lips, the sobbing only worsened.

"Just a few more minutes, sweetie. I promise." She pressed her nose into the crook of Christina's warm neck, inhaling the scent of the little person she loved more than anyone or anything in the world. "Put your head on my shoulder. It's going to be all right."

That's when Evelyn felt it. A prickly shock of alarm went through her body and she knew that someone had locked sights on her. As casually as possible, she glanced around, making sure she'd produced an all-purpose tourist smile as she searched for the source of her unease.

She saw him. The cop was standing ramrod straight, his right thumb hooked into a leather belt that held his gun. His dark gaze homed in on her. Luckily, the crowd blocked his view for a second, enough time for her to turn, duck, and keep walking. But she could feel him right behind her.

Dammit.

Christina continued to cry, then balled up one of her fists and hit Evelyn on her opposite shoulder.

Please . . . Evelyn's mind began to spin. Was it already over? Was this cop going to arrest her? Had she already failed Amanda? Christina? Pop-Pop Charlie? Had she already disappointed everyone she had ever loved?

"Welcome to Bayberry Island."

Evelyn turned toward the male voice, pretending she'd been caught off guard. Of course she did a piss-poor job of it. She was a sports therapist and fitness and nutrition blogger—not an actress. "Hello. Thank you." She adjusted Christina's weight on her hip. "It's been a long day," she said with an apologetic shrug.

The officer nodded.

"Is the fountain this way?" She pointed down Main Street, figuring he had to see right through her charade. If he was going to arrest her, she just wished he'd do it now and save everyone's time. Why didn't he just get it over with?

The police officer tipped his head and regarded her with a puzzled expression. But then his brow relaxed, and he unleashed a smile so warm it stole Evelyn's breath.

The noise of the crowd faded away. The dock seemed to vaporize under Evelyn's feet. Her heart did a back flip in her chest as the tingling shock wave of recognition hit her.

Those midnight blue eyes. That straight, white grin. The dark curly hair. She knew this man—well, once, briefly, a very long time ago she'd known him as a boy. Evelyn let her eyes roam to his name tag: CHIEF CLANCY FLYNN.

It took every bit of her remaining strength to stay standing.

Chapter Two

"I already told the sheriff everything I know." The old man sighed, looking like he barely had enough energy to shake his head. "Evelyn left to pick up Christina from Montessori school yesterday like she always does, but they never came home. I have no idea where she is. I'm just as confused as everyone else."

From where Richard Wahlman stood just outside the kitchen door, he could see Charlie McGuinness wipe his weathered face with a wide farmer's hand. The old guy's eyes were rimmed red and watery. Richard almost felt sorry that the FBI had to interrogate him in his own home like this. Almost.

If his four terms in the U.S. House had taught him anything, it was that no human being was one hundred percent honorable—not his fellow caucus members, not his devoted staff, and not his wife. That said, Richard had a hunch that old Charlie McGuinness was telling the truth. The shell-shocked look on his face revealed that his daughter hadn't shared her kidnapping plans with him. Richard had to hand it to Amanda's older sister, Evelyn. She'd been smart not to involve her father in a crime that would surely result in a lengthy federal prison sentence for everyone involved.

Richard smiled to himself, sliding his hands into the

pockets of his suit trousers. He knew the federal government didn't look kindly upon a noncustodial family member taking a child across state lines. The FBI's presence in Charlie McGuinness's kitchen was proof of that. And things could get a lot worse for the McGuinness family if the case landed in the lap of one of the many federal judges Richard knew personally. Evelyn had made a boneheaded move. If she'd done it without involving her father, she'd done him a huge favor.

"Was Miss McGuinness in a relationship? Was she seeing anyone?"

Charlie didn't bother to hide his disgust at the FBI agent's question. "None of my business. She was with the same fella for six years, but they broke up last fall. I don't stick my nose in my daughter's personal life, as a rule."

"His name?" Clearly, FBI Special Agent in Charge Teresa Apodaca wasn't a warm-and-fuzzy kind of gal. "You know, Mr. McGuinness, we are here as a courtesy to Congressman Wahlman, but we can easily move this conversation to the Boston field office."

The old guy's face flushed with anger. "You're some kind of hotshot federal investigator, aren't ya? Since I already pay your salary with my tax dollars, I'm sure as hell not going to do your job for ya, too."

Richard smiled at the old Mainer's approach to being interrogated. He liked him, mostly because he was an anomaly. Richard didn't spend much time with the likes of Charlie McGuinness, a guy who had no taste for bullshit. In fact, the opposite was true. Every waking second of Richard's life was spent in the company of men and women who swam in an ocean of bullshit and sunned themselves on bullshit beach, all while ordering fruity bullshit cocktails from a waitstaff composed of the general public.

No wonder he'd had a fucking heart attack at the age of fifty-four! He was utterly sick of it. All of it.

He just wanted his kid.

Richard took several slow and deep breaths in an attempt to keep his pulse steady and his blood pressure down. He needed to think of something else. Relax. Since this was the first time he'd been allowed inside the Mc-Guinness place, he decided to take advantage of the opportunity, and look around a bit. It certainly wasn't chic, but the only home his daughter had ever known was sturdy and comfortable. The floors were worn wide-plank pine. Its thick plaster walls were covered with faded wallpaper and its kitchen was right out of *Leave It to Beaver*.

As Richard had recently learned, the farm had been passed down the generations to Charlie, and both Mc-Guinness girls had been raised here. When Amanda left DC, she came back to her childhood home. And when Evelyn discovered her sister was pregnant, she sold her Augusta condo and moved in again, too. So that's how the place became the headquarters of the multigenerational McGuinness family.

Richard remembered when his driver had brought him here for the first time a month earlier. It had been a gloomy summer day, the sky heavy with impending rain, but the two-hundred-year-old farmhouse and its surroundings were picture-postcard perfection. The farm lane cut through rolling acres of fields and was framed in a low stone wall. Far off to the right, Richard had been able to see where the land curled up against a large mirror-calm lake.

His driver had parked directly in front of the house. Richard had stepped out of the backseat and evaluated the sprawling yellow clapboard saltbox with dormer windows and white trim. A cedar shake barn was attached directly to the side of the house for easy access during what he knew could be brutal winters here.

He'd decided that if Christina had received half as much attention as this old farm had, then his daughter had been lovingly cared for.

But on that first visit and every visit since, the Mc-Guinnesses refused to open the front door to him. Any contact he'd had with Christina had taken place in a ster-

ile playroom within the offices of the county's Child Protective Services. The only reason Richard stood inside
today was because the FBI had granted him access.

"Excuse me." He pushed aside the cluster of agents in
the farmhouse kitchen, and moved into the light. He
pulled out a chair and took a seat across the table from
Charlie McGuinness, studying the man in the diffuse
glow of the old ceiling light fixture. After a moment of
quiet thought, Richard said, "Well, this is a helluvah situation, isn't it, Charlie?"

The man said nothing.

"You know I have the child's interests at heart, correct? I only want what's best for her."

The old farmer lowered his chin and glared at Richard, his upper lip twitching just a bit. "Funny thing is, Mr.
Wahlberg—"

"It's Wahlman. Richard Wahlman."

He ignored the correction. "You see, we don't refer to
Christina as 'the child' in this house. We call her Chris or
Chrissy and sometimes we call her Jellybean. But no-
body calls her 'the child.' Do ya know why that is, Mr.
Wahlberg?"

Richard felt himself smile. This guy didn't give a damn
who was seated across the kitchen table from him, which
was admirable. Irritating, but admirable. He decided to
humor him.

"I had no idea Christina existed until one of my aides
showed me Amanda's obituary. You are well aware of
that. It breaks my heart that my daughter is nearly four
years old and I'm just now getting to know her."

Charlie tipped his head to the side. "She's not your
anything. Neither was her mother."

Richard blinked reflexively, but he let the jab go. He
had no idea how much Amanda had shared with her
family about her years on the Hill, though it was now
obvious to everyone that her contributions had gone far
beyond scheduling.

"That's where you're wrong, Mr. McGuinness." Richard leveled his gaze at Amanda's father but kept his voice kind. "Christina is my flesh and blood. She's my daughter. The DNA evidence is irrefutable. That doesn't make her any less your grandchild, certainly, and I am amenable to you having visitation privileges, but the court has already decided this matter. I am her biological father. I have sole custody. Your eldest daughter may have stolen her from me, but rest assured I will stop at nothing to find her."

The old farmer tapped his fingertips on the scrubbed oak tabletop and shook his head. "See, nobody knows how ya did it, but ya cheated us in that court, pure and simple. I don't know how you can live with yourself."

Richard felt his pulse race, which did worry him, but he could handle Charlie. "You missed the custody hearing, Mr. McGuinness. Court records show you received notice of the date and time, yet you and Evelyn didn't bother to show up. Of course, the judge saw that as an indication that the girl wasn't particularly important to you, and granted me custody by default. Only you know the reasons why you failed to—"

"You and ya people can go to hell." Charlie shot an angry glare toward Richard's chief of staff and attorney, who stood off in the dining room. "Ayuh, you're nothing but a bunch of liars and thieves perfectly happy to stomp all over a little girl's heart. Ya people have no shame."

"Where are Evelyn and Christina?" That came from Apodaca. "This is your last opportunity. If you don't answer, you could face obstruction charges."

Charlie shook his head at her. "I don't know where the hell they are. But if I did"—he glanced up into the light, blinking back tears—"I wouldn't tell ya. Sorry, now, but that's the God's truth. Go ahead and arrest me."

Richard was weighing his response when everyone's attention turned to the front staircase. Half a dozen FBI evidence techs tromped down the stairs with their search warrant bounty—several boxes of books and documents and what was obviously Evelyn's laptop and printer.

Charlie tilted up his chin defiantly. "Won't find much in that thing but her sports therapy appointments up in Augusta and the recipes and running diary and whatever she calls those stories she writes on the computer."

"Blogs," Apodaca snapped.

"Ayuh, that's right. Blogs. Cricket gets on her high horse sometimes about healthy eating and training for marathons. 'Feed the speed,' she likes to say. Even though some of it is strange stuff, she has lots of followers, apparently. I remember this one time, she made a dish for Jellybean that—" Charlie stopped himself. His chin trembled. He was clearly on the verge of tears. When he'd regained his composure, Charlie slapped his palms on the table and pushed himself to a stand, hiking up his worn blue jeans.

He spoke evenly. "Now, if you don't mind, I need a hot shower and a hot meal and unless you ladies and gentlemen would like to join me for both those things, I need to ask you to kindly leave."

The Special Agent in Charge placed her card on the worn wood table. "We expect that you'll remain in town."

Charlie McGuinness let go with a belly laugh. "I expect I will, too, miss. I was born in this town sixty-nine years ago, and they'll bury me next to the beautiful Ginny Dickinson McGuinness one day, not a mile down the road."

"You know what I mean," the agent said. "We'll be in touch."

Richard remained seated as the federal agents filed through the hall and out the front door. Once the crowd dispersed, he could see that his attorney and chief of staff remained in the dining room. Richard motioned for them to leave as well. "I'll catch up with you," he said, producing a reassuring nod.

M.J. Krawecki and Walt Henson produced twin scowls. Richard knew they were being extra cautious about the physical demands of his schedule these days.

It had been only ten weeks since his bypass surgery, and news of Amanda's death—and that she left behind a four-year-old child—had been a shock. The existence of one tiny little dark-eyed girl had been like a bomb going off in the middle of his recovery, his marriage, and his reelection campaign.

Walt did as Richard asked and reluctantly headed for the door, but M.J. stood in place, propping a fist on her hip and widening her stance like a gunslinger in a spaghetti Western. It almost made Richard laugh.

M.J. possessed a set of balls ten times bigger than his own. That's why he hired her when he was minority leader in the Massachusetts Senate and brought her along when elected to the U.S. House. But recently, there had been an unpleasant rift in their partnership. She wanted to make this paternity mess disappear—she'd do anything to avoid a scandal that would jeopardize his political future. Richard wanted only his daughter, and he was willing to risk everything to get her.

M.J. didn't understand, of course. How could she? She was in her late thirties. Married to her job. Ambitious. No kids. And in perfect health. Someone like that couldn't grasp how precarious life really was, or how a child could change a mortal man's priorities.

"Go on ahead, M.J. I'll be there shortly."

She wasn't happy about it, but she stepped outside, closing the heavy wooden door behind her. Richard knew he'd have to give the M.J. situation some thought once he and Christina were settled into their new routine as a family. The truth was that his chief of staff had defied him. He asked her to rig the custody ruling and she refused. He hadn't dared involve the squeaky-clean Walt in this sort of thing; the man would never condone it. This meant Richard had to take care of the matter himself.

M.J.'s snub put Richard in an uncomfortable position. Plausible deniability was always trickier when there was no middleman to take the fall, so there he was, his ass swinging in the breeze.

Richard had offered the local clerk a higher-paying post at the federal court of appeals down the road in Portland. In exchange, the clerk had changed the custody hearing date and didn't notify the McGuinnesses, though computer records showed she had. It had worked. All the judge had seen was that the grandfather and aunt never showed up to challenge Richard's petition for custody. He had won by default.

Richard now looked down at his hands folded on the McGuinnesses' kitchen table. Those hands had been dirty a long while now. A man couldn't hold elected office for more than twenty-five years without finessing the rules now and again. But that didn't prevent him from feeling a sickened twinge in his gut every time he thought about what he'd done up here in Maine. He'd won his daughter under false pretense. What did that say about the kind of man he was, the kind of father he would be?

The house had gone quiet. Charlie hadn't moved, but Richard could tell he was itching to speak. He turned his attention to the old farmer.

"Leave."

Richard smiled kindly. "I was hoping I might take you up on that offer of a hot meal. It would give us a chance to talk in private."

Charlie laughed again, and though the laugh was laced with bitterness, something about the sound reminded Richard of Amanda. There was once a time when he'd felt a sense of accomplishment every time he made the pretty, smart, and dangerously young Amanda McGuinness laugh.

"You know, Charlie, this heart attack and surgery thing has really made me take a hard look at my life, and I've got to say, I wish things had been different with Amanda. I wish she'd told me she was pregnant."

The old guy got up, the kitchen chair scraping across the wood floor. He began tidying up at the sink, his back to Richard.

"You see, I now understand that I've wanted a child all my adult life. I want to leave a flesh-and-blood legacy on this earth. But I willingly gave up the dream for public service."

Well, okay—that was stretching it. Richard had knowingly traded the idea of fatherhood for money. It wasn't his wife's fault. Tamara had made it clear from the beginning that she was unable to have children and had no interest in them. So when he married her, he released the idea of children and embraced the wealth and influence of his wife's family.

Richard cleared his throat. "I do think that perhaps everything would be different today if I had known about Christina from the start. Maybe I would have been with my daughter every day. Maybe Amanda and I would be in a relationship. Maybe she wouldn't have been in the path of that drunk driver."

Charlie spun around. He spoke slowly and distinctly. "You are a lying, crooked, heartless bastard. You threatened my precious Amanda, and for that I will never forgive you. I don't care who you are—you will never be welcome here."

"Mr. McGuinness—"

"My idealistic daughter was in love with you, and you threw her away like a piece of garbage. You didn't want Christina back then, but now that you've had health problems you suddenly decide to come steal her from us?" Charlie raised his right arm and pointed to the door, his hand shaking. "Let yourself out, Congressman."

"I don't know what you're talking about, Charlie. Why can't we—?"

"Don't make me get my Winchester."

"Have we met before?"

Evelyn swallowed hard at Clancy Flynn's question, but managed to answer. "I don't think so." She forced herself to sound as cheerful as possible, all the while thinking *don't figure it out, please don't figure it out.* . . . "I'm Cricket Dickinson, and this very tired little man needs a nap. This is our first festival."

He nodded calmly, but didn't look particularly convinced.

"I want ice cream!" Christina began to struggle in Evelyn's grasp.

"You know, we should probably get going. Someone is a little cranky after our trip. We've come a long way. We live in Indiana."

"Sure. Of course. Enjoy your stay."

That's when Christina suddenly decided her curiosity about the police officer outweighed her meltdown plans. She swung her head around, frowned at him, and pointed. "Who you?"

Clancy laughed, and the warm sound sent Evelyn back in time. She was hit with the remembered smell of salt water and sunscreen, the hot sun on her skin, and the taste of Clancy's lips on hers. She remembered that astonishing rush of her first love, how being with him had made her feel fully alive, tethered tight to life while soaring above it.

Of course she'd known Clancy Flynn was an island boy. But in her rush to get Christina to safety, it had never even occurred to her that he might still live here or that he would even remember her, let alone be chief of police! After all, it had been eighteen years. He'd never even written her back, so she couldn't have meant anything special to him.

He smiled at Christina. "I am Police Chief Clancy Flynn, at your service. And who are you?"

Evelyn stiffened, afraid that Christina would answer that question truthfully. How stupid of her to stand there in a fog like that, preoccupied with memories! She couldn't afford to lose her focus. "This is—"

"I'm a pirate boy!" Christina called out, wiggling to be let down. She stood on the boardwalk and looked up at him with big eyes. "I am Pirate Jellybean! Are you a policemans?"

Clancy leaned toward Christina, grinning. "I am." Kindness softened his dark blue gaze, and gentleness warmed his voice.

"Good, 'cause at school they say if I need help I can go see a policemans and he would help me. I want to be one of the policemans when I grow up."

Clancy glanced briefly at Evelyn, his expression bright with amusement. "You know, that sounds like an excellent plan. Maybe you could come visit the police station while you're on Bayberry Island."

Evelyn couldn't help but think that invitation was as much for her as it was Christina. "Thanks!" She hated how nervous she sounded, but she had to get out of there. "We should probably let you get back to work. Thank you very much, Officer."

She propped Christina on her hip once more, adjusted the bag's shoulder strap, and walked away. One foot in front of the other. Four blocks to go. Evelyn kept moving, not looking back, not glancing around, not giving Clancy Flynn another second to try to put the puzzle together.

Thank God she was wearing the sunglasses and hat.

Evelyn told herself she could do this. Everything would be all right. She would find a way.

Eighteen years ago ...

"Would you hurry up? Everybody's waiting!"
Evie resisted, digging heels into the sand and trying to yank her arm free from her sister's grip. Amanda might have been two years younger and four inches shorter, but she was strong. And stubborn. "I still don't think we should go. Mom said—"

"Mom said that Evelyn McGuinness needs to loosen up and not be such a pansy-ass. Mom said you only live once so you'd better have all the fun you possibly can while you're on vacation because you may never get back here again!"

Evie was shocked. "She didn't say that, did she?"

"Oh, my God. You're completely clueless." Amanda grabbed her by the crook of the elbow and started running. Evie jogged along, still not convinced.

"You know that *'no swimming'* areas exist for a reason, right? Sometimes there's a strong undertow or a rip current, and other times there are rocks you can't see and if the waves throw you against them—"

"But those boys were so cute! C'mon! If we don't hurry we won't know where everybody went!"

"So, wait. Where did you meet these kids? We just got here about an hour ago."

"You are so out of it, Evie. Didn't you see that group hanging out on the boardwalk when we waited for our taxi?"

She tried to remember. "No."

"Okay, well, that's because you're a complete airhead and boys don't matter to you. I think something's wrong with your hormones."

"Uh, no, my hormones are perfectly fine. Something's wrong with you. You're like a senior trapped in a seventh-grader's body."

"Thanks." Amanda thought that was a compliment. "So do you want to know how I got this invitation or not?"

"Doesn't matter to me. I'm not even listening to you anymore."

"Great. Well, there were about six boys and two girls. I think some of the guys live here year-round. So anyway, one guy asked me if we wanted to go swimming with them later somewhere really cool. I said yes, and he slipped me a piece of paper with 'Eagle Nest Point' on it."

Evie tried to slow down, but Amanda wouldn't let her. "Wait. Where was I when all this was going on? Didn't that boy know you were just twelve?"

Amanda groaned with exasperation. "You were busy helping to load the suitcases in the trunk, and if you tell anybody I'm only twelve I will make your life miserable."

Evie laughed because, honestly, Amanda already did that. "So how old are you supposed to be, then? I'm fourteen, and we're obviously not twins, but there's no way you're going to be older than me."

"Make me thirteen, then."

Evie couldn't believe how stupid this conversation was. "I hate to tell you this, but thirteen doesn't sound much older than twelve."

"Well, at least it has the 'teen' part in it."

She had a point. "Okay, so how do you know where this Eagle Nest place is?"

"I asked the motel owner."

Evie looked sideways at her little sister. "When did you do that?"

"When I went to the vending machines for ice."

She just shook her head. "How did you even turn out this way? How is it that you and I can be in the exact same place at the exact same time and you always find a way to get in trouble?"

"Simple!" She pulled Evie to get her to run faster. "You see it as trouble. I see it as fun!"

They arrived at a metal fence. A crooked and rusty No Trespassing sign hung by a single screw. Evie knew instantly that this was a bad idea. "We could get arrested," she said.

"Or, we could die of boredom."

They hopped over the fence and climbed up a dune dotted with sea grass, goldenrod, and a whole lot of bayberry plants. Duh—that was probably how the island got its name. Once at the top, they saw about a dozen kids hanging around a big piece of driftwood. Some were smoking. Some seemed uneasy, wrapped up in their towels and staring out at the water. This was obviously something that went on here every summer—the locals checked out the tourists and decided which ones would be fun to get in trouble.

Evie wanted no part of it.

"I'm going back to the motel."

"No!" Amanda grabbed her upper arm. "You can't! I'm just twelve! You have to stay and make sure I get home safely. What would Ginny and Charlie say if you abandoned me and left me with kids who were a bad influence?"

"*You're* the bad influence. I should be protecting the local kids from *you*. And Mom and Dad would ground you if they heard you call them by their first names."

They trotted down the sandy slope and walked up to the group. One of the boys announced, "Okay. Whoever's not here is shit out of luck, I guess."

"Oh, my God!" Amanda sucked in air dramatically. "That guy is a complete Baldwin."

Evie was so tired of her sister repeating lines from the movie *Clueless*. It had come out last summer and she and her little friends went to see it five times. Then she bought the video with her babysitting money and watched it on the VCR at least twice a week, memorizing the dialogue. Amanda thought that if she talked like a Valley Girl no one would know she was from Maine.

Well, she *was* from Maine. They both were. And the only valley they knew was the Moose Lake Valley so she might as well just admit it.

"Hi!" Amanda walked right up to the cute boy who seemed to be in charge. Evie hung back.

"Hey." The boy spoke to Amanda with a cigarette dangling from his mouth like he thought it made him look cool. It didn't. Evie already knew that with a boy like that in charge, this little social event was going to be a total disaster.

Suddenly, the boy looked over Amanda's head and waved. "Well, lookie who decided to show up after all. It's the Prince of Bayberry Island."

Evie turned around. This new boy took his time coming down the dune toward the water. He was about her height and really cute. He had dark hair. Although he looked to be about her age, there were already some muscles on his arms and chest. When he smiled, Evie felt hot, like she was going to melt from the inside out.

Ha. He was a boy and she noticed him. So there. And apparently nothing was wrong with her hormones, either, because they were now doing the Macarena inside her bathing suit.

This guy was way more Baldwin than any of the actual Baldwins, and he was looking right at her.

Chapter Three

"This coffee tastes like the bottom of my locker. It may not even be fit for human consumption."

Clancy glanced up from his laptop and grinned at his old Boston PD friend, Deon Ware, the first of his moonlighters to arrive for the briefing. "Haven't you had four cups?"

"Five." Deon eased his considerable heft into a conference room folding chair and sighed dramatically. "You know, Flynn, every year I sacrifice ten days of precious vacation time for this mermaid shit. I even agree to wear these damn Daisy Duke shorts. The least you could do is provide halfway-decent coffee, man."

Clancy laughed, knowing that was Deon's way of thanking him. First off, a stint of double shifts on Bayberry Island *was* a vacation compared to Deon's usual South Boston patrol, and, since each of the extra officers hired for festival week earned triple overtime, he'd be going home with a boatload of cash for his trouble.

Besides, Clancy had known Deon for a dozen years. They'd gone through the academy together. And he knew that though Deon was six feet four inches of concrete, he loved to bitch and moan like an eighth-grade girl.

"You're welcome," Clancy said.

Deon shook his head. "It's a damn good thing I got such nice legs, that's all I gotta say."

Each of the remaining members of the temporarily beefed-up Bayberry Island Police Department wandered in and found a folding chair. Sitting near Deon were four more of Clancy's BPD buddies and one longtime friend with the Massachusetts State Police. Clancy's only full-time employee, Assistant Chief Chip Bradford, joined him at the front of the room.

"You know the drill, gentlemen," Clancy said. "We'll do two-man teams with eight hours on an assigned patrol, eight hours as a floater and eight hours off. Both Chip and I will be on call twenty-four-seven and be available for backup whenever needed. You each received your schedules via e-mail a few weeks back. Any problems or questions?"

"It's on like Donkey Kong," Lowell Pernecky said.

"Good to know." Clancy clicked his laptop to view the Mermaid Festival event spreadsheet. "The schedule is the same as every year, with just a couple minor additions and changes I need you to be aware of."

"Did you finally get rid of the nudists?" Doug Lukovich raised his eyebrows in hopefulness. "I don't think I can handle going out there again."

The room erupted in laughter. Clancy knew poor Doug would never live down the emergency call he made to the nudist colony, when he'd been forced to provide first aid to an older gentleman who'd been stung by a hornet.

On his left nut.

And since Doug's mission of mercy included holding a frosty Diet Dr Pepper on the old guy's equipment, his coworkers left a six-pack of the soda in front of his door every night for the remainder of festival week. It was a good thing Doug was an easygoing dude.

Clancy motioned for Chip to answer the question. He knew his friend always got a kick out of being in the know.

"The island council held a zoning hearing in the off-season. They discussed the matter at length." Chip nodded with authority. "But in the end they decided to renew the group's operating permit. The Bayberry Freedom Colony is still going strong."

"Great," Doug mumbled.

"In fact"—Chip was on a roll—"they got two new clay tennis courts installed this spring. Top quality, too. Nice bounce and slower speed."

"Hold up." Deon straightened in his chair. "Let me see if I got this right. They play tennis butt-naked?"

Chip shrugged. "Well, yes. They do everything naked. That's why they call it a nudist colony."

"Okay, but see, what I'm wondering right about now is, how does a person serve while nude?" Deon looked around the room. "You know what I'm sayin'? Where are you supposed to keep the extra tennis balls? I mean, it's not like human beings have kangaroo pouches, right?"

Will Farney held up his hand, already laughing. "Doug should probably run out there and conduct an in-depth investigation."

Though it did Clancy's heart good to hear the raucous laughter of his old friends, he knew they had a job to do. The island's population went from about nine hundred year-round residents to close to twenty-five thousand visitors over the course of festival week. Six ferries arrived and departed daily, three originating from the Cape and three from the Nantucket–Martha's Vineyard route. Private sailboats and yachts jammed the marinas. Private planes flew in from the mainland, Nantucket, and the Vineyard all day and night. Along with the volunteer fire department, these men assembled in the conference room made up the first line of protection for every one of those visitors.

There would be time for cutting loose next weekend, after the festival wrapped up. Right now Clancy knew he needed to keep the briefing on track.

"Listen up. Tomorrow is Saturday, which is kickoff

day. The parade starts at fourteen-hundred, followed immediately by the opening ceremony at Fountain Square, my dad giving the official welcome."

"Is Rowan gonna be riding on the float? You know, in her mermaid costume?" That question came from a hungry-looking Jake Tedesco, who had never hidden his appreciation for Clancy's only sister.

"Yes, but she's practically engaged to Ash Wallace."

"They're still together?" Jake looked crestfallen.

"Big-time," Chip chimed in. "They live together at the Safe Haven and they're renovating it, bit by bit. I think Ash Wallace is going to propose soon. And you saw all the construction over there, right? His marine research foundation will be up and running by . . ." Chip suddenly stopped talking, realizing that question had been directed at Clancy. "Sorry, boss," he mumbled.

"Let's keep moving." Clancy cleared his throat. "Sunday is Island Day, as always. Monday is the clambake out at Safe Haven Beach. Tuesday is the reenactment and the museum tour. Wednesday is the children's play and, as usual, I will be off the radar from about seven to nine p.m. for family obligations, unless there's a major emergency."

"Your bro comin' home this year?"

Clancy shrugged at Deon. "I have no idea. We never have any idea." He continued with the itinerary. "We've got the officially sanctioned costume contests on Thursday and then the Mermaid Ball Thursday night, followed by closing ceremonies Friday at noon."

Cam Wilkins yawned. "What's the vehicle situation this year, Flynn?"

"We've got three extra Jeep Wranglers leased from the mainland, all four-doors. The keys are in the lockbox by the parking lot, as usual. The combination is the same. And the police boat got a much-needed face-lift in the off-season, so she's good to go."

"A cigar boat it ain't," Deon said, stretching his long legs out in front of him.

"What's the new stuff?" Lowell asked. "So far it just sounds like the same ole, same ole."

"Right." Clancy hooked his thumbs into his utility belt. "This year, the carnival is staying an extra day. Instead of being up and running through Sunday, they've extended their operating license until Monday, midnight." Several men expressed their dissatisfaction with that plan, but Clancy continued. "Also this year, we have added security considerations. As Chip just mentioned, construction has started on the Oceanaire Foundation's education center and research marina on Haven Cove. The site is clearly blocked off from the bed and breakfast traffic and the public beach, and they have their own round-the-clock private security team, but we are their backup. I have promised Ash our full cooperation."

Chip chimed in. "Whoever is on patrol out there should check in with security at least twice a shift."

"Gotcha," Doug said.

"Also, there are a couple BOLOs to be aware of. I've sent them to you on your tablets. As we know, festival week on Bayberry Island isn't exactly a den of felons, but we need to be kept up to date."

Will sighed. "What I wouldn't give for a normal felon instead of one of these fruit loops."

"Hey, did you see that half-woman-half-man mermaid?" Doug's eyes got huge. "He shaved half his damn chest! That's just not right!"

"It's called a mer*man*," Chip corrected him.

Clancy refreshed his laptop to be sure he had the latest bulletins. "As I was saying, there's an APB out for a double-homicide in P-town last night, an AMBER Alert out of Springfield with plates and vehicle description, and a BOLO on a preschooler from Maine, probably a custody-related abduction."

"But that one's not an AMBER Alert," Chip added, helpful as always. "Unlike the Springfield case, the girl's not believed to be in danger."

Deon shook his head. "Man, I don't care what the situation is—you just don't go around snatching kids. What the hell is wrong with people?"

Evelyn spooned with Christina on the motel bed, listening to the gentle rhythm of the little girl's breathing. The poor kid was zonked. Once they'd checked in, Evelyn had followed through on her promise of ice cream, but Christina's eyelids grew heavy after just a few licks of her vanilla soft-serve cone with rainbow sprinkles. So she carried her comatose niece back to the motel, removed her pirate patch and shoes, and tucked her in.

Evelyn let her eyes wander around the room absently, noting how a tiny sliver of evening light cut through the cheap plastic draperies. Though the windows were shut and the walls of The Sand Dollar were made of concrete block, she could still hear the rhythmic rush of the ocean and the occasional laughter of vacationers. The motel was just a couple blocks from Fountain Square, Ground Zero for partying. Eighteen years earlier, her mother had marched down to the manager's office to complain that the late-night laughter and music kept the family awake.

Evelyn smiled sadly to herself, thinking of that long-ago vacation. She was fourteen that summer. Amanda was twelve. And the McGuinness clan was whole, happy, and hopeful—a state of affairs she assumed would last forever. And why not? What kid with a happy life thinks it's temporary? And, really, Evelyn's world was far more than just happy. It was structured, safe, and part of a larger context of church, community, and roots two hundred years deep. The summer her family vacationed on Bayberry Island, everything was just as it should be, and in her teenaged heart she was sure nothing bad could ever penetrate the contentment and order.

Her mother died the next summer, just six weeks after being diagnosed with stomach cancer. Evelyn didn't need to be a psychiatrist to know that ever since, she'd been trying to re-create the certainty and structure of her childhood, and discovered her sanctuary in training and running. She liked the cause-and-effect relationship—excellent finish times were the direct result of pristine nutrition, disciplined training, and careful preparation. It was simple. It worked. It made sense.

Evelyn's eyes burned with fatigue and sadness. She hugged Christina tighter, inhaling the sweet summer smell of her niece's hair and skin, deciding that maybe now she could allow herself to cry. She'd been hiding her panic and fear for a week while she schemed and plotted about how she'd get her niece to safety. She'd done things she never would have believed herself capable of, and hid all of it from her father. She'd lied to him. Repeatedly.

The thought made Evelyn feel nauseated.

How had she become the kind of person who used a disposable cell phone, carried fake IDs, and relied on bribery to make it through the day? How about making Christina put on her pirate costume in the car before they entered that New Hampshire Burger King? Or cutting and dyeing her own hair in a motel room near an I-95 exit ramp? Holy crap! That was the kind of crazy spy shit that happened in movies starring Angelina Jolie or Will Smith—not in the real life of Evelyn Helena Mc-Guinness. Amanda, of all people, should be alive to see the transformation. But then again, if she were alive, the transformation wouldn't have been necessary.

Evelyn smiled to herself, thinking about her little sister. As soon as Amanda began to talk, she started trying to get Evelyn to be more carefree and less concerned about the rules. In other words, more like her. When they were younger, Amanda only wanted a companion to explore with—crawl under the fence, hide in the hayloft, or take their bikes out to the main road. But by the summer they went to Bayberry, Amanda was pushing the envelope and dragging Evelyn with her. Her reasoning: if they got caught, they would be in it together.

Evelyn's ex-boyfriend would likely find her current cloak-and-dagger routine entertaining, as well. Rory often complained she was too predictable, too tied down by her routines, too comfortable with how things had always been. And, yes, when they broke up last fall, he'd used the dreaded B-word: *bor-ring*.

Ha! Not anymore.

Her friend Hal's observations echoed in Evelyn's mind. When she called the reformed hacker to ask for help, he was quiet for a moment. Then he said, "Are you absolutely sure you want to do this? Once you start down this road, you have to stay on it or pay the price."

Evelyn had tried to convince him it wasn't that black-and-white. Or maybe she was trying to convince herself. "It's temporary," she told him. "I need some time to figure this out, find a way to prove he rigged the custody proceedings. I only want to get away from him long enough to come up with a plan."

"But she's his kid, Evie."

"I know. I know. But Amanda made me swear to her . . ."

"DNA crushes everything else." Hal interrupted her. "Look, I'm sorry. You know I love you to death and will do anything to help you, but listen to me. It doesn't matter how horrendous Wahlman was to your sister or how you promised Amanda you would keep him out of Chrissy's life should anything ever happen to her. Now that she's gone, the only thing that matters to the court is that Chrissy carries that rat bastard's DNA. She will always be his daughter. That is forever."

Evelyn felt hot tears run down her sunburned cheek, across her lips, and down into the crease of her neck. She buried her nose tighter to Christina's hair, knowing the last thing she wanted was to wake her up. She used her last bit of resolve to keep quiet as the tears ran. Silently, she prayed for strength. She prayed for luck. She prayed for sleep. She prayed that she was doing the right thing for her niece. But most of all, she prayed that Clancy Flynn wouldn't remember that week they'd shared so long ago.

She'd read somewhere that men didn't retain muscle

memory as sharply as women, at least the emotional component of it. If that were true, then Clancy wouldn't have struggled the way Evelyn had, remembering strong arms pulling her from the undertow, fingers brushing wet hair from her face, the scent of Coppertone and sea spray. It wouldn't have taken him years to forget holding hands by the bonfire, dancing under the fairy lights, and the kisses that started out as timid curiosity and flared into an explosion of awareness.

He was Evelyn's first. Her first kiss. Her first love. The first boy she let touch her like that. The fact that he never wrote back hurt like hell for many years, but now she was grateful. If Clancy Flynn didn't answer her letter, it meant he wasn't interested, and if he hadn't been interested back then there would be no reason for him to remember her now.

Don't remember me. Don't remember anything at all. I can't believe I'm thinking this, but I hope you forgot everything.

"So. You're never speaking to me again?"

Tamara looked up from her leather-bound planner, retrieved the eyeglasses hanging from a platinum chain around her neck, put them on, and then directed her attention to the doorway of her home office. She had no reaction whatsoever to seeing her husband for the first time in six days. She removed the glasses and went back to whatever she'd been working on, not bothering to respond.

Tonight, Richard refused to accept her cold-blooded indifference. Tonight, he was going to stand up for himself. "For God's sake. This is absurd."

Tamara popped up from the upholstered desk chair and marched toward him, her high heels clicking on the marble floor. She got inches from his face, so close he could see the feathering of her pink lipstick, how it ran into the tiny vertical crevices on her upper lip. She used to be so beautiful when she was young.

"I would never stop speaking to you, dear. Do you know why? Because *you would enjoy the silence.* So I plan to talk—talk, talk, talk, talk, talk—and then talk some more. You won't be able to shut me up. Care for a drink?"

She spun away from him and headed to the bookcase. That was what she called the piece of ornately carved furniture with glassed-in shelves, though Richard knew it was more of a book-themed liquor cabinet. "I'm not supposed to drink, darling."

"Yes, I am aware of that. So do you want one or not?"

Richard didn't answer. His wife was angry. He got it. Tamara wouldn't mind if he dropped dead right on the spot. He understood that as well. Richard wandered over to one of the white sofas arranged in the center of the room and sat down, trying to get comfortable. He'd always thought it was interesting how Tamara's things— her furnishings, her cars, her clothing, her jewelry, her hairstyles—everything was chosen for its visual appeal instead of its usefulness or comfort. That's why her sofas were quite chic but as comfortable as sitting on a steel girder. Her clothing was expensive but restricting, her cars were exotic but in need of constant repair, her jewelry too heavy for her earlobes, and her hairstyle crunchy to the touch. But it all looked fabulous.

She sat facing him and daintily crossed her ankles. One thing he could say for her—she knew all the steps to the dance. Always had. She was as refined and ladylike as any woman he'd ever known. She had a gift for people's names and faces. Tamara could talk to anyone about anything. She was an impeccable hostess, generous philanthropist, and sought-after board member.

Only Richard knew what she really was. He wanted this encounter to be quick. "Go ahead. Let me have it."

She raised her cut crystal highball to her wrinkly lips. Richard suspected she'd had some work done around her eyes, but he couldn't be sure. It wasn't the kind of thing she shared with him.

"I am thinking about divorcing you, Richard."

He shrugged. "It's unfortunate you feel that way."

Tamara downed the rest of her scotch in one swig and slammed the glass onto the coffee table. "You broke the rules, goddammit!"

What could he say? She was right. The only thing she'd demanded when they got married was that his extracurricular activities never reflect badly on her. She would not be made a fool of—period. Richard agreed to those terms. If Amanda hadn't gone and gotten herself killed, everything would still be copacetic. But she had died and left his child behind, and this could prove to be an exceptionally unflattering turn of events for Tamara Derrick Wahlman.

"I am sorry for how this played out. As you know, none of this was due to my own carelessness."

Tamara howled. It took her a moment to collect herself. "Oh, Dick, my darling. The level of your self-involvement never ceases to amaze me."

He adjusted his position on the steel girder, which he now suspected she purchased just to rupture one of his discs.

"Out of curiosity, Dick, while you were banging your intern, did you stop to consider that you might better serve your country by using a condom?"

"She was a staffer, not an intern."

"Ah, so she was on your payroll while you were ... What do the kids say today? *'Hittin' it'?*"

Richard twisted his face into a smile. "As much as I enjoy your verbal abuse and dirty talk, I must insist that you have an actual conversation with me this evening. You said you were willing to talk. So talk."

"Right. And did you ever consider that your obsession with teenagers might damage my name and all members of the Derrick family?"

"She was twenty-four. Maybe even twenty-five. And this isn't about your family or their deep-fried dynasty, Tamara."

She laughed again. "Everything about you serving in the U.S. House of Representatives is about the wealth and connections of Derrick Brand Restaurants. Let's not delude ourselves, dear, darling Dick. Your entire career has been built on chicken strips and fries."

Richard remained perched on the edge of the sofa and stared at his hands. He needed to conclude this bit of nasty business. "Do you have any idea what kind of time frame you're looking at with the divorce?"

"I'll wait until after the election. When are you going public with the child?"

"Well, it depends." He stood, knowing this would be the tricky part. "We're dealing with two separate issues here, I'm afraid. First, there are the things I have no control over."

Tamara's wrinkly upper lip twitched.

"There is always the danger of an anonymous tip, plus the grandfather despises me so much that he might launch a campaign to ruin my reputation."

"Ha! But you're doing so well by yourself!"

He moved right along. "Also, my legal name is on dockets, petitions, and the custody ruling. It would take a halfway decent reporter two minutes to connect the dots, since Gerhardt R. Wahlman isn't exactly the most common name in the universe. Thank God there aren't too many halfway decent investigative reporters out there anymore."

She crossed her arms over her chest and leaned back into the sofa. He hoped it bruised her kidneys. "I can't wait to hear about the second issue."

He cleared his throat. "Yes, well, my hope is that they find her soon and I can choose how and when to tell my story, giving me some control over how it plays out in the media. But that isn't so clear cut, I'm afraid."

"Exactly what are you implying?"

At that moment, Richard was positive she'd had work done. Tamara was trying her best to scowl, but her forehead looked as icy-smooth as a hockey rink after a Zamboni run. He wondered when she might get around to having her lip wrinkles removed. They really did age her.

He needed to refocus, because he wanted out of there. "I'm not implying anything. What I am, in fact, saying is that if the days drag on and the FBI can't locate her, then—"

"You wouldn't dare."

"The first days are crucial. If I came forward as her father, it might help bring attention to the case, darling. If I went public, the abduction of a congressman's child would become the lead news story and stay that way until she was found."

Tamara pressed a thumb and forefinger into the bridge of her nose. "Absolutely not. Not before we're divorced."

"This is the safety of a little child we're talking about."

Tamara's head snapped up. "And my dignity! And my family's name!"

He held out his hands. "Tamara, it might get to the point where I really have no choice."

"You always have a choice, darling." She got up and returned to her desk chair. "I would tell you to pack up your things and get out but you don't have much here these days, do you?"

"I never intended to hurt you. Believe me."

She folded her hands on the desk, her lips peeled back in a sneer. "I'm not hurt, darling. Not in the least."

"What are you, then?"

"I am thoroughly disgusted with myself for ever marrying you."

Chapter Four

Clancy hung out on his mother's porch while Tripod and Earl rolled around in the yard like they were still puppies. Unfortunately, he arrived while the meeting of the Bayberry Island Mermaid Society was still in full swing. He didn't want to interrupt. Scratch that. He didn't want anything to do with their mermaid crap.

On the other side of that bright blue painted door, the living room couches and chairs were packed with middle-aged women dressed in long wigs, sparkly spandex mermaid tails, and shell-shaped boob-catchers. That's what his brother had called them when they were kids, at any rate. Clancy closed his eyes and tried like hell not to think about the whole subject.

Detective skills weren't necessary to guess what was being talked about in there. Not only could he hear nearly every word being exchanged—these ladies were, and would forever be, loud—but they'd been having the same festival week discussion since he was born. There was certain to be bitching and moaning about last-minute changes to festival scheduling and who needed to be where, when, and doing what. They would certainly pledge not to make "the same mistake" next year, whatever this year's mistake happened to be. And there were surely complaints about parade logistics, disagreement

among the members of the clambake decoration committee, and any number of off-color comments about
God-knows-what. Rising above it all was his mother's
unmistakable voice, calm and no-nonsense, cutting through
the menopausal melee.

Though Mona Flynn had retired after thirty-five years
as principal of the island's only school, she hadn't managed to shake her principal tone of voice. Clancy suspected it was permanent.

"We are all grown women here," he heard her say. "I
am confident we will all be on our best behavior this
week. Remember, these seven days are the reason we
work so hard all year long. This is our holy week, ladies,
our sacred duty to the history of this island, the legend
of the Great Mermaid, and how the two have become
intertwined through the generations."

The room went quiet. Clancy raised his head, knowing
what was coming next. He waited . . . waited . . .

"Pass the merlot," Polly Estherhausen said.

Bing, bing, bing! He was damn good at this.

"All right. Gather 'round, ye maids. Let us recite our
sacred pledge of devotion."

At his mother's command, Clancy could imagine the
swish of mermaid skirts and mumbled complaints about
stiff joints. He decided to give them some space. After
all, this closing ritual was supposed to be secret. Most
everything Mona's Mermettes did behind closed doors
was supposed to be secret, but the Flynn kids had been
spying on these meetings since they were old enough to
get out of bed and sit on the main staircase at the Safe
Haven. Voices carried in that big old house, and when
Mona forgot to close the huge pocket doors to the formal dining room, they got to watch the proceedings, too.

For most children, it would be unnerving to see your
friends' moms hanging around your dining room every
Sunday evening dressed like mythological sea vixens, but
for the Flynn kids, it was just the way things were.

While the ladies finished their business, Clancy shoved

his hands in the pockets of his uniform shorts and wandered out toward Mona's front walkway, the dogs at his heels. He threw a stick toward the backyard and they raced off.

Clancy turned his gaze east, over the Atlantic. As he often did, he began searching for the breakthrough stars, the first few pinpoints of celestial light to leave their mark on the blank slate of nightfall. He widened and softened his gaze, and like magic, they appeared. As a kid he'd been fascinated by the idea that all those billions of stars and galaxies had been up there all day long, hidden from view by only a thin curtain of sunshine. The stars hadn't disappeared and reappeared—it was just the perspective that had changed.

Even now, as a cop, he found he returned to that certainty again and again. He often discovered that the truth was right there in front of him, visible only when he widened and softened his gaze and waited patiently for the glare to fade. A change of perspective worked wonders.

His thoughts went to the chick from the ferry, and he decided he'd rely on his tried-and-true method with her, as well. After all, he hadn't gotten anywhere by trying to force his memory to work. It still bugged the hell out of him that he knew her from someplace yet couldn't figure out where. So tomorrow, once the parade was over, he would get her name from the ferry manifest and find out where she was staying. Then, he'd pull back, relax, and wait for the spark of recognition to reveal itself.

Because, dammit, he did recognize her. And it was driving him crazy trying to figure out why she felt so *familiar*.

The front door of the cottage creaked open, spilling lamplight onto his mother's unruly rosebushes. The ladies filed out chatting and laughing. The dogs abandoned their stick and ran toward the voices.

"Spying on us again, Clancy?" Abigail Foster gave him a friendly wink. "Hey, boys," she said, bending down to pat the dogs' large heads.

"I could have you arrested for loitering," Izzy Mc-Cracken added.

"Hold on while I get my cuffs," Polly said, snorting in appreciation of her own wit. "Hello, Earl. Yo, Mr. T." She rubbed Earl's ear and kissed Tripod on his nose.

"Evening, 'maids." Clancy gave them a gallant tip of his ball cap, stepping aside and gesturing for them to pass him on the sand-strewn walkway. "Enjoy your stroll home. It's a lovely night."

"Yes, indeed," Layla O'Brien said.

"Good luck this week." Darinda Darswell stopped in front of Clancy, smiled, and gave him a peck on the cheek. "I know you've got a lot on your plate like every year, but do try to take a few minutes to enjoy it, too. Thank you for being such a wonderful chief of police." She squeezed his hand, turned, and walked through the garden gate.

"She's right, you know." Clancy felt his mother's soft touch on his back. "We are all very lucky you decided to come back to the island."

Clancy turned toward her, smiling to see she'd already exchanged her Spandex and wig for a pair of khaki slacks and a well-worn cotton blouse.

He wrapped an arm around his mother's shoulders and gently pulled her closer. She felt frail to him, tinier than just a couple months ago. Her latest rheumatology checkup on the mainland hadn't produced the best of news. Her lab results were high, and the doctor added yet another medication to combat painful swelling in her joints. Along with all the other pressure he felt during festival week, this year he was particularly concerned about his mother. The woman was sixty-seven but never stopped. She'd been at this mermaid thing most of her life, and he wished she'd just give it a rest, hand over the reins to someone else. It was starting to be too much for her.

"Would you like a cup of tea?"

"No, Ma. It's okay. I just stopped by to check on you."

"Care to take a walk with me, then? Do you have a few minutes?"

"For you, absolutely." Clancy whistled for the dogs and took his mother's elbow. The group passed through the gate and strolled out onto Idlewilde Lane, a narrow paved road blown over with sand and dotted with loose gravel.

"Careful where you step," Clancy said. "If the dogs start crowding you, just let me know."

His mother chuckled. "I've been walking these old crooked lanes for forty-five years and the dogs are perfect gentlemen, as always. You worry too much."

Clancy shook his head, though he suspected his mother was right. He worried quite a bit. With his parents living separately now for more than two years, he hated the idea that his mother was alone most of the time in her little rental cottage overlooking the sea. She refused to wear the safety alert device he bought for her last winter. Mona had always been the one to care for others, and the idea that she needed some kind of battery-operated alarm to keep her safe completely horrified her. Nobody could change her mind on this—not her fellow Mermettes, not Rowan, and not even Duncan, her favorite.

Mona denied having a favorite child, of course, but Clancy and Rowan would roll their eyes whenever she protested. They were aware of her soft spot for Duncan, the oldest, who had been sick most of his childhood with asthma, bronchitis, and severe allergies. Of course, their brother had made up for lost time after puberty. The sickly, skinny boy who spent most of the first thirteen years of his life in bed became a champion distance swimmer and quite the ladies' man, and as Duncan's ego swelled, so did the rivalry with Clancy. Duncan was now a Navy SEAL serving in. . . . hell if Clancy knew where. The family was never informed of Duncan's whereabouts or what, precisely, he was up to. Sometimes months could go by without a word from him. The only thing they could count on was that he'd show up at the last minute for the family cookout during festival week. It was an unbroken tradition.

"Is everything okay with your Boston boys this year?"

Clancy was drawn back to the moment, letting thoughts of his brother disperse into the breeze. He smiled at how his mother referred to his fellow officers as "boys" when they ranged in age from thirty to forty-one. "Yep. They're all good. We're working as backup for all the security out at the Oceanaire construction site, so that's really the only new thing going on this year."

"Isn't it amazing how fast things are coming together? Ash has poured his heart and soul into that project—and the Safe Haven, of course. Have you seen all the progress?"

"It looks fabulous, Ma. The best I've ever seen it."

Clancy wasn't exaggerating. He'd stopped by the family mansion two days ago, and Rowan and Ash were busy with preparations for the Safe Haven's last festival week as a bed-and-breakfast. It was mind-blowing how many changes had been made in just a year.

Last fall, Ash began bringing in an army of architectural preservation contractors from Boston to tackle restoration of the tile roof, gutters, spouting, storm shutters, cedar shingles and stone, porches, and windows. A zoned heating and cooling system that independently controlled each of the mansion's thirty-two rooms was installed. The Safe Haven's fourteen bathrooms were renovated, the kitchen modernized, and the oak floors refinished. They had even started to design a second-floor suite of rooms to serve as their private apartment.

Clancy couldn't imagine how much money Ash was throwing at the Safe Haven. It had to be staggering.

His mother cleared her throat. "Now, technically, I'm not supposed to say anything about this . . . ."

"When has that ever stopped you, Ma?"

Mona giggled. "Well, apparently, Ash and Rowan have had a change of heart. You know how they wanted to use the Safe Haven to house researchers and foundation members?"

Clancy nodded.

"Well, they've decided to experiment. They want to keep it functioning as a B and B—but only during high season—and see if it's manageable."

Clancy stopped in midstride, not even trying to hide his surprise. "What? After all the complaining Rowan's done about running that place?"

Mona laughed, nudging Clancy to keep moving. "Everything looks different when you're in love."

"If you say so."

She smiled up at him, so much happiness in her expression, which made perfect sense, because if love was part of a conversation she got downright giddy. But he could tell Mona was about to start one of her Mermaid-related pep talks, and he wanted no part of it.

Clancy spoke before she could. "Productive meeting tonight?"

Mona chuckled, aware that he was trying to change the subject. "I was simply saying that Ash has become quite passionate about that old house, and his enthusiasm seems to have rubbed off on Rowan. She told me they plan to clear out the attic this fall and add additional rooms for seasonal employees. I warned her it would be quite an undertaking, since nobody's touched that mess in at least ten years."

"Huh." His mother could be right. Maybe Rowan was so blinded by love that nothing bothered her. All he knew was that his sister had been completely overwhelmed with the job of managing that run-down old mansion before Ash entered the picture. It looked like he'd remodeled the house and his sister's attitude at the same time. "I'm really happy for her. For both of them, I guess."

Mona released a long sigh of pleasure. "So am I. But, sometimes . . ." She stopped herself, looking flustered. "I'm completely thrilled for Rowan and Ash and for the foundation and everything that's going on over there—it is wonderful. What I was thinking was, well, I wish Rowan would come around and serve as president of the Society."

Clancy knew this was why she'd held on so long. "But she's not."

Mona shook her head a little, deep ridges forming between her eyebrows. "I know."

"Ma?"

"I've just been thinking about how I spent all those years and all my energy trying to keep the Society together, the Safe Haven in Flynn hands, and Haven Cove undeveloped. I realize I've been kind of obsessed with my duties. And now I'm getting older. The Safe Haven is being used for the greater good and everyone's so happy with how things worked out . . . well, there's nothing left to fight for."

"So . . . you're saying you miss the battle?"

"Ha. Yes, I suppose. But I think the time has come for me to stop putting all my energy and time into other people—what they do or do not do—and concentrate on myself. I'd like to slow down, learn to relax, focus on my health."

He hugged her. "I think that's a wonderful idea. I'm sure the woman elected as the next Society president will do a great job. She will have you to advise her, right?"

They walked together in quiet for a moment, the dogs loping nearby. Clancy and Mona took in the view from the intersection of Idlewilde and Shoreline Road, one of the highest points on the island. Down below, the lights of the Ferris wheel sparkled, several varieties of live music competed for airtime, and laughter rose up the hill. Clancy knew that the police radio mounted on his left shoulder was bound to come alive any second, but he was grateful for the break.

Suddenly, he frowned. Something his mother had said bothered him. It echoed inside his head, but he couldn't quite name it.

"Something wrong, Clancy?"

The Mermaid Society . . . Rowan . . . the Safe Haven . . . that was it! The Safe Haven attic! Mona raised an eyebrow. "Care to share?"

The photo of the girl.

"Son?"

"It's nothing. I was thinking that I should get anything of mine out of the attic before Rowan tosses it on the garbage barge. Didn't you store some of my kid stuff up there?"

"Yes. Your school work, refrigerator art, and trophies for track events and the like." She tipped her head with curiosity and grinned. "Since when have you been the sentimental type?"

"Ma," he said, gently patting her back. "It's more practical than sentimental. If Rowan and Ash are going to live at the Safe Haven, then it's only right for me to get my junk out of their way and take it to my cottage. I do have my own home, you know."

She didn't seem satisfied with his answer. "All right. So nothing else is bothering you?"

Clancy shook his head. "It's just festival week. You know how it is."

His mother stopped and faced him. "All I want is for you to be happy."

Uh-oh.

"Someday you'll find her, and she will be exactly right for you. Everything you've been through will have been worth it."

"Hold up." Clancy laughed at how quickly she'd forgotten her promise to stay out of other people's business. "First off, I'm not looking for a woman, exactly right or completely wrong or anywhere in between. And I have no idea how your brain went in that direction, since we were talking about me getting my crap out of the attic."

She shrugged.

"The woman of my dreams isn't inside a mildewy cardboard box shoved under the rafters."

Mona chuckled. "I'm simply telling you that I'm here and I love you. If you ever want to talk about anything and everything or nothing at all, you know where to find me."

Clancy stopped walking. "You and the mermaid brigade do not have permission to mess with my personal life. No magic spells or true loves or anything. You're clear on this, right?"

"Of course! My gracious. I would never even dream of that, son."

Evelyn jolted awake in a panic, her eyes searching her surroundings and her brain spinning, struggling for traction. It took a few seconds before she put it together. They were in the motel on Bayberry Island and Richard Wahlman was hunting them down. Christina was sound asleep against her, one bony little knee poking into Evelyn's side. She breathed deeply and forced herself to relax, realizing that her niece's usual nighttime flailing had woken her from a deep sleep.

But just then, she heard it, an odd beeping sound coming from the corner of the room. Her mind began to race through all the worst-case scenarios—was Richard here? Had he found them already? Was the SWAT team at the door, or FBI agents? Evelyn's heart pounded as the beeping continued.

Then it dawned on her. She rolled her eyes at her own ridiculousness. It was her phone, the disposable phone she'd purchased from the variety store in Augusta. And the only person in the world who had the number was Hal.

She'd completely forgotten to call him.

As carefully as possible, Evelyn pulled away from Christina. Her niece grumbled a bit then turned over on her side, but she remained asleep. Evelyn rose from the bed, tiptoed across the room, and grabbed the duffel from the floor. She rushed into the bathroom and closed the door, then went rummaging around in the bag for the phone. Finally! She found it tucked into a pair of Christina's socks. As soon as she flipped open the no-frills device, she apologized.

"I'm so sorry, Hal!" she whispered.

"Christ on a cracker! I've been worried sick about you guys!"

"Sorry."

"It's nearly one a.m. I haven't seen anything on Justice Department or state police sites, but I hadn't heard from you, so I didn't know what to think."

Evelyn sat on the edge of the bathtub. "It was kinda rocky when we first got here, and then Christina fell asleep."

She heard Hal sigh with relief. "Good, but why did it take you so long to answer?"

Evelyn rested her forehead in her hand. "I couldn't figure out what the beeping sound was."

He laughed.

"Hey, I've never heard this phone ring before! But we're fine. Thank you for making sure we're okay."

"Of course. So you followed the plan? You waited for the teenager to check you in?"

"Yes. Everything worked out. I waited for the owner to turn over the front desk to the summer help, just like you said. And God, he snatched up the cash without a second of hesitation."

"Good."

"And, from what I could tell, he changed the guest records to the name on my ID, and he knows he'll get more money when I check out without incident."

Hal made a humming sound. "Yeah, well, he sort of changed the records. I had to tie up a few loose strings."

"What? You didn't—"

"Yeah, I hacked into the Sand Dollar computer system, if you could call it that. Listen, that place is a joke. If anyone wanted to, they could extract the credit card information for every guest who's stayed there in the last decade."

"Hal . . . ?"

He chuckled. "I only use my powers for good. You know that."

Evelyn did. She'd met Hal at a New England wellness convention six years before, where she was slated to give a presentation. At the time, he'd been an overweight type 2 diabetic who'd just learned he was playing Russian roulette with his blood pressure and cholesterol. He was only thirty-nine. Today, Hal was a marathoner, in prime shape, and off all medication.

It had taken years for Hal to admit he'd been part of a vigilante computer hacker group dedicated to exposing what he called "information injustice." Evelyn had told him she never wanted to know the details. But he got himself out of that shady world and started a successful Internet security consulting business. Hal was now among the small group of people she considered her closest friends, and for that reason, it was impossible to lie to him.

"I do have an issue. It's nothing huge, but I want to run it by you."

Hal was quiet for a moment. "Let's hear it."

This would be embarrassing. She worried she'd sound ridiculous telling the story, like some kind of heartsick teenager. Come to think of it, that's exactly what she had been all those years ago. She took a deep breath and steeled herself.

"Evie?"

"All right. All right." She glanced up at the old bathroom ceiling fixture, which was not a smart thing to do. A layer of dead insects had piled up inside the cradle of the light's frosted globe. "Oh, gross. There are dead bugs in the bathroom light."

"That's your issue?"

Evelyn giggled, relaxing a bit. "I wish. But, um, you know how Amanda had been planning this trip as a surprise for Pop-Pop's seventieth birthday?"

"Yeah."

"You know how we used to read all those mermaid storybooks to Christina and told her we came to see the beautiful mermaid as kids?"

"Yes."

"And how Christina begged to see the mermaid for herself?"

"Yeah, but what are you getting at?"

"Well, what I didn't tell you is that when we were here eighteen years ago, I had a . . . well, I sort of met a boy."

"Uh, are we headed into Annette Funicello territory? 'Cause I need to prepare myself if we are."

"Please, Hal. This is no joke."

"Sorry. Go ahead."

"I was fourteen. He was an island kid. The first day we were here, Amanda dragged me down the beach to meet up with a group of kids going swimming on a no-trespassing beach. We swam out to these rocks and started diving into the waves. I knew it was stupid, but I did it anyway, and . . . well, I almost drowned in the undertow."

"Oh, my God!"

"The local boy saved my life. He dove under and pulled me out, and later he told me he hadn't even planned to be there that day but changed his mind at the last minute."

"Wow."

"So for the rest of the week, we were inseparable."

"Does he still live there? Is that where you're going with this?"

"It's not that simple."

"Uh-oh."

"So this boy was my first love, right? He gave me his address and I promised I would write him and give him all my information so he could write me back. So just days after I got home, I poured my heart out to him. He never wrote back."

"Ouch."

"Yeah. It felt like I'd been punched in the face, you know? So he was my very first love, and my very first broken heart. It was a two-for-one deal."

"Give me his name and I'll check him out."

"No need, Hal. He's the Bayberry Island Chief of Police."

The line went quiet for a beat. Then Hal said, *"Ohhh, shiiit."*

"Yep, he saw us get off the ferry and walked right over

to me to welcome us to festival week. It took me a minute to figure out why he looked familiar, but then I saw his badge. This is really bad, isn't it? I think we need to leave tomorrow and go somewhere else."

Hal made a deep growl of frustration, and Evelyn could hear the lightning-fast clicking of computer keys in the background. "Well, it's certainly not good. Okay, well, it looks like the police chief of Bayberry Island is not just some chowderhead. Clancy Flynn graduated with honors from the Mass State Police Academy and was a decorated Boston patrol officer, six years on the beat." The keys kept clicking. "Check this out—he got a meritorious service award for pulling victims from the rubble of a gas explosion and two years later got a community service award for working with neighborhood watch groups. Looks like your man is a frickin' Eagle Scout."

"He is?"

"That was just a turn of phrase, but if you hold on a moment I can check—"

"No! Stop!" Evelyn sighed deeply. "We'll leave tomorrow. I'll pack us up and we'll take the first ferry out."

"And go where?"

She closed her eyes. "I have no idea."

"This is not the way to do it, Evie. Especially with a traumatized little kid in tow."

"Do you have a better plan?"

Hal was quiet for a long moment. "I am still trying to figure out how Wahlman got custody. I'll need to drive to Maine and track down the clerk of courts in your county, do some human interface."

"That's a four-hour drive from Burlington!"

"Four hours is just four hours, honey. I'll do a little detective work. In the meantime—"

"We'll leave the island."

"Hold up! Listen. Are you sure this dude recognized you?"

"Actually, I don't think he did. Not yet, anyway."

"Good." Hal made his humming sound again, and Evelyn knew he was thinking. "Listen, Evie. If your hair turned out anything like the Photoshopped ID, then you look nothing like you did when you were a teenager, right?"

"God, no. I had wavy brown hair past my shoulder blades back then, and I hadn't yet discovered the magic of eyebrow tweezers."

He snickered.

"And now I look like that eighties chick, what's-her-name, the one who used to hang out with Sylvester Stallone."

"Brigitte Nielsen?"

"Yeah. Her."

Hal laughed hard. "Sweetie, don't panic quite yet. Here's what we'll do. I'll keep monitoring FBI and state police activity and let you know if there's any indication they have a lead. I'll also keep an eye on your hottie police chief. If I see him doing any online snooping on Evelyn McGuinness or the so-called kidnapping, I'll get in touch with you immediately. Even if he searches for Cricket Dickinson, you should be okay—unless he decides to dig deeper than the first couple levels. Let's hope he's satisfied with what I had time to throw together. Keep your phone with you."

"I will."

"In the meantime, don't make any rash decisions. Do you promise me?"

"Sure."

"Good. Wear your sunglasses and hat or get yourself a costume. Put Chrissy in her pirate getup and just blend in at the parade. Hide in plain sight. Try to avoid talking with the cop. I'll touch base with you tomorrow night."

"Okay."

"Bye."

"Hey, wait, Hal. How do you know he's a hottie? I never told you what he looked like."

Hal snorted. "I'm staring at his BPD photo right now. Dude's got a penetrating gaze and a set of guns on him."

"Sheesh."

"Do you want to know if he's married?"

Evie clicked her tongue. "I can't believe you asked me that! It doesn't matter one way or the other. Why would it?"

"Right. Well, just as an FYI—he's divorced."

Thank God. "Good night, Hal."

"'Nite, Evie. Sweet dreams."

No, no, no. He would not. He could not. He refused to touch the hand of the bronze sea goddess and say the words. He hated the words. He knew that anyone who believed this shit—including his own mother—had a screw loose.

A sane, rational man had no business here. He decided to go.

So odd . . . his feet made no contact with the ground. They pedaled along as if treading water. No matter how hard he willed his legs to churn, he didn't move an inch. He was trapped in Fountain Square, staring directly at the mermaid, the one place he swore he would never be.

Suddenly his feet hit solid ground, but they froze in place. When the wind picked up, fountain spray misted his face and chest.

She beckoned to him again.

No!

She didn't seem offended by his refusal. The metal maiden smiled down upon him as if she knew every doubt in his head, every regret in his heart.

He heard her speak, which was impossible, of course, since her lips remained welded shut, cold, and lifeless. He would not believe. He refused.

"Enough, Clancy Flynn. It is time for you to see that I am not your enemy."

Oh, *hell* no. Of course he was dreaming.

"There is only love. And now you are ready for it."

Okay. Since this was his nightmare, he would simply

make himself wake up and be done with the whole hideous hallucination.

Wake up.

Wake up!

Wake the fuck up!

"You are a son of the island, part of a story far bigger than you realize. You now face the most important decision of your life, Clancy. Soften your gaze. Calm your mind. Follow your heart, and the choice will be clear."

Suddenly, he was no longer at the square. He stood on the dock instead, watching the girl go. Her soft hair lifted in the breeze, her long and tanned legs carried her away from him. But wait. What was happening? Someone—or something—grabbed her and began dragging her toward the ferry. She struggled, freeing one arm enough to turn and reach out to him, eyes sharp with terror. "Clancy! Help me! Please!"

Time to wake up. Now.

He gasped, a desperate rush of air slamming into his lungs as he shot upright. Clancy was in his own bed, in the dark, the sound of the sea crashing nearby and the ceiling fan whirring above. He touched his chest, neck, and face, finding his bare skin dripping with sweat. Or was it fountain spray? His heart thudded behind his ribs.

Clancy threw off the sheet and stumbled into the bathroom, where he flipped on the light and threw cold water on his face. He tried to shake the dream, the vision of the metallic mermaid towering over him, alive but unmoving. And all that crap she'd said! Enemy? She was a statue, not an enemy. He was facing the most important decision of his life? Please.

And what about the girl calling out for help? How bizarre. He almost felt guilty, like he'd let her down somehow.

Shit. Once festival week was over, he would be going back to decaf.

Clancy stood in front of his mirror, hands on the edge

of the sink, trying to catch his breath. He heard the brisk clicking of dog paws on hardwood and a rhythmic panting—which turned out to be his, not the dogs'.

"It's okay, boys. Go back to sleep."

They sat in the open doorway. Tripod yawned first, then Earl. They blinked at him like he was nuts for being up so early. And, hey, since it was only five a.m., they had a point. And as far as him being nuts was concerned? Maybe they nailed that one, too, because normal men don't have nightmares about talking mermaid statues.

"Go to your bed, fellas."

They did, tails swinging wildly, excited to be alive— like every Lab Clancy ever had the pleasure to know.

Just then, his police radio crackled to life on the bedroom nightstand. Within ten minutes, he was behind the wheel of his Jeep, chugging coffee, driving through the dark toward a rental house on the north shore. Doug Lukovich had called for his assistance with a domestic dispute with minor injuries. Was that the perfect kickoff to festival week, or what?

Clancy raised his mug for a mock toast. "Here's to true love," he said. "Here's to the magical mermaid of Bayberry Island!"

Mickey usually did a halfway decent job picking out the tourist cuties, and the new crop was no exception. Clancy spotted four girls off to one side and two guys standing around looking lost. Somebody's brother always seemed to tag along, unfortunately. He did the math. Clancy and five of his friends had to divvy up four girls. The ratio didn't bother him too much. If nobody seemed worth spending time with, he'd just head back to Haven Beach and get something to eat.

His eyes made a quick sweep over the options. He saw her right away. His stomach got all nervous and tingly. Clancy decided to save her for last after he'd checked out the other girls. One was blond and smiley and looked like trouble but he had a feeling she was way too young. The girl with pale skin and red hair was gorgeous, but Clancy figured she'd be burned to a crisp by tomorrow and wouldn't be much fun for the rest of the week. Another girl had long blond hair and a perfect body, and he could already tell by the way she stood there looking bored that she thought she was too good for anyone. He'd pass.

Clancy went back to the one who had first caught his

attention. She was about his height, fairly thin, but athletic. She probably played volleyball, or maybe lacrosse.
She wore a pink and orange Hawaiian print bikini that
showed off her shape but didn't make her look like she
was trying too hard. She had long and curly light brown
hair pulled back in a tight ponytail. He decided he liked
the curve of her neck—it was really graceful looking.
And then she turned to face him.

Oh, man. What a face! She was the prettiest girl he'd
ever seen in his life. And those eyes . . . he'd have to be
standing right in front of her to decide what color they
were, but from his position halfway down the dune they
looked see-through green, like an old-fashioned soda
bottle, no, wait . . . he'd just come within about three feet
of her, and decided she had eyes the color of sea glass.

Since he didn't want to be an uncool dweeb and just
stare at her, Clancy gave a quick nod of his chin and said,
"Hey," then headed over to Mickey. Clancy didn't speak
to her while the group walked to the lighthouse ruins, but
he felt her nearby and knew her eyes were on him. It was
kind of a weird sensation, not one he'd ever had before
with a girl. He felt her even when he couldn't see her.

The ruins were Mickey's favorite forbidden spot. Technically, it was on the outer edge of the wildlife refuge, and
it was known for its heavy surf and wicked dangerous
rocks. Duncan always said only serious athletes should
even try to swim near the ruins, but Clancy ignored him.
His brother was now training for triathlons and distance
swimming events and thought he was some hot-shit su-
perhero or something.

Kids who had towels or sunglasses tossed them onto
the dune before they got in the water. Clancy kicked off
his sandals and followed close behind. He swam out toward Mickey and immediately started messing with him.
"That blond girl is jailbait."

"Yeah? Well, she told me she's thirteen, asshole."
Mickey smacked him in the face with a decent amount
of seawater.

"She's bullshitting you." Clancy returned the favor.

He let it slide, and swam away. He needed to clear his head. His parents were fighting about money again and he couldn't swing a dead cat without hitting somebody dressed like a mermaid, and he just wanted to hide until festival week was over. It had been a good three years since he actually had any fun during the Mermaid Festival. Now it was just *work*—his parents called it doing them favors . . . do stuff for his mom's goofy group or to help his dad with city and festival duties. *Help me real quick with the copying. Do the dishes for me—we're having an emergency meeting. Give me a hand with the clambake setup, would you? And could you run down to the warehouse and get . . .*

Clancy suddenly became aware that the current had carried him pretty far offshore while he wasn't paying attention. It didn't worry him—he'd been swimming in the Atlantic since before he was out of diapers, and knew exactly how to handle the situation. He began a leisurely, but steady, freestyle stroke parallel to the shore. Once he passed the rocks he knew he could make a direct turn toward land and encounter no resistance from the current.

He heard the kids shouting but didn't pay much attention to them. Mickey was fun, but he could be loud and obnoxious sometimes and he just wore Clancy out. His mom had once commented that the three friends were like the Three Little Bears—Chip was too soft, Mickey too hard, and Clancy just right.

Yeah, well, all moms said shit like that about their own kids.

In a watery distortion of sound, he thought he heard his name being called. Clancy lifted his head and saw almost all the group standing on the beach waving their arms and yelling. Something was wrong. He stopped swimming.

"My sister!" The little jailbait girl was hysterical. "She's caught in the riptide!"

Clancy saw the girl's head bobbing along with the waves and knew she was on a collision course with the rocks. She'd get smacked around good if nobody helped her.

Ah, shit.

He resumed his freestyle but put on the afterburners. Clancy calculated in his head how many minutes he had before she'd start banging against the rocks. He'd seen kids get mangled up pretty bad by those things, and couldn't even imagine that pretty face and body of hers covered with gashes and bruises.

Clancy made his cut toward shore. He started flying through the water, the screaming and yelling intensifying. Above all the voices and the roar of the water, he heard a girl's solo plea.

"I'm in a little trouble over here!"

Clancy nearly laughed at how casual she sounded. She was pretty tough for a girl. Most girls he knew would be buggin' out the way her little sister was. Clancy reached the girl with only inches to spare before she hit the boulders, immediately flipping her on her back, slipping his arm across her chest and gripping her side. He shoved off from one of the rocks and began a hard-core rescue sidestroke, hauling her skinny little ass out of the rip current. And while he did it, even though this was an actual emergency, he couldn't help but think about how close his right hand was to her left boob. He considered "accidentally" slipping so he could get a feel, but he thought better of it. The first time he put his hand on a pretty girl's breast, he wanted it to be because she invited him—or at least at a time when she could tell him to stop if she wanted. Would it be wrong to cop a feel during a crisis? He wasn't even sure it would count.

Clancy loosened his cross-body carry, only because it was obvious they were out of danger. She slipped from his grasp and floated a few feet away. They stayed there, bobbing together in the sea, staring at each other and gasping for breath.

"Thank you. I owe you one."

"Na. It was nothing. I do it all the time."

They both laughed at that.

It got a little awkward after they finished laughing. Clancy didn't even know her name and he suddenly found that he'd lost his ability to speak.

"I'm Evie," she said, sticking her hand out above the waves.

"I'm Clancy." He shook it. Funny how just shaking her hand made him want more—a lot more.

"Awesome," she said.

"Cool. Let's swim in."

It took a few minutes to make it back to shore. It was a high-drama situation, with Evie's sister in tears and the other girls in a general state of freaking out. Clancy wasn't into that sort of thing, so he slipped on his sandals and began to walk up the dune. It was so weird, but he knew the exact second Evie started following him. He felt her.

"I'm staying at the Sand Dollar."

"I live here on Bayberry."

"I kind of figured you did. So maybe we'll see each other around this week?"

"I hope so. Later, Evie."

Clancy walked along Shore Road about a mile until he reached the Safe Haven. The whole way back he couldn't decide—was the buzz he felt from saving someone's life, or was it from meeting Evie—touching her skin, talking to her, looking into her eyes, and feeling her even when he couldn't see her?

He had no friggin' idea. He'd never saved anyone's life for real like that, the way Duncan had shown him. And he'd never met anyone quite like her.

God, he wished he knew what to say to a girl as cool and as pretty as Evie.

Chapter Five

"I can't see her! I can't see the pretty mermaid!" Chrissy began to jump up and down on the sidewalk. "I want up! Put me on your shoulders, Aunt Cricket!"

Evelyn made a hasty calculation. Rationally, she knew that there were so many kids balanced on so many adult shoulders along the parade route that one little pirate boy wouldn't draw attention. Besides, she hadn't seen Clancy Flynn at all.

But she'd taken a quick peek at the morning cable news shows while Christina slept. Though the volume was off, she'd seen all she needed to. As expected, Evelyn's and Chrissy's faces and names were now all over the place. So if she put Chrissy on her shoulders she'd be taking a risk.

"I want to do shoulders! Please, Aunt Cricket! I only want to see the mermaid!"

"Okay. Okay."

She turned around, crouched down, and felt Christina climb on board. They had done this so many times back home—at the beach, at the farm, and hiking in the mountains around Moose Lake—that it was second nature to both of them. With Christina's hands gripped in hers, Evelyn stood up.

"There she is! There's the pretty mermaid!"

Evelyn began to move farther back from the street but toward the parade float that had captivated her niece's attention. At least that way, she'd have several rows of people in front of her along the route.

"What does it say? What are the letters?"

Evelyn smiled at Christina's question. She was so smart. She loved this little person so much. Without warning, her throat tightened and her chest became overwhelmed with the crush of sadness. Amanda, her beautiful sister, was gone forever, and she would never see her funny, spirited, and intelligent daughter grow up. That was now all Evelyn's responsibility—and her privilege.

Oh, God! What had she done? If they were caught, she'd never be allowed to see Chrissy again! And that was the exact opposite of what Amanda had asked of her!

Evelyn knew she had to keep it together. She pushed down the sadness and doubt and focused her eyes on the parade float sign. "The letters say that she is the Mermaid Queen of the Safe Haven Bed and Breakfast."

"What's that? Is that a castle under the sea? Can we go see her there?"

Evelyn smiled a little, thinking that the bed and breakfast's owners had such a fearless sense of parade-float design that God knew what the inside of the place would look like. The Safe Haven float was a flatbed version of a Johnny Weir figure-skating costume. It was blinged-out with glitter, rhinestones, and even a few oversized feathers adding pizzazz to the display of sea grass and giant fake shells. She answered Christina. "Bed-and-breakfasts are like hotels. Maybe we can visit there."

"She's so pretty! Is she Ariel?"

The woman sitting in the huge, sparkly clamshell waved like a princess, smiled like a beauty queen, and tossed candy to the kids lining the Main Street curb. Christina was right—she was very pretty, even in the shell bikini top, skintight mermaid tail, and overly long wig.

"I don't know her name, sweetie. Maybe she really is the Little Mermaid."

Just then, the mermaid queen turned to smile at the parade float directly behind her. Large script along its side advertised The Oceanaire Foundation, whatever that was, but the mermaid wasn't smiling at the elaborate marine-life decorations. She smiled at the devastatingly handsome sea captain at the helm of the float, and he smiled back.

Clearly, those two were an item. Maybe Evelyn was getting caught up in the vibe of the Mermaid Festival, but seeing how the couple looked at each other made her sigh. Perhaps one day she would look at a man like that, reminding him that she was all his, that her heart was fully open to him alone, and that with him she was exactly where she belonged.

Evelyn's eyes widened behind her shades. What the hell was wrong with her? Why was her brain going in that direction? She had never gotten carried away with love and she'd certainly never looked at a man the way the mermaid just did. Not her boyfriends in college, not the few men she'd had relationships with since, and certainly not in her six years with Rory.

Rory Sobrato wasn't the type of man who inspired surrender. Well, to be fair, Evelyn wasn't exactly the type of woman who felt like surrendering.

Wait. That wasn't entirely true. Once, she had been the surrendering type. Back when she was a kid. Right here on this island. With Clancy Flynn. Before she knew better.

At that instant, her body flared with an electric charge—a warning. A quick scan of her surroundings brought her eye to eye with the police chief.

He flashed a genuine smile, then motioned for her to stay put. Evelyn pretended she hadn't seen him, shifting her attention to the Falmouth High School marching band and its jarring rendition of "U Can't Touch This." Without warning, she pulled Christina from her shoulders, set her on her feet, then took her by the hand.

"No! I want to see! I want shoulders!"

Evelyn tried her best not to show her anxiety. "In a minute, Chris. We're going over here. Maybe we can see the parade better."

"I see it better when we do shoulders!"

Evelyn soon realized she'd dragged them into a crowded area of the public dock, where she was unable to make much progress through the throng. But she needed to stay focused. Not only did she have to avoid Clancy, but she needed to make sure Christina remained right next to her in the middle of all these people.

"Let me go!"

"In a minute, Jellybean."

Evelyn turned her head to the right. Dammit! There he was, heading in their direction. She ducked, pulling Christina along. She could see nothing but the hairy knees and sandals of tourists.

Chrissy began crying. "No! No! Take me back to the mermaid, Aunt Cricket!"

"That's where we're going. There are a lot more mermaids coming in the parade."

"No! I want that one! The pretty one!"

She straightened, picked up Christina, and propped her on her hip. Evelyn pulled on the canvas brim hat, ensuring that it hid at least part of the side of her face. "You need to be patient. It's very crowded and I'm trying to get us to a better spot to watch the parade."

The little girl glared at Evelyn. A deep furrow appeared between Christina's one brown eye and her pirate patch. "I don't like it when you do that."

"Yeah, well, sometimes we have to do things we don't like, Pirate Jellybean." Evelyn gave her a peck on her cheek and hugged her. "Now, how about we head over—"

"Excuse me."

She stopped. Her heart sank. *Dammit, dammit, dammit!*

Christina announced with a cheerful voice, "It's the policemans!"

As she turned toward the deep, friendly voice, she pasted on a smile. "Well, hello," she said, as if she didn't have a care in the world.

"Hello to you, too. Are you enjoying the parade?"

Christina nodded. "I saw the pretty mermaid!"

Clancy laughed, smiling down at the little girl. "Yeah, there are quite a few of those here today, aren't there?" He turned his attention to Evelyn, and shook his head. "You know, for a minute there I thought you were running from the law."

Her blood froze. Her mouth opened, but nothing came out.

"That's a joke." He studied her for a second. "I could have sworn you saw me back there. It was almost as if you were trying to avoid me."

"Of course not!" Evelyn's mind was buzzing with chaos. Oh, God. This was it. He was going to arrest her.

But Clancy's body seemed to relax, and his eyes crinkled with delight. "I have something I wanted to give to Pirate Jellybean."

"You mean you're not . . . ?" She had to have misunderstood him, which would be an easy thing to do over the high school band's rendition of M.C. Hammer and the hammering of her own heart. "I'm sorry, but what did you say?"

He raised his voice. "I said that your pirate might need this to protect himself out on the high seas." With as much flourish as he could produce in the crowd, Clancy held out a cheap plastic sword with a scabbard and jewel-covered belt.

Christina's mouth fell open and her eyes widened with delight. "That's for me?"

Clancy nodded. "You're the only little boy pirate standing in front of me right now, right?"

She nodded. "I want to wear it!"

"Here you go, big guy."

Evelyn touched Clancy's arm to stop him. As soon as she did it, she knew it was an incredibly stupid move. But there she was, with her hand on the short sleeve of Clancy's uniform shirt, his body heat spreading into her palm. She'd only wanted to tell him they couldn't accept the gift but her brain buzzed with remembered sensations, each one as fresh and sharp as if it had happened only moments ago. She saw the handsome boy's smile flashing in the sun, heard the rumble of his laughter, watched how he ran effortlessly through the sand, and remembered that tentative touch of his lips against hers the first time they kissed. But most of all, she felt that long, tight hug he'd given her right on this very dock, just before she boarded the ferry. He'd grabbed her like he hadn't wanted her to go.

Evelyn drew in a big breath, then pulled her hand away like she'd been burned.

Clancy looked equally stunned.

She had no idea how long they stood like that, just gazing at each other. Maybe a few seconds, maybe a couple minutes. But while it was happening, the world receded around them, sounds dampened, sights dulled. The only thing that existed was a rush of energy filling the space between them and swirling around them.

Evelyn forced herself to snap out of it. She tried to pinpoint what was wrong, because something was most definitely wrong.

Christina!

She spun around. The little girl was nowhere to be seen. Evelyn scanned the crowd, focused on a level about three and a half feet above the ground. She was desperate for a flash of the red pirate bandanna or the sword, or the sweet curve of a little sun-browned arm, or the Nikes with neon green laces.

"Oh, my God!"

Clancy was at her side.

"We'll find him. It's okay. He's got to be close."

Evelyn paid no attention to him, and began to run. But she was grateful for the reminder—she had been on the verge of calling out the name Christina, which only would have added to the disaster. She ran, pushing through people, spinning, weaving, and all the while her heart was exploding with self-loathing. How could she? How could she have been playing googly-eyes with that man while Christina ran off?

The mermaid. She probably ran after the mermaid.

"Oh, shit."

Evelyn stopped at the sound of Clancy's voice. She jerked her head to follow the direction of his gaze and saw her niece, balanced precariously on the middle railing at the edge of the dock. Both of them were already running toward her.

"Chris!" Evelyn screamed.

Christina didn't hear her. She was busy waving her new sword over her head, shouting out warnings to some imaginary foe at sea. Her niece's body stretched farther, her knees pushing against the middle rail while the rest of her tilted over the water.

"Chris!"

She tumbled over, just inches from Evelyn's grasp.

"Stay." Clancy had already removed his utility belt and dropped it to the deck. "I've got him."

"No!" As Evelyn shrugged off her small daypack, Clancy balanced a hand on the top rail and pivoted his body into the water. She was right behind him. Evelyn hit the surface, shocked by the temperature, salt water stinging her open eyes, panic threatening to overwhelm her. She would not let it. She would find Christina.

She took a big gulp of air, diving down into the churning green sea, her eyes bulging, searching for any sign of Christina's small body. At least her niece knew how to swim. She was a good swimmer for a four-year-old. Amanda and Evelyn had made sure of that, taking her out into the shallow part of the lake, right off the beach, before she'd even turned one. But Moose Lake wasn't the Atlantic, and Evelyn began to choke with fear, still swimming, still digging through the water, deeper, but nothing . . . Her lungs burned with pain and pressure. She had no choice but to get more oxygen.

She broke the surface, gulping air, and was about to go under again when she heard a man's voice.

"I've got him! He's okay!"

Evelyn twisted around in the water in time to see Clancy handing Christina over to another police officer reaching from the dock. Though immediately relieved beyond measure, she swam as fast as she'd ever done the freestyle in her life, her only objective to get to her niece.

"Let me help you, Cricket. I got you."

Clancy had already pulled himself onto the dock and was seated on the edge, holding out his hand to her. She gripped her fingers around his muscular wrist as he grasped hers. He pulled her up from the water, and though Evelyn tried to get leverage on the dock with her foot, she slipped. He grabbed her, and for a moment she was caught there, tight against him, body to body, his lips an inch from her own. Evelyn felt his warm breath brush her face. His body pressed into hers and she felt him— firm and solid. She remembered him. Oh, God, even for that brief flash of contact, it was as if those eighteen years had never happened.

This was not good.

She twisted from his grasp and reached for the lowest rail, pulling herself up and swinging her body through onto the dock. And then, finally, she had her arms around Christina.

"Are you all right?"

Through the sobs she managed a singular, loud, "No!"

Evelyn's heart nearly burst. "Where are you hurt?"

"No! My sword! My sword is in the water!"

"He seems to be fine." That was the second police officer, now crouching nearby. Evelyn swore he looked familiar too. She must be hallucinating. "I've called the rescue squad as a precaution. Do you want to get him to the hospital on Nantucket and have him checked out?"

"My new sword!" Christina yelled out.

Evelyn loosened her grip on her niece and held her out in front of her. "Did you swallow any water?"

"My pretty new sword! My pirate costume!"

That's when Evelyn noticed Christina was missing her bandanna, and eye patch, and one of her shoes. Thank God her breeches had stayed on, since her niece chose a pair of pink-flowered underpants that morning.

"We will get you a new sword and everything else. Please answer me—did you swallow water?"

She shook her head, her ultrashort hair flinging out drops of water. "I did what you said and always keep my mouth closed and blow out my nose."

Evelyn hugged her tight again, but Chris pushed against her. "I want to go home," she said, her bottom lip trembling.

"Okay, Jellybean. Okay." Just then, Evelyn realized that though she'd jettisoned her daypack, she'd forgotten to remove her hat and sunglasses before she dove into the water. She smiled at Christina. "Look! I lost my costume, too! We'll go shopping together!"

Her niece pouted, not convinced.

"All right, kiddo." Evelyn stood, pulling Christina to a stand. "Let's go change our clothes."

"I'll go with you to Nantucket."

Evelyn twisted around to see Clancy, soaked to the skin, standing tall and serious, his arm outstretched as he handed her the daypack. In any other circumstance, she would have hugged and kissed him and told him she was indebted to him forever. But all she did was accept the pack and shake her head. "Thanks, but no."

He looked puzzled.

"I'll call her doctor at home first. Back in Bloomington." She grabbed her daypack, slipped it on, and picked up Christina from the boardwalk. Just then she noticed that a small crowd had gathered to watch the drama. "He's fine," she said to everyone. "We're good."

She turned to go, took one step, and stopped. Evelyn

slowly spun around on her squeaky sandals and sought out Clancy. He stood next to his colleague, hair dripping and his uniform clinging to every plane and swell on his gorgeous body, concern in those deep blue eyes, jaw set tight. In that moment she saw all of him—the fourteen-year-old she'd loved, the beautiful man he'd become, the quick-on-his-feet lifesaver, decorated police officer, and Eagle Scout, if only in a manner of speaking. It made her smile.

God, how she wished they'd met again under more normal circumstances.

"I truly thank you, Chief Flynn. For everything."

She walked away, Christina's head on her shoulder, both of them weighed down with seawater. She knew in her heart that she'd blown it. Not only had she failed to provide even the most basic safety for Christina, she'd made a spectacle of them both. As soon as they got back to the Sand Dollar, she would examine her niece to make sure she didn't need medical attention. If she did, so be it. Christina's health was the most important thing. But the ruse would be over the second doctors discovered she was a girl.

Evelyn would turn herself in.

But if her niece seemed okay, then Evelyn would get her in some dry clothes and start to pack. Either way, they needed to get off this island and go . . . somewhere. Anywhere but here.

Clancy strolled through the small parking lot and entered the Bayberry Police Department through the back door. As with every other moving part in this nineteenth-century building, finesse was required to get it to function as intended. Clancy jiggled the key while simultaneously lifting upward on the knob and the thick wooden door finally opened.

He took a moment to close his eyes and appreciate the relief of central air-conditioning flowing down the narrow hallway. The evening had turned hot and muggy and rain was in the forecast for tomorrow, which always threw Island Day organizers and vendors into a tizzy. Only minutes ago, an artist had called Clancy's cell phone to express her disdain for the weather report.

"Isn't there anything you can do about this?" She sounded completely serious. "As you might imagine, my origami creations don't fare well in a downpour, and I forgot to bring my plastic rain shields with me from the mainland this year. Does the police department have extras?"

On one hand, Clancy was pleased that Island Day merchants felt comfortable coming to him with their questions and concerns—small-town cooperation was what had made the event so successful over the years. Unfortunately, he had to tell the owner of "Mâché Madness" in Provincetown that the police department didn't stock rain shields for vendor tents and hadn't yet found a way to control the climate.

She groaned in frustration and hung up on him.

"You're two minutes late, great leader."

Clancy chuckled as he moved through the open doorway of the department's conference room. "Yeah, sorry about that, Officers."

Deon raised both his eyebrows. "First day and you already look like you got a beat-down."

Clancy nodded. "I did, indeed. Chip, you ready with roll call?"

"Yes, Chief Flynn."

As Chip read aloud every name on the beefed-up police roster, Clancy checked his laptop for bulletin updates. But his mind wasn't on police work. It was on the lovely, and inexplicably familiar, Cricket. After all the drama at the dock that afternoon, he decided he needed to know a little more about the standoffish visitor. It was simple enough to find out she was staying at the Sand Dollar, and that's where he'd start in his quest to dig a little deeper. Once he was caught up on paperwork.

Within ten minutes, everyone had been brought up to

speed on the day's events, the status of ongoing investigations, and the two men in the lockup waiting for transport to the mainland. Precisely at seven p.m., Deon and Jake switched over to assigned patrol, Doug and Will were on station duty and would provide backup where it was needed, and Lowell and Cam would be off duty, getting some much-needed sleep. The last item on the agenda was updating the team on the custody-related kidnapping out of Maine.

"Good job today, gentlemen. Everyone have a safe evening. I'll be in the office a bit longer, then reachable by radio or cell, as always. Chip will handle the overnight roll call. See you tomorrow." He prepared to head out.

"How's the little boy from the dock?"

Clancy shrugged, wondering how he would answer Jake. What could he say? That he knew the kid's aunt but couldn't figure out how? That the woman had some kind of effect on him? That seeing her today felt like a punch to his gut? "I really don't know," was his answer. "Haven't talked to the kid or his aunt since it happened."

"He seemed fine," Chip said. "I got there right after it happened and all the witnesses said the boy popped up and started treading water. Never even panicked. That's one tough little man."

Eventually, the room cleared. Clancy wandered down the hall to his office. He put his feet on the desk and rocked back in his chair, hands behind his head. He decided now was the time. He needed to step back, away from the glare. He would soften his gaze and keep his mind occupied with police business. And sooner or later, it would come to him. The Cricket situation would solve itself.

The phone rang. It was Rowan. "Hey, Clancy. You doing good?"

"Never better. And may I just say that you were stunning as the Safe Haven Mermaid Queen today. And my man Ashley looked dapper at the helm of the Oceanaire float."

His sister laughed, amused by his intentional mispronunciation of Ashton's name. Clancy had enjoyed yanking his chain since their first meeting, and saw no reason to stop.

"Yeah, well, thanks so much," Rowan said. "I'll pass it along to Ashley."

"So what's up?"

"I'm almost afraid to ask, but . . . any word from Duncan?"

"Nah, but you know how he is."

"Yeah, unfortunately. I thought Ma was going to have a heart attack last year. I just don't want her to get all worked up again."

The thought had crossed Clancy's mind, too. Their mother had worried all last summer about Duncan because she hadn't heard from him. No one had any idea where—or how—he was. True to form, Duncan arrived the evening of the annual Flynn family cookout on the last ferry, without a word of warning. He called Clancy to pick him up and drive him directly to their mother's cottage.

It had always struck Clancy as funny how his brother's job required him to slip unnoticed into hostile territories, yet he loved making an entrance when he came home—the bigger, the better.

Clancy smiled to himself. "Hey, Row, maybe this year a Navy helicopter will fly directly over Ma's backyard, you know, and just air drop the bastard right into the crudités platter."

Rowan laughed. "Don't joke. It could happen."

"I'm prepared for anything. Well, sis, I'd better go."

"Wait a sec. The other reason I called is that Ma told me you wanted your boxes that were in the attic."

He took his feet off the desk and sat up straight.

"*Were* in the attic? You already threw them out?"

"What? No, of course not. What's the big deal—you looking for a long-lost lotto ticket or something?"

He chuckled. "I wish."

"Anyway, we found three boxes of your stuff—trophies and kid junk and even some college crap. I put it all in the carriage house . . ."

Clancy was already on his feet.

". . . So come over anytime after festival week. Maybe you can join Ash and me for supper."

He put on his cap. "I'll take a rain check on the meal, but I'll be right over to get the boxes." He grabbed the keys to the Jeep.

"Uh . . . now? Seriously? Aren't you just a little busy?"

"See ya in five."

Eighteen years ago . . .

Amanda grabbed Evelyn's wrist so hard it hurt. "Oh, my God. There he is!"

"Where?" She looked all around but didn't see him. There were thousands of people crammed onto the boardwalk and the edge of Main Street for the parade. How was she supposed to pick out one single teenage boy in this craziness?

"Don't do that!"

"Don't do what?"

"Look around like that, like a gopher on a PBS nature show or something."

"How am I supposed to find him if I don't look for him?"

"Oh, my God. You just don't know anything, do you?"

"So I'm supposed to use ESP to find him? Or Baldwin radar?"

Amanda cracked up. "God, that would be great, wouldn't it? But, no. I'm just saying you need to be low-key. If he sees you looking for him, he'll think you're dying to see him again."

Evelyn *was* dying to see Clancy again, but decided to keep it to herself. If Amanda knew how interested she really was, this vacation would be a living hell. Could there be anything in the world more embarrassing than having your twelve-year-old sister teach you about the art of seduction?

"He's looking over here. He sees you."

Evelyn puffed up her hair with her fingers and tried to appear casual. She must have been crazy, but she actually let Amanda help her get ready that morning. On her sister's advice, she'd applied mousse to her damp hair and let it dry naturally. After Amanda borrowed a pair of scissors from the front desk, she cut off the bottom of two T-shirts so they both could wear crop tops to the parade. They had to hide this from their parents, of course, because people from Maine thought stuff like that was indecent.

So there she was, hanging out on the boardwalk waiting for the parade to start, pretending not to be looking for the boy she was desperately looking for, all while having big hair and an exposed belly. Evelyn felt kind of silly.

"Don't look. Don't look. He's coming over here!"

The parade started. Evelyn tried to appear really, really into the high school band now playing "Achy Breaky Heart," something that was almost impossible to do.

"Hey!"

She turned to see Clancy standing in front of Amanda and herself. She smiled like she was surprised to see him.

"Hey!"

"Want to go for a walk?"

"Sure." Evelyn shot Amanda a silent look that screamed *Oh, my God!* and said, "Tell Ginny and Charlie I'll see them later."

They pushed their way through a dozen rows of people and Clancy gestured for her to follow him. Finally they broke into a patch of clear boardwalk where they could actually talk to each other.

"Who are Ginny and Charlie?"

"Oh. My parents."

"You call them by their first names?"

Wow—she felt pretty stupid. "No. Not really."

They walked down the dock toward the marina and the two of them made more small talk—school, family, sports, music, TV—just trying to figure each other out. They went for ice cream cones and Clancy took her back behind Main Street to a beach access he said only the locals knew about, and they went for a walk.

"I think you're really pretty and smart," Clancy said.

Of course, Evelyn had just taken a giant lick of butter brickle and it got all over her lips. She shook her head while licking it off, feeling more awkward than she ever had in her life. "Hmm. I'm just average."

He laughed. "Trust me. I see girls come and go all the time here and you're *way* above average."

She couldn't stop herself from smiling, which meant she was now embarrassed about three things: that she was sloppy with her ice cream, that he thought she was above average, and that she couldn't stop herself from smiling. This boy thing was hard. She didn't even know if she was doing it right.

"I think you're really special, too."

Clancy shrugged, licking a dribble of rocky road ice cream from the side of his cone. "Thanks."

"Really. You're cute and brave and an excellent swimmer. And totally strong. Plus, you're super nice."

That was such a stupid thing to say! Evelyn wished she could turn into a pile of sand and be blown away by the breeze. Had she admitted too much? Did the compliments sound fake? They were *real*. She honestly felt that way about him.

But Clancy turned toward her and his face exploded into a smile. It was the most beautiful thing she'd ever seen—a straight, white grin that pushed up his eyes and cheeks. For just a second, it was difficult to get air. Her feet seemed nailed down, but her insides—her chest and stomach and heart—were so light that she felt she could fly right up over the beach. This was weird. She was wiggin' out.

Clancy reached over and took her hand in his. It wasn't like he demanded it, or was afraid she'd say no. It was more like he just knew it would be there and she would be fine with it. And she was.

Evelyn was holding hands with the cutest guy in the world! He liked her. And she liked him. This was the bomb!

Chapter Six

What he wanted wasn't near the top of any of the boxes, of course, so Clancy had to dump their contents onto the living room floor. Once he pulled out all the trophies and set them on the fireplace mantel, he went to the kitchen for a cup of coffee. When he returned, his dogs were using his memorabilia as a wrestling mat.

"Fellas! Off!" The two large dogs froze. Tripod was on his back, his pale belly exposed, his three remaining legs sticking straight up in the air. Earl's chocolate brown butt was aimed toward the ceiling and his elbows were on the floor, and his wide, expressive eyes revealed his guilt. Tripod seemed oblivious as always, eyes crazy, tongue lolling out of the side of his mouth.

Clancy couldn't help but chuckle at his companions. A few years back, Duncan had christened them Dipshit and Doofus, which he thought was a bit harsh. But adopting those two rescue dogs had been one of the best decisions he'd ever made. Somehow, it made perfect sense that Barbie couldn't stand them. The world sorts itself out in mysterious ways. Hard-hearted Barbie was long gone and these two loving, harebrained creatures made him laugh and smile every damn day.

He placed his coffee cup on an end table and picked

a spot on the floor away from the spilled contents of the boxes. "All right. Come on over." Both dogs spun and twisted, trying to get traction on the slick papers, and eventually piled into Clancy's lap—two hundred pounds of in-the-moment happiness. He rubbed their ears and scratched their backs and roughhoused with them for a few minutes. "I know I'm not around much this week, but hang in there, all right? Now, listen up. I need to find this damn photo and get some sleep. Okay by you?" Clancy gave them each one last scratch and pointed toward the back of the house. "Outside. Dog door."

They happily clambered down the bare pine hallway and squeezed themselves through the cutout. The heavy plastic flap closed behind them.

Clancy started in on the mess scattered in front of him, deciding that he might as well organize as he searched. Clearly, Mona hadn't been overly choosy about what she decided was worth squirreling away for posterity. Clancy found programs from elementary school band recitals, science fair honorable mentions, his kindergarten report card, and his first communion photo from Our Lady of the Isle Catholic Church. But some of the junk was highly entertaining, like an essay he wrote for Mrs. Schmidt's third-grade class with this unique title: "A Mermaid." His essay read, "The mermaid is dum and ugly. The legend is really stuped." Clancy tossed the wide-ruled paper into a box, somehow proud that, though his spelling had improved, his opinion of the mermaid hadn't changed much in the last twenty-five years.

He uncovered several track ribbons, including a handful from his junior varsity year, and one for his third-place finish in the ten-thousand-meter event at the state high school championships. He found a bunch of shells and sea glass, and a drawing he'd done of his family when he'd been in fifth grade. He stared at it for a moment, deciding it was both sweet and sad. Everyone was standing on the deck of his dad's old Bermuda sloop, ready to head out for a day sail. His father loomed large over the family the way he always had, and his mother had Duncan pressed into her side, like she was afraid he'd be blown over by the wind. Clancy had drawn himself smiling and making peace signs while Rowan had a bratty look on her face. All in all, fairly accurate, he'd have to say.

That was the year Clancy turned twelve. Flynn Fisheries was still hanging on and the mansion was still their private home. But soon, everything would change. In a few years the fishery would close, they'd open the house as a bed-and-breakfast, and his parents would begin arguing over whether they should sell the family home and acreage to hotel developers. Though it was no longer an issue—thanks to Ash's plan to restore the Safe Haven and build a marine research institute on a piece of the land— his parents couldn't find a way to stop arguing. It was as if they couldn't remember any other way of communicating.

Clancy tossed the drawing into the box he'd designated for school stuff, and kept going. It took about ten minutes, but he spotted it. It was a color photo his mother had taken with her auto-focus 35 mm camera. His dance partner was exactly his height and equally lean, her brown hair hanging loose down her back, just as Clancy remembered. He studied the picture, examining the dynamics of it. They were laughing, the girl arched away from him just enough that they could look into each other's eyes. Clancy had managed to pull her close on the dance floor, holding her hand against his chest while slipping his other arm around her waist.

Not bad for a fourteen-year-old. Not bad at all.

At that instant, he remembered her name. *Evie.* One look at this picture and his mind was filled with the sound of the word.

Evie.

The rush of memory and emotion came on so hard and fast that he had to laugh at himself. No wonder he'd forgotten her name—he'd buried it on purpose so he wouldn't have to remember how much he had loved her.

But there she was in the photo, beautiful in a pale yellow sundress with thin straps and decoration around the bottom. She had on a pair of those hideous, but popular, jelly shoes. He found something fascinating in the delicate curve of her face and the shape of her chin. Clancy popped to a stand and took the photo into the kitchen, where the light was better.

She really was beautiful, and it was obvious that she would grow into a gorgeous woman one day. Though the photo captured her mostly in profile, he could see Evie's long, elegant neck, pretty skin, and nice eyes. But why hadn't she written him? It made no sense. She really seemed to like him—the photo was proof that she'd liked him.

Suddenly, Clancy squinted. He tilted the snapshot into the light and pulled back. What the hell? There was no way. It wasn't possible . . . was it?

To be certain, he imagined that lean and tanned body slightly more muscular and in shorts and sport sandals. Then he pictured the elegant neck and pretty eyes topped off with a spiky blond haircut.

Clancy was so stunned he forgot to breathe for a moment. He couldn't move. Couldn't think. He yanked himself out of his shock and flipped the picture over in his hand. There in the bottom right corner was his own juvenile handwriting. *Evie and me, Mermaid Ball.*

The years fell away, and Clancy was laughing with her, inhaling her flowery, warm skin, and making plans to go visit her in Maine over Christmas break. At least he thought it was Maine. But now she lived in Indiana and called herself Cricket.

Though it ate up a few minutes of precious time, Clancy ran to his printer and scanned the photo into his home computer. He needed a backup image in case anything happened to the original. Then he shoved the photo in the pocket of his uniform shorts, threw some dog chow in two large stainless steel bowls, and grabbed his duty belt and ball cap. Though the Sand Dollar was a short walk, he took the Jeep in case he got a request for backup. Moments later, Clancy pulled up in the no parking zone and opened the lobby door, a bell tinkling.

"May I help you, Officer?"

He quickly scanned the name tag of a small, dark-haired kid on a J-1 summer visa. He'd seen him around, and had always thought him to be polite. "Hello, there ... Bujar. How are you this evening?"

"Fine, sir. And you?"

"Great. So where are you from originally?"

"Albania."

"Enjoying it here?"

"Oh, yes. It is wonderful. Except I must do cleaning rooms three days a week—I like work at desk better."

"Can't say I blame you." Clancy could now add Albania to his list. At this point, there were few countries that hadn't been represented in Bayberry's summer workforce at some point. "So, Bujar, if you have a moment, I was hoping you could help me out. I have a quick question about one of your guests."

The kid's dark brown eyes got big. "Yes? Yes, sir. I'll get Mister Cosmo. Please wait." He ran off to the office tucked behind the wall, and Clancy heard him on the phone, apologizing several times for disturbing Cosmo Katsakis during his dinner.

Within minutes, Cosmo appeared, coming from his apartment in the back. He was still buttoning a cotton shirt over his tomato sauce–stained wife beater and sucking food from his teeth. "Hey, Chief! What a pleasant surprise! What can I help you with tonight?"

No, the motel owner would never be elected Bayberry's most eligible bachelor—or businessman of the year. Cosmo had resisted improving the motel's amenities and furnishings, which angered his fellow Bayberry Island merchants. More than once, Clancy had been called in to officiate at a Chamber of Commerce meeting at which Cosmo referred to his fellow islanders as "communists" and told them exactly where they could stick their five-year tourism development plan.

Clancy's aversion to Mr. Katsakis had nothing to do with his appearance or business practices, however. It was personal. In Clancy's mind, Cosmo would always be linked to the worst night of his life. The motel owner smirked every time they crossed paths, as if to remind Clancy that he was in on the joke. Which, in a sense, he was.

It had happened during festival week three years before. Clancy had asked Cosmo to open the door to room forty-seven. Inside was Clancy's wife, Barbie, knockin' flip-flops with a tourist. The image was forever burned into Clancy's corneas—Barbie's spandex mermaid costume crumpled on the floor while a naked man in a jaunty sea captain's cap rode her like she was high tide.

The next morning, Clancy had the very bruised tourist in custody for assaulting an officer and purchased Barbie a one-way ferry passage back to the mainland. Her parting words had been, "I hate this ridiculous island! There's one week of fun, and the rest of the year I'm bored out of my skull! I'm going back to Boston where I belong!"

Separation papers were drawn up that week. Within two months, the divorce was final and the sea captain had wisely dropped the idea of filing police brutality charges.

In an attempt to lift Clancy's spirits and help put the whole disaster behind him, his dad had taken him to the Rusty Scupper Tavern for a pint. Frasier had raised a glass in his honor.

"She wasn't good enough for ya, son. Besides, you've dodged the menopause bullet, and that makes you a lucky, lucky man."

Right on cue, Cosmo smirked. "Let me guess, Chief Flynn. You need me to open up another door for you? I didn't know you had remarried."

Clancy glared at Cosmo, making sure he saw his complete lack of amusement. "I need to ask a few questions about Cricket Dickinson, one of your guests."

"Dickinson?" Cosmo let his eyeglasses fall down the

bridge of his nose so he could see the computer screen. "Yeah. Adjoining rooms. Fourteen and sixteen."

"Two rooms? For an adult and young child?"

"A . . . who? Now, hold on." He clicked a few keys on the computer. "They checked in yesterday . . . paid cash for the whole week in advance . . . This don't make no sense." He looked up over the rim of his eyeglasses at Clancy. "I don't know what's going on with this reservation, but I swear that's not who I rented these rooms to last fall. I always require a credit card on file but there's nothing here, just a copy of her license. Something's not right."

"I'd have to agree with that," Clancy said. "I'd like a printout of that license if you don't mind."

Cosmo clicked a key and the printer whirred to life. He resumed his perusal of the computer screen. "This had to be a reservation for a party of four originally, because I have a rule—a minimum of two people per room rule during festival week. No exceptions."

"So what happened?"

Cosmo suddenly lost enthusiasm for the issue, and shrugged. "What do I know?" He retrieved the black-and-white page from the printer and handed it to Clancy. "I'm an old man and half the time I can't even find my own wallet. Computers don't make mistakes, right? So I guess I don't remember so good. As long as the bill is paid, I got no problems."

Clancy decided he'd be coming back for a chat with his new Albanian friend when Cosmo was otherwise occupied.

"Well, thanks for your help, Mr. Katsakis."

"I don't want no trouble here, Chief. I run a nice family operation, no funny business—well, most of the time, that is. But I don't need to tell you that."

Clancy tipped his cap and walked out of the lobby, feeling Cosmo's smirk burning through the back of his uniform shirt.

* * *

There was a knock at the door. Evelyn jumped off the bed and ran to press her eye to the peephole. Though it was difficult to get a clear look in the glare of the security light, it was obviously a young woman. Maybe one of the motel maids.

She unlatched the chain lock and cracked the door open, putting a finger up to her lips. "Shhhh. My nephew is asleep."

"Oh." The girl tried to peek inside.

Evelyn blocked her view, suddenly uncomfortable. "Is there something I can help you with?"

The girl smiled. "Did I wake you, too?"

Evelyn glanced down to see she was wearing nothing but a stretchy camisole and pajama shorts. Okay. Now she was irritated. "It is almost ten p.m., and families with children are asleep by now. What did you say you wanted?"

She reached in the pocket of her khakis and handed Evelyn a business card. "I'm Hillary Hewes, editor of the *Bayberry Island Bulletin*, and I'm here to interview you and your boy about the near-drowning at the dock today."

Evelyn felt her jaw fall open. She pushed the card back into Hillary's palm. "Sorry. Not interested."

"I already have the police report." She produced a smug little wobble of her head. "Don't you want to add your side of the story? Maybe get your photo in Friday's festival week wrap-up edition?"

"My side of the story?" Evelyn laughed sarcastically. Shit. They should have left on the last evening ferry as she'd planned, but Jellybean had been so worn out and grumpy that Evelyn decided they'd leave first thing in the morning instead. Huge mistake.

"If you'd prefer, I can interview you on camera. I'm a freelance broadcast journalist, too, trying to break into the big leagues, you know?"

Evelyn blinked. "Uh, no. Good-bye."

"Wait!" Hillary put her gym shoe in the crack of the door. "Is the boy all right?"

That was it. Evelyn stomped on the reporter's shoe with her own bare foot, pressing down hard until the girl retreated from the threshold. "Good night." She shut, chained, and dead-bolted the door.

Even after all that, a small, white business card got shoved under the door. *People!*

Evelyn twisted around to check on Christina, relieved to see she was still asleep and breathing peacefully. She decided that while she was up she might as well call Hal, so she grabbed her cell phone and headed toward the bathroom.

There was another knock at the door, this time much softer. Evelyn was completely pissed off at that point and her mind was spinning . . . *Sure! Come on in! I'm a wanted kidnapper! Since the news coverage hasn't gotten me arrested yet, let's put my frickin' picture on the front page of your newspaper and see what happens!*

Evelyn opened the door while keeping the chain in place. She stuck only her lips through the crack. "If you do not stop harassing me, I will call the police."

Someone with a deep voice cleared his throat. "It's always nice to be needed."

Evelyn's spine stiffened. Her heart began to slam behind her ribs. It was him. Un-bee-*leeve*-able! Now what was she going to do?

"I . . . I'm sorry, Chief Flynn. Chris is asleep and I'm not dressed."

"I'll wait."

"Wait for what?"

"For you to come out here and sit on the bench with me. We need to talk."

Evelyn let her forehead drop to the motel wall. So what now? This could be a trap. In the hours since the parade, Clancy could have figured out who she was, contacted the FBI, and flown in a SWAT team. There might be a dozen specially trained officers with automatic weapons just outside the door. Christina could be whisked away to Richard Wahlman while Evelyn was being thrown to the ground and handcuffed. And she wouldn't be able to stop any of it. She wouldn't even get a chance to say good-bye.

Evelyn raised her head from the wall. On the other hand, maybe Clancy Flynn simply wanted to talk to her.

"It's pretty late. I really shouldn't. Chris will be—"

"He'll be fine. We'll be right outside."

She slowly moved her eyes so she could see out the crack in the door. Clancy had his head tipped to the side, his hands in his pockets. He seemed pretty mellow for someone coordinating a SWAT raid. Suddenly, he raised his eyes and locked his gaze with hers.

"Come on out. We have a lot of catching up to do."

Richard was one of the anointed few, and if he ever needed to be reminded of that, all he had to do was look out his office window. For the last two terms, he'd been situated on the second floor of the Rayburn Building, where the view, especially on a night like this one, was nothing short of intoxicating.

He could see the Capitol dome, the thirty-six windows of the rotunda shedding golden light into the darkness. He enjoyed the vast geometric display of the District of Columbia spread out at his feet, as if it had been designed for his pleasure alone. Sometimes, just the view from up here could give him a hard-on.

Not tonight.

He reached for the cut glass decanter and poured two fingers of cognac. In the darkness, he sipped slowly, appreciating the rich combination of flavors—caramel, grape, and ancient oak. His cardiologist would bitch-slap him if he knew he was drinking, but then again, tonight wasn't about his cardiologist. Or his furious wife, or his terrible mistakes, or his position as one of the anointed. Tonight, he was just a man alone, having a heart-to-bypassed-heart with himself.

Though Congress would be back in session in just two weeks, no one was working late that night, not even his most overachieving legislative assistants. Members of his staff were at home with their families or significant others, sweating and worrying. The faint odor of scandal had already begun to cling to the draperies around here. Richard's media relations guy said rumors were all over town that Tamara was leaving him. His constituent services director asked if it was true that he missed two meetings because of health complications. Richard knew how it worked—as the congressman goes, so goes the staff. On the Hill, the concept of "job security" was an oxymoron.

He took another delicious sip, savoring the pleasure to be had in his only noncompliant behavior since surgery. The wood-paneled walls and thick carpet absorbed the heavy silence. Darkness hid him. The room felt lifeless, the perfect setting for a man on the edge. This was it. It was time to make a decision.

When he said his daughter was more important than his career or marriage, was that the truth? Was he really willing to pay the price for such a choice? He couldn't afford to stew about it any longer—yet another day of bulletins, evidence review, and interviews of potential eyewitnesses had gone by and the FBI still had jack. The girl had been missing for more than two days now, and the special agent in charge informed him that they were now fifty percent less likely to ever find Christina.

Richard jolted at the sound of a single rap on his door. "Who the hell is it?"

"It's me."

Of course it was M.J. The woman didn't even have a cat to feed. Or a plant to water.

"Come on in." The door cracked, spilling hallway light across the royal blue plush carpet.

"Drinking in the dark, Congressman?"

"Yeah. Care to join me?"

She shrugged. "Why not?"

As was customary, M.J. took a seat in one of the overstuffed armchairs cozied up to his eighteenth-century cherry desk, turning on his desk lamp. She accepted the drink and raised her glass. "To eighteen great years."

Richard swallowed another mouthful and smiled at her, puzzled. "You have something to say, I take it."

"Not at the moment, but I'm trying to plan for my future. I thought I'd better get a bead on what was going on in your head."

"Ahh."

"Tamara's leaving you, isn't she?"

"Yes."

M.J. swished the cognac around in her mouth, pondering the information. "Do you have a strategy in mind?"

Richard's laughter continued for several seconds before it faded into a drawn-out sigh. "Sure. My strategy is to sign and date whatever the fuck her lawyers put in front of me."

That managed to get a chuckle out of M.J. "Will she wait until after the reelection to file?"

Richard set the glass on his desk. He looked in her eyes, knowing he had to be straight with her about this. "Tamara will wait until after the reelection. But there's another matter that I'm afraid may not be able to wait."

M.J.'s entire demeanor changed in an instant. One moment she was plotting political strategy and the next she sat, her face blank and frozen. But her empty stare soon turned to an expression of horror. As usual, M.J. had already made the cognitive leap. She'd been working for Richard so long that she knew how his brain worked. And in this particular situation, he could see that she was already grasping for how to convince him to change his mind.

"She's been gone more than forty-eight hours now, M.J."

"No, Richard. You can't. Absolutely not. Not before the reelection."

"That's well over two months away. They'll be living in Bora Bora by then."

M.J.'s ears turned red. She was more pissed than Richard had ever seen her.

"Please try to understand. Right now, Christina's case is simply a custody-related abduction out of a tiny town in Maine. It is not particularly news. But the minute I go public and reveal she's my child, the precious four-year-old daughter I never knew I had—"

"Your career is over?"

He ignored her snarky interruption. "When I go public, the faces of Evelyn and Christina McGuinness get plastered all over the Web and featured on every damn TV news channel in the nation. And, *bam*, we find her."

"This is pure insanity."

"Be realistic." Richard rose from his leather chair and made his way to the tall windows. He rattled a bit of loose change in his trouser pockets, watching his partial reflection in the glass. He looked a bit like a ghost. How perfect. "We both know the truth will ooze out before the election, one way or another. Charlie McGuinness is angry enough to serve up my head on a platter."

"I can handle Charlie McGuinness."

"And if it's not him, it could be any number of people who have knowledge about my paternity. Perhaps a court employee or even an agent assigned to the case who happens to loathe my politics. You know how nasty this life is. One anonymous tip is all it would take to cause a crap avalanche."

"You simply can't do it."

"If it's all going to fall apart anyway, I should go public sooner rather than later, proactively cut through the scandal and take responsibility. At least that way my confession might help find Christina. Some good might come out of this whole mess."

"This is political suicide."

He turned from the windows in time to see M.J. stand. The woman was irate.

"It's within reach, Richard. We can almost touch it." M.J. was trying so hard to keep it together that her voice cracked. "You said if I came to Washington with you I would have a desk in the West Wing one day. And now we're closer than we've ever been. You're on the short list for VP in two years. This is the promise you gave me. Why would you blow it all to hell and back now?"

"I know the timing isn't good."

M.J. produced a foul-tempered cackle. For the first time in their partnership, she reminded him of Tamara. He shuddered.

"I've sacrificed my life for you. Every day and week and month of the last eighteen years I gave to you. Why? Because you made me a promise. How stupid I was! I actually believed you!"

"I never intended for this to happen."

"You are making a huge mistake. You will regret it."

"I'm sorry."

"Not as sorry as you will be, and very soon."

"M.J., please."

"You'll have my resignation by the end of the week."

Eighteen years ago . . .

"So, do you believe in the mermaid?"

Evie asked that as she brushed a wind chime with her long fingers, smiling when it released a random series of dings, tinkles, and hollow notes. Clancy knew it was one of a million like it hanging from display racks in Island Day vendor tents up and down Main Street, but to Evie it was exotic.

They'd spent the day together and he'd actually had fun, even though he'd been through fourteen of these events in his life. And that was one of the reasons—everything was an adventure for Evie. She asked questions. She oohed and awed over stuff that surprised her. Since Evie was seeing everything for the first time, it made everything a lot less boring than usual for Clancy.

"Ooh! I think this one is really pretty, do you?"

Clancy checked it out. The chime was made of blown glass shaped like mermaids and dolphins and decorated with shiny abalone beads, pieces of sea glass, and tiny shells. "Sure. It's nice. But I was busy staring at something much prettier."

Evelyn smiled shyly, but didn't make eye contact with him. In the two days he'd been hanging out with her, he decided she wasn't like most of the tourist girls he'd met. She didn't talk about Madonna or her tan lines or that she cried when New Kids on the Block broke up. Evie was a Red Sox fan. She played soccer, ran track, and rode horses. She wanted to be a doctor when she grew up and was a fan of *Star Trek: The Next Generation*. But while all this awesome stuff was going on with her, she was still one hundred percent girl. She smelled like sea air and wildflowers after it rained. Her skin was soft. She was curvy where curves were nice and flat where flat was fine. And she was nice to people. When Clancy bought her a funnel cake a while ago, Evie thanked him and then thanked the food truck dude who handed it to her.

But the best thing about Evie had to be that she had no idea how beautiful and great she really was. She wasn't stuck on herself. He wasn't sure how she'd managed to live so long without her head swelling up. He wondered if maybe all the guys in Maine were blind dweebs. But Clancy was happy Evie was so . . . cool.

"I bet you see a thousand wind chimes like this one every summer, don't you?"

"Nah."

"No?"

Clancy shook his head. "More like a million."

Each time Evie laughed the way she just did, some kind of electrical storm went off inside him. His blood was filled with hot sparks that went zooming around all over his body, and he got light-headed. Yeah, he'd asked the mermaid for his first piece of ass, but as stupid as he sounded to himself inside his head right at that moment, he had to admit that this was even better—Evie was so much more than that.

She slipped her hand inside his and they continued their slow, romantic tour of Island Day. He felt kind of guilty about it, but all he could think about was kissing her. She had such pretty and soft lips. They looked like they'd be real delicate to the touch, like a ripe nectarine or something. He wondered what she tasted like, or how it would feel to hold all of her against him, standing up or sitting down or, God, what would it feel like to lie down with her? He thought he might pass out.

"Yo."

Great. It was Mickey Flaherty and Chip was with him. Why Chip hung out with a dude who called him names and made fun of him he would never understand. But then again, Clancy had ditched his best friend for the last couple days to be with Evie, so what else was he supposed to do?

Clancy didn't let Evie take her hand away. He gave it a soft squeeze to let her know that he didn't care who saw. She felt her fingers relax and weave together with his.

"These are my homies. You met Mickey at the point. This is my best friend, Chip."

"Hey, Chip." She offered him her hand. "Nice to meet you." Then, Evie looked at Mickey but looked away without saying anything. Clancy just saw Evie be not so nice to somebody, and she'd picked Flaherty. It made him laugh.

"Why don't you come with us?" Mickey gave Clancy a look that was definitely a challenge. He was telling him that if he didn't choose his friends over this tourist girl, then it wouldn't be cool.

"Nah. I'm good. We're gonna hang here."

Mickey put an unlit cigarette between his lips and rummaged around in his jeans pocket for his Bic lighter. When he lit up, Evie coughed. "Well, excuuuuuse me," he said, the Marlboro hanging between his lips. "We're out."

Chip lingered a moment after Mickey walked away.

"It was really nice to meet you," he said to Evie. "I heard Clancy saved you from the rocks."

"He did." Evie made an effort to stop from smiling but couldn't do it. "You know, in the Kung Fu tradition, if you save someone's life you are responsible for their safety and happiness forever."

Chip's mouth fell open. "I saw that episode!"

"Chipster!" Mickey yelled for him to hurry up.

"I gotta go. But, yeah. Awesome. Have fun today." Poor guy looked a little dazed.

"Catch you later, Chip," Clancy said.

Evie said she needed to find a ladies' room, so they agreed to meet up at the seafood taco stand when she was done. Clancy used the opportunity to run back to the wind chime tent and buy the one she liked. His plan was to give it to her before she left on Friday.

She was leaving.

Clancy paid the woman and while she wrapped it in tissue paper so it wouldn't break, that's all Clancy could think about. Evie would be leaving at the end of the Mermaid Festival. That was five days away. Could that be right? He had only five more days with her. . . .

She met him as planned and insisted their next stop be the Fountain Square, which, of course, was the last place in the universe Clancy wanted to be. He was still creeped out every time he thought about that psycho whisper he heard. But what kind of personal tour guide would he be if he refused to show Evie the statue, the reason for all this festival week crap?

Honestly, there was no one on Earth he would do this for except Evie. And she'd never even know.

People were packed around the fountain shoulder to shoulder. If his dad was here—and he was glad he wasn't—he would have called it a real hoobanger. To Clancy, it was just a real pain in the ass.

Evie waited her turn and then pressed in so that she could read the plaque. Clancy stood right next to her, but it took everything in him not to run. He kept his eyes away from the mermaid. "Oh, wow! So Rutherford Flynn's fishing fleet was saved by a mermaid—is he an ancestor of yours?"

"Uh, yeah. My dad's great-grandfather or something like that." Clancy looked around to make sure no one he knew saw him there, since only dorky tourists and New

Age woo-woos hung out at the mermaid fountain. God, this was embarrassing.

Evie began mumbling out loud as she read. "So Rutherford tries to swim back into the storm to thank the mermaid, and almost dies. Holy crap. An innkeeper's daughter named Serena nurses him back to health and he wakes up and thinks she's the mermaid! Ha! Awesome!" Evie turned to him and must have detected his impatience. "We can go if you want."

"No." Clancy put his arm around her shoulders. "We'll stay as long as you like."

Evie got this look on her face he'd never seen before. Like she might cry or something. Then she kissed him on his cheek. It was quick but he'd been right—her lips were silky and warm and his skin was on fire where she kissed him.

"Thank you, Clancy. You are so nice to me."

At that moment, he would have done anything, *anything in the world* for that girl.

"So do you believe in the mermaid? You never said."

Anything but talk about that. "Uh, well, sort of, maybe, but not really. I mean, not literally. But it's cool. Sort of."

Evie went back to skimming over the history. "So they marry, he gets rich with a fishery company and he builds this fountain in Serena's honor. Oh! After fifteen years of marriage he still thinks she's the mermaid! That's wild!"

"Yeah. Wild."

"So, okay, here comes the legend part. People start believing that if you take the mermaid's hand and kiss it, asking for true love with an open heart, she will grant you your wish. But . . ." Evie quickly turned to look at Clancy and found his face right up near hers. He was busted.

"Oh." Evie got red in the face and returned her attention to the plaque. "So, you're not supposed to ask her to send you true love if you have someone specific in mind, someone you already know, and if you do . . . jeesh, that's harsh. 'Happiness will elude you,' it says."

"Let's walk over here and see her up close."

Clancy held Evie's hand and pushed through to the front of the crowd. The two of them stood just off to the mermaid's side. Her gaze was focused directly over them, out to the sea. Evie raised her chin and looked straight up. Clancy couldn't help it. He must have been swept away or something, because he looked up, too, just so his eyes could see what Evie was seeing. Mist from the fountain rained over their hair and clothes. They didn't say anything for a minute or two. Then Evie whispered.

"She's so incredibly beautiful." Her mouth parted slightly and her eyes were as big as sea scallops. "Very strong. Powerful, but, I don't know. It's hard to describe."

"She's strong but she's all girl."

Evie swung her head around and stared at him. Where the hell had that stupid comment come from? He was such a loser.

"Exactly."

Nope, he was a frickin' genius.

Whoa. Just then, the hot sparks were going completely nutso inside him. All he wanted to do was get out of this crowd of socks-and-sandals-wearing dads and get Evie alone. But, since he was trying to be a gentleman and all, he had to give her the opportunity to do what all the tourists did on Bayberry Island.

"Do you want to kiss her hand and ask for your true love or something?"

Evie shook her head back and forth slowly. "Nuh-uh." Her lips curled up into a small smile. "If I did that, happiness would elude me."

Without thinking, Clancy grabbed her hand and, like a tight end clearing the path for a running back, he led her through the socks-and-sandaled mob to safety. He knew exactly where he was going, though he could hardly admit it to himself.

Of course he'd always wondered what it would be like to kiss a girl. He'd thought about it a lot. But whenever he pictured it in his mind the big event took place on the beach, or on the boardwalk, or in her bedroom, or under the parade reviewing stand or anywhere, really—except where he was headed at the moment.

Clancy rounded a row of bayberry bushes, and immediately plopped down on the perfectly mowed grass. He knew it was perfect because he'd mowed it. And then he guided Evie onto his lap.

"I have to kiss you."

"I think I have to kiss you, too."

"I've never kissed a girl before."

"Neither have I." They both laughed. "A boy, I mean."

This was going to be everything, *everything* he ever wanted his first kiss to be. She angled her head and Clancy pulled her close, then pressed his lips to hers. Oh, God, Evie smelled like Coppertone and roses and the bayberries that kept them hidden from the crowds. She was like nothing he'd ever experienced—warm and soft and fleshy in places only girls were fleshy. Her lips were wet and smooth.

But the kiss ended.

They looked at each other. Neither said anything, but it was clear she'd liked it as much as he had. Oh, yes, God, she wrapped her arms around his neck. He put his hands in her long brown hair. And together, they melted.

Though Clancy reminded himself that he really had no idea what he was doing, it didn't seem to matter. He just let go, and somehow they figured it out together— the breathing, the moving, and even a little bit of tongue. It didn't last as long as he might have liked, but Clancy hoped this was just a warm-up for things to come.

All of a sudden, Evie frowned and reached toward the underside of her thigh. "What is that poking into me?"

Oh God, this was a nightmare. She'd just felt him get hard! He wanted to die. And then he felt her hand patting the large side pocket of his cargo shorts. Oh, thank baby Jesus it was the wind chime instead of his pecker!

Yes, Clancy intended to give the gift to her at the end of the week, but did it really matter when she got it? He only wanted to make her happy. So he fished it out and handed it to her, hoping to hell it wasn't broken.

Her fingers trembled slightly as she peeled open layers of white tissue. Evie pinched the small ring at the very top between her thumb and forefinger and pulled. It unfolded, perfect, unbroken, and already singing all its notes. Tears plopped onto her cheeks.

"Thank you, Clancy. This is the nicest thing a boy has ever done for me."

"I . . . you're very welcome. I like you, you know? I mean I *really, really like you*."

She nodded, sniffing. "I know. I really, really like you, too. So now what do we do?"

"I'm not sure, but we can kiss some more while we try to decide."

Chapter Seven

Clancy watched as Evie slipped from the motel room, turning her back toward him to double-check the lock. The instant she glanced over her shoulder, there was no longer any doubt in his mind—she knew who Clancy was, and she remembered the week they'd spent together when they were kids, probably in more detail than he did. But, for whatever reason, she'd chosen to avoid him and lie about it, and the time had come to find out why.

Cricket—Evie—faced him but remained at the door. Her hands hung straight at her sides, balled up into fists. Her eyes darted around the motel courtyard, almost as if she expected someone to jump from the bushes.

"Please come sit." Clancy patted the concrete bench under a loblolly pine, just outside of the range of the security light.

She had changed from the revealing pajama shorts and was now covered head to toe. Despite the humidity, she wore a baggy pair of jeans and a too-big—brand-new—Indiana University hoodie sweatshirt. Clancy didn't know what the hell she was up to, but he had to give her points for choosing a story and sticking to it.

"How's your nephew?"

She frowned, pulling her mouth tight. She tried not to

look at him but kept returning her gaze to his, expecting the worst. She was afraid of him, for some reason.

"He's fine."

Evelyn glanced down at the ground and Clancy did the same. She'd ditched the sport sandals for a pair of top-of-the-line Asics running shoes, a model he'd seen on many women athletes. It was difficult to be sure in the limited light, but they certainly didn't appear as new as the sweatshirt.

"I should probably go."

"Who was harassing you?"

"What?" Her head snapped up.

"At the door. You were about to call the police, re-member?"

"Oh!" She brightened up. "You know, uh, it was just the Mormons."

Clancy couldn't hold back his laugh. "Yeah, they're a rough crowd. Our jail is pretty much wall-to-wall Mormons as we speak."

She burst out laughing, then turned her face away to hide the one honest thing she'd shared with him in the last eighteen years. Score. Clancy made her laugh! And, oh, did he remember that laugh.

She faced him again, embarrassed. She was adorable. How could he have not known her the second she stepped off the ferry? Those eyes—such a pale, ethereal green curtained with dark lashes. As a clueless adolescent, he'd been mesmerized by those eyes. And as a grown-ass cop, he was still mesmerized, still defenseless when it came to her.

As a reflex, he let his eyes travel down to her mouth, pink and full. He wanted to kiss her. Just one more time.

"I need to go."

He smiled at her. "Do you still wear sundresses?"

Her eyes widened.

"You looked so beautiful in that yellow dress, but those shoes . . . I never liked those plastic shoes." With that, Clancy reached into his pocket and pulled out the photograph.

She arched away from him, holding on to the edge of the bench. He could see her chest rise and fall.

"It's good to see you again, Evie." He kept his voice gentle, not wanting to cause her to freak out any more than she already was. But why was she? "Please tell me what's going on, okay? I just want to understand why you took all the trouble to come back to Bayberry Island, and then didn't want me to know it was you. You are literally hiding from me."

Her body tightened, but she responded as casually as if he'd just asked her to pass the salt. "Sorry, but I'm not following you."

Clancy laughed softly at her stubbornness. "Okay. I'll make it real easy. You were here the summer we were both fourteen. I fell in love with you."

She blinked. Evie leaned in, took the photograph, and studied it, the faintest tremble visible in her hand. "That's pretty interesting. I mean, the girl does kind of look like me, doesn't she? A little bit, anyway. Her eyebrows are completely different, though."

"You don't have to . . ."

"And I've always had blond hair. Sorry." She glanced up and smiled casually at him. "Was she important to you, this girl? Are you searching for her for personal reasons, or is it, you know, a police thing?"

Clancy felt one of his eyebrows arch high, not even sure how to respond to that loaded set of absurd questions. First off, it didn't take a cop to see that she was lying about her hair. She'd recently bleached it, and not all that evenly, either. And she'd managed to ask about his feelings for her while fishing around for whether he suspected her of wrongdoing. This was getting more interesting by the second.

Just then, she slipped the photo into the pouch of her sweatshirt. He pretended not to notice.

"Why didn't you write me, Evie?"

He watched a dozen different emotions rush across her pretty face. Surprise, anger, frustration, fear ... she wanted to say something. Her lips parted. It was killing her not to be able to say it. A bead of perspiration appeared on her upper lip.

"I think you've mistaken me for someone else." She wiped her palms on the front of her jeans. "Whoever that girl was, she cared a lot for you—you can see it in the picture. I'm sure she wrote you. I mean, why wouldn't she?"

With that, she jumped up and returned to the motel, already reaching to put the key in the door.

Clancy would not let it end like this. Evie was going to bolt the first opportunity she got. She felt threatened that he was a cop and terrified because he'd figured out who she was. He saw how she struggled, how she wished she could tell him what was going on ... if only she trusted him.

He jumped off the bench and in an instant stood behind her. Her back was so close he could feel her heat radiate through the sweatshirt and onto his chest. He lowered his mouth to her ear. "Evie." He touched her hair. He softly placed his lips on the back of her neck.

She spun around. Evie raised her face and leaned forward tentatively, touching her mouth to his. Almost immediately, she pulled away, her eyes filling with tears. "Good-bye, Clancy. It was nice to see you again—today. Since earlier today. Thank you for saving my nephew."

The force of his response surprised him. He pulled her against his body and kissed her, hot and slick and over and over again. Instead of pushing him away, she fitted her body against his, threw her arms around his neck, and kissed him back with a desperation he'd never felt from a woman in all his life. Her hands were in his hair; then her fingers dug into his shoulders. She moaned into his mouth. She allowed him to back her against the motel room door.

Clancy was out of his head. He was gone, completely lost inside the kiss, only wanting more of her, anything and everything she had to give. His hands pushed up inside the sweatshirt and grasped her firm waist, caressed her straight back, pressed against the hot, smooth skin of her belly. Christ, he hadn't wrestled with this kind of raw need since . . . never. Not like this, ripe and hot and full-to-bursting from the first touch.

It was completely insane how much he wanted her.

She began to push him away, tentatively at first, then with force. He let her go. They stared at each other for several seconds, breathing hard, bewildered, and amazed.

She touched her fingers to her lips, as if she couldn't believe what she'd just done. "I have to go."

"I can help you. Whatever it is, you can trust me."

She opened the door and slipped inside.

And just like that, it was over.

As exhausted as Clancy was, there was no way he could go home. Not like this, with ten thousand questions swirling around his brain. He knew how it worked. If he went home with a head full of loose ends, he would only lie in his bed and stare out the window, unable to sleep. He might as well get to it.

He grabbed a cup of locker-bottom coffee, placed the driver's license information on his desk, and logged on to the police department's mainframe. He began a database search for one Cricket Dickinson, twenty-nine, of 3448 Jinni Lynn Court, Bloomington, Indiana. It sure didn't take long to find her. Everything was right at the top of the search results, like it had been placed there for his convenience. Interesting.

She was an IU graduate, a self-employed vitamin and supplement distributor, a registered voter, YMCA member, good credit, and legal guardian to her nephew Chris Dickinson, a four-year-old enrolled at a Montessori preschool down the street. According to tax records, she owned a three-bedroom bungalow at that address, which she'd purchased two years earlier for two hundred ninety-eight thousand dollars.

Fine. It all looked perfectly fine. And that was what bothered him. Why did a chick with such a tidy little life give herself a quickie dye job and leave town? How did she find herself a thousand miles from home, on Bayberry Island during festival week, hiding from the police chief? What made her so frightened that she couldn't admit she was his summer love from eighteen years before?

Why was she even here?

At this point, Clancy knew that was the only thing he was sure of—Cricket was Evie, they were one in the same. No doubt in his mind. Her touch, her kiss, her laugh, how she fit in his arms, the way he felt when he was with her ... those things were real. The rest of it? He shook his head as he scrolled through the database search. The rest of it made no sense.

There were a couple possibilities. She could be an innocent, law-abiding woman hiding from a spouse or boyfriend who had harmed her. The kind of domestic dispute Clancy had responded to just that morning was more commonplace than people wanted to admit, and Evie could simply be another woman who had reached the point of no return, unable to take one more punch or one more degrading comment. It would have taken planning and advanced IT skills, but maybe her new identity had been in the works for a long time.

Or, she may be on the run for reasons far more sinister. Maybe she embezzled from her business, or orchestrated a pyramid scheme out of her home and the SEC caught up with her. Possibilities like that were endless.

Clancy's mind did a double take. On the run. The way she moved down the ferry gangway. The long, lean, muscular legs. Those shoes.

He opened a new window on his laptop and searched for the make and model of running shoe she'd been wearing. It retailed for one-fifty, and just as he thought, it was the go-to shoe for serious women runners. Clancy smiled. Now this was a subject he knew a little bit about.

He logged on to a members-only Web site that tracked amateur race results from all over the country, members and nonmembers, everything from 5Ks to ultra-marathons. First he checked Indiana races—no finishing times for a Cricket Dickinson were listed. He broadened his search. He saw nothing at first, but kept digging. There she was! San Diego's Rock 'n' Roll half marathon, 2009, where she finished twelfth in her category—the seventy and up age group.

Huh?

He tried for another half hour and though he encountered the senior citizen version of Cricket Dickinson a few more times, he didn't find his Cricket. She simply did not exist in the data-hoarding world of running, which implied that her lies were several layers deep. And that bothered him. A lot.

Clancy was so tired his body hurt. He took the Jeep home, played with the dogs for a few minutes, grabbed a quick shower, then collapsed in bed. His mind wasn't racing with unanswered questions anymore. It was heavy with dread and regret for what had to be done come morning. When Evie boarded the first ferry—and he was sure she would—Chief Flynn would be waiting for her with a boatload of questions.

She wouldn't be leaving Bayberry until every one of them had been answered to his satisfaction.

"The FBI just found your car."

Evelyn let her head drop into the crook of her elbow. "No! Oh, God!"

"They went public with a snippet of video footage. They caught you leaving the parking structure at Logan, and again taking the T. They don't know for sure, but they've told the public that you may have caught a bus to the Cape."

"No! Hal!" Her body had already started to shake. "I had my hat on! My shades! I changed shirts in the ladies room before we got on the bus! I changed Chrissy's clothes twice! How did they . . . ?"

"Manpower. From what I've been able to tell, they put hundreds of agents on this, and they scoured thousands of hours of video from hell and back. They used facial recognition and the latest body recognition software. We were out-manned and out-teched."

"Shit."

"I'm so sorry, Evie. I know it sucks."

She groaned.

"There's a ferry at eight a.m., and you need to be on it. Cover up and wear the baggiest clothes you've got and try to remember to skip or swing your arms differently. The software is still rudimentary enough that you'll get away with it."

"Okay."

"Keep Chrissy in your arms whenever possible so they can't scan for her movement, either. I will contact you once you get back on the mainland, and I'll have some ideas how we can switch things up."

Evelyn stared at the bug-encrusted light fixture again. She felt limp. Her brain had glazed over. "What am I going to do?" The pitiful voice she heard was her own. "This is a total disaster."

"You're not alone. I am helping you every step of the way. And don't you dare give up. Stay pissed! Wahlman is a scummy, lying dickhead who rigged the custody decision. Don't forget that."

Evelyn broke down. She tried to keep the noise to a minimum by burying her mouth in the crook of her arm, then realized it probably didn't matter much—Chrissy would soon be hearing a lot of crying.

"Evie. Please."

"Why are you doing this for me, Hal?" Her sob came out as a hiccup. "You're putting your own future at risk."

He laughed. "Honey, first of all, we've been over this—no one will ever find me. Remember, this is what I do. It's my thing. And second of all . . ." Hal got choked up. It took him a moment to find his voice. "You saved my life, Miss Evelyn 'Feed The Speed' McGuinness. I was killing myself. I was thirty-nine and I was fucking killing myself with junk food and sitting on my ass in front of a bank of computers. You took me under your wing and—"

"Hal—"

"You asked, so let me answer." He cleared his throat. "Evie, you taught me how to shop and cook and eat. You stood by me when I stumbled—and you know I stumbled a lot—then you picked me up each time. You shared everything you knew about training, fitness, equipment, mental preparation, physiology, and race strategy. Basically, you held my hand for six long months until I got my act together! My health and happiness are because of you. I owe you my life."

She shook her head, reaching for a strip of bathroom tissue to blow her nose. "I care about you. You're my friend. And all that stuff, the nutrition and training stuff, it is just what I do."

"Right on, sister. Right on."

Chapter Eight

Crazy-crackers-reckless-stupid insanity. That's what M.J.'s night had been made of.

And now it was six forty-two a.m. and she sat in the greenroom at the Boston CBS affiliate with her politically brain-damaged boss and his ice bitch of a soon-to-be ex-wife.

M.J.'s letter of resignation was, at that very moment, burning a hole in her briefcase.

The situation was pretty clear. If M.J. couldn't pull a game-changer out of her ass in the next ten minutes, Richard would be destroying her career before a live television audience, Tamara at his side. Apparently, after her unpleasant visit to his office last night, M.J.'s boss was spurred to action. The FBI had a major breakthrough with evidence, and Richard decided he would never forgive himself if he didn't contribute to the momentum. He decided to go public first thing in the morning.

Richard now sat across the room from M.J., wearing a suit slightly too big for his post-surgery body. She noticed that instead of a dress shirt and tie, he wore a polo shirt with an open collar. That was his signal to the country that he wasn't on official business, simply there as a regular Joe. Richard hadn't spoken in the last few minutes, so M.J. knew he was rehearsing the talking points in his mind. She could just imagine:

Unknowingly, I fathered a child with a young scheduling assistant a few years back:

1. Tragically, the mother has died;
2. Fortunately, I won custody of the product of that union;
3. Shockingly, the child has been kidnapped!

Now, I will do anything to get her back safely.

And, most importantly, he would add this:

I am not here to answer questions or respond to speculation about my political career. I am only here to ask—no, beg—for everyone's help in locating my daughter.

M.J. had already tried to talk some sense into him, of course. First, she tried on the phone. Next, it was at the Jefferson, on the private jet to Boston, then in the limo, and again while coming in the back entrance to the studio. But his mind was made up. He was about to kill his reelection bid and snuff out any chance for a vice-presidential nom—over some kid.

She silenced a groan of frustration that began in her toes and rose up into her throat. How dare he keep her from the kind of power she deserved, the kind she was promised? She longed for the delicious feel of digging her fingers into his neck and cutting off his air.

A production assistant stuck his head through the greenroom door. "Five minutes, Congressman and Mrs. Wahlman. You can follow me to the set."

"Just a minute." M.J. held up her hand. "Go on. We'll be there." She closed the door in the kid's face.

"Don't do it, Richard. One last time, I'm begging you."

He shook his head. "I have to."

"See, that's where you're wrong. You don't *have* to do anything. You're Richard Wahlman, four-term congressman from Massachusetts, cosponsor of groundbreaking debt ceiling legislation, chairman of the Ways and Means subcommittee on oversight, philanthropist—"

"Father."

M.J. closed her eyes. This was a fucking catastrophe!

It was almost as if he didn't care! Out of utter desperation, M.J. looked to Tamara. The oh so chic blonde sat in the corner with a glass of sparkling water balanced on her bony Lanvin-covered knee. She wanted no part of this.

Ha! If M.J. thought about strangling Richard, then Tamara was probably fantasizing about breaking his neck, slapping him silly, and cutting off his Johnson—just to warm up! Not for the first time, M.J. wondered whether the roles within that union were backward— Tamara should have served in Congress while Richard hosted dinner parties and charity fund-raisers. Things might have turned out better.

The limo ride to the studio had been, by far, the most cringe-worthy twenty minutes of M.J.'s life. Unfortunately, she had been privy to everything the Wahlmans had said to each other. How could she avoid it? Was she supposed to open the sliding window, crawl headfirst through the divider, and sit up front with the driver? She needed a hot shower and a tequila slammer after the experience.

"This is utterly ridiculous, Dick." That's how it had started. Tamara had said that as she finished off what was left of her second early-morning scotch, leaving a shiny pink lipstick stamp along the rim of the glass. "This is a debacle. At this point in your career? Really, Richard? Couldn't you have found some other way to help look for this pitiful urchin of yours? Perhaps walk through fields with neighbors and their tracking hounds or something? Anything that didn't involve dragging the Derrick family name through the muck?"

"I told you—this isn't about the Derricks."

"Oh, darling, you are my very favorite pathological narcissist."

"Stop it, Tamara."

"You truly don't give a rat's ass about the impact this may have on Derrick Brand Restaurants, which I find ironic, since you would be nothing without us."

"That's enough."

"I despise you for this, Dick."

"You've despised me for twenty-five years."

"True." She had thrown a few ice cubes into the glass and freshened her drink. "Well, at least now you have the baby I could never give you."

"I won't even respond to that."

"But why this way, Dick? Why can't you deal with this problem quietly? Why are you making a spectacle of yourself ten weeks before the election? Why are you throwing away your shot at the vice presidency? Do you want to ruin your life? Is that what's going on? Are you just so insecure about yourself that you want the world to know your penis works?"

M.J. had contemplated hurling herself out the window at that point.

Richard had kept his fury bottled in, however. No wonder he'd had a heart attack. "I simply want to find Christina."

"How noble of you."

"It's the right goddamn thing to do!"

Tamara had blinked in surprise at her husband's sudden outburst, then turned her claws on M.J. "This is your idea, I take it?"

It was a good thing M.J. had long ago perfected the art of saying "fuck off" without using the word "fuck" or the word "off." She had smiled pleasantly at Tamara. "As much as I appreciate your confidence in my skills, I assure you, you couldn't be more wrong. I've advised Richard to keep the matter as private as possible. I think what he's doing is a horrible mistake. There is a chance some of his base would admire how he's stepped up to his responsibility here, but that is a gigantic risk." M.J. had then pretended to be checking her text messages.

Tamara had laughed again. "Oh, I find that hard to believe, Mary Jane. I've known you for a long time, and I've seen you use anything and anyone for political gain." She had looked toward her husband and cocked her head to the side. "So let me take a wild stab at it, darling—you think voters will see that behind that nasty old scar of yours is a heart of gold. Is that it? Just weeks out of the hospital and Congressman Richard Wahlman is willing to sacrifice his health and his reputation to find his long-lost bastard child? Or maybe you're proving to the world that you're still healthy and vibrant enough to be the parent of a toddler!" She raised her glass. "Fabulous."

"Shut up, Tamara."

"Go to hell, Dick."

They had ridden in silence for about five minutes before Richard said to Tamara, "You don't need to say anything today. Just look supportive."

Tamara had drained her glass. "Of course, darling. We both know how good I am at faking it."

Now the three of them sat in the greenroom like cattle penned before slaughter, the seconds ticking by, and M.J. knew this was her last chance to stop the freak show.

"Linking your name to the girl is unnecessary. The FBI has solid leads now. They will find her without the endorsement of Congressman Richard Wahlman. Once she's home you can quietly maintain custody and go on to have a lovely life with your daughter, without destroying everything you've worked for all these years."

He stood and smoothed his shirt. "Neither of you can possibly understand where I'm coming from." He turned his steady gaze toward M.J. "I know this will make things difficult for you professionally, which is something you clearly don't deserve. You've always gone above and beyond. I appreciate that."

On his way out the door, Richard stopped and gave her a stiff hug. It was the only time in eighteen years he'd touched her.

"Stop."

"I've made up my mind."

"Richard, seriously. There's something you need to know before you go on the air."

A frantic voice echoed down the hallway. "Congressman and Mrs. Wahlman! We need you on the set!"

Richard was clearly irritated. "Your story will have to wait, M.J. Call me tomorrow." He held out his hand to Tamara. "Darling?"

The power couple met up with the production assistant, who hurried them along to the sound tech. They were clipped with their lapel mics and ushered out onto the set.

M.J. hated him at that moment. Rage scalded the inside of her throat. Her brain felt like it was in danger of exploding. That idiot! There wasn't enough money inside the beltway to pay for the kind of dedication she'd shown Richard Wahlman, but in the end it didn't even matter to him. All he cared about was the kid.

Someday, he would learn to what lengths M.J. had gone on his behalf five years ago, and on that day he would completely lose his shit. Richard was so oblivious that he believed his perky little paramour quit her job and slipped out of town without a peep because she was homesick. How simpleminded could a man be?

M.J. told the pregnant girl that Richard insisted she have an abortion, and handed her six hundred dollars in an envelope. Next, M.J. made vague threats about how some young women in Washington who found themselves in her situation were never seen or heard from again. Oh, how Amanda cried. She threw the money back at M.J. and slammed her door. And she was gone the next day.

M.J. smiled to herself at the memory. When Richard found all this out, he would hate M.J. as much as she hated him. Funny how one little girl could flip the script like this.

She gathered her briefcase and headed for the TV studio's back door. M.J. wasn't sure what her next step would be. Maybe she'd take a week off. Start packing up her apartment. Or maybe she'd go somewhere—she hadn't taken a real vacation since she got to Washington.

Her thoughts went to poor little Amanda McGuinness—just another exceptional girl who hit the Hill with big dreams and open legs. Surely she didn't deserve what she got. M.J. had actually liked her. She was high-energy, cheerful, and the first in line to take on extra tasks. But what was done was done. There was no such thing as a do-over. And she regretted nothing. As everyone knew, the rules were different in Washington.

Above and beyond? Richard had no fucking idea.

He woke to a headache lit up by a bolt of lightning and head-butted by a crash of thunder. His scaredy-cat dogs hurled themselves onto the bed for protection, and somebody's bony elbow dug right into Clancy's diaphragm.

"C'mon, guys. You're too big for this. How many times do I have to tell you?" He snapped his fingers and pointed to the floor, and, to their credit, they jumped off without complaint, though their ears were pinned back and tails curled up between their legs. After giving his face a quick scouring with his hands, Clancy rolled over to check his cell phone—five thirty-two a.m., Sunday of festival week, Island Day—and it was raining like a son of a bitch.

But that wasn't his biggest problem. Today was the day he had to deal with Evie.

Just then it dawned on him—he'd dreamed of her. Clancy let his head fall on the pillow and allowed the images to take him back. Evie was running down the beach, her laughter clear and joyous in the wind. Her little nephew giggled as Tripod and Earl nudged and licked him. And that was pretty much the whole dream—

no plot, no Freudian symbols, no screaming for help, nothing even remotely sexual. It was simply Clancy being aware of that moment and how good it felt to share it with Evie and Chris. He felt lucky in the dream. He actually felt happy—and lucky in love.

He'd had enough of these dreams. He didn't have the spare brain energy to deal with them right now.

He jumped up, made coffee, and got dressed. He was out the door by six—both skittish dogs in tow—and at his desk by six fifteen, pools of water forming by his feet. It never failed—at least one day during the Mermaid Festival was a partial washout, but if it happened on Island Day it was a major problem.

Two hundred craftspeople, artists, and food vendors descended on Main Street on Island Day, and carnival attractions occupied the dock and museum lot. In decent weather, Island Day would be the most crowded and popular of all festival week events. Thousands of daytrippers arrived in the morning and left in the evening, exhausted, stuffed with lobster rolls and fried blueberry pies, and holding their just-purchased watercolor painting, carved jade necklace, or giant origami dolphin. But if a storm front moved in and didn't blow over, a lot of people would lose a lot of money today. And the Bayberry municipal government would miss out on a crapton of tax revenue.

Clancy's head pounded. He turned on his preferred early-morning TV news, deciding he would listen in while he finished paperwork.

"Morning, Chief." Chip stood just outside the office door, soaked through to the skin. "What are you doing here so early?"

He pointed to Tripod and Earl spooning together in their dog bed in the corner. "My alarm clocks went off early."

Chip laughed. "Poor fellas. Yeah, it's a loud one—that's for sure."

Clancy started in on the stacks of work on his desk.

Though a lot of the police station's reporting was now completed digitally, they were still slaves to a variety of forms, charts, and reports—all of which required his signature. "So what's happening, Chip? Busy night?"

He shook his head. "Pretty quiet, but the evening shift had to break up a party on a private yacht down at the marina—bunch of investment bankers."

"Naturally."

"We think they tossed the evidence overboard before we got there, you know, the standard rock-in-a-baggie trick."

"Gotcha." Clancy kept at his paperwork.

Chip continued. "The rain kept people off the beach and streets and sent them into the taverns, so it was a controlled chaos."

"Sounds good."

That's when Clancy's brain nudged him, telling him to pay attention to something that had just been said—not by Chip, but by someone on the news. He looked up to see a Massachusetts congressman by the name of Richard Wahlman in tears on live TV, talking about his kidnapped daughter. Clancy turned up the volume.

"My heartbreak is that I only just met her. Tragically, her mother was killed by a drunk driver, and that's when I learned she left a child behind. DNA testing shows she's mine. And now I have lost her before I had a chance to show her how much I love her."

"Oh, crap!" Chip started for the door. "I forgot about that alert!"

"All I ask is that if anyone, anywhere, has seen Evelyn McGuinness with my precious and innocent daughter, please contact the FBI immediately."

"Uh, Chief?"

Clancy held his palm toward Chip. "I gotta hear this. Hold on just a second."

The news host laid it on thick. "First let me say that we are keeping you and Christina in our thoughts and prayers and hope the suspect is found soon."

"Thank you." The politician touched his wife's leg as if asking for support.

"I know this is an indelicate question, Congressman, and forgive me, Mrs. Wahlman, but do you worry about how this will affect your reelection bid? Your opponent has been trailing significantly in the polls, but with this kind of shocking revelation about your sexual relationship with a—"

"I'd prefer not to talk about my campaign right now and instead focus on finding my daughter."

The congressman's wife grabbed his hand with both of hers and broke the awkward silence. "As you know, Richard has recently undergone open-heart surgery. Finding out he had a daughter and then having that child abducted . . . well, that would be extremely difficult for anyone, let alone someone who has charged back from the brink of death."

"So you *are* abandoning your reelection plans?"

"I didn't say that," Richard snapped. "I said I'm not here this morning to talk about politics. I'm here because my little girl has been taken across state lines by someone with absolutely no right to do so. I want her home safely."

"But your campaign . . ."

"That's it. I'm done." The congressman tore off his mic and left the set, his wife following behind.

Clancy turned off the TV, heavy dread already lodged in the pit of his stomach. He had a bad feeling—nauseatingly bad.

"You need to see this!"

Clancy had known Chip a long time, and he was a reliable sort. When Chip's voice got squeaky, it meant something really important was going on, and his voice just went up a full octave.

"This FBI alert came in about twenty minutes ago, specifically for Nantucket, the Vineyard, and Bayberry. I can't remember the last time we've been included in one of these."

Clancy knew what was coming.

"The congressman's kid! The child-custody BOLO out of Maine. They think she might be here!" Chip handed him a printout.

Before he read the first word, it was obvious. Maine. Child. Secrets. Lies.

Evie's a kidnapper.

His eyes raced over the alert, immediately drawn to the photos. First, there was the suspect, with those pale green eyes, lovely lips, and the soft brown hair. Evelyn H. McGuinness, age thirty-two, of Bridgton, Maine was described as Caucasian, five foot nine, one hundred twenty-eight pounds, no identifying tattoos or scars. They'd used a post-race photo from the New York Marathon for identification, both a close-up of her face and a full-body shot. She looked exhausted but triumphant in that picture. And she wore the exact same model of running shoe he'd seen on "Cricket."

Next, he looked at the photo of the victim. Chris was no pirate boy with a buzz cut. She was a girl with wispy brown curls pulled back with barrettes. Christina G. McGuinness, age four, of Bridgton, Maine, was Evelyn's niece. She also was Caucasian, and three feet four inches tall, about forty-three pounds.

Clancy's chest burned with confusion. He didn't want to read any more, but he did, hitting only on the words that jumped out at him: *violation of court-ordered custody ruling . . . car recovered . . . Logan remote parking lot . . . dummy plate and tag . . . security video footage . . . altered appearance . . . short blond hair . . . facial and body recognition software identified the suspect . . .*

Clancy jumped to his feet and spun around, not sure what he was looking for, but aware that it sure as hell wasn't in his office. Dummy plate and tag? That was awfully sophisticated.

"You okay, Chief?"

Fuck, no, he wasn't okay.

He continued reading. *Additional video . . . boarding*

*the MBTA red line train with the girl ... exiting at South
Station ... may have boarded a Peter Pan bus to Woods
Hole, Massachusetts ... possibly intending to travel via
ferry ... current location unknown ... may be traveling
under the alias "Cricket Dickinson."*

Clancy raised his eyes from the paper and stared at
Chip, his thoughts circling around his next step. What
would it be and how would he do it?

"Wouldn't it be wild if she's here?" Chip's face lit up
and his voice went even higher. "I mean, think about it.
What better place to hide? Just put on some costumes
and run around with all the other whacky people—who's
gonna notice? I bet you she and the girl are here, right
under our noses!"

Clancy's brain spun too fast for his mouth to catch up,
but Chip was absolutely correct. *Right under our noses.*
There had to be a back door out of this situation, a hidden
exit, some way he wouldn't have to do what had to be
done, but he didn't see it. Clancy was a police officer, sworn
to uphold the laws of the State of Massachusetts and the
municipality of Bayberry Island, and bound to standards
of mutual assistance and cooperation with all federal agen-
cies. He had no choice but to take Evie into custody. And
why was that concept such a big deal, anyway? Clancy
might have been crazy about her years ago, but he barely
knew her now. And a warrant was a warrant, right?

And yet ...

"What time is it, Chip?"

He checked his phone. "Six forty-four."

"Are the ferries running on schedule?"

"We haven't received notice of delays on any of the
lines."

"Good. Good." Clancy sorted it out in his head—if
the first ferry Evie could possibly catch pulled in at seven
thirty and left at eight, that meant he had just over an
hour to figure out what he was going to do. With Evie.
With his duties. With his principles.

His heart told him the sweet, fun, and affectionate girl

he met eighteen years ago must have her reasons, and might very well have done nothing wrong. But that wasn't his call. Guilt or innocence was determined by a judge or jury. His only responsibility was to accept that some judge, somewhere, believed there was enough evidence to support a felony warrant. His sworn obligation was to arrest and detain the subject of that warrant.

But, damn. He had an unshakable feeling that taking her into custody would be the absolute wrong thing to do. Why, he couldn't say, but he knew that failing to help her would be the biggest mistake of his life.

But the evidence ...

"A felony criminal arrest warrant has been issued by the State of Maine for McGuinness, the child's maternal aunt ..."

Clancy wanted to scream. So what if he had a hunch there was more to the story? This wasn't the first time he'd wrestled with finding a balance between intuition and reason, and it wouldn't be the last. All cops went through this—good cops, anyway. Balancing evidence with gut feeling was part of the investigation process. In Clancy's experience, evidence always mattered most, but whenever he completely ignored his gut he got himself in trouble.

But this? His intuition wasn't just whispering to him— it was screaming at the top of its lungs.

He closed his eyes. Ah, God, it was obvious Evie took the girl because she didn't want to give her to the congressman. And her actions were clearly premeditated. The plate and tags. The zigzag modes of transportation. The haircuts and dye job. The fake ID, the false Internet presence, and the motel switcheroo. He didn't know how all the strings were tied together but it was certainly a tangled mess. So where did all this leave him?

Only one thing was certain—aiding and abetting a fugitive wouldn't be a wise career move.

"Chief? Are you sure you're all right?"

Clancy opened his eyes, looked at his friend, and

laughed in a way that sounded a bit unbalanced, even to his own ears. "Our first priority is helping the vendors set up and deal with the weather in whatever way we can. Please remind both soundstages not to plug in while it's raining."

"Will do."

"Latest forecast?"

"Reports say it's supposed to clear by ten a.m., but you know how that goes."

"Yep, things don't go as expected sometimes." He patted Chip on the shoulder. "All right. I have a few things I need to do before I head down to greet the ferry." He checked his dogs, both in the corner together, sound asleep.

"We'll keep an eye on them here, Chief. No problem."

"Thanks. And as far as this goes"—he held up the FBI alert—"do *not* make a move unless I am present. If you think you see this woman and little girl, observe only, and notify me immediately of her location. Do not approach the suspect or the child, or take either into custody without my okay. Do not process the suspect. Most importantly, do not contact the FBI until I give you the go-ahead. I am very serious about this. Please tell me you understand."

Chip frowned with the gravity of his duty. "Of course, Chief. This would be the biggest arrest in Bayberry's history, and all eyes of the world would be on our little island. This has to be executed with perfection."

"Yes! That's right!" God, he loved Chip.

"I'll give everyone else the same instructions, Chief."

"Thank you."

Just then, the old building shook with a deep growl of thunder and the dogs began to howl.

"Well." Chip shoved his hands in the pockets of his uniform shorts, his voice squeaking with excitement. "This is sure shaping up to be an interesting day!"

Chapter Nine

The sun was trying to show itself through the rain clouds. Clancy took the turn onto Idlewilde Lane so quickly that arcs of mud went shooting out from the Jeep's back tires. He ran through the rain to the front door and pounded. "Ma! Hello?"

Mona answered her door. Clearly, he'd caught her in the middle of dressing for the festival. Everything from the waist down was Grand Poobah mermaid. Everything from the waist up was early-morning mom—she wore an old T-shirt, her hair was sticking up every which way, and she was still working on her first cup of coffee.

"Well, this is a surprise!" She opened the door while trying to smooth down her hair. Suddenly, she narrowed her eyes. "Is everything all right? Is it Duncan?"

He hugged her. Of course she would think that. The family cookout was four days away and no one had heard a peep from him. "Everything's fine, Ma. No crisis. I haven't heard anything from Duncan. I came over because I have a favor to ask. I kind of need your help."

"Coffee?" She toddled off into the kitchen, her mermaid tail flapping around her ankles with each step.

"I'm good, Ma." He took off his damp ball cap.

His mother replaced the coffee carafe and leaned her elbows on the kitchen island. She studied Clancy carefully while she blew over the top of her mug. The thorough going-over he was getting made him feel uncomfortable.

"Tell me what's wrong."

"Nothing! I just have a favor to ask. It's important, but before I get into it, I need to be sure you won't hit me with a lot of questions and please, please—promise me you'll keep this to yourself."

She popped up, her back going ramrod straight.

Clancy answered before she asked. "Nuh-uh. Not even the Mermaid Society. Nobody."

Her eyebrows arched.

"I know it's a lot to ask. If you can't do it, tell me now, and I'll be on my way. I'll understand and get someone else to help me."

"This is about a woman, isn't it?"

Clancy replaced his ball cap and headed to the front door. "Well, obviously, this isn't going to work."

His mother blocked his progress and pointed to her sofa. "Sit." He did, and she joined him.

"Of course you can trust me," she said. "I understand this is just between the two of us and you have my word. I also understand that you are here for help, but not advice, so I'll try my best not to give any."

He took off his hat again. "Thanks, Ma."

Mona patted his hand. "You know I'll do whatever I can do, my wonderful son. Whatever you need, if it's in my power to give it to you, I will. I love you with all my heart and I'm so proud of you. You are an exceptionally good man."

Clancy nodded and gave her a quick kiss on her cheek. "Thanks."

"What can I do for you?"

"Well, I need a mermaid costume for an adult woman— five nine, one twenty-eight, size small to medium. I want the whole thing—hair, shells, accessories."

His mother looked temporarily stunned.

"And I need a really over-the-top pirate costume for a four-year-old, a tricorner hat, eye patch, sword, white puffy shirt, whatever you can scrape up. I want the works."

"Oh, my. You really are in trouble."

He laughed, raking a hand over his face to make sure he wasn't having another nightmare. "Not yet, though things might get interesting in the next couple days. Can you stop with the questions, now?"

Mona nodded.

"So do you have any of that crap here? Or would it all be in storage in the museum warehouse? I'm kinda in a hurry."

"I'll be right back." She set her coffee mug on a side table and disappeared into the cottage's only bedroom. She came out with her giant key ring, which probably unlocked every damn door on the island. She removed an irregularly shaped brass key. "This is for the warehouse loading dock door. It might be a big mess in there since the parade was just yesterday and most of the floats are in some stage of disassembly. You know where the costume section is? Where we keep the stuff for the reenactment and the children's play?"

"Yeah."

"There's a combination lock on the big metal doors. The combination is forty-two, twenty-eight, thirty-eight, and, yes, your father came up with that. The kids' sizes are on the right and the adults' on the left. But"—she placed the key in his palm—"you know what? Hold on. Let me check on something."

Clancy waited, twisting the key in his hand, knowing the minutes were ticking by. Eventually his mother came out carrying a long zippered garment bag with a clear plastic pouch tied around the hanger. "I won't ask who this is for. Depending on how large her bosom is, and pardon me for bringing this up but it is important, you might have to adjust the straps. Or she can adjust the straps. It's none of my business who's doing the adjusting. . . ."

"Ma."

"And because she's tall, the skirt may have to be

pulled lower than it's usually worn, even below the belly button. But not too low, because that would mean that in the back—" She stopped. "I'm sure the two of you can find a happy medium."

"Ma!"

"Well, I'm only trying to follow the rules. Here." Clancy stood as she draped the nylon bag over his forearm. "She'll need to wear her own shoes."

"Of course."

"It might be slim pickings in the kid area of the warehouse, since they've started rehearsals for the children's play. But I'm sure you'll find something for a little one."

"You're the best. I gotta go."

He started for the door.

"Clancy?"

He turned, holding the front door open with his foot. "Yeah?"

"Whatever this is about, I hope it works out well. I've always hoped that one day you would find . . ." Mona waved her hand as if she wanted him to forget she'd just said that. "I just want you to stay safe and know that your family is always here for you. We've got your back."

Clancy smiled. It was his first legitimate smile of the day, and for some reason, he let himself believe it was a good omen.

"Chrissy, we need to get moving."

Her niece shook her head again, crossing her arms over her chest with such determination that the flesh of her forearms turned white.

"Now, Jellybean."

"I want to stay! I want to see the pretty mermaid! You promised we could go see her at the Save Heaven Castle!"

This was no time to get into it with a grumpy, sleep-deprived preschooler, but what was Evelyn going to do? Leave the island without her? Drag her kicking and screaming to the dock so that anyone who may not yet have noticed them would get a real good look?

Just then she heard it—the long, one-note sound of the ferry horn. It was arriving, which meant they had exactly a half hour to get there and get boarded. Evelyn peeked out the curtains to see some bad news and some good news. Unfortunately, the rain was coming down in a steady sheet of water, which meant they would be soaking wet by the time they reached the public dock. But the rain would keep the streets emptier than normal, especially at this hour, giving them a smaller audience for their mad dash.

Evelyn sat down on the floor in front of Christina. She held out her arms and the little girl crawled into her lap, snuggling deep. Evelyn gently rocked her back and forth and kissed the top of her head. Her thoughts wandered to how long it might take for Christina's hair to grow back, and whether she would get to see it happen.

Oh, God! Evelyn closed her eyes and pressed her lips to Christina. She had put this poor child through hell. She'd only been trying to do what Amanda had begged her to do—keep Wahlman out of her daughter's life—but it had been unfair to expect a four-year-old to remain cheerful through an odyssey like this. Christina had lost a lot more than her hair. She'd lost her mother, her grandfather, her animals, her home, and her preschool friends. She'd lost the knowledge that her world was safe.

Evelyn had dared to watch a few minutes of early-morning cable news while Christina slept. The volume was turned almost completely down, but she still got the gist of what was going on. The FBI was on their tail and Wahlman had gone public. His tears were obscene—how could he pretend to cry for a child he never wanted to be born? He made her sick. She had to turn it off.

What if Hal didn't come through for her? What if he couldn't find evidence that Wahlman cheated his way to full custody? Without that proof, she had no defense. And then what? Would she keep running forever, depriving Christina of her grandfather and home? She felt crushed by the weight of what she'd done.

"Sing the mussels song, Aunt Cricket. Please?"

She smiled sadly, thinking how she began singing the traditional song to her niece soon after she was born, just as Evelyn and Amanda's mother had done when they were young. After Amanda died, Chrissy began requesting the song whenever she needed reassurance. It broke Evelyn's heart.

"Sure, sweetie. And thank you for using the word 'please.'"

"You're welcome."

"Thank you for saying 'you're welcome.'"

Christina giggled, and Evelyn joined her. Well, why not? Maybe giggling was the best option at a time like this. Eventually, their laughter drifted away. Evelyn held her niece tighter and began to sing, her voice barely above a whisper.

In Dublin's fair city,
Where the girls are so pretty,
I first set my eyes on sweet Molly Malone.
As she wheeled her wheel-barrow,
Through streets broad and narrow,
Crying . . .

"Cockles!" Christina sang, right on cue.

And . . .

"Mussels!"

Alive, alive, oh!

Evelyn stopped there. "Hey, Chrissy?"

"Mmm?" Her face was still pressed to Evelyn's chest.

"I need your help with something."

The little girl lifted up and studied Evelyn, narrowing her eyes. "Did you forget the words to the song?"

"No. But I need your help with something important. I need you to be a big, brave girl this morning. Do you think you can do that?"

She gave it some thought, then nodded.

"Do you know I love you bunches?"

"Yes. I love you bunches, too."

She kissed her warm forehead. "I know you do, Jellybean. So here's how you can be big and brave for me. Do you have your listening ears on?"

She nodded.

"Good. We're going to get our stuff right now and run through the rain all the way to the dock. You can ride piggyback. We've never done that before, have we?"

She pursed her lips and shook her head.

"Let's see how fast we can go, okay? And I promise that I'll sing the mussels song the whole way. Are you willing to try?"

Suddenly, her eyes widened. "Are we going to get wet?"

"Oh, yes, we sure are. Soaking wet. Have you ever gotten that wet in the rain before?"

She shook her head again.

"We'll change our clothes once we get on the boat. And then we'll go on a ferry ride! Are you ready?"

Evelyn placed Christina on her feet, jumped to a stand, and checked that her shoes were laced securely. Since she had everything ready to go, it took only a minute or so to get it all together. Evelyn pulled her hoodie over her head. She strapped the duffel across her body. She patted the pocket of her shorts to make sure her wallet was there, then zipped up Christina's little jacket and covered her head with the attached hood. She knelt on the carpet and told her to climb on.

"Shoulders?"

"Not today. Just piggyback."

With a quick check to make sure she left the keys on the bed, she opened the door and they were in the rain.

"Ahhh!" Christina hunkered down on her back. "I can't see!"

Evelyn started to jog, alternating her attention between what was below and what was ahead. Tripping wasn't an option. Her first priority was keeping Christina secure. Speed was secondary.

"Hold on tight! Don't let go!"

"Okay!"

Once Evelyn made it to the paved road, she increased her pace, careful where she stepped, peering through the curtain of rain.

She was a fishmonger,
But sure 'twas no wonder,
For so were her father and mother before.

"Your voice sounds funny and bouncy, Aunt Cricket!" She laughed.

And they each wheeled their barrows,
Through streets broad and narrow,
Crying . . .

"Cockles!"

And

"Mussels!"

Alive, alive, oh!

Unfortunately, a large bandstand with scaffolding had been erected in front of Fountain Square, which meant Evelyn had to loop around the mermaid statue to access Main Street. She adjusted her sweatshirt hood so that she could take a quick sideways glance at the majestic creature. The mermaid appeared serene and wise, immune to the rain or time itself. She smiled kindly, and for the oddest instant, Evelyn was sure that smile was meant especially for her.

Stop running. Trust him.

Evelyn pulled the hoodie to her face and picked up her pace. Her footfalls, her breath, the rush of the rain, the warm weight of her precious niece against her back — these things would keep her focused on what was real and get them to the dock safely. Because ... *of course the mermaid did not just speak to her!*

Evelyn knew how high levels of stress could do a job on a person's senses, but c'mon. If she had to have a hallucination, couldn't it be something that could actually help her and not some random, off-topic mermaid lecture? And really. Stop running? As in stop running in the rain? Or stop racing? No problem. There weren't too many marathons in prison. And the trust him thing? She was supposed to trust Richard Wahlman with Christina?

Not in this lifetime.

"Later, babe," Evelyn muttered to the mermaid, merging once again with Main Street. She immediately realized this would be more of an obstacle course event than road race. On both sides of the street, along the two blocks from the fountain to the dock, were rows of craft show tents, some wrapped entirely in plastic to keep their treasures dry. People ran through the rain pulling carts, calling out to one another or unloading pickup trucks. She inhaled the beginnings of kielbasa and sauerkraut, barbecue, hot grease, and chili. Of course! Today was the big street fair, and that meant she'd have to run along the Main Street boardwalk, now slick with rain.

"I'm wet!" Chrissy nearly busted her eardrum with her shouting.

She ran. She picked up at the chorus.

Alive, alive oh!
Alive alive, oh!
Crying ...

Silence. Evelyn tried again.

Crying ...

"Cockles." It came out as a pathetic whine. Evelyn felt her pain. This little jog was flat-out miserable.

And . . .

"Mussels."

They reached the dock and she slowed her pace, careful not to slide on the treated wood. Evelyn had no idea what time it was, but thank God, she could see the ferry's running lights in the mist. That sight flooded her with such a rush of relief that she felt tears forming in her eyes. Just a few more seconds. Just a few more feet. "Time to take our boat ride!" She knelt on the dock to let Christina climb down.

"All aboard!"

Evelyn's head snapped up. No! She stood quickly, grabbed Christina's hand, and began shouting over the rumble of the ferry engine. "Wait!" She waved her free arm as she ran again. Christina dragged her feet and began to whine.

"Wait! Please!"

The conductor couldn't hear her, not with the storm, the engine noise, and the bright yellow oilskin rain hat he had yanked over his ears. She could see him prepare to shove off. But this was their only chance—they absolutely had to get on the ferry!

The instant she reached the gangway, she stomped on the aluminum as hard as she could. The vibration alerted the conductor that he had two last-minute fares, and he secured the ramp again and waved them aboard.

They ran up, raced across the outside deck and pushed open the door to the passenger seating area. This particular ferry was en route from Martha's Vineyard to Nantucket before it would head back to the mainland. Everyone who was going to the Mermaid Festival had already disembarked. The dozen or so passengers continuing on were dry, comfortable, and slightly annoyed by the messy, unruly, last-second arrivals. Evelyn knew how pitiful they must appear. Both of them were drenched to the bone. She was breathing hard and her hoodie was plastered to her head. She surely had a wild look in her eyes. Chrissy was trembling and complaining that she was wet and cold.

Ignoring their stares, Evelyn dropped the heavy duffel bag onto an empty bench, then collapsed right next to it. Her shoulder ached. Her heart was banging against her ribs. But as bad as she felt, Christina looked worse.

"I'm so sorry, baby." She had just reached out to remove the layers of wet clothes from her niece when the conductor approached, already free of his yellow slicker and hat. He stood over her. "ID, please. Where ya headed?"

"Two one-way fares to Woods Hole, please." She unzipped Christina's coat. "One child under five and one adult." Evelyn pulled off Chrissy's little jacket and tossed it onto the empty bench in front of them, motioning for Christina to crawl past her and sit next to the window. Only then could Evelyn begin digging into her shorts pocket, eventually pulling out a water-logged wallet. "Here you go." Smiling, she handed him her Indiana driver's license and two twenties. He nodded, but didn't return the smile. "Why don't you hold on to those fares for just a moment. I'll be right back."

She didn't know what time it was but wondered why the ferry wasn't moving. She searched the interior of the ferry until she found a large clock positioned over the door to the outdoor seating area. It was 8:07.

"We're already late," said a woman two benches away.

No. Oh please, no. Evelyn stiffened. Something was wrong. They should be in open water by now.

Just then, Christina started to sob. Her shoulders shook and she couldn't catch her breath. Evelyn pulled at the wet clothes sticking to her skin and stared out the ferry window at the hard rain and the gray-green sea.

"Mommy." It came out between great gulps of air. "I want to see Pop-Pop, Mommy. Can we see Pop-Pop and Reba and Tussy? Take me home, Mommy."

Her niece looked up at Evelyn, her big brown eyes filled with longing. "Please? I want to go home."

Evelyn froze. She didn't know what to say. Her niece had just called her "mommy." Three times. And it devastated her. Could it be that her little-girl memories of Amanda were already starting to fade? Maybe it was just a slip of the tongue. Or maybe she simply needed Evelyn to play that role for the time being, just to get her through this latest frightening and exhausting experience.

More importantly, she had no idea how to respond to her request to go home. Christina wanted the things she would never have again—a home with her grandfather, feeding her favorite goat and helping to milk the family's dairy cow. She wanted her life back, but she would never get it, because her future could go either of two ways: she would be on the run the rest of her childhood, or she would live in a fancy Back Bay mansion with her rich old father, who would send her to boarding school as soon as the novelty of having a child began to wear thin.

"I know you're sad. I'm so sorry you're hurting, Christina. I'm hurting, too." She put her fingers under her niece's chin and tipped her face. She wanted to look directly in her eyes when she said the words. "Everyone loves you more than you will ever know. Your mommy loves you from heaven. Pop-Pop Charlie loves you with all his heart. And all the animals, too, they love you. See, people still love you even if you aren't with them. Love never goes away."

Christina's chin began to tremble.

"And Jellybean, I love you so much that you are the most important thing in the world to me. You matter more to me than anything."

Her niece lifted her arms and Evelyn picked her up. Christina wrapped her small legs around Evelyn's waist, pressed into the crook of her arm, and began to cry. Hard. It was a gasping sound full of sorrow. Evelyn couldn't take it. She buried her face in Christina's neck and cried right along with her. So much sadness ... so much grief ... as deep as the ocean. Evelyn doubted they'd ever find the bottom of it.

Some time passed. Maybe two or three minutes, and Evelyn looked up when she heard the passenger cabin door open. She wasn't particularly surprised. In fact, she felt nothing. No fear. No panic. It was almost as if she knew he was out there, waiting for them.

Clancy Flynn was draped in a deep blue rain suit. He wore no hat. He probably had his uniform under it all, but at first glance, he didn't look like a police officer. He just looked like a guy who'd run through the rain to catch the ferry.

He walked to the center of the cabin and stopped. Evelyn met his gaze, knowing she was still crying but not caring anymore. She'd failed. She'd given up. It was almost funny—the girl who planned and trained and worked her ass off so that she always finished the race had just quit.

She shook her head at Clancy. "Not in front of her," she whispered. "Please. That's all I ask."

Clancy said nothing, just came close to the bench, grabbed the duffel and put the strap on his shoulder. He touched Evelyn's elbow, helped her stand, and grabbed their wet coats. "It will be okay. Everything will be all right."

She felt like she was sleepwalking. They stepped over the threshold and were back in the rain, but Clancy produced a large umbrella and it sprang open over their heads. He gently held on to Evelyn's arm. This wasn't like any arrest she'd ever seen on TV. He wasn't reciting her Miranda rights or yelling for her to put her hands up. He was simply accompanying them down the gangway to the dock, trying to keep the rain from pummeling them. Christina hung on to her so tightly that Evelyn worried she would cut off her circulation.

Right there, in the middle of the dock, was a police department Jeep. No lights were flashing and there was no siren wailing. He unlocked the passenger door with his key fob and helped them inside, Christina still hanging on for dear life. Clancy reached over and squeezed himself between Evelyn and Christina and a police scanner, computer, and all sorts of devices mounted inside the vehicle. She wondered what he was doing when she felt the comforting *click* of the seat belt, which he'd pulled around them both. He began to pull back but paused a moment, hovering not an inch from her face, those intense blue eyes searching hers. Without a doubt, she saw concern in his expression, and something else. Maybe it was pity. He might even feel a twinge of guilt for turning her over to the executioners. "I'm sorry," he said.

She shrugged. What could she say?

"I don't have a booster seat, but it's a short ride."

With that, he backed out, and shut and locked the door.

Her heart was pounding and her mind grasped for a clue . . . what next? Where were they going? Who would make the arrest? Would Wahlman be there to take Christina away on the spot?

She watched Clancy drop the duffel bag into the back and walk around to the driver's seat. Soon they were moving, winding their way through an access road along the dock and approaching a huge redbrick building. Faded white block letters along the side said FLYNN FISHERIES but the large sign out front welcomed visitors to the BAYBERRY ISLAND MUSEUM AND HISTORICAL SOCIETY.

She looked sideways at him. He kept his eyes on his driving, which was probably wise. The rain was coming down even harder and the Jeep's windshield wipers were racing to maintain visibility, yet Clancy was cutting through parking lots and zipping down one-way side streets designed for horse and buggy. They came to a STOP sign. To her right there was a squat white clapboard building with tiny windows capped with metal latticework. The sign said BAYBERRY POLICE AND MUNICIPAL LOCKUP. She hugged Chrissy tighter.

He turned right at the STOP sign, heading down the narrow street that ran alongside the building. Evelyn figured he would be pulling up to a back door, so when he drove on by, she jerked her head in surprise.

"Where are you taking us?" Only then did she realize he hadn't spoken one word since buckling them in at the dock. "Say something!"

"I'm taking you home."

"You're sending us back to Maine?"

Clancy turned his head to meet Evelyn's gaze. If she didn't know better, she'd say he looked relieved. "We'll talk very soon." He inclined his head toward Christina, indicating he didn't want to discuss her fate in front of her. "It'll just be another couple minutes."

Evelyn felt foolish—he was doing only what she'd asked. "Thank you for that." She meant it. "I'm sorry for yelling at you."

He gave her a small smile. "Perfectly understandable," he said.

The Jeep bumped along, continuing past a congregational church, a school, and the volunteer fire department. The road curved, then suddenly opened up. Gone was the tight squeeze of the town streets, and though it was difficult to tell with the rain, Evelyn thought they might be on a hill overlooking the ocean. Of course, she'd lost her orientation and had no idea where on the island they were. Where was he taking them?

Clancy pulled into a gravel driveway of a small house that seemed to have been painted red at some point in the past—the distant past. He turned off the engine.

"What is this? What the hell's going on?"

Christina raised her head and looked around, blinking.

She must have fallen asleep, even in her wet clothes.

"I'll get your bag." He opened the door for her and motioned for them to head up the front steps ahead of him. "It's unlocked. The dogs aren't here at the moment," he said.

She pulled the screen handle and turned the old brass knob to the wooden door. It opened with a lot of complaining, and she stepped inside. It was dim, but Clancy was right behind them, and reached around to flip a switch just inside the door. "I wasn't expecting company. Sorry if it's a little messy."

"But—" Evelyn's mind went blank.

"Let's get you guys out of those wet clothes first, okay?" He moved in front of them and headed down the hallway. He dropped the duffel on the floor and disappeared inside an open door, reappearing just seconds later with his arms full of dirty clothes. "There're clean towels on the shelf and plenty of hot water. Feel free to give her a bath if she prefers that, but I'm sorry—you're probably going to have to give the tub a quick rinse first. Cleaning supplies are under the sink." He motioned with his head for her and Christina to go into the bathroom. "I'll give you guys your space and get the guest bed made. Looks like she might need a nap."

Evelyn couldn't move. She stood, frozen, at the juncture of the living room and hallway. Her mouth fell open as she tried to sort out this whole bizarre situation. When he said he was taking her home, he meant to *his house.* She was baffled. Why would he do this? Did he want them to be warm, dry, and well rested before he handed them over to the FBI?

"I'm sorry, but I just don't—" Evelyn stopped, suddenly figuring it out. "Oh. This is for the benefit of the news cameras? You don't want a crying, miserable little girl and a drowned rat of a woman making Bayberry Island look bad?"

Clancy backed away, and toed her duffel bag so he could get around it. "Are you hungry?"

"What?"

"Can I have pancakes?" Chrissy was awake.

"Sure." Clancy smiled at her. "Do you like the blueberry kind?"

She nodded with enthusiasm. "And milk, please."

"You got it." Slowly, Clancy raised his eyes to meet Evelyn's. It felt as if they were locked in a Wild West standoff, each waiting for the other to flinch before they reached for their weapons. In this particular duel, however, the lawman's arms were full of dirty laundry and the outlaw held a hungry four-year-old.

Evelyn tilted her head and stared at the handsome tall man in the rain suit. She was confused, unsure of what was next or where this was going, and she still couldn't decipher that expression in his eyes.

Despite everything, she felt a tiny flicker of hope ignite in her chest.

"Trust me," was all he said.

Eighteen years ago ...

It was a close call. Evie almost wasn't allowed to go to the clambake, and if that happened, she knew she would completely drop dead in a hysterical, spastic mess. Though she could hardly believe it, it was Amanda who saved her.

"Oh, Mom, you should let her go. He's super nice." As usual, her little sister inserted herself into a conversation that didn't involve her, but this time, Evie appreciated what a complete nudge she was. "We met him at the beach the other day and he hung out with us at the parade. He's very polite and intelligent and he and Evie get along great. You know, he reminds me a lot of Ross."

Wow. Amanda was good at this. Ross was a cousin on their father's side, a valedictorian who had been accepted to West Point, and their mom and dad believed he could do no wrong.

"That's wonderful, but you're too young to date, Evelyn." Her father look worried. "I don't want you out at night by yourself."

"It's not a date, Dad!" Uh-oh, he now had that stern "don't argue with me" look on his face. She needed to be more mature. "What I'm saying is that I agree completely—I am too young to date. But this isn't a boy-girl kind of date, so there's nothing to worry about." Evie knew her whole life hung in the balance. If this conversation didn't go well, she might never see Clancy Flynn again, and she couldn't accept a world without him in it. Besides, she'd promised she'd be there!

He didn't look impressed. "If it isn't a date to a beach party, then what is it?"

That was Amanda's cue to pour on the crap. "It's a Bayberry Island tradition, a beach clambake with music and dancing. They've been having one at Haven Beach since the late 1800s—isn't that amazing? And Dad, there'll be a lot of locals with their kids. We might even be asked to do some babysitting. Tickets are expensive and hard to come by, but Evie's friend can get her in."

Their mother and father exchanged knowing looks.

"You know the consequences for drinking."

Evie gasped. "Mom! I don't drink!" She was already freaking out with joy. *She was almost there! They were going to say yes!* "Alcohol will never touch my lips. Drinking rots your brain and I have big plans for my future. I just want to go and enjoy the music. And the clams."

Her mother pursed her lips. "I just don't know."

"I'll go with her!" Amanda smiled innocently at their parents. "That way you won't have to worry. Evie and I will stick together the whole night and we'll both be home by ten."

Okay. Now she wanted to totally kill Amanda. She'd planned to stay out way later than ten, and besides, she had absolutely no intention of hanging out with her twelve-year-old sister when the cutest guy on Earth was holding her hand. But, if her choice was between taking her along or not going at all, she'd figure out a way to get around it.

"All right," their father said. "Ten o'clock and not a minute after."

"Please, please can you make it eleven?" Evie knew

that begging was unattractive, but Clancy Flynn's kisses were worth begging for.

Her mother shook her head, annoyed. "Ten thirty. That's it. No discussion."

So, with their freedom granted for exactly four hours, Evie and Amanda hustled from the Sand Dollar up to Haven Beach. It turned out they were part of a line of people heading up the hill from town, and Evie noticed that many of them were dressed in summer whites.

"Do we look okay in jeans?"

Amanda made a face. "Derrr. This is the nineties. We're teenagers. Jeans are acceptable anywhere. We could even wear them to a wedding if we wanted."

"Uh, not. First off, you're twelve. And jeans at a wedding? I don't think so, unless somebody's getting married in a barn."

"Uh, thirteen, remember?" Amanda imitated Evie's tone of voice and then rolled her eyes. "Jeans are fine. Besides, we've got our bikini tops on under our shirts."

"Stop a second." Evie tugged on Amanda's arm, leading them into the beach grass along Shore Road. "Once we get there, you are on your own. You understand that, right? I don't want you to talk to me even one single time until a quarter after ten. Then we'll run back to the motel. Got it?"

"Chill out, would ya? I don't want to hang with you and your little Baldwin boy. I have my own plans tonight."

Evie laughed. "Oh yeah? Let me guess. Brad Pitt, maybe? Johnny Depp?"

"Ha! Wouldn't you like to know."

They walked past a huge mansion on the way to the beach, and Evie couldn't stop staring at it. It was stone and cedar, with a huge front porch, a roof that rose to a point in several places and then leveled off in others, all of it topped off with at least a dozen chimneys. She decided it was beautiful and interesting to see in the evening light, but it would probably creep her out after dark.

"We should take off our shirts before we get close to the beach."

"Why?" Evie looked at her sister like she was insane.

"So we can arrive at the party already in our bikini tops. That's cooler than taking them off in front of everybody and basically announcing to the world that our parents wanted us covered up like nuns."

"Oh." Evie removed her shirt. "Now what? Do we just throw them in the grass or something?"

"God." Amanda grabbed her shirt and balled it up with her own, then shoved them into a mailbox by the road. She flipped up the red flag. "That's so we don't forget them on the way home."

Eventually, they made it to the public access stairs to Haven Beach. Clancy was waiting at the top of the steps, leaning against the railing with his hands in his pockets.

Evie's heart skipped at least two beats at the sight of him. He was so totally cute. He wore jeans, too, thank God, and an old and faded Red Sox baseball jersey. His face busted out into a happy grin as soon as he saw her, but when he noticed Amanda, he couldn't hide his disappointment.

"I know. I'm sorry. The only way I could come tonight is if I brought Amanda."

Clancy shrugged. "Hey. No problem. I'll make it work." The girls followed him down to the beach, and Evie already knew deep down in her soul that this would be a night she would remember for the rest of her life.

Clancy walked up to a woman in a mermaid costume sitting at a table. "These are my guests, Ma. Evie and Amanda."

"Welcome, girls." She snapped a neon green wristband on each of them and gave them a friendly smile. Evie thought his mom was pretty. "The bracelet lets you into the buffet and drink station." Then she stamped the top of their hands with big red letters: UNDER AGE. Gee. Embarrassing enough?

"Thank you so much," Evie said.

True to her word, Amanda was off like a shot, already heading up the beach. "I wonder where she's going."

"There's a party up there. A bonfire."

"How did she know about it, though?"

Clancy shrugged. "We can go check on her later if you want, make sure she's safe. It's not too wild of a party, but you never know what young kids will get into."

Evie glanced around the crowded beach. Once she knew no one was looking at them, she kissed Clancy softly right on his lips and gently touched his chin. She felt a little stubble, which made her strangely warm all over. "You're so sweet to me."

Clancy shrugged again. "Of course I am. You're sweet to me."

Oh, how her spirit twirled, her legs danced, and her heart sang that night. She barely talked to another soul for the entire four hours. It was all Clancy Flynn, everywhere she went. They ate together at a little folding table. He devoured three ears of corn and refilled her lemonade without even being asked. They walked at least a mile down the beach, holding hands and talking, and turned around and headed to the bonfire to check on Amanda. She was dancing but not drinking, thank goodness, and Evie reminded her what time she needed to be ready to go.

On their way back to the clambake, the moon appeared over the ocean, sprinkling silvery light across the water. In that perfectly romantic moment, Clancy turned Evie to him, put his hands on her waist, and kissed her. It was the bomb of all kisses that had happened anywhere, anytime. Evie couldn't imagine that a girl had ever been kissed like this in the history of the earth—sweet and tender, full of emotion, full of hunger. It dawned on her that this is what girls meant when they warned of *going too far to stop*. She'd never understood the concept before. She always figured that if a person wanted to stop, they just said, "Hey. I think we should stop." But right at that moment, if Clancy had pressed the issue, Evie might have said yes.

The kiss was *that* good.

Fortunately, he didn't push. He was too much of a gentleman. And that made her love him even more.

"You are special, Evie. I'm so glad you came here this summer and that I had a chance to meet you." He played with her hair and let his eyes take her in, all the way from her hands and fingers to her bikini top, belly, jeans, and bare feet. She felt a little shy and it must have shown. "Don't ever be embarrassed about how gorgeous you are. I can't stop looking at you, you're so beautiful."

Evie ran her fingers through his curls and slipped her fingers inside the neckline of his shirt, just to feel more of his bare skin. "You are the most wonderful person I've ever met, Clancy. I love kissing you, touching you, laughing with you—just being with you makes me happy."

They dropped into the sand. They rolled, kissed, and stroked each other, right there in the sand on the dark beach. At one point, he rolled with her so that she was on top of him, with her legs spread. She started breathing fast. And then she let him put his hand on her jeans, right on her butt! And a few minutes later, when they'd reversed positions, she did the same to him! Evie couldn't believe she had the nerve to do something like that! To think—a few days ago she didn't even know how to kiss, and now look at her, touching a guy's butt!

When they returned to the clambake, the DJ was rockin' the crowd. He picked some truly lame music for the old people, like the Rolling Stones and even the Eagles. Evie and Clancy sat those out. But when he got around to the real stuff, like Hootie and the Blowfish, LL Cool J, Mariah Carey, and the Goo Goo Dolls, they danced nonstop.

A slow song came on. After just the first few lines, it became clear to Evie that it was their story, their song, drifting down on them as they danced on the sand under the fairy lights. Clancy slipped both his arms around her waist and Evie wrapped hers around his neck. They gazed into each other's eyes as the music said it all—in a moment in time, a boy and girl became one, and time or distance would never erase that.

Clancy put his lips to her ear and sang along, telling Evie the words she was hoping and praying he would say to her. "Our love will never end."

At ten minutes after ten, Amanda showed up. Clancy offered to walk them to the Sand Dollar, to make sure they got back safely. Unfortunately, they lost track of time and had to break into an all-out run for the last block.

Amanda straggled behind, which gave Clancy enough time to pull Evie into the motel courtyard to steal one last kiss.

"Tomorrow?"

"Of course. Thank you for tonight. I had a wonderful time."

"Meet you in front of Frankie's at noon."

"Okay."

"Evie?"

She turned back. He blew her a kiss before he slipped into the shadows and ran off.

Amanda arrived breathless at the motel room door just as Evie slipped into place at her side. They counted to three and Evie opened the door. Their mom and dad were waiting for them.

"You're thirty seconds early," their father said. "But where the hell are your shirts?"

Chapter Ten

Just as Richard suspected, Charlie was in the barn. It was a particularly warm morning for Maine, well into the eighties. When Charlie heard him approach and glanced up in surprise, Richard could see his frayed work shirt was soaked with sweat.

"Good morning, Mr. McGuinness. I was wondering if you'd have a minute to talk."

Charlie blinked, turned away, and continued what he was doing—tossing fresh hay into a barn stall. It was as if no one had spoken to him.

Richard never spent much time in the country until he was forced to campaign in the rural reaches of his adopted state. He grew up in Hartford and then transitioned immediately to Manhattan, getting his undergraduate at Columbia. Then it was on to Boston, law school, and Tamara. So as he looked around this quaint Maine barn, he couldn't even guess what kind of farming, if any, might be done on a property like this, or what kind of animals might be roaming about. Charlie disappeared into the stall without a word.

"So, do you have horses? Do you ride?" Richard made this inquiry as he stepped into the shade of the two-hundred-year-old barn, aware that he hadn't been invited to do so. He hoped casual conversation might loosen up the farmer, since Charlie McGuinness was about as stoic and cantankerous as any New Englander he'd ever run across. Richard heard Charlie clanging around with water and a bucket but he didn't answer his question. He decided to try again. "Perhaps you have cows. I think I hear chickens, too, is that right?"

Nothing.

Well, this was awkward. Suddenly, Richard realized he must look out of place standing on a dirt floor in six-hundred-dollar Italian leather shoes and his custom-tailored, triple-pleated pants. But he'd come straight from the station in Boston. Changing his clothes hadn't even occurred to him.

He had come to Maine to have a chat with Charlie. So far, he'd made no progress. Richard decided to step outside the barn and wait until the old guy felt like talking, because he didn't want to piss him off any more than he already had.

As he turned to leave, Charlie exited the stall. "Why are you asking about this farm, Congressman?"

Richard was about to respond when Charlie's laughter cut him off—apparently that had been a rhetorical question.

"Have you come to steal poor old Tussy now? Has 'the child' not been enough and now you want all our critters? How many chickens are you planning to take? We got four goats, too, and a cranky old mare. Do you want to ride her out of here? Should I tack her up for ya, Congressman?"

Richard had never heard Charlie McGuinness speak so many words at one time. And every one of them was dripping with sarcasm and disgust. He tried to soften the tone of the conversation. "Now, Charlie—"

"You want it all, you say?" McGuinness laughed again, resting his dirty hands on the hips of his cotton work pants. "You've come to grab the whole place out from under us? The house, the barn, the hay crop, the tractor?"

"I believe we should move on from the sarcasm," Richard said. "I've simply come to talk. Can I take you into town and maybe we could have a cold beer? You look like you could use a break."

"It isn't even noon yet and I don't drink, but if I did, you'd be the last soul on Earth I'd want to imbibe with."

Richard nearly laughed. Could this have started off any worse? He sincerely doubted it. "Iced tea, then? Lemonade?"

Charlie peered around Richard toward the open barn door and the yard beyond. He craned his neck. "Where are your minions? I only see one car out there, though I know my FBI friends are where they always are, parked at the end of my lane."

"I came alone."

"What, no driver? No lawyers and aides and press people? Tell me you didn't leave the house without your royal ass-wiper!"

Richard shoved his hands into his pockets and stared at his shoes. This little get-together was going nowhere, and if he couldn't find a way to defuse the old guy's rage, then the trip would have been a waste of time. It might even make things worse.

Richard raised his gaze to Charlie's reddened face. "I chose Christina over my career and reputation. Her safety was so important to me that I went public with my paternity, though it might very well cost me my political future and my marriage."

Charlie tipped his chin, frowning. "Is that why you're here? To tell me how inconvenient it's been for you since you stole my granddaughter?"

"I was alluding to the fact that the media exposure has been tremendous already, and I am optimistic we're close to finding her."

"Ayuh, I have a TV, Wahlman. I saw how they're tracking down Evelyn like some kind of terrorist, and I caught your little dog and pony show, too."

"Please, Mr. McGuinness." Richard made his voice as

soothing and understanding as he could. "I only came to check on you."

"Check on me?"

"Yes, I was concerned about how you're holding up. I know you must be worried sick about her. I know I am. I can barely sleep."

It happened fast—Charlie planted a left to his gut and right cross to his cheekbone. Richard hit the hard-packed dirt with a thud. He lay there stunned, mute, trying to get his lungs to work again.

"I've had the idea of doing that since the day we got served with your paternity claim, you slimy bastard!"

Richard opened one eye to see the old farmer staring down, nostrils flaring. He looked as if he were about to kick him just for the hell of it.

"You come up here from away, pushin' your case through like you did, runnin' us over before we knew what hit us, with your high-priced lawyers and your demands, just like you were king of the hill! You should be ashamed of yourself!"

Richard tried to speak but he couldn't get enough air.

Charlie pointed down at him. "How am I holding up? Are you joking, man? Look at me!" He waved his arm around the barn. "I have lost every single member of my family! I am by myself in this world and my heart has broken! My neighbors and friends feel so sorry for me that my house is stacked to the rafters with floral arrangements and casseroles!" Charlie's face twisted with pain and his chin bunched up. The old man began to cry. "All my girls are gone."

"I—"

"By God, man, shut up and listen for once!" He rubbed his eyes, trying to pull himself together. "Losing Ginny nearly killed me, but I had my two daughters to live for, and we made a happy life. And then four years ago, I was blessed enough to become a grandfather. Do you know Christina looks just like my wife?"

"No. I—"

"Of course you don't! You don't know anything about my beautiful family, and that's the worst part of it all. You are just some stranger who's walked in and destroyed our lives—first you hurt my dear Amanda, and now you've put Evelyn and Christina in a horrible, unfair position. Damn ya!"

Charlie spun on his work boots and marched off, leaving Richard on his back in the dirt. He turned his face enough to watch Charlie disappear down the slope of the hill, and tried to assess the damage. That crusty old lobster had the strength of a man half his age. Richard brushed his fingertips along his cheekbone and pulled back with a gasp. It hurt like hell, and might even be broken. As for the rest of his body, he was most worried about the stitches from his bypass surgery. He was essentially healed, but his doctor hadn't yet given him clearance to play squash, let alone engage in hand-to-hand combat.

With a loud groan, Richard pushed up to a sitting position, then managed to pull himself up off the dirt floor of the barn. On the opposite wall was an old mirror framed in leather, so he staggered over and pulled up on the hem of his polo shirt. He froze at what he saw.

Who the hell was that? A used-up senior citizen looked back at Richard. The stranger was a geezer with a gut, gray hair, and a swelling red welt under his left eye. The stitches seemed fine, if you didn't mind having a chest sewn together like leather on a baseball. Honestly, Richard didn't like what he saw in that reflection. He didn't like what he'd become.

His salvation was his daughter. Christina would keep his memory alive. Because of her, Richard Wahlman would leave a legacy bigger than Ways and Means, his philanthropy, and his party leadership. He would have a flesh and blood monument to the vital man he once had been.

Richard tucked in his shirt, wiped off his trousers, and was headed across the yard toward the rental car when he had an epiphany. For the first time in nearly thirty years of corporate law practice and serving Boston in state and national elected offices, he had nowhere in particular to go and no one who was expecting his arrival. He had no meetings. No dinners. No cocktail parties for the sole purpose of sweet-talking donors and flattering lobbyists. In fact, it was possible that he'd never return to that life. Polls conducted after his television appearance had shown an instant decline in voter support, and within hours, Washington had decided he was an embarrassment. Contagious. An unpleasant reminder to his colleagues of just how easily the game could go awry, how close they all were to disgrace. Already, some of his longtime colleagues had turned on him.

And "home" was no longer an option, of course. Tamara had made it clear that she was done. He was on his own.

He would catch a flight to Reagan National this afternoon and hunker down at the Jefferson for a while. He could set up shop and avoid the media. His cardiologist could stop by. He could meet with his broker and his attorney. They would discuss establishing a trust for his daughter, ensuring that she would have everything she would ever need. And, while he was in town, he'd find a discreet real estate agent to help him locate a perfect house. He wanted something with a yard for Christina, and perhaps a pool. Maybe there would be enough land that she could have a pony if she wanted. Where would they live? Massachusetts? Northern Virginia? Connecticut? Of course, the house would need extra rooms for housekeeping staff and the nanny.

"I'm not usually a violent man."

Richard jumped. He had been so lost in his own thoughts that he hadn't noticed Charlie. But there he sat, about twenty feet away on a front-porch rocking chair, his hands gripping the armrests.

Richard collected himself. "You were upset. I happened to be the sucker standing in front of you. I'll survive." He cautiously moved closer to the porch.

Charlie nodded in time with the rocking chair, obviously giving careful consideration to his next words. "I've been thinking about what you said, Wahlman. You do seem very protective of Christina, worried about her welfare."

Richard breathed in relief. Charlie had turned the corner. He was finally willing to have the conversation they desperately needed to have.

"Yes, Mr. McGuinness. Of course I'm protective. She's my daughter. I only want her to be happy and safe and have the best life possible."

"Ayuh, see what I mean? Now that's a protective parent speakin'."

"Absolutely!" Richard propped a foot on the lowest porch step and tried to smile, but his face hurt too much. "I think about whether she's warm and what she's eating and if she's in a place that frightens her. I wish I could see her, just to know she's all right. Or even hear her voice on the phone. I may not have known her for very long but she has become precious to me."

Charlie smiled faintly, then leaned forward, propping his elbows on his knees. "I think I understand."

"I so hoped you would."

"Ayuh, I really do. So here's what I want you to do. Are you followin' me?"

Yes. Charlie McGuinness was ready to give in—thank God this difficulty was over. The old man would ask for a boatload of money, of course—these kinds of things were always about money in the end. Richard was sure they could find a mutually agreeable settlement. And if Charlie wanted to spend time with Christina, or even take her to visit Evelyn in prison, that might be workable as well. Richard was no scrooge. He nodded enthusiastically. "I'm listening, Charlie."

"Good. So what I want is for you to take all that worry you have for 'the child,' all those protective feelings, and the concern for her safety and comfort and happiness, and then multiply it a million times over and add love and family. Then, you might have a *hint* of how I feel about Christina Ginnifer McGuinness, you ass!"

Richard's mouth hung open. He took his foot off the step and backed away.

Charlie wasn't finished. "You know, before Amanda died she made her sister swear that if anything should ever happen to her you were not to come within a hundred miles of Chrissy. My girl was smart. Ayuh, it might look like you have a right to be in her life somehow, some way, because you're her biological father, but you know what, Wahlman?" Charlie pushed himself to a stand on the porch. "You don't deserve her. You aren't a good enough man to be a father to her. Do you realize that you've twisted this around to make it all about *you*? Well, by God it's not! It's about a little girl who has just lost her mother! How can you be such a selfish bastard that you can't even see that?"

It took a full ten seconds for Richard to find his voice. In all the years he'd been debating on the House floor, no one—not even the most outrageously wrongheaded and belligerent elected official—had left him speechless the way this farmer just had.

"Now get off my property."

Richard rebounded. "You're making a mistake, Charlie. It's my decision how much time—if any—Christina gets to spend with you. You forgot that."

McGuinness turned his back to Richard and headed for the door.

"The FBI is going to find them very soon. We've got several solid leads. It's probably only a matter of hours at this point." No response. Richard loathed this stubborn rube. "You will regret this little display of physical violence."

"Doubt it." Charlie reached for the screen-door handle. "That was the most satisfying thing I've done in years."

Clancy's head was inside the hall linen closet, and he found himself regretting that he wasn't more domestically inclined. So far, he'd located one bottom sheet of unknown size, two mismatched pillowcases, and a partially chewed-up dog blanket. He would have to figure something out, fast.

He pulled his head from the deep shelves and heard splashing sounds echoing from the bathroom, followed by a high-pitched giggle. It was the little girl, and she sounded happy. The hum of Evie's lower, gentler voice could be heard as well, though the words were indistinct. Clancy stood in the hallway, mesmerized by the beautiful sound. It had been three years since he'd heard a female voice or felt embraced by female energy in this house. Barbie's unpleasant tone of voice and vibe had been the last. No, he hadn't been exactly celibate since then—there were weekends in Boston and an occasional blind date in Nantucket or the Vineyard—but no woman had set foot in this house in the three years since his divorce except for his mother and sister. Even his damn dogs were male. At that moment, Clancy realized he'd missed it, the sense of being balanced out, and maybe even smoothed down, by the softness a female brought to a space.

But how hilarious was this? He finally found a woman he wanted to bring home but she happened to be a wanted felon with a child in tow, the obsession of every news team, special report, and political blog on the Eastern Seaboard. In fact, because Richard Wahlman had some big-shot assignment in Congress and had even been named as a possible vice president contender, her story had gone nationwide and global. That giggling little girl in his bathtub was Wahlman's child. Evie had kidnapped her. Countless state, federal, and regional law enforcement professionals were searching for her.

Hey, every woman has *some* kind of baggage, right?

Clancy leaned his forehead against the painted pine door of the guest room and tried to make peace with the reality of what he'd taken on. Evelyn McGuinness would go to prison if convicted. That was the bottom line. And by deciding to help her, Clancy had changed the course of his life as well.

He opened the door and did a quick job of straightening up. His last houseguest had been Duncan, almost exactly one year before, and in the fifty-one weeks since, the space had been used as a haphazard storage bin. Clancy opened the window a crack, enough to let in some fresh air without flooding the windowsill with rain, and began taking everything off the bed and piling it against the wall. There were books, law enforcement journals, winter coats and hats, and even a supersized container of Milk-Bones. Then he looked at the bed. Shit! No wonder he couldn't find the sheets—they were still where Duncan left them a year ago! Clancy ripped the bed apart and headed toward the laundry room off the kitchen. At least the linens would be freshly washed.

Next he removed the trophies from the mantel and tackled the gigantic mess still dumped in the middle of his living room floor, randomly throwing the jumble into the boxes and depositing them in his bedroom closet. So much for his organization plan. He went on to conduct a search-and-destroy cleanup of the dining room, kitchen, and even his bedroom. He was grateful for the burst of activity, because if he'd had a moment to stand still and second-guess himself, then he'd be in a heap of trouble.

As he headed toward the refrigerator for pancake ingredients, his cell phone rang. It was Chip.

"Flynn here."

"Chief, what is your ETA at the station? Will you be here for roll call?" Clancy realized he'd neglected to check in with Chip as he usually did. It had been more than two hours since his last contact with his second-in-command. That was a piss-poor example of leadership.

"Sorry, Chip. The time got away from me. Is there anything I need to be aware of?"

"Not really, but"—Chip hesitated—"there's been some scuttlebutt about the fugitive and the abducted juvenile, but we're getting conflicting reports."

Clancy's heart flew into his throat. "What do you mean?"

"Well, someone on the morning Nantucket ferry called to say she saw the suspect come on board and get dragged out by an undercover police officer. But her husband said she always overdramatized things, that it was just a typical vacation marital disagreement. He said the lady's husband came on board to tell her to stop with all the drama and come back to the hotel."

"You don't say?" Clancy set the milk carton on the kitchen counter, then went to find a couple eggs, his pulse going crazy. "Did the woman make an official statement?"

"No, Chief. She said she didn't want to get involved."

He couldn't help but laugh. Witnesses were an interesting bunch. Two people at the same place at the same time could see two completely different events. Sometimes, a witness with valuable information had to be subpoenaed to ensure justice was done. In this case, Clancy was glad the woman was skittish.

"How did you follow up on this, Chip?"

"I called Old John, the conductor working that run, and he said he had no idea what the people could be talking about. He said there was no record of a woman and child fare from Bayberry. He said he'd fax over the manifest."

Clancy leaned his head back and closed his eyes in gratitude. Not only had his longtime friend held up a departure for Clancy, he'd covered his ass without even being asked. He owed the conductor a big favor, and he knew just what it would be. Since his wife had died, Old John had become so desperate for companionship that he could drive passengers crazy with his aimless chatter. Clancy decided he would invite him to the house for a meal, a game of checkers, and a leisurely chat.

"Well, there you go." Clancy tried to sound matter-of-fact. "Since we don't have an official witness statement, let's not bother the FBI with it—I'm sure they're completely overwhelmed with rumors at this point. Oh, and speaking of the case, are there any FBI updates?"

"None at the moment."

"Ten-four, Chip. Thanks for checking in. I'll be there a little before eleven. Are the boys causing you any trouble?"

"Nah. Mostly just sleeping."

"Excellent. See you soon."

"Chief?"

Clancy's finger pulled away from the END CALL button. "Yep?"

"Is everything all right? I mean, I don't mean to pry, but this morning you seemed real upset about something, and, well, I can't remember the last time you forgot to check in. Is Mona all right? Has something happened to Duncan?"

"Everything's good with the Flynns, Chip. No worries. I'm just running low on sleep. You know how it is during festival week—and my canine alarm clocks sure aren't helping."

Mercifully, Chip seemed satisfied with his answer and said good-bye.

Clancy pulled out the electric skillet, started some sausage patties, and began to whip up the batter. Just then, the bathroom door opened. He heard little bare feet run across the floorboards.

"I know you. You're the policemans from the water!"

He smiled down at the cute little girl. Her short dark hair smelled like shampoo and her eyes sparkled. She was dressed in another unisex kind of T-shirt and a pair of cargo shorts. He wasn't sure how to play this—would he continue pretending she was a boy? Could he call her Christina? Should he stick with Chris? He couldn't help but think that if this was a challenge for him—a grown man—it had had to be confusing as hell for a little kid her age. Yet she seemed perfectly at ease.

"That's me, kiddo. On land and on sea, I'm always a police officer." Clancy let his eyes flash to Evie. She looked refreshed, too. Her face was smooth and dry, and for a woman in her thirties wearing no makeup and being hunted down by the feds, she looked damn good. Rosy and soft—but not exactly relaxed.

There were deep grooves between her light brown eyebrows. Her pretty mouth was pulled tight. And she stood about as stiff as a mainsail. It was then that Clancy remembered he was in uniform.

"Anybody a vegetarian?"

"Not us," Evie said softly. She cautiously entered the kitchen space and picked up Christina, propping her on a perfectly shaped hip. Clearly, Evie didn't want to let the little girl out of her sight. "Is there any way I might use your washer and dryer?"

"Please do. They're right in here." He nodded to the mudroom. "The load in there right now will be done shortly." Clancy gave Evie a friendly smile, and she responded with a small upward twitch of her lips. In an attempt to break the ice a bit, he pushed a kitchen stool to the sink and retrieved a colander from an overhead shelf. He turned to Christina. "Would you like to help with the blueberries?"

"Yes! Yes! I love blueberries!" She wiggled out of Evie's grasp and climbed up on the stool. Clancy placed the pint of fresh blueberries in her hands and wrapped her fingers around the cardboard container. "Can you dump all the berries in here?"

She hurled those suckers in the colander without a second of hesitation. Clancy laughed. "That was wicked good, kiddo. Now your next job is to take this sprayer"— he pulled the faucet extension as far as it would reach— "then sprinkle the berries until they're clean." The kid yanked the nozzle out of Clancy's hands.

"Chris likes to help in the kitchen," Evie said from behind the butcher block. Clancy noticed that she'd used the genderless name and continued to keep her distance.

"We cook a lot together, and we always make pancakes on Sundays back in . . ."

Clancy pretended he hadn't noticed her awkward pause. He busied himself with flipping the sausage while keeping an eye on his kitchen assistant, who was drowning the living hell out of those berries. He began talking to himself, hoping Evie would share in the conversation. "This is freshly ground turkey sausage from a butcher here on the island. No antibiotics or growth hormones, free-range kind of bird raised on the mainland. Perfectly spiced, too." He glanced over his shoulder. "There's even fresh sage . . ."

Evie had taken a seat at the butcher-block island. She had her hands gripped together and her head lowered. The sight of her shoulders hunched like that hit Clancy hard. He studied the elegant line of her neck, bent low, and couldn't imagine how desperate and afraid she must feel. If everything went well, Clancy would know soon enough. He'd know everything. And he would do whatever he could to help her.

"The blueberries look good, Chef Jellybean."

"Hey! That's my name!"

"I know!" Clancy grinned at her. "Now let me turn this off, okay?" He had to wrestle the faucet from the death grip of his sous chef. For the next fifteen minutes his assistant was indispensable—she helped set the table, flip the pancakes, and pour the milk, all while Evelyn sat in silence, trying to smile pleasantly when it was obvious she was about to lose it. They ate at the island, but since he had only two stools, Clancy had to pull up a dining room chair for himself. He sat so low that his chin barely cleared the butcher-block surface, which Christina thought was hilarious. Her aunt said almost nothing through the meal.

When they'd finished eating, Evelyn volunteered to clean up, which gave Clancy a chance to grab the sheets from the dryer and make the guest bed. With that task completed, he had to go. Roll call was in just a few minutes.

"Evie, may I have a quick word with you, please?"

She turned slowly from her work at the sink. Christina was busy at the dining room table, humming to herself as she used a dishtowel to dry every plastic cup or bowl Clancy owned, though not a single one had been used in the course of making breakfast. Evelyn was a smart cookie.

She joined him at the juncture of the hallway and living room, but immediately circled around so that she would have both Christina and the front door in her line of sight. Clancy raised an eyebrow. Did she think this chat was a trap? Maybe she still thought this whole thing was a trap, and that he was setting her up.

He sighed and smiled sadly. "Look, Evie, I have to go into work and I don't know when I'll be back. I never know, unfortunately. But I want you to know you are welcome to stay. I want you to stay. Just don't answer the door or the phone and you'll be fine."

Evelyn raised her ethereal green eyes to his, and Clancy saw tears begin to form. She shook her head.

"So? Will you be here when I get back?"

"I"—she looked around his house—"I don't know."

"Fair enough," Clancy said.

"We don't have anywhere else to go at the moment, but I . . ."

Clancy stretched out his hand to hers. He didn't know what the gesture meant or even why he did it, but it seemed she needed to be reassured. Softly, he stroked her fingers with his, and he was astonished when she unfolded her palm to his touch. If there was a word big enough for what this woman did to him, he'd never heard it. There was a power circling him whenever she was near. Her presence somehow made everything sharper and sweeter. Clancy felt as if he knew her—and not just as the fuzzy memory of a long-ago summer fling. He understood her. She was familiar to him. It almost felt as if she were supposed to be here, in his house and in his life. But there was just one little problem . . .

"I'm going to need to know everything, Evie. You can't hold anything back if I'm going to help you."

She pulled her hand away.

"I can't force you to stay, but if you do, you must tell me exactly what's going on. No more secrets. There's too much at stake here."

Her eyes darted quickly toward Christina. "I . . . right. I understand."

"If you're gone when I get back, I will keep you in my thoughts, always. I hope everything works out for the best for you."

She nodded but said nothing.

Clancy headed to the front door, patting Christina on the head. "See ya later, alligator."

"Bye!"

The rain had stopped and the sun was making its debut, which was excellent news for Island Day. Clancy tried to focus on that. He had a job to do today. He had a responsibility to this island.

He was harboring a fugitive.

"Jesus, what am I doing?"

As Clancy headed for the Jeep he heard crunching gravel on the drive behind him. He spun around.

Evie rushed forward. She kissed him. Hard. She popped up on her toes and cradled his head in her hands and just laid one on him. Then she hugged his body so tight his spine cracked. Then she stepped back. It ended just as abruptly as it began.

Clancy felt dizzy. And deliriously happy. He found himself laughing. "Now that was a wicked sick kiss."

"Glad you liked it." When Evie made eye contact with him, Clancy could see how torn and sad she was. "I need to go back inside with Chris."

"Wait." He touched her upper arm. "Is that your usual 'have-a-good-day-at-work' kind of kiss? Because if it is, I can pretend I forgot something, go back in the house, and come out again."

She did manage a smile, but it didn't spread to her eyes. It was a start, though. And he'd take it.

"I think that kiss was a first. I just wanted you to

know . . ." Evie didn't finish her thought, but she didn't have to.

"I feel the same." He brushed the back of his hand down her cheek. "Despite everything and no matter what happens, I am grateful we got to see each other again."

Chapter Eleven

"Gather 'round, ye 'maids." Mona gestured for everyone to sit. "As we know, the Island Day opening has been delayed two hours. This has thrown us off schedule." She inclined her head toward Darinda Darswell. "Thankfully, Darinda has reworked our assignment flowchart. Darinda?"

Mona knew she was being sly. Every member present would notice that seemingly innocent statement and it would be fun to watch their reactions. Slowly, it began to dawn on them. Some women dropped their jaws. Some scrunched their faces in confusion. Some looked as if their eyeballs would spring from their sockets.

By turning over festival-week scheduling to Darinda, Mona had made the first, blatant indication that she was ready to step down. After thirty-six years, she had decided this tourist season would be her last as the president of the Bayberry Island Mermaid Society. In Darinda, she had finally found a natural leader who both understood the sacred nature of the job and possessed the skills to pull it off.

Most important, she had agreed to put her name on the ballot.

"What the fuuuh . . . ?" Polly Estherhausen caught herself, slapping a hand over her mouth.

At least she was trying. Mona recently received a formal complaint about Polly's language penned by Izzy McCracken and signed by eight other members. They claimed curse words had no place in the spiritual domain of the mermaid. They said Polly's fondness for the "F" word, in particular, tainted their rituals and diminished the sacred nature of true love itself, although her frequent use of the "sh" word and the "a-hole" word weren't so great either.

Abigail jumped to her fins. "Shit just got real up in here, people!"

"For crying out loud!" Izzy threw her hands around in exasperation. "I give up. Maybe this group should abandon all pretense of decorum. I know—let's forgo the costumes and run around in obscene T-shirts. Something like ... YEAH, WE GOT A FUCKIN' MERMAID."

After a moment of stunned silence, Layla O'Brien raised her hand. "If you order twenty or more you can get a discount."

Darinda glanced at Mona with a wide-eyed and worried expression.

"You'll do just fine," Mona whispered to her, patting Darinda's hand. "But it does look a little different from this angle, doesn't it?"

Darinda nodded.

"Hold up." Polly stiff-armed the room as a whole. "Let's get back to the point. Mona—what's going on?"

Mona took a deep breath and turned to address her dearest friends in the world. "Ladies, I think the time has come for a transition. Darinda is thirty years my junior, full of energy and wonderful ideas, and she has excellent organizational skills. She'll be on the ticket come our October election. I am going to hang up my shells."

It took a while for the general shouting, jumping, and hugging to stop so that Mona could continue. "We've talked about this many times, 'maids. The leadership role has become too much for me, and God knows Rowan has no interest in continuing the tradition and taking over as president. She doesn't even want to be among our general membership."

Abby laughed. "Am I the only one who finds that ironic? Rowan is with her heart-mate because of the Great Mermaid's intervention. As a matter of fact, so is her best friend, Annie! We authenticated both cases, did we not? And yet they both still refuse to *believe*!"

Sadly, Abigail was right. Despite benefiting directly from the mermaid's good works, the young women had no desire to join the Society. While it was disappointing that Annie Parker wasn't interested, it was a *tragedy* that Rowan felt that way.

As the only Flynn woman of her generation, Rowan should have been the next Mermaid Society president. It was a tradition that stretched back to the 1890s, when the eldest daughter of Rutherford and Serena Flynn created the society in her mother's honor. Since neither of Mona's sons were anywhere near married, Rowan was the only one who could continue the unbroken line of Flynns to serve the mermaid.

There was no convincing these young women that their good fortune was the handiwork of the sea goddess. Rowan and Annie believed that garden-variety coincidence and good luck were behind their love stories. How flat it must be for them to go through everyday life without the spark of the Great Mermaid's magic. How dull it must feel.

All that said, Mona had finally accepted that there was no reaching them. There was no forcing it. The decision to open oneself to the mermaid had to come from the heart, like all life's most worthwhile choices.

Izzy raised a finger. "I do have one small question."

"Me, too," Polly said. "Is this meeting going to go on indefinitely? Because I gotta pee like a pregnant racehorse."

Mona gave Izzy the floor while ignoring Polly.

"I don't question Darinda's abilities or dedication—I truly do think you'll be a wonderful president—but do our election eligibility guidelines allow us to put a former fairy on the ballot?"

A hush went through the room. This was a sensitive topic for the society. Many years back, several members defected, deciding to create a new organization, one that honored the *alleged* existence of woodland fairies in the island's nature preserve. Most mermaid devotees considered it a slap in the face, and possibly even a tongue-in-cheek lampoon of the island's sacred legend.

Darinda cleared her throat. "I was a member of the Fairy Brigade when I first moved here, but it didn't last."

Polly headed for Mona's bathroom. "Well, nobody else has shown the slightest interest in being on the ballot for the last three decades! So fairy or not, I say we let the girl chase her dream."

Layla jumped up and hugged Darinda. "I think you'll be terrific!"

Mona agreed the matter was settled and asked Darinda to proceed with scheduling. Just before the meeting ended, Mona placed her hand upon the stack of colorful brochures on the coffee table. "Please remember that in addition to the beauty of the legend itself, these brochures are our best recruiting tools, and I don't have to remind you that we are in desperate need of new members."

Abigail sighed. "We know, Mona."

The meeting adjourned and the mermaids scattered to their Island Day assignments. As Mona closed her front door, her thoughts went to Clancy's visit that morning. If she said anything to him about this, he would tell her she was a fruitcake, but the fact remained—her son's vibration had undergone a dramatic change in just twelve hours.

Last evening, he seemed preoccupied and unfocused. This morning, he was exhilarated. She sensed a joy in Clancy she hadn't seen since he was a kid, spiced with a pinch of danger. When she sat with him on the couch, she had known he was on the verge of transformation.

Surely, this change in his vibe was not due to his police work. He never got wound up about his job, not even during festival week.

Mona went around her house turning off lights, checking that the coffeepot was unplugged, and giving a last-minute tug on her long blond wig. It was unheard of—Clancy just walking in and announcing he needed help. He was self-sufficient to a fault. Even something as overwhelming as his cottage renovation was primarily a solo endeavor. It was how Clancy saw himself—a man who gave help instead of asking for it. As police chief, he spent his life assisting others. As the only Flynn son on the island, he was forever helping his family.

And this was why she was so puzzled. What revolution was taking place in the spirit of her unflappable middle child? And the mermaid ensemble for a tall and slender woman? And a kid's pirate costume? What was that all about?

Mona smiled in the hallway mirror. Of course it was a woman. A woman with a child.

Mona grabbed her tote bag and headed out for her busy day as ambassador of the Mermaid Society. She had to remind herself that she would not get involved with Clancy's personal life, at least not directly. Her days trying to coordinate her children's happiness were behind her, but, that said, she was curious to see what would happen with the costume she'd given him.

He had no way of knowing, but the mermaid ensemble he'd borrowed was more than just spandex and sequins. It was the regalia Mona had worn for her last six swearing-in ceremonies. She had renewed her devotion to the legend six times in that tail, and believed it had absorbed the purest of light, been infused with love energy, and now hummed at an advanced, openhearted frequency. In short, any woman who wore that ensemble would receive protection and strength from none other than the Great Mermaid herself, the goddess of the sea, the patroness of true love.

Mona hoped whoever this girl was, she would make the most of it.

Clancy had been right. Christina needed a nap. The little girl was so tired that she conked out within five minutes, despite the unfamiliar environment. The lovely ocean breeze moving through the window soothed both of them, and forced Evelyn to admit that the motel had felt more like a prison cell than a rented room. She lay next to Christina on the bed until her niece's breathing fell into the settled rhythm of deep sleep.

Evelyn then stood and went to the back deck of Clancy's house, watching the sunshine burn through the clouds. His place was small but comfortable, and it was clear he'd put a lot of effort and time into making it his own. The kitchen and bathroom looked recently modernized, both rooms featuring light gray marble counters and a variety of repurposed antique cabinets and shelves of all kinds of shapes and sizes. They were all painted the same glossy off-white, giving them a harmonious appearance despite their differences. Then he'd added touches of color with backsplash tile in blues and grays. She was impressed. Clancy had an eye for detail, and the colors and textures inside blended seamlessly with the beach house setting.

She was enjoying the view from that beach house now. Sea grass and squat pine trees fringed Clancy's property, and a crooked walking path wound its way from his yard down to the waterline. But all that was window dressing for the spectacular, front-row seat at seaside. With the sun's help, she could see that Clancy's house actually sat on the highest point of a little spit of land jutting into the water. Off to the left, breakers crashed up against an outcropping of sharp and foreboding boulders, but on the other side, waves spilled peacefully on a couple acres' worth of pretty beach. Funny how such extremes existed side by side on one sliver of land.

Evelyn gazed out over the expanse of blue, green, and gray sea stretching into forever.

Like most Mainers, Evelyn knew and loved the state's lacy edge of seashore, but because she grew up in the foothills and worked in the state capital, she never felt as if the ocean dominated her surroundings. It was easy to forget that nearly two-thirds of the earth was covered in water when you lived inland. Not here. The view from Clancy's little backyard gave Evelyn a to-scale view of the world: she was a tiny speck, standing on a small rock, surrounded on all sides by a vast ocean. Wasn't it interesting that only a few days before she had imagined Bayberry to be the ideal place to hide? Now she realized she might have backed herself into a corner. If it wasn't for Clancy Flynn, she'd already be in handcuffs.

"Son, I need your help at the chili cook-off. It's an emergency." Clancy could tell by his father's authoritative tone of voice that Frasier Flynn was in official mayoral mode.

"What's up?"

"I think one of these smart-asses from the mainland put psychedelic mushrooms in his entry. Dammit! I hate when this happens!"

"Can I send one of my crew over?"

"Are you *nuts*?" Frasier caught himself in midshout and lowered his voice to as much of a whisper as he could manage, which was none at all. The Flynn kids had always snickered at the "Irish whisper" their father was known for.

"We must keep this quiet, son. Come alone. Act casual. The story they ran in the *Bulletin* two years ago nearly shut this whole pop stand down and you know it. We . . ." Frasier stopped suddenly to dole out a few hearty greetings to passersby. "I'm back," he said with a loud sigh. "We simply can't have the cook-off judges wandering around Island Day tripping on 'shrooms again. I need you to take care of this."

Clancy rolled his eyes. His father had been known to become slightly paranoid executing his official duties during festival week. Rowan had long ago given it a nick-name: "Mayornoia."

"Relax, Da. I'll be there as soon as the one o'clock unloads."

"Fine. Fine."

Clancy finished greeting the latest batch of tourists as they disembarked from the ferry, shaking hands and get-ting hugs from repeat visitors. All the while his mind was on his two houseguests. What were they doing? Were they staying inside out of sight? Had they watched the news on his TV? Was she finding anything there to keep Christina occupied? The Flynns didn't have any little kids around. He didn't know much about children—especially little girls—and what they might like to play with.

Were they even still there?

As Clancy headed over to the cook-off stage, he de-cided he needed to be clear in his own head about what he was doing. Did he regret the situation he'd put him-self in? No. In fact, he knew from the second he saw Evie what was ahead for him. Even when he didn't realize who she was, he felt compelled to help her carry what-ever burdened her.

After Clancy had finished roll call and shift change that morning, he managed to catch a few moments in his office with the door shut. An FBI memo said they planned to sweep through Bayberry in the afternoon and would contact Clancy when they were en route via helicopter from the Vineyard. In the meantime, video of the congressman making a spectacle of himself was be-ing replayed everywhere on TV and online. He issued a formal statement in which he took full responsibility for seducing Amanda McGuinness, admitting he had abused his position of authority with a staff member. He went on to claim he would gladly abandon his political career if it brought his daughter back safely. The guy even ad-dressed rumors of his impending divorce, saying that whatever his wife chose to do he couldn't blame her. "I haven't been a very good husband. I don't deserve her."

Clancy didn't trust a word that came out of either side of that man's mouth. Nobody got to serve four terms in Congress by baring his soul. Politics didn't work that way. Richard Wahlman was doing this for a reason. He had to gain something from his public shaming, either politically, financially, or personally.

It took time for Clancy to wind his way through the Island Day crowds, not only because Main Street was packed but because he was on alert. It was his job. Every time he nodded toward someone, caught someone's eye, or returned a smile or friendly greeting, he was checking for any sign of illegal or dangerous activity. It's just what cops did—a lost kid, concealed weapons, shoplifting, narcotics possession, indecent exposure, young men on the verge of fistfights, public intox. The vast majority of visitors to Bayberry Island were there simply to commune with the mermaid while letting their inner oddball out to play. Yet it was his job to find anyone who could potentially pose a threat to public safety.

Clancy caught himself, and laughed out loud. Here he was, worried about someone stealing an origami seagull when the nation's most-wanted kidnapper was hanging out at his place doing a load of laundry. Sometimes, you just had to believe everything would work out fine. Otherwise, life could make you crazy.

Clancy had been there a few times. There were mornings when he woke up and assumed it would be just another day, only to find himself living a different life by the time the sun set. Some changes were good, some bad, and others would take years before he knew what the hell had happened. The day Frasier told the family that the fishery was bankrupt was a bad day. The day he—and Mr. Katsakis— found Barbie in room forty-seven of the Sand Dollar Motel appeared to be a bad day at first, but Clancy soon saw it was a blessing. But never had his life been tossed up in the air and turned upside down as it was the day Evie returned to Bayberry Island. He chose to have faith—because the alternative was unthinkable.

All that said, Clancy had to be honest with himself. He wanted her. In the middle of this giant shit storm, he wanted to touch her more, kiss her longer, and discover what her life had been like through the years.

He needed to know if that summer had ever meant anything to her.

Clancy wasn't proud of the level of his frustration. It took everything he had not to stare at Evie like a starving man, and it was downright painful to not be able to talk to her freely. It wasn't Christina's fault, but the little girl's presence complicated things, big-time.

Clancy saw his father waving.

"Oh thank God!" Frasier clomped down the steps of the cook-off stage and gestured for Clancy to meet him behind the Island Day command center, otherwise known as the family's 1978 Winnebago trailer. He pointed to a covered lobster pot sitting on the grass. "Here it is. Exhibit A."

Clancy was confused. "Uh, what am I supposed to do with a giant-assed tub of chili? Why don't you just dispose of it?"

Frasier shook his head. "If I poured it down the sewer the whole island would be seeing tie-dyed dolphins."

"I don't think that's how it works, Da."

"I want arrests made. I need you to take this in for evidence."

"Take it where?" Clancy chuckled. "You know I don't work for NCIS, right? I don't have some cute Goth chick in pigtails in the basement, fiddling with every technology known to forensic science. If I took this chili in as evidence, I'd have to ship it to the state police lab in Sudbury, and it could take months to get results back."

"Are you sure?"

Clancy put his arm around his father's shoulder and grinned. "Well, now, you might have a point. Seeing as how there's no actual crime associated with this pot of allegedly tainted chili, it could take years."

Frasier's mouth fell open. "So . . . that's it? That's all you're going to do?"

Clancy patted his dad's back. "I'm afraid so." Just then, he was struck with an idea. "Unless we can work out a deal."

Frasier narrowed his eyes. "Does this have anything to do with your mother?"

"Uh, wow. No." Clancy shook his head nice and slow. "I don't want anywhere near that subject."

Frasier glanced up to the heavens and said, "Thank Jesus, Mary, Joseph, and the wee donkey." Then he returned his attention to Clancy. "What do you propose?"

"I'll take the hallucinogenic chili back to the station if you fill in for me the rest of the week at the dock."

Frasier grimaced. "The rest of the week? Ah, son. That's harsh."

"Remember that year you made me clean bird shit from the mermaid scales?"

His father narrowed one eye.

"Payback is a bitch, Da."

"You drive a hard bargain." Frasier held out his hand to shake on the deal. "Done. Thank you. We're gonna throw the book at them."

Clancy carried the heavy chili pot a full block before he reached the police Jeep. He tucked it between the passenger seat and the dash, moving the sun hat and baseball cap far away just in case there was any chili spillage. He wanted to be careful even though the hats weren't anything fancy. He'd stopped by a couple vendor tents so he'd have something to give the girls. For Evie he got a generic straw hat with a wide brim and a flowery ribbon. It was a lot more girlie-girlie than the one she lost in the water, and much larger, and it would hide her face better. And for Christina—*Chris*—he found a kid-sized Red Sox cap, which he hoped would check the "unisex" box because he had to cut his Island Day shopping trip short.

A few minutes later, Clancy let himself in the back entrance of the police station and went immediately to the break room. He transferred a decent amount of the chili to a plastic container and poured the rest down the garbage disposal, public acid trips be damned. He placed the container into an evidence bag and scrawled on a Post-it Note, which he stuck to the bag. It read: *"Do not eat. May be tainted. Sending to Sudbury for analysis."* He stuck the bag in the freezer.

He went into the front office, where he found a solo Jake. "What's up?"

"Hey, Chief."

The dogs burst from their sleeping spot under the desk, nearly knocking Jake onto his ass.

"Whoa. Settle down," Clancy said, petting them. "Where is everyone today. Anything going on?"

"Just sent Deon out to check on a couple cyclists who crashed into each other on the southern side of the bike trail."

"Injuries?"

"Scraped knees. EMTs responding."

"Ordinance violations?"

"Deon says they were wearing helmets and didn't appear to be intoxicated, so unless we're citing people for being dumbshits, then no."

"Ha. All right. Look, I'd like to be off the grid for a couple hours. Call if it's an emergency. I'll be back for the dogs later."

"Got it, Chief."

"Any news on the kidnapping suspect?"

"Not a peep."

On the drive home, Clancy realized he should be feeling relieved that there were no Evie sightings. Instead, the closer he got to his house, the more wound-up he felt. His emotions and thoughts were whipping around like an invisible cyclone. This was it. If Evie was still there, then he was about to cross a line. Clancy had already pledged to help her—and now he was going to discover just what he'd signed up for. He was a man of his word, but what would she tell him? How would he find a way to help her without compromising everything he believed in?

He had butterflies, too. Jesus, he actually had butterflies in his stomach at the idea that Evie could be there when he opened the door.

He'd felt like this only one other time, the summer he was fourteen. He would jump out of bed each morning and race to see the pretty tourist girl. They would meet at the boat dock, or at Haven Beach, or in front of Frankie's, and then spend every possible second with each other. Every day it was the same—butterflies in his belly, his brain charged with the thrill of sexual chemistry, and his heart exploding with something powerful and strange.

Over the years, Clancy told himself the experience had been nothing but the chemical mirage of puberty, a cocktail of hormones, summertime freedom, and the ego boost of being crazy about a girl who was crazy about him, too. Turned out he was wrong.

It wasn't hormones or ego—it was Evie.

Clancy pulled the Jeep into the drive and took a deep steadying breath. The situation was far more complicated this go-round. It was time for them to sort it all out.

Eighteen years ago . . .

As much fun as he was having with Evie, and as crazy as he was about her, Clancy wouldn't be able to see her that evening. Technically, he *could* see her, but that would mean he'd have to invite her to his family's annual festival-week cookout—something he wouldn't do even to his worst enemy.

It just wouldn't work. There would be relatives there from the mainland and all kinds of nosy questions and comments—*ooh, do you have a girlfriend? She's a tourist girl? Well aren't you Mr. Hot Stuff!* He didn't want to embarrass her like that. Also, he didn't want Evie to meet Duncan. She'd probably be offended by the shit he would say to Clancy, right in front of her, and he might even try to hit on Evie just to see if he could steal her away. Sometimes, he wished his big brother was still sick and stuck in bed. He'd been a lot easier to deal with back then. Duncan had gotten a fat head on him lately. He thought he was the shit.

Clancy walked toward the boatyard, where they'd planned to meet to go for a run on the beach together. When they discovered that they both competed in distance events for their track teams, it opened a whole world in common. It gave him yet another reason to want to spend time with her.

But he really shouldn't have said he could go out with her tonight to watch the reenactment. He just didn't want to hurt her feelings or make her think he wasn't into her. Because he was. He was seriously into Evie.

It was hard to believe that he'd known her for only five days. It seemed like forever to him, like there was nothing but a big blank before she showed up on the island and tried to drown herself at the Point. Clancy asked himself many times when exactly he knew she was special. He always came up with the same answer: the moment she reached out through the waves to shake his hand and thank him for saving her. Most other girls would have been hanging on him, crying and shaking and gulping for air because they'd almost died. Not Evie.

Just then he saw her off in the distance. He wanted to ask her to the Mermaid Ball. A real date. But he was scared shitless. Why? Because he was crazy about her, and if she said no, it would crush him. He might not live through it.

Man, this love thing was hard.

But why her? Why was it suddenly this girl that made him light up? One thing was probably the delicate way she touched him—the same way she'd touched the wind chime—like he was one in a million. Like he was priceless. And her kisses were sweet but they meant business. He lived for that first brush of her lips against his, and then the rush he felt when things got wild. He could tell she was really into it, but was holding back because she didn't want to look like she was a bad girl.

God, that was hot.

Sometimes, Clancy wondered what would happen between the two of them if the situation were different—no parents, no curfews, no siblings, and hours of privacy. Nuclear meltdown, probably. They'd generate enough heat to melt the beaches into glass.

Damn. He needed to stop his imagination from heading in that direction. It only tortured him, because he knew it was true—he would do it with Evie in a heartbeat if he thought she was cool with it and they wouldn't get caught.

Evie waved to him. He waved back, groaning in frustration. Why did the world make it almost impossible for teenagers to experiment with sex? At least on Bayberry Island, anyway? He couldn't believe that news of their hot beach make-out session got back to his mom. She was sort of chill about it, asking him if he needed his dad to buy him protection. *But oh my God*—Clancy would rather die than have to talk about the details of his sex life with either of his parents ever again. *Just shoot me now.*

Evie was perched on the boardwalk railing, near the public boat dock office. She wore a pair of dark blue nylon running shorts that showed off her long and lightly tanned legs, a sports bra running top, and had her hair pulled back in a ponytail, like the first day he'd met her. She waited for him, watching as he approached her. As soon as he got close, she widened her legs so he could stand between them. He kissed her.

Uh-oh. Since he wasn't packin' a wind chime that day, he needed to back away a bit.

"Hey, Clancy."

"Hey, Evie. Ready to run?"

"If you're sure you can keep up with me."

"Well, baby, if anyone could get the better of me, it would be you."

They helped each other stretch out. Clancy tried his best not to stare at her butt and thighs and hips, but failed. Once they started out, they wound their way through the alleys to the beach path, headed down to the hard-packed sand.

"It's exactly two-point-six miles until it becomes private property. So I figured we'd go the length, then run up to Shoreline Road, down the bike path, and back into town. Just shy of six miles in all."

"Sounds great."

They smiled at each other quickly, Clancy admiring how her ponytail would swing back and forth with her stride. He had to say that her running form was excellent—efficient and relaxed. Her gaze was forward, her shoulders were straight but not tight, and her torso and hips were perfectly aligned, upright but not rigid. She looked perfectly at home running. In fact, Clancy decided he'd never seen a sight more beautiful than Evie in full stride, the green-blue of the ocean behind her.

Once they reached Shoreline, they headed to the bike path, parts of which were in shade and caught the southern cross-breeze.

Evie spoke as they kept running. "I'm sorry, but I have to tell you something."

"What's wrong? Do you have a cramp?"

"Ha! No. Do you?"

They both laughed, recognizing the friendly competition that existed between them on this run. It turned Clancy on so much that he wished he could just throw her down in the pine needles and get jiggy with her.

"I can't go to the reenactment with you tonight. I'm sorry. It's my dad's birthday, and my mom wants us all together to celebrate while we're on vacation."

"Seriously?"

"Are you mad?"

Clancy laughed, knowing he'd dodged a bullet. "Of course not. I was getting ready to tell you the same thing—tonight is my family's stupid annual cookout. I thought about inviting you, but you'd have to meet everyone, including my brother, who is a complete ass."

She laughed. "I guess we're cool, then."

Clancy reached out and gave her ponytail a friendly tug. "I have a feeling that we're always going to be cool with each other, no matter what."

For some reason, he just couldn't spit it out about the Mermaid Ball. He was crazy nervous. But the more they ran the more time was running out. If he didn't do it now, it wouldn't happen.

After their run was over, Clancy saw Evie to the motel and pulled her behind the loblolly pines. He asked for a good-bye kiss, and it was one for the record books.

"Will you go to the Mermaid Ball with me tomorrow night?"

Evie stared at him and said nothing at first.

"It's okay if you don't want to go."

"No! Yes! Yes, I do want to go! It's just that—I don't have anything to wear. Isn't it a costume ball?"

Clancy kissed her again. He could kiss her forever. "Nah. It's not required. It will be your last night on the island, you know? I really want to spend it together."

Oh, no. She was going to cry. God, he didn't mean to do that, but how was he supposed to know what would send her over the edge and what wouldn't bother her at all? Evie almost died and didn't even whine, but he gave her a ten-dollar wind chime and she needed a Kleenex.

"I'm sorry." She shook her head, trying to pull herself together. "I didn't mean to do that. It's just the idea of it being our last night."

"It's the last night of your vacation on Bayberry Island," Clancy corrected her. "It won't be our last night, period. I know it."

He gave her one last sweaty good-bye kiss, then jogged back home. About halfway, he heard a horn and the sputtering of the beater 1985 Toyota 4-Runner Duncan was so proud of. Clancy ignored him as his brother slowed the car and pulled alongside him with the window open.

"Hey, who's the brown-haired cutie I saw you runnin' with?"

Clancy kept his eyes ahead.

"She looks like that Felicity chick from TV. Real nice."

He didn't pay any attention to Duncan—sometimes it seemed like his big brother's only reason for being alive was to try to jump Clancy's case. Suddenly, the SUV swerved in front of him and nearly ran him over. That was the end of his patience.

"What is your friggin' problem, dude?"

Duncan draped his arm over the front seat and looked down at him, laughing. "I was just going to ask you the same thing, lover boy. Don't you think fourteen is a little early to be sinkin' the salmon?"

Clancy shook his head and walked around the car, slamming a fist into the hood as he went.

"Hey, moron! You just put a dent in my ride!"

Clancy laughed. "No, I just put a repair in your dent."

"Fine. You wanna fuck up my car? Then I'll make sure I get the chance to spend some time with Felicity."

Clancy knew it was the absolute stupidest thing he could do, because if he reacted, Duncan would see how easy he could get to him through Evie. But he couldn't help himself. It was like he'd gone blind and deaf with anger. He whipped around.

"I swear to God, Duncan. If you speak to her or even look at her, I will kick your asthmatic ass to Kennebunk and back!"

"Bwaa-haaa-haaa!" Duncan turned his steering wheel and peeled off onto the road, waving. "Later, you pussy-whipped girlie-man!"

Chapter Twelve

She did it. While Christina was asleep, she turned on the television and faced reality. The two of them were quite the celebrities. In the five minutes Evelyn allowed herself to flip through the channels, she heard Wahlman's interview recounted several times, saw his face on four channels, and listened to two separate interviews with FBI agents. When federal investigators described her as "quiet" and "disciplined," she just about threw up. They might as well have called her a psychopath and be done with it.

If that wasn't bad enough, the world now knew she was traveling under the name Cricket Dickinson. Now her ID was worthless.

She turned off Clancy's television. She refused to let this destroy her, but she knew how shattered her father must be. It had to be killing him. This whole drawn-out saga was putting him through hell. And he didn't deserve it.

Evelyn squeezed her eyes shut, trying to stop the memory from flooding her mind, but she couldn't. Maybe the details of that summer day would never leave her, no matter how hard she tried to forget.

Richard Wahlman's fancy lawyer had shown up at the farm before noon on a sunny July afternoon. Evelyn,

Pop-Pop, and Chrissy had just returned from a successful berry-picking adventure, and had arrived home with quarts and quarts of boysenberries, raspberries, black-berries, and blueberries. As always, the next couple days would be devoted to baking, canning, freezing, and jam making. Though everyone was choked with grief over Amanda's death, Evelyn thought Christina needed to see that the rhythm of life would go on.

When they heard a loud and impatient banging at the front door, Evelyn knew she needed to answer it—Pop-Pop was out in the back garden picking snap peas and digging potatoes for dinner. She hurried toward the front of the house with a berry-smeared Chrissy on her heels.

The man in the suit was a stranger.

"Evelyn McGuinness?"

Her stomach fell to the ground. Had something else horrible happened? What now? "Yes." Christina ran behind her legs.

He shoved folded-up papers into her sticky hands.

"But—"

"You are hereby subpoenaed to comply with an emergency order for determination of paternity, and you are required to make any response within ten days to this petition for custody."

Pop-Pop came running in from the garden, horror in his eyes. It had been just over a month since State Police arrived to inform them Amanda had been killed. Evelyn saw her father's expression and immediately knew what he was thinking, because she had asked herself the same question: *everyone was right here—who else was left to die?*

Her father turned bright red when he unfolded the papers. Evelyn's body trembled. Christina began to cry, not because she understood any of what was happening but because she was emotionally raw and the only people in the world she had left were clearly in distress.

Her father didn't do well with any of it. It had devastated him to learn of Amanda's affair with the congressman. The custody ruling left him livid. And Evelyn knew that running off with Christina likely caused him to experience both those emotions all over again, and for that she was truly sorry. She hadn't even given her dad a chance to say good-bye. And now, with the FBI surely keeping him under a microscope, she couldn't risk sending him a message that they were all right. That was, by far, the worst part of all this.

Evelyn had no idea how long Christina would sleep in Clancy Flynn's guest room, but eventually, she would wake up. And then what? Would Evelyn and the police chief play house, neither acknowledging that she was a wanted felon? Would she bolt before he returned home tonight? And go where?

She decided to call Hal. She sat at the dining room table, which put the guest room door directly in her line of vision. She would end this call at the first sign her niece was awake.

While the phone rang on Hal's end, she glanced at the slew of family pictures on Clancy's walls—this man's normal life looked like other people's vacation pictures. There was deep-sea fishing, beach bonfires, sailing, people tanned and fit and laughing, and an adorable photo of three kids under ten, sitting on the steps of a fabulous old mansion. She spotted Clancy right away. He was the one in the middle, the one who looked like he was up to no good. He had that same glint in his eye, even back then. She could see the man in the boy, just as she now saw the boy in the man.

"Christ, where the hell are you?" Hal said by way of greeting as soon as he picked up the call.

"Still on Bayberry Island."

"You're still at the *motel*?"

"We left early this morning."

"I'll make a quick cyber visit to the Sand Dollar and remove any record of your reservation."

"Thanks."

"So if you're not there, where are you? Are you okay?"

"We're safe for the moment."

"Want to tell me how that is possible? Because I was just watching *Headline News*, and the FBI is spreading out on Martha's Vineyard, Nantucket, and Bayberry, searching for a tallish, athletic woman who looks a lot like Brigitte Nielsen. And Wahlman, that scum, is whoring himself out to any media outlet that will take him. I wouldn't be surprised to see him make a guest appearance on *Here Comes Honey Boo-Boo*."

"Please, Hal. Stop. I really don't feel like—"

"I just wanted to hear you laugh. You must be worn to a frazzle."

"I . . . I'm okay. At least right now."

Hal remained quiet for a moment. "Something's different with you. What's going on? You sound sort of—I don't know—calm, I guess, which is the last thing I expected. Where exactly are you on Bayberry? Where's Chrissy?"

Evelyn sighed and propped her forehead in her hand. "I don't really know what's going on, but Chris is napping. We're at Clancy Flynn's place while he's at work."

Hal gasped. "What? Did you break in or something? What the hell?"

Now that made her laugh, and Hal had been right—it felt good. "We were invited."

"All-right-tee then."

"We left the motel early and ran through a rainstorm, making the ferry by the skin of our teeth. But the boat didn't push off on time, and then Clancy calmly walks on board, grabs our stuff, and escorts us off. I thought for sure we were being taken into custody, but he took us home with him and made us pancakes."

"He arrested you and then made you breakfast?"

"No. It wasn't an arrest. His uniform was covered in rain gear and he didn't flash his badge or anything when he got us off the ferry. He just took us to his Jeep."

"And he knows who you are?"

"We haven't exactly had time for a heart-to-heart about it, but I know he does. I can see it in his eyes, like he's worried about me. He told me he wanted us to stay. He told me to trust him."

Hal groaned. "Hold up. I don't get it, Evie. What the hell are you doing?"

"I'm not completely sure."

"Uh, yeah. So what is your immediate plan—to stay there until the FBI has come and gone?"

"I don't have a plan."

"Sweetie, I'm not sure this is such a great idea. Are you putting your fate in this cop's hands? Do you really trust this dude?"

Evie had no idea how to answer that question. There was no logical reason why she should, and yet . . . "I don't know if I trust him, Hal. But it's the best offer I've had today. Do you have a better idea?"

No comment.

Once she promised Hal that she would check in with him that night, Evelyn went back out on the deck, and continued to stare across the sea.

Clancy opened the front door and encountered silence. No little girl running barefoot down the hall. No Evie.

She was gone.

He tossed the costume bags on a chair and simply stood there. He let the emotions slam into him like a rough shore break, hitting his chest so hard that it knocked the air out of him. Up until right that moment, Clancy hadn't realized how desperately he wanted her to be here.

And now what? He was afraid for Evie and intensely sad for Christina. Why did she run? Why didn't she even give him a chance to help her? Immediately, Clancy began playing it out in his head—maybe he could still find her before the FBI did, and at the very least be a friendly face and a shoulder to cry on when the feds took her into custody.

Enough.

Evie left because she didn't want his help. She never wrote to him all those years ago because she didn't feel the way he did. It was all pretty simple. But dammit, it hurt like hell. It felt like torture to see her after all this time, only to watch her disappear again.

Yeah, his thoughts wandered to *her*, the stone-faced harpy, and he had to laugh at himself. So it had come to this—eighteen years on, Police Chief Clancy Flynn now stood in his own living room, revving up to give the mermaid the beat-down she deserved.

"Still having fun with me, huh? Never found anyone as satisfying to screw with? Is that it?" He didn't know where to look because, well, the fountain was a mile away. So he just spun around and looked everywhere. "Don't you think I'm all paid up now—principal, penalties, *and* interest? Give me a fuckin' break!"

He shoved his ball cap in place and turned to go, catching a flash of movement out of the corner of his eye. Off to the left, on the deck beyond the dining room double doors, he saw a ripple of a blue-and-white-striped shirt.

She was here.

At that instant, Evie moved into the frame of the doorway, looking out to the ocean. Clancy's heart jumped to see the shock of white blond hair, the long neck, and those legs. God, it was so wrong to be looking at her legs at a time like this! But he was only a man, and for eighteen years now he'd been walking the earth with the image of Evie's legs permanently burned into his brain, the standard bearer for every woman he would encounter. No one ever came close.

Evie turned, peered through the glass, and caught him staring. Her face remained blank, just a hint of sadness in her expression, but she didn't shy away from his gaze.

He went to her.

"Chris is napping."

"Good."

"Have you seen the news?" Evie wouldn't make eye

contact with him, her voice sounding as blank as her face appeared.

"Look at me, Evie."

"Don't ask me to do that."

"Please." Clancy placed his hand on her shoulder, then let his fingers trail down her left arm. "You need to tell me everything. It doesn't matter what this looks like on the news or what anyone else is saying. I want to hear it directly from you—what's real, what's politics, what's complete bullshit. Just tell me what is going on and we'll go from there. Whatever I can do, I'll do it."

"Chris won't be asleep for much longer."

"All the more reason to not waste any more time." Clancy eased her around so that she faced him. So much pain in those pale green eyes, so much fear etched in her beautiful face. It was obvious how alone she felt, and it wasn't right. The girl he once loved so deeply shouldn't feel that way.

"First, I need to ask you to do something for me. It's important."

"If I can, I will," Clancy said.

"I need you to somehow get a message to my father, telling him we're okay. But it's not safe to call or e-mail or even write. I think the FBI is—"

"I'll take care of it."

Her eyes widened. "You will?"

Clancy put his fingertip under her chin and forced her to look up at him. "I can safely get a message to your family that you and Chris are all right. It will just take a little ingenuity."

Evelyn grabbed Clancy's forearm for support, as if she felt light-headed. "You'll do that for me? It's only my dad. I know he's going crazy right now, not knowing what's happened to—"

"I didn't know your mom passed away." Clancy couldn't begin to imagine the weight of the grief she carried. Both her sister and her mother were gone, and he hadn't been there to help her through any of it.

Again . . . her choice. So why was it still so hard for him to remember that? Why did he have to keep reminding himself that Evie chose not to write to him, not to have him in her life?

She nodded. "The summer after you and I . . . she had cancer. It was very quick. Dad, Chris, and I are what's left of the family."

"I wish I would have known, Evie. I'm so sorry. About your sister, too."

She didn't say anything, just dropped her eyes to her feet.

"Evie, you've got to tell me what's going on. Right now."

Her head snapped up. "I . . ." Tears began to well in her eyes. She tried to stay in control but her chin trembled. Ah, shit. It was obvious she needed to be kissed more than she needed to be interrogated.

He put his hands on her upper arms and pulled her tight to him, lowering his mouth to hers without delay. Damn, she was delicious. She was Evie, silky, sweet Evie from so long ago. Clancy slid his arms around her body and lifted her off the deck, still kissing, still holding, still doing whatever it took to get her to come out of hiding. He waited. . . . Evie didn't shove him away or take her lips from his. In fact, Clancy felt her clutch on to him for dear life, her hands gripping his back, her muscular legs flying up to grip him around his waist—which wasn't recommended for a utility belt outfitted with a loaded Glock, handcuffs, Mag flashlight, mace, and a Taser, among other things.

"Evie. I gotta put you down. Hold on just a second."

She wouldn't let go. Her lips moved on his and she tightened her thighs. Ah, God it felt so damn good, but it was crazy unsafe. "Evie?" She only grabbed him tighter.

Clancy managed to pull her off, and guided her to the top of the deck railing, where he plopped her down.

"Give me a second. My gun is loaded."

Evie looked down the front of his body and smiled. "It sure is."

They both laughed as he unhooked his utility belt and laid it across one of the deck chairs. He returned to Evie, and when he got close enough she opened her legs and pulled him in to stand between her thighs. Just like so long ago.

"Keep kissing me. Please."

Clancy brushed the side of her cheek. It was almost too wonderful to believe. She was right here with him, after so much time. Evie gazed into his eyes, and suddenly, she didn't even look like the same woman. Her face had opened in softness, her eyes were so wide and vulnerable that she looked fourteen again.

Clancy feathered his lips against hers, trying to be gentle when all he wanted was to disappear deep inside her, bite down into her flesh and consume her. It took everything he had to hold back, to simply enjoy her gifts of sweet, soft, luscious kisses. His hands went around her firm waist. Evie gently held the backs of his thighs, pressing him a little closer, demanding a bit more from his kiss.

They were on the edge and they both knew it. His hands went to her hips, back, thighs—oh, God—these kisses and these touches were not the cautious exploration of two kids. This was the real deal. Evie's flesh felt firm and hot and her legs were open to him. She wanted him. And he wanted her so badly he was about to explode.

"This is very dangerous," he said.

"Danger is my middle name nowadays." She slapped her hands on his ass.

They went there again—raging, hot, and wild, her legs flying around his waist. Clancy felt all of her, the delicate juncture between her thighs, her perfect breasts pressed up against his chest, her heat, her need, the muscle strength of those thighs and calves claiming him. He kissed the living hell out of her until they were both gasping for breath.

So this was Evie—all grown up.

They panted, staring at each other in silence. She looked stunned, and Clancy was sure he did, too. There was no logical explanation for what was happening. They hadn't said a word to each other for nearly two decades. She was a fugitive on the run and he was a cop who had decided to risk everything to help her. This detonation of lust made little sense.

Clancy smiled at her. All he had intended to do was comfort her, ease her sadness. Instead, he'd unleashed eighteen years of desire. Clearly, it was mutual.

"Oh, dear God," Evelyn whispered.

"Yeah."

"Where do we even start?"

"Wherever you want."

She bit her lip and looked past Clancy into the house. "She won't be asleep too much longer—maybe a half hour at the most."

"We can cover a lot of ground in a half hour."

"If the last three minutes are any indication, you're right."

"Talk to me, Evie."

"All right." She sighed, her moment of soft vulnerability gone. Once again her face was etched with mistrust and fear. "Why did you bring us here? What are you doing?"

"I want to help however I can."

"But you know I'm wanted for kidnapping, right? That I've committed a federal felony and broken the heart of a doting father."

"If you say so."

She laughed bitterly. "Everything's right out there for you and the whole world to see. All my friends, my patients, blog readers . . ." She stopped, then imitated the deep and serious tone of a news anchor. " 'Neighbors and coworkers of this otherwise law-abiding sports therapist and blogger called her 'quiet' and 'disciplined.' "

"Yeah. It did have a serial killer ring to it."

"And this doesn't bother you?"

"Of course it does, Evie! I look at you. Then I see the FBI bulletins and TV reports and I know something doesn't fit. You're in a seriously shitty situation, but I believe there's got to be a good reason you took Christina and ran. And now's your chance to tell me what it is."

Evie breathed deeply, then rubbed her hands over her face. When she looked up at Clancy again, there was intense grief in her expression. "I was living and working in Augusta when my father called to tell me Amanda had come home unexpectedly and refused to tell him why. Within a few weeks, she admitted she was pregnant. She told us the identity of the father wasn't important and she would give us that information when—and if—she thought it was necessary. She asked my dad and me to drop the subject, so we did. We just assumed the father was some young professional she met on the job, another overworked, ambitious, too-smart-for-their-own-good twentysomething who wanted to be at the center of it all. We thought maybe he was married."

Clancy reached out for her hand. "You're doing great. Go on."

"Well, one day, when Christina was about a year old, Amanda and I went out to the main road to get the mail like we sometimes did, and on our walk back to the house, she just pulled me to the stone wall, set me down, and it all came spilling out.

"She was twenty-five when she started working as Wahlman's personal assistant in DC. She described how she had admired him, saw him as eloquent and sexy and larger than life. Everything started out as innocent flirting, she said, but Wahlman began slipping in an innuendo or two whenever they were alone for more than a few seconds. He seemed to really enjoy how smart she was and how she could go toe-to-toe with him in conversation. Soon they were sharing ideas and confidences.

My sister said Wahlman treated her more like a colleague than a scheduling assistant."

"I'm sure that wasn't the first time he'd done something like that," Clancy said.

Evie nodded sadly. "Amanda said there were rumors, you know, that he had a thing for much younger women, but she told herself that she was different. She convinced herself that they shared something real and she wasn't just another diversion."

"Ugh, poor kid."

Evie laughed a little. "She said he told her he loved her and would leave his wife for her."

"Oh, God. What a bastard."

"She really beat herself up for being so naive."

"I'm sorry she went through all that, but how does that justify you running away with Christina?"

Evie's mouth pulled tight. "It *doesn't*."

"So . . ."

"So that day Amanda cried her guts to me, she told me she'd made me legal guardian of Christina in case anything happened to her. And she made me swear I would never, ever let Wahlman be a part of her life."

Clancy felt his eyes widen. "That's pretty intense. Did she say why?"

Evie turned her head away, trying to compose herself.

"Sure. Amanda said that when Wahlman found out she was pregnant, he tried to give her an envelope full of money, insisted she get an abortion, and made reference to how young women in her situation had been known to disappear from Capitol Hill and are never heard from again."

"What?" Clancy's jaw dropped. "He threatened to physically harm her?"

"The conversation took place between my sister and Wahlman's chief of staff. He sent her to Amanda's apartment to deal with the situation because he didn't have the balls to do it himself."

"But Wahlman claims he never knew your sister was pregnant."

Evie laughed bitterly. "Yeah. He says a lot of things that aren't true. Like that he won custody."

"He didn't?"

"No. I can't figure out what he did, but he used his influence somehow to steamroll us. He basically stole Christina from her family."

Clancy stared at her. She did have her reasons. And they were good ones, if they could be proven.

"So." Evie lowered her chin and frowned at him. "Why would you automatically assume I'm not guilty as charged? You don't even know me."

Clancy realized he had just become the subject of this interrogation. "I *did* know you, once, a long time ago, and I am looking at you right now. You're right here in front of me. I've watched how devoted you are to Christina, how much she loves you. And I see you carrying the weight of the world on your shoulders, more crap than any one person should have to deal with. But you know what I *don't* see when I look at you?"

She shook her head.

"I don't see a ruthless kidnapper. And I will do whatever I can to help you sort this out."

Evie's chin trembled. It took her a moment to pull herself together enough to speak, and when she was ready, she lifted her sea-glass eyes to Clancy. "So you're not going to turn us in?"

"Ah, Evie. No. I'm not. But we've got our work cut out for us." Clancy held out his arms and she fell into his embrace. He felt her begin to shake slightly. He knew she was trying not to cry.

"It's going to be all right."

She shook her head against his chest, then sat upright, wiping her eyes. "I really do need your help. I have nobody else to turn to."

"You've already got it."

"What are we going to do about my name? My alias is all over TV. I picked Cricket because that's Chris's nickname for me, which only my immediate family knows. Dickinson is my mother's maiden name. But now I can't be Cricket *or* Evelyn."

"I guess you're Evie again." Clancy gave her a gentle smile. "At least until we sort this out."

She blew out air and looked away for a moment, like she was summoning courage. "Before we go any farther, I have to know—did you ever think of me? Even just a little?"

Clancy wasn't sure he'd heard right. "Of course I did. For a very long time."

"Then why the hell didn't you ever write me back?"

He took a step away. Apparently, she was serious, which made absolutely no sense. Tears began to flow down her cheeks. He was baffled. "I'm sorry . . . *what*?"

"Clancy, I've missed you. I think I've missed you my whole life."

His pager went off, and before he could answer it, his cell phone rang. Clancy shook off the mind-blurring confusion and retrieved his utility belt off the deck chair. He answered the phone at the same time he checked the beeper.

"Flynn here."

"Chief, it's Jake. They're on their way from the Vineyard. ETA is fifteen minutes. We're meeting them at the airstrip."

Clancy spun around on his heels, checking out the horizon. At the same time he motioned for Evie to go inside. "I'm on my way."

"We were told to expect media, too. Everybody's got a helicopter these days."

"Great." He opened the door for Evie and placed his hand on the small of her back, hurrying her along. She flashed him a confused look but didn't resist.

"And the congressman is traveling with the FBI."

Ugh. "On my way."

Once they were inside, Clancy locked the double doors and jogged into his bedroom to batten down the dog door. He found Evie standing in the kitchen, leaning up against the cabinets, arms crossed.

He walked right over to her. "Listen to me." Her eyes widened. "Do not leave the house. Do not answer the door for anyone but me."

"What's happening?" Her voice sounded shaky.

"Come over here a second." He took her hand and pulled her with him into the living room. "Look, I'm sorry to be dragging you around but I've got very little time." Clancy yanked on his police department cap and grabbed his keys from the hook, then picked up the costume bags.

"What's this?"

"It's a mermaid costume for you and a pirate costume for Jellybean. If, for whatever reason, you think you absolutely must leave the house—as in a dire emergency— these will give you something to hide behind. I don't know when I'll be back. You should be able to find stuff to eat."

"Who was that on the phone?"

He wouldn't bullshit her. "The FBI and Wahlman are on their way. Please lie low."

She pulled her lips tight.

"Do you have any hard evidence about how Wahlman gamed the custody system?"

"Not yet."

He nodded. "We'll continue our conversation later." Clancy grabbed her by the upper arms and kissed the bejesus out of her. "But there's one thing you need to hear before I leave. Please listen to what I'm telling you."

"Okay."

"I never got a letter from you, Evie. I didn't write you back because I never heard from you. I thought you weren't interested in me. I'm sorry, but I have to go." He gave her a quick peck on the cheek and was gone.

A bewildered Evie stood in the doorway. He waved to her as he peeled out from the gravel drive.

Richard always enjoyed the drama inherent in helicopter travel. Disembarking involved ducking to avoid being beheaded, feeling the violent whip of trouser fabric against his legs, and being escorted off across the tarmac or landing pad. Today was no exception.

A few of the local yokel police officers were at the airstrip to meet them. Richard and six FBI agents endured quick greetings and were given the keys to two Jeeps they could use while they were on the island. But it was the same story they'd heard on Martha's Vineyard— no witness sightings, no photos or smartphone videos, no credit card use, no cell phone pings, no conclusive store videos, and no indication that Evelyn and her niece had ever been there. But they would look anyway.

Special Agent in Charge Teresa Apodaca rattled off a list of questions directed at the head yokel, who seemed friendly and cooperative enough.

"Any reports of squatters in any of the boats in the harbor?"

"No, Agent. Every boat is occupied by owners or rented out during festival week. The marina is fenced and locked. Slip tenants aren't very welcoming to strangers."

"Any empty buildings?"

"Some industrial space by the shore is unused. Feel free to check it out for signs of habitation, but it is secure and we do patrol the area. I don't think it would be the first choice for a woman and child, since there is no power or water and you'd have to scale the walls to access the interior."

The agent frowned at him. "The suspect is a trained athlete and she's desperate—anything is possible." She went back to her list. "I've been told the girl and her captor may be dressed in costumes for this, whatever it's called. . . ."

"Mermaid Festival."

"Yes."

"Of course," the Chief said. "We have thousands of visitors each day, and a good number of them are in costume—mermaids, sea captains, pirates, sailors, and sea creatures of all varieties. Plus we have our share of fairies and just plain unidentifiable stuff."

She rolled her eyes. "Sounds like Miami on a Tuesday. So what about the beaches? Do you conduct a sweep every night? Is there any chance they're camping out illegally?"

"We do patrol via boat, vehicle, and on foot, but we have limited staff and the island has six miles of beaches. Three of those miles are owned privately—by an invitation-only club, the marine research facility, or individual residential landowners. Only the club has camping facilities—you know, running water, fire pits, electric hookups."

Richard had to give the chief credit—he sounded on the ball.

The agent in charge nodded and took notes. "We'll be headed there first. The name of this club?"

Chief Flynn pursed his lips. He seemed to have a hard time spitting it out.

"The club, Chief?"

"Yeah. It's the Bayberry Freedom Colony. Ask for Chet and Willa Chester, and they'll be glad to show you absolutely *everything*."

"Yeah, and don't forget your tennis racket."

That mumbled comment came from one of the local cops, the big one in the middle, who was now casually gazing up toward the sky. Richard figured the place must be a private tennis club.

Just then, Chief Flynn shot a sideways glance at Richard. There was no warmth whatsoever in his expression. In fact, it looked like the cop wanted to rip out his throat.

He decided to kill him with kindness. "Thank you for your assistance, Chief. It's much appreciated. I am desperate to find my daughter."

He got silence in response.

It was agreed that everyone would meet at the Bay-berry Police Department at six p.m., and if there were enough media outlets present to warrant it, the FBI would conduct a short news conference at that time. Before then, local cops were instructed to respond to any inquiries in the usual way: "We cannot comment on an ongoing FBI investigation."

The agents split into two groups and set out in the borrowed Jeeps, Richard accompanying Apodaca and her second fiddle. He had to say that after a few minutes, he began to enjoy the view of the pretty little island as it zipped past the open passenger window.

"Strange place," the agent in the backseat said.

Apodaca laughed. "I've seen much stranger."

"It appears they're annoyed we're here, though," Richard said.

"Yeah, it happens." Apodaca took a hard left onto something called Shoreline Road without even slowing down. "Locals can get a little territorial when we show up. They think we're questioning their abilities, or stealing their thunder. You know—stepping on their toes."

Richard decided he would let that analysis go without comment. In this case, he knew it was more than that. The police chief's demeanor had gone far beyond territorial. When he looked Richard in the eye, his dislike felt personal.

It felt like a warning.

Chapter Thirteen

The police station's front door flew open with such force that it cracked the plaster wall behind it. Clancy, Deon, Jake, and Cam automatically reached for their weapons, then put them away as soon as they saw who it was.

"I know her! The criminal! She was my mystery guest!"

Deon leaned toward Clancy. "The motel dude, right?"

Clancy sighed like this was just another tedious encounter with Cosmo Katsakis, but his heart raced and his palms began to sweat. *Shit.* Katsakis was a loose end— he'd given Clancy a copy of Evie's fake ID. Somehow, Clancy had to convince him to keep his mouth shut.

Cam smiled at their visitor. "Why don't you come on in and we'll get you a cup of coffee?"

"I don't want your bad coffee! I *know* her, that's what I'm trying to tell you! That kidnapper girl! And she broke into my computer system!"

Cosmo was so out of breath Clancy worried he was having a heart attack. Did he run all the way from the motel? He peeked out the window. No—Cosmo ran all the way from his golf cart, now illegally parked directly in front of the station.

"Mr. Katsakis, you need to relax." Clancy took a step

toward him. "Maybe some water would be better." Deon headed off to the break room.

"I don't need no coffee, no water, no treatment like I'm a crazy man! I need to talk to the FBI! It's a conspiracy, I tell you, and I don't trust you chowderheads to take my testimony!"

Cam let go with a long and low whistle.

"Get me the FBI on the phone!"

"We can do better than that, sir." Jake gave him a pleasant smile. "The FBI is here on the island. They will be back to the station within the hour. You can talk to them personally."

"Good!" Cosmo crossed his arms over his stained shirt. "'Cause I'm not gonna move nowhere until I speak to them!"

"Here's your water, sir." Deon handed him a paper cup, which he did not accept.

Deon set it down, looked at Clancy, and rolled his eyes.

"All right, Mr. Katsakis." Clancy sat down in the chair nearest to him. "Here are your options. You can wait here with us, make new friends in one of the holding cells, or relax in our luxurious break room, which has a TV."

"Show me the way."

They escorted him to the lunch room and handed him the remote control.

"Hey! You said it was luxurious. This is disgusting!"

Cam closed the door and whispered, "That guy thinks our break room is disgusting. What does that say about us?"

Jake asked, "Is he on something?"

Clancy shook his head. "It's his God-given charm."

"Hmph," Deon said. "I'd say he ranks about a six on the cray-cray scale."

Only minutes after they had returned to their posts, the door opened again, this time politely.

"Hi, guys."

Clancy smiled patiently at Heather Hewes, the local

press barnacle. Heather was an earnest young woman with big dreams—she was determined to be a *60 Minutes* producer one day. What she lacked in spelling skills, camera work, and factual accuracy, she more than made up for with enthusiasm. "What's happening, Heather?"

"I was hoping you'd tell me. I need something sexy or this festival week will be a washout."

"We don't do it for you?"

She shook her head at Deon. "In the biz we use that word to mean exciting, something to catch the public's attention. Not, you know, actual sex."

"Gotcha."

"So, can you give me an exclusive on the kidnapper, Chief?"

He almost laughed—*why, yes, he could, and no, he wouldn't.* "Now, Heather, you know our policy. We don't comment on ongoing criminal investigations, especially those coordinated by the FBI."

"Well, crap." She sighed, pushing up her glasses. "I'm just not finding anything good to write about. This has got to be the most boring Mermaid Festival in the history of Bayberry Island."

"Yeah." Clancy sighed. "One for the record books, I'm afraid."

"How about that pirate boy who almost drowned yesterday? Any word on him? I tried to interview the family but they weren't very cooperative. Are they even still on the island?"

Clancy shrugged. "I don't know what to tell you, Heather. There are a lot of kids running around this place right now."

She groaned in frustration. "One last thing. An anonymous tipster called the paper today. The message he left was pretty shocking."

Clancy's spine straightened. Was this the husband from the ferry? Katsakis? Old John, even? He made sure he sounded only marginally interested. "Oh? What was the message?"

"He said one of the chili cook-off entries was tainted with 'shrooms again. Is there any truth to this allegation?"

"*Day*-um." Deon shook his head.

"I have no evidence to support that claim, Heather. I'll let you know if there are developments we can share in either matter."

She sighed. "See? Dull, dull, dull!" Heather left.

Not much later, Clancy went to check on Katsakis. He poked his head in the break room to find him sitting with his arms crossed over his sauce stains, watching *Headline News*. A can of diet Dr Pepper sat in front of him on the lunch table. "Doing okay, Mr. Katsakis?"

"I'm not talking to you. Only the FBI."

"Well, they should be here in about twenty minutes." Clancy suddenly noticed a lingering scent of spicy food. There was nothing in the microwave or on the stove, however, so he figured it was just the way Katsakis smelled in a closed room. "I see you already located the soda. There might be some chips in the cabinet."

"I already found something to eat. Leave me alone, Flynn."

Something to eat . . . oh, hell no! As casually as he could, Clancy strolled inside the break room, opened the freezer, and found it empty save for the ice cube trays, a freezer-burned tub of ice cream, and a frosty Post-it note, which had fallen off the evidence bag.

Clancy shut the freezer. He looked into the garbage can. Yep, the bag was in the trash. He looked into the sink. Yep, the plastic container was empty. He took a moment to compose himself.

"Hey, Flynn. If that was your lunch, then I guess I'm sorry. But you're not a very good cook. It had a strange taste. Needed more cinnamon. The Greeks put cinnamon, cumin, and sometimes cocoa in their chili—did you know that?"

"How much did you eat?"

"I said I was sorry!"

"How much, Mr. Katsakis?"

"I ate it all! So shoot me!"

Clancy thought this through. On the off chance his father had been right and the contest entry was tainted, then it might be wise to call the EMTs. "Are you good? You feeling all right?"

"Why do you care how I'm feeling? I'm a little gassy. There. Now you know."

Suddenly, it dawned on him that if the chili was, in fact, psychogenic, the credibility of anything Cosmo might say to the FBI would suffer. Could he really have gotten this lucky? For the first time in recent memory, he hoped his father's "mayornoia" was legit.

"I'll let you know when the federal agents arrive." He shut the break room door.

Fifteen minutes later, the borrowed Jeeps rolled into the parking lot. Clancy, Deon, and Cam glanced at each other, barely able to keep from laughing. They were about to learn how the agents enjoyed their sightseeing tour of the island.

The three special agents who canvassed the industrial area, boardwalk businesses, and Island Day vendors looked no worse for the wear. But Congressman Wahlman, Apodaca, and her sidekick appeared shell-shocked.

"How did it go?" Deon came off as business-as-usual, but no one answered him. "Uncover anything noteworthy?"

Clancy had to momentarily turn his attention to some papers on the front desk or he was going to lose it.

"Thank you for asking." The Special Agent in Charge sounded noticeably snippy. "The answer would be, 'fuck no, we are not okay.' "

"I may never be okay again," her sidekick said.

Clancy looked up just as Wahlman glared at him. He seemed somewhat less stunned than his friends, but certainly not happy. "You might have had the courtesy to tell us exactly what kind of private club the Bayberry Freedom Colony is."

Clancy looked surprised. "What? I thought you knew! I am so sorry."

"I just bet," Wahlman said.

Cam got Clancy's attention and nodded his head toward the break room.

"Ah, yes." Clancy addressed Apodaca. "We have a witness here who claims he saw the kidnapper. He's in our break room."

"Finally—something normal."

"Don't know if I'd go that far, Agent," Deon said. "He came in here acting a little woo-woo. Something about a computer conspiracy."

Deon and Clancy led Wahlman and the agents to the break room. As Clancy opened the door he thought to himself, *Please, please let there be shroomers!*

Mr. Katsakis sat with his head bent low over the table, his index finger making tiny shapes on the cracked enamel surface. He was having a conversation with ... his fingernail.

Yes!

"This is Cosmo Katsakis, he owns the Sand Dollar Motel. Mr. Katsakis? The FBI is here to take your statement."

He raised his head with an agonizing slowness and smiled. "Thank you for bringing me the beautiful tray of *dolmades* last year," he said, immediately crossing himself three times.

The agent in charge cocked her head at Clancy. "Really? The naked old people weren't enough?"

One of the other agents sat down next to Cosmo. "What did we bring you last year, Mr. Katsakis?"

"The stuffed leaves of the precious grape, with lamb and rice and spices, all kinds of beautiful colors dancing on the platter and spinning in the wind like—" He suddenly pointed at the break room wall and let go with a horrified scream. "It's on fire! Everything's on fire!" His panic stopped as quickly as it started. Now calm, Cosmo glanced up at Clancy apologetically. "I thought it was on fire. I really did."

"Yeeaahh." The special agent got out her notebook. "What is your statement about the suspect, sir?"

Katsakis seemed to snap back to reality. His eyes focused.

Uh-oh.

"She checked into adjoining rooms with a fake ID and dressed the girl up like a boy. She paid cash. Probably bribed my Albanian, but he won't confess."

No one spoke.

"You don't believe me, do you? Well, I saw her license, but now"—he pointed an accusatory finger at Clancy—"right after *you* asked for a copy it just disappeared! Poof! It was zapped out of our computers, like it was never even there! She might even be a spy!"

"I see." The agent turned to Clancy. "I'll need you to provide me with his contact information."

"Of course."

"Thank you for your time, sir." She shoved her little notebook back in her pocket.

Clancy whispered to Deon, "I think maybe we should call the EMTs."

"No shit."

A half hour later, Mr. Katsakis was on his way to the hospital in Nantucket and the news conference was over. Clancy couldn't believe how lucky he'd been. The FBI would be leaving without finding anything on Bayberry linked to the kidnapping case. When everyone was loaded in the helicopter and ready to take off, Clancy started to breathe easier. But a door flew open. Out popped Congressman Wahlman, who marched right up to Clancy.

"A word, if you don't mind." He grabbed Clancy by the arm and pulled him farther from the helicopter. He still had to shout over the propeller noise. "You have a grievance with me, Chief?"

Clancy shouted back. "Should I? Have you done something against the law?"

Wahlman's eyes narrowed. "Excuse me?"

Clancy shrugged. "I asked if you'd violated the laws of the Commonwealth of Massachusetts in some way, because that would be the only reason I'd have a grievance with you. Is there something you'd like to confess for the greater good of society?"

Wahlman laughed. "So you're a social worker, too?"

"Nope." Clancy got right in his face. "I'm a cop. And as a cop, I am always looking out for public safety and the integrity of our legal system."

Wahlman's face fell. He was about to respond, but decided against it. The congressman marched back to the helicopter.

Clancy shook his head and watched him go, and Deon sidled up next to him. "What was that all about?"

"Maybe someday I'll tell you the whole story." He slapped Deon on the back. "Right now we're late for shift change."

The sun was still bright when Evelyn saw Clancy's Jeep pull up the gravel drive. She jumped from the chair and quickly checked her reflection in the mirror over the fireplace. She looked as worn-out as she felt. There was no way around it—her face advertised stress and exhaustion and it was time to admit that the Brigitte Nielsen look didn't work for her. Of course, being attractive hadn't exactly been at the top of her list for the last couple months. It still wasn't. But with Clancy around, it was now at least *on* the list.

She watched him exit the Jeep and pull the seat forward. Two large Labrador retrievers, one black and one chocolate, tumbled onto the ground and began an out-of-control dance of happiness. They were so cute! On closer inspection, it looked as if the black dog was missing a leg. It sure didn't seem to slow him down any. The dogs went running along the side of the house and headed toward the backyard.

Christina's head popped up from her coloring project. "That him? That the guy?" Mercifully, Evelyn had found some markers in the kitchen junk drawer and printer paper on a living room bookshelf, and set up her niece at the dining room table. The activity had kept her busy for at least a half an hour, which was a half hour during which Christina didn't obsess about the pretty mermaid—she just would not let it drop.

"Yes, that's him. He brought his dogs, too. So let's be gentle and give them a chance to smell us, okay?"

"Okay!" She flew off the chair and ran toward the door.

"And remember how we decided to be polite and call him 'Officer Clancy'?"

She nodded, wiggling with excitement. "Yep!"

The door opened, and Clancy stuck his head in tentatively, as if he was unsure what he would find in his own home.

"Hi, Sir Clancy!"

His attention snapped to Christina and then to Evelyn. He burst out with a surprised chuckle. "Finally—the recognition I deserve!"

He bent to give Christina a pat on the head. "And hello to you, fair maiden . . . er, I mean knight."

"I am Pirate Jellybean!" Christina began hopping up and down.

"You look more like a jumping bean to me."

Unfortunately, Christina interpreted that as an invitation to bounce around his house. "We're going to see the pretty mermaid! We're going to the Save Heaven! She lives there when she's not under the sea!"

"Yikes." Evelyn hurried over to where Christina had hopped too close to an antique curio cabinet. "Sorry." Evelyn glanced up at Clancy, still standing by the front door with an amused look on his face. "I think she needs some play time. She's a little, well, *pent-up*."

"I know the feeling well."

Evelyn straightened, holding her niece's hand, and

mirrored the slow, teasing smile that broke over Clancy's face. *Oh, my.* She couldn't wait for her next fifteen minutes alone with him.

"So." Clancy headed into the kitchen and poured himself a glass of water, drinking it down in a few ravenous gulps. "Somebody wants to see the mermaid from the Safe Haven parade float?"

"I do! I love the mermaid! We're going to see the mermaid!"

Evelyn widened her eyes at Clancy, hoping that he saw how desperately she wanted to change the subject.

He laughed. "I might be able to help with that. I happen to know her personally."

"Oh?" Evelyn asked.

"Back in two minutes."

Evelyn watched him jog down the hall and into his room, where he was probably changing clothes, and she found herself wondering . . . was the beautiful mermaid his ex-wife? A former girlfriend? She embarrassed herself at how inappropriate her thinking was. The history of Clancy Flynn's personal life could wait. She needed to stay focused on the many critically important issues right in front of her.

He came out barefoot, in a well-worn Sam Adams T-shirt and a frayed pair of olive green cargo shorts and she thought, *the hell with propriety*. "Have you known the mermaid for a long time?"

"Yep, since the day our mother brought her home from the hospital and I drove a Hot Wheel over her face."

"Whaa?" Evelyn laughed with surprise. The mermaid was his sister!

"She owes me a favor or two, and Chris is such a good . . . kid, maybe a visit could be arranged."

Chrissy jumped up and down some more. "We going now?"

Evelyn put a hand on Christina's head to keep her from bouncing around. "Everyone agrees that Chris is a

very good kid." She paused to make sure Clancy understood that for the sake of consistency, Chris was a boy,
and he would remain a boy until a slipup would no longer have dire consequences.

Clancy smiled gently at Evelyn, as if reassuring her he
understood. "How about we try to see the mermaid tomorrow. In the meantime, would you like to meet the
dogs?" He gestured toward the back sliding door to the
deck.

"Are they well behaved? Will they jump on Chris?"

"They get pretty excited, so they'll have to sit first. That's
all the 'well behaved' we got. Is Chris afraid of dogs?"

Evelyn smiled sadly. "No. She loves them. We had a
border collie for fourteen years. When Jordi died, we
buried him under the apple tree near someone's bedroom window, as requested." Evie inclined her head
toward her niece.

"Gotcha."

"Look at those silly dogs!" Chrissy exclaimed with
delight.

Both retrievers pressed so close to the door that their
breath left condensation on the glass. Their tails swished
in unison. Evelyn grabbed Christina and propped her on
her hip.

"I'll go first." Clancy opened the door and told both
dogs to follow him to the far side of the deck. "Sit." They
managed, though they were so thrilled to see Evelyn and
Christina that they could barely keep their butts on the
wood. Clancy got behind the dogs and squatted between
them, his hands gently touching their collars. "Good
boys. Stay." He looked up at Evelyn. "Come on over
whenever you'd like."

Evelyn moved cautiously toward the dogs, holding
Christina. Her niece's eyes went wide and she immediately started wiggling to escape.

"Chris will be fine, Evie. Really. I'll make sure of it."

There it was again, the reassurance that everything

would be all right if she just trusted him. Evelyn let her squirming niece climb down. "Be gentle, Chris."

"Hi, doggies." Chrissy bent at the waist to peer at them. They quivered with eagerness.

"Hold out your hand and let them smell you, okay, Pirate Jellybean?"

Christina did as Clancy asked. She stuck out her arm, palm up, and immediately fell into a fit of giggles as the dogs licked her fingers. "They're wet!"

Clancy began with the introductions. "The black one is Tripod, but we call him Mr. T, and the brown one is Earl. Boys, these are our guests, Pirate Jellybean and Aunt Cricket."

"Mr. T, huh?"

Clancy glanced toward Evelyn and chuckled. "Yeah, my brother came up with that. He said he didn't think it was right to focus on his disability."

"Gotcha. That would be Duncan, right?"

Clancy's eyes widened. "You remembered."

"I remember everything."

His gaze darkened for an instant and she understood exactly what he was telling her—*I can't wait to get you alone.*

Clancy stood, and the dogs stayed in place. "Would you like to go down to the beach? It's not big, but it's private. We could take a walk."

Evelyn swept her gaze over the ocean, feeling the sunset warm her face. Her first instinct was to calculate the chances of being spotted on that beach—from what direction could someone see her and Christina? Was there an amphibious landing planned? A satellite orbiting over Bayberry? What could she use as an escape route if one was needed?

She hated this. She hated the paranoid calculations that constantly lived in her head, and wondered if they would stop once this ordeal ended. *If* it ended.

Evelyn tried to sound enthusiastic. "Sure."

"Oh! Hey, wait. I have something for you. I left it in the Jeep. Be right back." Clancy ran around the side of the house while the two gentle giants sat patiently, waiting for him to return, happy to let Christina coo at them and pat their heads. Clancy was back in a flash. Evelyn saw him round the corner carrying a big sun hat.

"This is for you. To replace the one you lost when you jumped off the dock."

Evelyn blinked, completely surprised. She looked up at him and shook her head as if she didn't understand. "You got this for me?"

"I figured you could use a new one, you know, since it's important these days to keep your face and hair protected when you're in the bright daylight."

Evelyn thought she may cry and laugh at the same time. The idea that Clancy took time in the middle of all this chaos to replace her hat was probably the sweetest thing any man had ever done for her. And he'd found a perfectly innocent way to tell her she still needed to hide herself beneath it.

"You hate it."

"No! I love it!" She grabbed it from Clancy and popped it on her head, then used a fingertip to push up the brim so she could see him again. "And it does a bang-up job of protecting me."

A huge smile broke out on his face. "Hey, and I got this for you, Jellybean." He held out a child-sized Red Sox cap, but Christina didn't even notice. She was in love. Her face was between the two dogs and they licked and sniffed at her neck and arms while she giggled.

"Beach!" Clancy's voice was no-nonsense. The dogs immediately forgot their new friend and bounded across the yard to the walking path.

"They going swimming?" Christina took off after them, Clancy and Evelyn right behind. Clancy grabbed a half-buried ball from the sandy soil on their way.

At the top of the path, Evelyn hesitated, noticing how

it dropped off. She grabbed Christina's hand. "It's pretty steep."

"Would it be okay if I carried Chris?"

Evelyn brought her gaze to Clancy's. He looked so serious.

"I'll get her down safely. I promise."

Again—there it was. It was remarkable how many times and in how many ways he'd managed to ask her that question in the last couple days.

Do you trust me?

It seemed she did. She was still here. Clancy hadn't ambushed her with the SWAT team or dragged her off the ferry in handcuffs. He'd welcomed her and Chrissy to his home, and, of course, he'd saved Chrissy's life, the way he'd saved her own, so many years before.

Evelyn took one more look down the beach path. This was it. She had already let down her guard, but the time had come to commit to a plan of action. She was about to hand Christina's future and her fate to a man she hadn't spoken to in eighteen years. She would trust him—absolutely—or she would leave.

"I'll be holding up the rear," Evelyn said.

"Hop on, Pirate Jellybean!" Clancy crouched in front of her and Chrissy automatically climbed on his shoulders. Evelyn was about to suggest just a piggyback ride for safety's sake but changed her mind. Christina squealed with delight as she rode on Clancy's shoulders down the path.

Look at him—so strong and capable and steady. Evelyn suspected he would need all those things in the days to come.

Clancy delivered Christina safely to the sand and tossed the ball down the beach. The dogs raced after it, sand flying, crashing together into the calm waves to ferret it out. Christina was in awe.

"They can swim! The dogs can swim!" She jumped up and down and began to spin in circles, arms wide. She was simply happy to be outside, glad to make noise and stretch out her arms and legs and run around. How lovely to be free in the world for the first time in days, without her aunt gripping on to her, anxiety and fear the undercurrent of everything she said and did.

Christina ripped off her shoes and socks so she could run in the waves, and Evelyn did the same. She luxuriated in the feel of the sand between her toes, the sea in her nostrils, and the low sun on her arms. Clancy jogged forward and backward along the water's edge, tossing the ball again and again, keeping an eye on Evelyn and Chrissy as they kicked around in the surf. Eventually, all three of them met up at the same spot, Clancy shoulder-to-shoulder with Evelyn. He gave her a sideways glance and broke into a smile right out of her memory—white, straight, gorgeous, and spreading into those midnight blue eyes of his.

A flash went through her. It was a sizzling rush of sensuality, yearning, recognition, and relief. She felt it when she recognized him Friday, when they sat together on the bench at the motel, and most certainly that morning, when his kisses made her lose the ability to reason. But the first time she had felt any of those things had been eighteen years ago, the summer she was fourteen.

He threw the ball. The dogs ran. Christina laughed and swept her hands through the water.

"Are you doing okay?"

Evelyn kept her eyes on Christina but answered him. "Better."

"Wahlman's gone. The FBI didn't find any evidence you were ever here."

She exhaled, only then realizing how much breath she'd been holding in. "Thank you."

"How do you know Wahlman fixed the court proceedings?"

She checked to make sure Christina was occupied. "He must have. The court never notified us that the custody hearing date had been changed, though computer records indicate they did. Wahlman won custody by default because we never showed up to object. I have a friend who works in IT who's trying to unravel it for us, but so far, nothing."

"IT?" Clancy raised his eyebrows and laughed. "By any chance, is this the same friend who vaporized your booking information from the Sand Dollar computer today?"

Evelyn stopped walking. Her heart crashed in her chest. "How . . . ?"

"The motel owner says it disappeared, but no one believed him because he . . . well, his behavior has been erratic lately. Your friend is good, though. Tell her I said thanks for helping you."

"It's a he."

"Oh?"

Evelyn laughed. "No—not that kind of 'he.' But you and Hal have a lot in common. You're both putting your asses on the line to help me."

"Who's got the nicer ass?"

She linked her arm with his. "Let me put it this way— I'm not even sure Hal has an ass. I've never noticed."

"Hmm." Clancy bumped his hip against hers. "But you've noticed mine?"

"Maybe."

Christina now squatted at the edge of a small tidal pool, perfectly content to be making sand pies and carrying on an animated play conversation with herself. Evie kept her eyes on Christina as they continued their conversation.

"Is your friend in Maine?"

"Vermont."

"I'll need to talk to him. I know someone up that way who does freelance investigation. Maybe together they can help me figure this out. You'll give me Hal's number?"

"Of course."

"Evie?"

She looked up at him, knowing she was about to face more questions.

"There's one thing I don't think I understand."

"Okay."

"You could have complied with the order, let Richard have custody, and then fight the ruling in the courts. Is there a reason why you didn't take the . . . well, the perfectly legal route?"

Evelyn bit her tongue. Of course Clancy couldn't understand. He'd never had kids of his own, and she couldn't fault him for that. "The reason is right there." She pointed to Christina, slapping and patting sand and now singing to herself.

Clancy stopped walking and Evelyn leaned against his side.

"That little person lost her mother, and her whole world collapsed. I know how she feels. The only constants left in her life are me, my dad, and the farm. So imagine the day a wealthy and powerful politician decides to claim her, without even giving us a chance to state our case. Imagine that this is the same man who never wanted Christina to be born in the first place. Imagine he's up for reelection. Wouldn't you have a few questions about his motives?"

"I would."

"But here's the biggest question, and it's the only one that really matters: what kind of aunt would I be if I let him take her, even temporarily, and further confuse her and break her heart? And what kind of sister would I be if I didn't follow through on the only promise Amanda ever asked me to make?"

The dogs tore up the beach toward Clancy. Earl dropped the ball, and they both sat and waited as patiently as they could.

Clancy leaned in and kissed Evelyn sweetly. Then he threw the red ball down the beach in the opposite direction, into the wind. She couldn't believe how high it went, how it sailed past the end of the beach and out into the water.

"You've got quite an arm on you. Did you switch from track to baseball?"

"You remembered!" He gave her a shy smile, which struck her as charming. A smile like that didn't fit with his grown-up, rugged, and got-everything-covered cop personality. Evelyn took it as a compliment—even after all this time, he was still willing to let her see him. "Nah," Clancy said. "I stayed with track. I knew a good thing when I saw it."

Evelyn stared at him in wonder for a second. Could they have ever competed at the same event? "I ran women's distance for Middlebury College. We were regional champions while I was there."

Clancy's mouth fell open. "I ran the five thousand meter for Amherst. You *know* we had to be at the same Division III meets many times over."

"You're right."

"Fancy that." Clancy put his arm around Evelyn's shoulder. "This okay with you?"

She nodded, slipping her arm around his waist. "This okay with you?"

"Oh, yeah." Clancy remained silent for a few strides, then squeezed Evelyn tightly. "Thank you for sharing your reasoning with me, Evie. I'm sorry I was slow on the uptake, but I do understand now. You love that kid fiercely, and Christina is incredibly lucky to have you."

"Look! Look! What is it, Sir Clancy? A frog?" Christina jumped to a stand and pointed into the tidal pool.

"Well, look at that!" Clancy reached down and gently removed a partially buried horseshoe crab.

Christina let go with one of her high-pitched screams.

"It won't hurt you." Clancy squatted so he was at her level. "It's strange-looking but it's just the shell of a harmless sea creature."

"What its name?"

"A horseshoe crab, probably a girl crab, and she got

too big for her shell so she had to leave it behind. Have you ever seen one of these?"

Chrissy reared back and shook her head slowly.

"She has, actually, back home at the shore. But it wasn't anywhere near that big."

Chrissy reached out her hand tentatively and Clancy held the shell, turning it so she could see it from all angles. He didn't push it on her, which made Evelyn smile. He was doing it again, but this time it was a one-on-one question directed only to Christina. *Do you trust me?*

Evelyn decided to step back and see what happened. The dogs suddenly realized no one was paying them any attention, so they ran over and began to sniff the shell, which made Chrissy laugh. "Do they want to eat it and chew it?"

"Nah. They're just sniffing it because they're curious. Remember how they snuffled and licked you when you first met?" From his squatting position, Clancy threw the ball and the dogs forgot all about the crab shell.

Christina leaned forward and began taking big sniffs, though she kept a good two feet away.

Clancy glanced up at Evelyn, his eyes crinkling with laughter, his face golden in the setting sun. She felt her heart drop. It was as if she were fourteen again, coming alive in the company of a boy who fit her, made her laugh, kissed her lips, and touched her soul. It had been the sweetest summer of her life. Though they'd both changed in many respects over the years, that feeling remained.

The physical differences in Clancy were obvious. On his way to becoming a man, his bones had lengthened and his muscles filled out. He face was still boyishly handsome, but with a harder edge to it and a lot more than the beginnings of peach fuzz. His hair was shorter than it had been as a wild island child. And he was far more confident than he'd been as a gangly fourteen-year-old. The kinks had been smoothed out in the way he moved, spoke, and filled a room with his presence.

Clancy's eyes, though, were exactly the same. Hal was

right—he did have a penetrating gaze. They were the same intense dark blue, set deep behind dark lashes, and still flashed with intelligence and kindness.

But the thing that most obviously connected the boy to the man was an underlying sweetness about him. That, more than anything, took her back in time.

Evelyn suddenly felt her throat tighten. Here she was, letting herself feel the old attraction, but the fact remained: he claimed he never got her letter. How could that have happened? It took years for her to talk herself into believing she'd been naive for falling in love with Clancy Flynn. With the help of her friends and Amanda, she finally decided her instincts had been wrong about him, that he'd only used her as a festival week distraction, and that he probably lied to all the tourist girls.

Or was it possible the only mistake she'd made was to doubt him? Could the whole thing really have been some stupid mix-up with the mail?

Evelyn couldn't keep it in a second longer. "You *had* to have received a letter from me. I sent you one. I spilled my guts to you. I told you I loved you."

His smile faded. He gave her a barely there nod.

"I want to hold it? Can I hold it?"

Clancy returned his attention to the excited Christina. "How about I put it down right here in the sand for you? That way, you can touch it if you want but you don't have to hold it. Does that sound good?"

She began bouncing and twirling again. "Yep, yep, yep!"

Clancy stood and moved toward Evelyn. He walked with determination, serious and focused, and he kept his eyes locked on hers until he was close enough that she could reach out and touch him if she dared.

"I never got a letter, Evie. I waited and waited, for years, really."

"What?"

"Finally, when I went off to school on the mainland, I told myself I had to let you go. By the time I started the police academy, I thought of you only occasionally. And then, life got ahold of me."

"But ... I waited for years, too! It crushed me that you never wrote back!"

A high-pitched screech jolted them. Christina was running in the surf after the dogs, her arms flailing in alarm. "They took it! They got the horse crap!"

Clancy kissed Evelyn's forehead. "Someday we'll know what happened. The important thing now is that you don't waste another second of your life doubting me, because I meant every word I ever said to you, Evie."

Evelyn's spirit lifted and her mind stilled. There was so much happiness in that moment—Clancy, Christina, the dogs, the sunset. She didn't know if her heart could carry it all. Now she knew. Clancy had not dismissed her.

"I've been thinking." He took her hand and they resumed their walk. "It's not a mistake you're here, you know. You're here for a reason."

"Ya think?"

They both laughed and he pulled her tighter. "Not only because of your current ... *difficulty*."

"Okay."

"I think you're back because there's a lot of unfinished business between us, Evie. Maybe we're getting another chance."

"A second chance at a first love?"

"Exactly."

Eighteen years ago ...

So this is what it felt like. Clancy hadn't said the words yet, but Evie knew by the way he held her close as they danced, and touched his lips so softly to her neck. He loved her. She was fine with that. Because she loved him back.

There were almost too many emotions to handle that night, and too many things going on in the background. For one, her parents were at the Mermaid Ball, too, and every once in a while, she'd feel her mom or dad's eyes on her, evaluating the danger their daughter might be in. *As if.* Clancy was a complete gentleman, and they had no idea how wonderful he was compared to some of the boys she knew at home.

Clancy's family was there, too, wandering around. His little sister, it turned out, was the same age as Amanda, and they'd been hanging out together much of the week. After some observation, Evie decided that Clancy was right about his brother, Duncan. He did act like an ass. He was one of those brainy superjocks who thought they were all that, the kind of guy who strutted around totally sure that girls were staring at him and fighting over him.

Duncan had been smiling at Evie all evening, even

when he was out on the dance floor with a girl of his own. Right now he sat at one of the side tables, trying to get her attention. She definitely sensed some serious competition going on between the brothers—Duncan was daring her to ditch Clancy and come hang with him. Ugh. She didn't understand boys sometimes, but she did know that guys like Duncan weren't her type *at all*.

Her type was Clancy—a boy with smarts, a sense of humor, and good looks. He was sweet, kind, and a blast to be with. And all of this came without a hint of being conceited. That is what made him special.

"You look so beautiful tonight, Evie. This is the first time I've ever seen you in a dress, and it was totally worth waiting for."

Oh, she was so happy to hear that! She had debated with herself whether to take up space in her suitcase for something as useless as a dress because, really, who wore a dress on vacation? But at the last minute she balled it up and stuffed it inside. Maybe somewhere in the back of her mind she'd known she would meet her true love that week.

"Thank you." She slid her arms lazily over his shoulders and cocked her head, just enjoying that handsome face in the twinkling lights. The only shadow on the evening was the fact that by tomorrow morning she would be gone.

"I wish I didn't have to go."

"Ah, man, so do I." A shadow moved across his expression, and Evie saw he was as bummed out as she was. "Hey!" Clancy perked up. "Do you think my parents could adopt you so you could stay on Bayberry forever?"

They both chuckled.

Just then, a flash of light surrounded them, leaving black spots in Evie's vision. They glanced over to see Clancy's mother with her camera, giving them a thumbs-up and a big grin. She wandered off to catch another couple unawares.

"Sorry about that. My mom's kind of in charge of the

festival and likes to document all the events with pictures."

"I'm not sorry at all." Evie kissed his cheek, not caring who saw her do it. "Now you'll have a picture of us together. It will help you remember me."

He whispered in her ear. "I won't need a picture for that."

As if on cue, the DJ played their song. It wasn't exactly a shock, since it was pretty much *the* love song of the summer and the Mermaid Ball was coming to an end, but to Evie it was a sign. The lyrics flowed through the breeze. The paper lanterns along the dock began to dance. They held each other tighter. *We'll always be a part of each other ... our love will never die ... I will always be your baby ...*

After the Mermaid Ball ended, she went to her parents and begged for a little extra time.

"I just want to take one last walk on the beach. Please, please, please let me. Just a few minutes."

Her parents shared a glance, and her dad looked at his watch. *Oh, great. She'd be lucky to get five minutes and thirty seconds.*

"Be back by eleven thirty."

Evie's mouth hung loose with surprise. Eleven thirty?

Amanda rolled her eyes. "God! I *hate* being twelve!"

Evie hugged her mom and dad, not sure what had just happened. They must have had pity on her, or maybe the fact that she was hopelessly in love was so obvious it was ridiculous. But she didn't care why her usually uncool parents had just been totally chill and given her a whole hour! She was taking it!

"Remember, we're leaving on the morning ferry, so you need to get your rest."

She nodded at her mom. How could she forget? As of tomorrow morning, the dream would be over. The best week of her life would be history.

Evie met Clancy at the public marina. He was so relieved and excited to see her that he picked her up and swung her around like they did in the movies, and Evie's legs flew in a circle around them.

Most of their time together was spent in silence. Neither of them seemed to know what to say as they took their last nighttime stroll along the beach, water tickling their feet. Clancy had his arm tight around Evie's waist, and she rested her head on his shoulder.

"Do you think you'll grow any taller?"

That surprised Evie—what a strange question for the kind of important moment they were sharing. "Probably not much. Why?"

"Because." Clancy tilted his head so that his temple touched her hair. "I'd like to be a couple inches taller than you eventually, you know, in a few years. I always pictured myself with a girl who was just a little shorter than me."

Evie raised her face. Clancy smiled shyly, gazing down on her. They stopped walking.

"What are you saying, Clancy?"

"I'm saying that I love you. I know kids our age aren't supposed to fall in love—except maybe for Romeo and Juliet—but it happened. And I really don't think one week is going to be the end for us."

Her bones weakened and her heart slammed in her ears. This was it—the most important moment of her life. He just said he loved her!

"Oh, Clancy. I love you, too. Don't *ever* forget it."

He grabbed her face in his hands and they kissed ferociously. Evie felt Clancy's tears on her own cheeks and it made her cry, too, and this was after she'd successfully avoided crying the whole night long.

Clancy held her hand in his all the way back to the motel. He got her there right on time. "I'll be at the dock in the morning to see you off."

He kissed her one last time, with so much tenderness and love. Then she slipped inside the motel door.

Evie had never been so sad in her life. She told her parents she was fine, just tired and a little sunburned, but her mom knew better. Evie cried while she washed her face and brushed her teeth, and she cried herself to sleep as silently as she could, wishing the morning would never come.

Chapter Fourteen

Evelyn eased from the guest room bed. Exhausted from their beach day, Chrissy had fallen into a deep sleep. Now Evelyn tiptoed across the room, shut the door, and slipped into the hallway. Silently, she disappeared into the bathroom.

The reflection she saw in the mirror startled her, but trying to do something with her hair was pointless. Maybe one day she could grow it out again, let it return to its natural brown. But for now, this was it. No matter what her hair looked like or what she wore or how frazzled she was, Clancy was in the living room waiting for her. The moment she'd thought about for her entire adult life had finally arrived, and it was nothing like she'd pictured.

Evelyn smoothed out her shirt and turned off the light. She was greeted in the hallway by a happy Earl and an even happier Mr. T, and the threesome headed toward the living room.

Clancy was sprawled out on the couch, all six-feet-something of him golden under the light of a floor lamp, sound asleep. His sandy bare feet hung off the edge of the cushions while a loose hand cupped his cell phone. She couldn't blame him. It had to be well past ten and in addition to everything else he'd dealt with that day,

Clancy told her this had been his very first evening routine with a four-year-old. That would wear anyone out.

Evelyn studied him for a long moment, thinking about their evening. They'd returned to the beach just before the sun disappeared. She'd whipped together a dinner using stuff she found in his pantry and freezer—a brown rice pilaf with chicken and spinach, and a fruit salad for dessert. The three of them ate at the butcher block, as they'd done at breakfast. Then Evelyn got Christina ready for bed while Clancy cleaned up, and afterward, he volunteered for story duty. Evelyn watched as her niece and the police chief snuggled together in the big living room chair, his deep voice becoming tender as he said good night to the moon, the mittens, the socks, and the stars, only to do it all over again at least three times. Christina was so worn out and happy that it took just minutes for her to fall asleep.

Apparently, it had been the same for Clancy.

Evelyn sat cross-legged on the living room rug and leaned against the chair. The dogs joined her, each resting a big, bony head in her lap. She scratched their ears as the exhaustion hit. It was a type of tired she had never felt before, not even after the most grueling marathons. The weariness cut down to the marrow of her mind and heart as much as her body. She let her eyelids close.

She could not fail. It had been the only thing Amanda ever asked of her. Evelyn remembered the day she made the promise. The air was bracing and the sky deep blue, and Amanda asked her to have a seat on the stone wall. It wasn't like her sister to reveal her deepest feelings, so Evelyn let her talk. She broke apart, releasing everything she'd been carrying by herself.

Though five years had gone by, Amanda's words were as clear as if they'd just been spoken.

"If anything ever happens to me, you cannot let him get his hands on her. He threw her away. Please promise me you will not let that bastard near Christina."

The memory faded. Evelyn felt as if she were floating

through the air. Had she fallen asleep? Where was Amanda? Christina? Had she been dreaming? Remembering? Who was carrying her?

"It's okay, Evie. Go back to sleep."

It was Clancy, taking her into his bedroom. She wanted it. She wanted to sleep with him at her side. Christina was happy and safe. Evelyn was not alone anymore. She had hope. So when Clancy gently placed her on his mattress and snuggled up behind her, she melted in bliss.

Oh, the relief of his arms around her, the comforting heat of his body, the knowledge that she could truly relax. She could sink into nothing yet be protected ... from ... everything. ...

He opened his eyes, immediately sensing that his bed and his life were different. This was not Mr. T shoved up against his left hip. This was Evie, and her arm was flung loosely across his chest while a firm thigh pressed into the front of his shorts. He lay in the dark, listening to the soft rhythm of her breath, letting the uniquely female essence of Evelyn McGuinness wash over him. His brain had remembered the exactness of the scent for eighteen years—sea breeze over wildflowers—and it now flooded him with memories. The scent was a deeper and richer version now, that of a woman, not a girl.

Just then he realized this hadn't been such a great idea. Yes, they were fully clothed and had done nothing but sleep for the last several hours, but now what? Evie was *in his bed*. For real. He was awake and she'd soon be, too.

Oh, God, she just shifted and made a sweet little moan in her sleep. Evie's knee slid higher on his body, her long calf muscle pressing directly onto his cock. Clancy tried everything to avoid the inevitable: he thought of Cosmo Katsakis's stained wife beater, the Bayberry Freedom Colony, the mountain of paperwork on his desk. But nothing prevented his body from doing what nature intended.

"Good morning, Sir Clancy."

He froze.

"Yes, I'm awake and you are, too. I can tell."

Slowly, Clancy turned to face her. With the barest hint of light in the room, he could make out the lovely shape of her face and the curve of her smile. He traced his fingertips along her cheek. "Good morning, sweet Evie." He leaned forward and placed a gentle kiss on her lips.

Evie pressed tighter to his hip while pulling her leg away, as if she realized what she'd done to him. "This is the first time we've ever woken up together. It's pretty nice."

"I'm not so sure about that."

"Say what?"

"Yeah. See, waking up with Earl is *pretty nice,* and you're way hotter than him."

They giggled together, then busted into full-out goofy laughter, holding on to each other while trying to keep the noise level down.

"Shhh."

"What time does Christina usually wake up?"

"Six thirty or so. What time is it?"

Clancy reached for his smartphone by the bed. "Four fifteen. I need to be at work by seven."

Evie placed her lips against the side of his neck. He heard himself groan with the pure pleasure of her silky flesh and warm breath. He imagined how incredible it would be to feel that sensation everywhere on his body.

Clancy turned on his side and propped his head on an elbow. He traced the outline of her body from shoulder to knee and back again. "It pains me to say this . . ."

"I agree."

"I figured."

Evie nodded slowly. "It wouldn't be smart. Everything has been so strange for Christina lately. If she were to see or hear something, it would scare and confuse her. Thank you for understanding, Clancy."

He decided to keep his frustration to himself.

"I don't think I could be quiet, anyway," Evie said.

"That makes two of us."

She propped up on her elbow as well. They remained like that, sharing the dim light with each other as the breeze from the open windows brushed over their skin and clothing.

"I wrote you exactly two days after I got home from vacation, the day before school started. I remember it clearly."

"What did you say?"

She shrugged. "I'm not sure about the exact words, but I talked about starting tenth grade and how much fun I'd had on Bayberry Island. I told you I thought you were the love of my life and we would always be together. And I said that if you didn't write me back, I'd know you didn't feel the same."

Clancy wasn't sure why, but a flash of memory came to him. It wasn't of their summer together—it was his dream encounter with the mermaid. Had she been trying to tell him something? That she had never cursed him? That Evie had always been there and now she needed him? She'd mentioned he was facing the most important decision of his life . . . what the *hell*? Clancy laughed to himself.

"What?" Evie straightened a bit.

"I don't know how to put this into words because it's going to sound completely crazy, but I think I've always carried you with me somehow. In the back of my mind, in my dreams."

"Seriously?"

"It was the sweetest summer of my life, Evie."

She smiled. "Mine, too. Without a doubt." She slowly brushed a foot up and down his calf. "What do you remember most about that week?"

Clancy raised his eyebrows. "You mean besides the fact that you blew up my world?"

Evie grinned.

"Well, I'd have to start with that day we ran on the beach together. I was in awe of you. So graceful. And you were incredibly easy to be with. You never made me feel awkward or clueless. You were nice to people. You were cool and smart but very much a girl—exactly the way you are now. I had fun with you, Evelyn McGuinness."

"I had fun with you, too, and I remember being amazed at how easily we fit. It was effortless. Remember the wind chime you gave me?"

"Absolutely. It was one in a million."

She laughed. "Yes, and I still have it back home." Evie paused. "Do you realize that you saved my life the first time we met, just like you saved Chrissy?"

Clancy felt his eyes go big. "I guess you're right. That's pretty weird."

"And the way we danced, talked, and kissed . . . those kisses were *da bomb*."

"They still are."

"Do you think it's possible the connection is still there, after all this time? I'm not sure there's any other explanation for how we've . . . reacted to each other."

"It's there." Clancy tipped up her chin and kissed her again. "You will always be the girl who showed me the meaning of life."

Evie sighed. "It really was that big of a deal, wasn't it? I know that for me, the girl who left for vacation was *not* the girl who came home to Maine."

"I wonder . . ."

"What?" She waited. "Tell me, Clancy. Don't stop."

He took a deep breath. "I've been thinking that what happened with us that summer wasn't just because you were *a* girl and I was *a* boy, do you know what I mean?"

"I do. You were *the* boy."

"You were *the* girl. I don't think I really understood that until today."

Evie sat up on the bed, running her fingers through her short spiky hair. "It would be easy to make yourself insane wondering how things would have been different if you'd gotten my letter. Maybe we would have been together all this time."

Clancy sat up, too. "Or, maybe we would have been in

too much of a rush and burned out right away. What if this is the exact time and the exact way we're supposed to meet up with each other again?"

"True." She smiled at him. "All we have is right now. It's all anyone has."

They sat in the quiet for a long moment.

"Clancy?"

"Hmm?"

"I know this might sound terrible."

"You might be thinking the same thing I am."

Evelyn bit her bottom lip. "Really? Because I'm going completely nuts being so close to you and not being able to"—she looked up—"you know . . . *express myself* with you."

He smiled, trailing his fingers down her bare arm. "Yeah. I think we both need to express the hell out of each other."

"I'm afraid I'm going to explode if I have to wait much longer."

"I've been a little worried about the spontaneous human combustion thing, myself."

They stared at each other in the dim light.

"How would you feel about hiring the world's best babysitter so we can have a date this afternoon, just you and me?" he asked.

Evie looked thrilled—for about one second. Then she scrunched her brows together. "I can't even . . . no. I couldn't do that under the best of circumstances, but now? No way. They would call the police."

Clancy smiled. "You've forgotten that I *am* the police. And the babysitter I had in mind would be my sister, the pretty mermaid."

Evie gasped. "Seriously?"

"We can go to the house together, see how comfortable Christina is with Rowan. Maybe she'd enjoy hanging out with the mermaid for a couple hours."

"But—"

"Rowan and I have always been there for each other.

I trust her completely and have no doubt she would come to me directly with any concerns. You have nothing to worry about."

Evie lay down again and he did, too, snuggling against her and gently bringing her head to rest on his chest. They stayed like for a long while, so long that he thought she had fallen back asleep.

"Clancy?" Evie's voice sounded small and tense. "I'm going to get out of this mess, aren't I?"

"You are." He hugged her tight. "I'll speak to your IT friend today, then do some snooping around on my own. If Wahlman used money or favors to get his way in the custody case, there will be a trail somewhere—somebody with a new job or a new car or a big deposit in their savings account."

"Thank you."

Clancy kissed her hair. "We'll get that message to your dad today, before we go see the mermaid. I know how important it is to you that he knows you're safe."

Evie raised her head from his chest and kissed him. It was sweet and sensuous. She was saying thank you, the way she always seemed to do.

"There's one other thing."

"Oh, yeah?"

"We should dye your hair."

Evie laughed. "I know. I hate it, too."

"That's not it. I think it's kind of funky. But you should change the style and go darker, so you don't match the surveillance video from Logan Airport that's now playing on every TV in the nation."

"I'll give it my best shot, but obviously, hairstyling is not my specialty."

Clancy chuckled.

"Now it's my turn to ask for something."

"Shoot."

"I want to watch the sun come up with you."

He smiled down on her. "Ah, sweet Evie, sometimes I think you really can read my mind."

*   *   *

After talking to Hal and spending three hours digging on his own, Clancy shut the door to his office and dialed the numbers he had memorized a long time ago. The call was picked up but there was no voice on the other end.

"Flaherty. It's Clancy Flynn."

"The Prince of Bayberry Island! I haven't heard this voice in a while."

"Mickey, I need your help."

"Shoot."

"It involves a congressman, an alleged child abduction, the FBI, and a possible bribe of a public official."

"Just my kind of party."

"It's the middle of festival week, and I'm stuck here. I'm asking you to be my feet on the ground in Maine, Boston, and DC for a couple days. Can you do it?"

"That's why I gave you this number, Flynn. You're in luck—I happen to be in between projects. Tell me what you need."

Charlie signed for the delivery. There were so many fresh flowers, potted plants, and casseroles in the place by now that he could open his own combination restaurant/garden center.

"Thank you, son." He checked out the white panel van parked just steps from the house. It had one of those large magnetic business signs slapped on its side. "Never got a delivery from you people before."

"It's a new shop."

"All the way from Augusta, eh?"

"Yes, sir."

There was something fishy going on. The man standing at his door was stiff as a fence post and well into his thirties. He was dressed in jeans but was acting all business—barely cracked a smile. He was probably another damn FBI agent. In fact, Charlie figured there was a listening device shoved down into the Shasta daisies. He was sick of this whole business.

"Long drive to deliver some flowers."

"I just go where they tell me, Mr. McGuinness."

Charlie looked past the deliveryman and waved to the FBI agents at the end of the farm lane. Every night and every day, they sat there in the blue government-issued sedan, staring at him. God knows it had to be the most boring assignment in the history of their careers.

"Say hello to your buddies for me."

"What buddies?" The man stiffened.

"Joe and Fred down there at the end of the lane."

"They're not my buddies, sir."

Charlie laughed. "Whatever you say. Bye, now." He tried to shut the door but a large leather shoe prevented it from closing.

"Be sure to read the card," the man said.

Charlie glanced at the small white envelope stuck inside the arrangement. It was probably some kind of FBI trick, a fake note from Evie, begging for help. They hoped he would take them right to her. They must really think he was stupid.

He put his lips directly into the flowers. "I don't know where they are, dammit!" He looked up to see the stiff man smiling.

"Jordi is under the apple tree, Mr. McGuinness."

Charlie froze, staring at the man as if seeing him for the first time. Of course, no one would know that but the girls. His heart flipped with joy as he suddenly understood—these flowers weren't another sign of support from loyal friends and neighbors or an FBI trap. This guy wasn't acting like a floral deliveryman because he wasn't one. He was a messenger. A man others counted on to slip under the radar.

Charlie couldn't help it. Tears formed in his eyes. "Thank you, son."

"Call us for all your floral needs." The man handed Charlie a slip of plain paper with an 800 number and a name penned in ink: *Flaherty.*

"Have a pleasant day."

"Ayuh, you as well. Thank you, again. Truly!"

Charlie shook his head in wonder, closing the door. The second he was inside he ripped open the tiny envelope. It wasn't her handwriting, but they were her words.

Pop-Pop,
  We are safe and have help. Forgive me! It will work out and we'll see each other soon. We love you and miss you and are sad we can't share your birthday. I will stay in touch.

  Love, C&J

Charlie wandered into the kitchen, lit the gas stove, and stuck the card in the flame. He tossed it into the kitchen sink and watched it shrivel into a wisp of ash. Note? What note?

Take that, FBI!

Clancy stayed in the mudroom and kept his voice down as he waited for his sister to pick up the line.

"Hi."

"Hey. Whatcha doin'?"

"Serving coffee for guests. Hold on. *What?*" He'd heard his sister mumbling in the background. "Mellie says she misses you."

"Tell her we'll do the fandango next time I'm over there, which will be soon." When Rowan had repeated his response, he heard Imelda Silva's familiar laugh.

Mellie came to work as the family cook and housekeeper soon after Clancy was born, and stayed on when the Safe Haven became a bed-and-breakfast. Though her wealthy daughter insisted she retire, she had no interest in it. Mellie said she knew too many people who died soon after they put in their last day on the job.

"What's up?" Rowan sounded busy.

"I'll just get right to the point. I need a favor."

"Oookay." She hesitated. "As long as it doesn't have anything to do with Mona and Frasier, because I don't want anywhere near that."

Gee, that sounded familiar. "I just need you to put on your mermaid costume and entertain a four-year-old for a few hours. Nothing major. Make cookies or something. This kid has been obsessed with your beauty since the parade and has been begging to meet you."

It got quiet for a moment. "You're not supposed to drink on duty."

He chuckled. "How many times have I asked you for a favor this big?"

"This is a first."

"So you'll do it?"

He heard his sister sigh. "You didn't forget that to-night is the clambake, right?"

Damn! He had forgotten. "Of course not. But we'll be out of your hair by four or five."

Rowan groaned. "Can't we do this some other day?"

"I really need your help today." Clancy didn't want to pique his sister's curiosity by sounding desperate, but, hey, he was. "It's important."

"Okay, okay. How can I say no? You've saved my bacon so many times it's not even funny. Honestly, I don't remember the last time you asked me to do anything for you."

"I don't either."

"But out of all the requests you could have made—why does it have to involve me getting dressed up like the damn Mermaid Queen? You know I hate it. Can't I just keep an eye on this kid dressed like a human being?"

"You're the best mermaid ever. We'll be over after lunch." He tried to hang up.

"Wait! Who's 'we'? Who is this kid, anyway? What's going on?"

"Tell you later. Just don't mention anything about this to Ma."

"Um, Clancy? She's—"

"See you soon."

"Are you ready, Officer Clancy?"

He shoved his cell phone in his pocket and retreated from the mudroom. "I'm right here."

"Go sit on the couch." Clancy had no idea four-year-old girls could be so bossy. "Then close your eyes, 'cause it's a suuuu—perize!"

He did as instructed. "I'm ready."

Clancy heard giggling and shuffling until it stopped directly in front of the fireplace.

"You can open."

Mission accomplished—they looked nothing like the photos of the suspected kidnapper and missing girl now being splashed all over creation. He would be thanking his mother.

"Very nice," he said.

"I know!" It was so good to see Evie's face light up with laughter. It had to be the most beautiful sight in the world.

"Watch out for the scary pirate!" Christina began a jerky freestyle dance that caused her tricornered hat and attached curly wig to list to port. "I will fight you for the treasure!"

As Evie tightened the headgear, he had to admit that Christina's outfit beat her previous pirate costume all to hell. Clancy had been forced to climb shelves and root through plastic storage tubs, but he had found it all—ruffled shirt, vest and short pants, pull-on vinyl boots and a plastic sword with matching scabbard and belt. He even found a new eye patch.

However, it was Evie who stole this particular costume show. Mona had been right—the shells needed adjusting and the spandex mermaid skirt was damn near scandalous.

He liked it. A lot.

"I'm not sure I can go out in public in this." Evie ran her hands down her hips, looking worried.

"It'll just be for a while."

"Yeah, but"—she mouthed the next sentence—*"Your sister will think I'm a pole dancer."*

He laughed. "And here I thought you were a sports therapist and blogger."

"We have some catching up to do, like you said."

Clancy got everyone in the Jeep and headed out to the Safe Haven. Chris was singing happily in the backseat and Evie sat with her hands folded on top of her spandex scales.

"You sure Rowan is okay with this?"

"Oh, she's thrilled!" Maybe that was an exaggeration, but at least she hadn't refused.

As they drove, Clancy glanced at Evie sitting in the passenger seat of the Jeep. She looked so goddamn hot he could hardly steer. He was probably this worked up because of the knowledge that—if all went according to plan—they'd be alone soon.

She looked over at him, sunlight in her pale green eyes. "You know, the last man I dated called my wardrobe 'predictable.'"

"He never had the privilege of seeing you in a mermaid skirt, I take it."

When she laughed, he wanted her so much it hurt—pure torture. He was a grown man, and a beautiful, wonderful woman had been sleeping in his bed and walking around his house and he couldn't have her. The images had been hijacking his brain all day. Evie in a state of abandon, wild and uninhibited and rolling on top of the sheets with him. Evie panting because she wanted him so badly. Evie naked and wet in the shower with him, in the surf, kissing him in the kitchen, sitting in his lap.

Evie. Naked. Everywhere.

"Whoops." He overshot the Safe Haven's front gate and had to bang a U-ie on Shoreline Road. "Sorry. Here we are."

A painfully high screech rose from the backseat. "Look! The castle! It's the mermaid's castle!"

Eighteen years ago . . .

For maybe the first time in her life, Evie was up before her parents. She left a note so they wouldn't freak out. *"Went for a quick run. Will be back by seven, plenty of time to finish packing."*

She needed to move, feel the sea air in her lungs, sense the oxygen fueling her blood. She took off, headed to nowhere but inside her own thoughts. She wished she knew where Clancy lived, but it suddenly occurred to her that she didn't have a clue. It was like she was waking from a dream, where nothing had existed but Clancy, the boy—and now that she was ready to leave she wanted to know more about his life. Talk about bad timing. She knew almost nothing about the guy except that he had a brother and a sister and his ancestor thought he'd married a mermaid.

Oh, and one other thing—she was completely, totally, crazy in love with him.

Evie ran, pushing herself to go harder, driven to beat the sadness out of her body. She didn't want to leave here, but so what? She was only fourteen, and her parents would make her go back to Maine. Besides, she had high school and college ahead of her, and if everything went according to plan the next stop would be medical school, then residency . . . she had goals. Her life was well organized.

Then why, deep down inside her spirit, did she think she was supposed to be on Bayberry Island, with Clancy? Totally crazy of course. She would never tell anyone the thought had crossed her mind—not her mom, Amanda, or any of her friends. It would sound psycho coming from a girl like her, someone grown-ups liked to point to and say, "Now that's a girl with her feet on the ground and her head on her shoulders."

What did that even mean? It felt like she was being praised for not accidentally doing it the other way around. The expression made her sound as exciting as watching paint dry.

She cut through Fountain Square on her way back to the motel. The mermaid towered above everything, lit up by the first glow of sun. She watched the light brighten as it poured through the sailboat masts and over the brick warehouses at the water's edge. All was still, strangely quiet. The island was just starting to wake up to the last day of festival week. For most tourists it was a sad day, the day they had to leave.

She listened closely, but the only sounds she heard were the tap of her own feet on the street, the rhythm of her breath, and the call of seabirds.

Cautiously, she raised her eyes to the Great Mermaid. Yeah, it was nuts, but it really felt like the statue knew she was there. But of course she didn't. For more than a hundred years the metal mermaid had been gazing in one direction—right out to sea—and still was.

Evie slowed to a walk, deciding to begin her cooldown in the mermaid's company. She approached the fountain with hands on hips, breath slowing down. She stretched her arms and waist, all the while examining her. For a big bronze statue, she sure looked lifelike. It didn't take much imagination to see the way she would move through the rolling ocean, surface out of a wave only to dive down again. She would let her arms trail along her sides while she sliced through the sea with whips of her strong tail, her hair flowing behind her like a web of watery silk.

Evie stood directly below the mermaid. She experienced something so strange—a sudden rush that felt like her heart would burst open with love and gratitude—for Clancy, for the beauty of this place, for her family. Just for a second, everything normal and boring felt priceless.

Oh, man, she knew this didn't make any sense but she did it anyway. "Dear mermaid, I need to talk to you. I know I'm not supposed to do this when I have a particular boy in my head, but I can't help it. His name is Clancy. He lives here. You probably know him. Just please listen while I tell you why you should bend your rules for us."

Evie quickly checked her surroundings. She wanted to be sure there were no witnesses for what was about to happen. Satisfied, she reached up for the beautiful creature's hand.

"Save him for me." Her heart was pounding in her throat. "I'm not asking that you force him to feel a certain way, or stop him from having adventures or fun life experiences—because he's only fourteen—but please, dear lady—if you think I am the right girl for him, save his true heart for me. My name is Evelyn McGuinness and I live in Bridgton, Maine, and one day I will come back to Bayberry Island."

She kissed the mermaid's hand, closing her eyes tightly. *Please, oh Great Mermaid, let him still love me when I do.*

Chapter Fifteen

"Welcome to the Safe Haven!"

Christina gasped at the sight of the mermaid, as sparkling and sleek as she'd looked sitting on her float in the parade.

Evelyn nearly gasped, too—when she saw the crowd gathered at the mansion's front door. Those in costume were Rowan, the dashing sea captain from the parade, and an older mermaid who was likely Clancy's mother. The others—a pretty blonde about Evelyn's age, the good-looking guy who held her hand, and a small, dark-haired woman wearing an apron and a curious frown—had opted for street clothes.

"Ah, God." Clancy squeezed his eyes shut.

"I tried to tell you, but you hung up!"

Clancy gave his sister a flat smile. "Well, then, everyone, this is Pirate Jellybean, who has become the scourge of the seas at only four, and Evie, who is an old friend of mine. Jellybean and Evie, this is eighty percent of my family."

The group was pleasant and welcoming. It took a minute to learn who everyone was. Clancy's mother, Mona, was indeed there, along with Rowan and her husband, Ash, Rowan's best friend, Annie, and her husband, Nat, and Mellie, whose dark eyes evaluated Evelyn's mermaid/pole dancer outfit.

Ugh.

"So nice to meet everyone." Evelyn shook hands with Nat and Ash, and received hugs from all the women. "Thank you for having us."

Once they were inside the house, Evelyn had trouble keeping her jaw from falling open as she took in the shining wood, sparkling crystal lights, and impeccable furnishings. Everyone moved toward a sitting room off the main hall.

"Would you like a cookie, Jellybean?" Mona held out her hand to Christina, who took it without hesitation.

Evelyn was encouraged to make herself comfortable, and Annie offered her iced tea. On a round table was an assortment of treats: everything from chocolate chip cookies to what appeared to be homemade scones. Christina dropped Mona's hand, walked right past the goodies, and stood in front of Rowan, her eyes as big as sand dollars.

"Are you real?" It came out in a breathless whisper.

"Of course I am, Jellybean."

Christina touched the mermaid's stretchy scales, then spun around to look at Evelyn's similarly made skirt. She checked out Evelyn's running shoes and then Rowan's sandals.

"Then why you got feet?"

She smiled sweetly. "Because I'm on land instead of swimming in the ocean, and mermaids need feet if they want to walk around."

Christina squinted her eyes. "Are you Ariel?"

"No. My name is Rowan."

"You are so pretty." Christina suddenly pointed at Ash. "So who dat guy?"

Everyone chuckled, clearly enjoying Christina's no-nonsense social graces. Evelyn accepted the tea Annie handed her and took a seat. *Relax. Relax.*

But, really, how bizarre could a situation be? She was

a wanted kidnapper hiding in a slutty mermaid costume while meeting the family of the police chief she was shacking up with, in the hopes that they would babysit for the kidnapping victim so she and the cop could *express themselves* for a few hours back at his place.

The ice cubes rattled in her glass.

That's when Clancy joined her on the divan, sitting right up against her spandex-covered thigh. He reached for her free hand and held it tight.

Of course, not a soul in the room missed his gesture, except for Chrissy, who was fixated on Rowan and intrigued by Mona. Evelyn took a sip of iced tea to wash down her nervousness.

The little party moved along smoothly. Christina hopped around the parlor and did her pirate dance while Evelyn carried on several conversations.

"Would you like a tour of the house, Evie?"

She felt Clancy's body stiffen next to her, and she caught his eye. He didn't seem thrilled with Evelyn having alone time with his mother.

"Thank you, Mona, but I'm sure you have things to do to get ready for the clambake tonight."

"Don't be silly." Mona removed the iced-tea glass from Evie's hand. "The place really does have a fascinating history and is quite lovely."

Evelyn was up on her feet and being ushered out into the foyer before she could protest. She looked back at Clancy and shrugged.

Mona had been right. The house was beautiful and had an interesting story behind it. It had been built in 1885 by Rutherford Flynn, Clancy's great-great-grandfather, after his fishery became prosperous.

"Did you know that during the first part of the twentieth century, nearly fifteen percent of all the seafood served in the finest East Coast restaurants originated on a Flynn Fisheries boat?"

"Uh, no. But wow."

"This house has been in our family for all that time—

Well, of course, I married into the Flynns. I met Clancy's father as a tourist here one summer. Fancy that, eh?"

Evelyn felt her mouth go dry. "So is this the same Rutherford Flynn who built the mermaid fountain for his wife?"

They had just entered the kitchen when Evelyn asked this. Mona stopped, grabbed her arm, and gasped. "Yes! Yes, it is! You know the legend, then?"

Evie was a bit surprised by the woman's enthusiasm. "Just some of it."

For the next half hour, Evelyn was brought up to speed, not only about the Flynns, the Safe Haven, the Mermaid Society, and the history of Bayberry Island itself, but about the mermaid legend as well. It almost seemed like Mona was selling Evelyn on one, or every one, of the topics.

Eventually, they finished the tour of all rooms not occupied by guests. As they descended the grand staircase in their tight mermaid skirts, Mona asked, "Have you ever sought her guidance in matters of love?"

"Whose guidance?"

"The mermaid's, my dear."

Based on the seriousness of her tone, Evelyn couldn't help but think the whole sightseeing trip had been a setup for that single question.

"Uh . . ." Yes, she'd talked to the mermaid that summer long ago, but she couldn't remember the conversation. She might have asked for a favor, but not guidance. "Not really, no."

Mona's expression was intense, and her eyes searched Evelyn's face. Clearly, this point was important to her. "Well, let me ask you this: do you believe in true love?"

"Yes, I do." Evelyn smiled at Clancy's mom. "My parents loved each other very much. I love Chri— Jellybean."

"In the realm of romantic love, the bond of a man and a woman, do you accept that there may be unseen forces that guide people toward their heart-mates?"

"I guess. Sure." She thought about what Clancy had said—*you came back for a reason.* "But what exactly is a heart-mate?"

Mona nodded. "That is an excellent question, and the answer is different for each individual. Only you know the exact vibrations—the combination, balance, and overall frequency—that complements your own."

"I see." Evelyn smiled. Of course she appreciated the mechanics of energy flow through the human body—it was part of her training in sports therapy—but she'd reached her maximum daily capacity for New Age hippie talk. "Well, thank you for the tour, Mrs. Flynn. It really is an extraordinary—"

Mona grasped her hand. "You might ask yourself these things: is life more colorful, peaceful, and infused with light when you two are together? Do you have a sense of oneness in his company? Do you sleep better when he is near? Do you trust him with your life? And, most important—could you imagine your life without him?"

Evelyn promised Mona she'd keep all those things in mind. Her head was spinning by the time they returned to the front foyer. Though Clancy's mom was sweet, she was definitely *different.* She'd even asked Evelyn to consider becoming a member of "the mermaid sisterhood."

And, hey, why not? Every women's club needed at least one wanted felon in its ranks. Evelyn told her she'd think about it.

The sitting room was empty, and for an instant Evelyn's blood buzzed with fear. Then she heard laughing and music somewhere, and she and Mona wound their way through the first floor. A kitchen party was in full swing. Somebody's iPod was blanketing the room with pop tunes. Ash, Nat, and Clancy were gathered at the center island, talking and laughing. Mellie, Rowan, and Annie were at the sink with Chrissy.

Evelyn paused in the doorway to observe her niece. The tricornered hat and wig were gone, along with the plastic slip-on boots and vest. She'd taken off her Velcro water sandals and was barefoot. Who would look at that child and not see a little girl? It was right there—in the shape of her leg, the curve of her neck, and the set of her shoulders. And her delicate little face—the truth was the short hair did nothing but make her seem more feminine.

She felt Clancy's gaze on her. He gave her a gentle smile and inclined his chin, as if to say everything was fine. At that moment, Evelyn realized if she applied Mona's formula for love, she knew that her life would be flat and colorless without both Christina *and* Clancy. Now that she had found him again, she couldn't imagine letting him go.

"Hey!" Christina jumped off the stool and ran to Evelyn. "Mr. Ass taught me how to swordfight!"

The room went silent as everyone strained not to laugh.

Evie smiled, too. "Sorry about that, Ash. We're into creative pronunciation sometimes."

"That's absolutely fine. Right, Sir Clancy?"

"Indeed, Mr. Ass."

"Can I stay?" Christina began jumping up and down. "Rowan and Annie said they'll play mermaids with me. I want to stay! Stay, stay, stay!"

Evelyn glanced up at the women, and they were beaming at her. "Everybody's getting along wonderfully," Annie reassured her. Rowan gave her a thumbs-up.

"Sure, sweetie. Would it be okay if I left for a little bit? I'll come right back if—"

"Bye!" Chrissy gripped Evelyn's legs for a quick hug, then ran back to the sink and climbed the stool.

Evelyn thanked everyone, then Ash and Nat walked them to the front door. "See you tonight," Ash said as they left.

"Will do!" Clancy held the door open for Evelyn.

She made her way to the car slowly, and with her legs pinned together as they were, it took some core strength to tuck herself inside the Jeep.

The trip back was much quieter.

"I hate to ask, but did Mona mermatize you?"

Evelyn laughed. "Yeah. She wanted me to join her group and asked me if I believed in love."

"Ah, God. Sorry." Clancy shook his head. "You know, it's funny about my mom. She's a brilliant lady, retired school administrator, the most organized woman I've ever known—but she loses her freakin' common sense when it comes to the mermaid."

"It's her passion, I guess. People have accused me of the same thing with all the stuff I'm into."

Clancy gave her a sideways grin. "I had a chance to check out your blog at work this morning. You are killin' it, Evie. Forty thousand followers? That's amazing."

"Thank you." She felt a little shy.

"I just hope my mom didn't scare you away."

"Scare me away? From what—*you*?"

Clancy shrugged, pulling into the drive of his house. "Yeah. Me. This island. I know we're a little unusual around here. It takes some getting used to."

He cut the engine, and they sat quietly in the Jeep, simply looking at each other. She reached for his hand.

"What happened with your wife?"

Clancy nodded mechanically, as if he were expecting that question. "Barbie and I met in Boston and got married after just six months together. Mistake number one. When I wanted to come back and take over as chief of police, she fought me every step of the way. She hated Bayberry Island, and she came to hate me for dragging her here."

"That sounds awful. I'm sorry."

"Nothing to be sorry about."

"Clancy, I have something to confess."

He raised an eyebrow.

"The day I had to leave Bayberry when I was fourteen, I had a . . . I don't know how to describe it, really. It wasn't a premonition or anything that dramatic, but I had a *feeling* I was supposed to stay and *would* end up staying somehow. Of course, back then I couldn't and didn't, but I'm here now. And the weird thing is, this trip wasn't even my idea. It was Amanda's. She wanted to bring our dad here for his birthday, to relive a happy moment from our past, and she wanted Christina to see the festival."

"That's why you had the two rooms."

"Yeah. Amanda booked them, maybe nine or ten months ago. When all this happened with Richard and I was freaking out trying to decide what to do and where to go, I remembered the arrangements."

Clancy cocked his head. "So it was almost as if you were sent here."

"Here's my confession: no matter why or how I came back, the truth is that this island—the way things are here, the people, you—it fits me, Clancy. I'm not scared away. I'm scared I'll be dragged off in handcuffs and never see you or this place again."

He leaned over the gearshift and lifted her chin with a fingertip. "Not gonna happen, sweet Evie." He placed a soft kiss on her lips. "I guess we're officially on our date."

"It seems like years since our last one."

Clancy laughed. "How about we go inside and you can slip into something, you know . . . ?"

"Without fins and a wig?"

"Exactly."

"Gather 'round, ye maids."

Not everyone was settled, but Mona couldn't delay. A half hour had already been wasted simply pulling people from their clambake assignments and getting them in her living room. This concern had to be addressed now or never at all. The window of opportunity was closing.

"Is this meeting gonna take long? Because I gotta—"

"Can it, Polly!" Mona immediately regretted snapping at her friend. "I'm sorry, but this is an *emergency* emergency meeting. As president, I am calling for a concurrent intervention ceremony."

The whole room inhaled at the same time.

"Oh, my Lord! We haven't done one of those in years!" Abigail scanned the room. "Does anyone remember . . . ?"

"It was Maureen Dulvaney in 2006. She put her house on the market to move in with that Rhode Island man she met on the Internet, the one who sent her a picture of his . . . *member*."

"No, Izzy. Maureen was back in the nineties. The most recent was Cloris Buchnell in 2010. Remember? Her best friend slept with Cloris's fiancé, but Cloris was sure all three of them could live together in harmony."

"No, Abigail. It was Maureen and it was 2006. People didn't even put photos of their members online in the nineties. That started much later."

"And you know this *how*?" Polly slapped her knee and snorted, and Mona's living room erupted into a cacophony of disagreement and peals of laughter.

Mona decided to just get down to business. "I am making this request for Clancy."

It went quiet.

"Yes, you heard right."

"But . . ." Darinda paused, then pushed on. "I don't mean to second-guess the president, but didn't you say that you were done trying to orchestrate your children's relationships?"

Damn Darinda and her attention to detail.

"This is a highly unusual situation, 'maids. Please hear me out."

Everyone stilled.

"Clancy needs the mermaid's assistance at this very moment. I can't tell you the specifics of the situation because I gave him my word I wouldn't."

Mona took a deep breath. "Before I go further, I must remind everyone that we took a vow of secrecy. You need to know that in this case, keeping your word could very well be a matter of life and death."

Everyone nodded solemnly—except for Polly. "Hold

up. Since when is Clancy's love life a matter of national security?"

"'Maids, I tell you I am in a predicament. I swore I would not reveal the details, and yet he needs us to rally behind him."

"Why the *emergency* emergency?"

Mona sighed and rubbed her forehead. "My son and his heart-mate are together right this moment. I believe that on some level, they know what they are to each other. However, there are grave issues that must be resolved before they can live in happiness."

"She's a married woman."

Polly rolled her eyes at Abigail. "Good God. Do you really think Mona would want us to help Clancy in his quest to diddle a married woman?"

Layla gasped, tears in her eyes. "Is she suffering from a fatal disease? Oh, my God—how much time does she have?"

"Is she a daughter of the island?" Polly asked.

Mona shook her head. "I don't mean to be coy, but it's no to all those things."

Izzy leaned forward, resting her elbows on her scales. "If these problems are so serious, how do you know they are each other's beloved? What evidence do you have?"

"Excellent question." Mona took a deep breath. "Without going into the specifics, this is a girl Clancy knew when he was a teenager. I remember seeing them together as kids. The vibrational frequency they created together was unusually high, but she was a tourist, and she never wrote or came back."

"But she's here now?"

"Yes, Izzy. She's here. But I don't know for how long—and that is why we need the intervention. She's in trouble with the law, and Clancy is secretly helping her."

The room erupted in chaos.

"Ladies!" It was the first time anyone had heard Darinda's president-elect voice. "Calm down and let Mona finish."

"My, my." Izzy tossed her wig dramatically.

Layla gasped. "Clancy could end up in prison for the rest of his life!"

"I know my son, and I assure you he wouldn't defy the law unless he believed he was serving a greater justice."

"Or he's doing all this thinkin' with his . . ." Polly hesitated. "What did you call it, Iz?"

"Member."

"Right. His *member*."

"Oh, the attraction is there, most definitely," Mona said. "The air around them crackles with it. But I am certain we must do everything in our power as members of the sisterhood to help them on their journey."

Abigail looked puzzled. "Are you saying the mermaid has already had a hand in how it's unfolded?"

"Absolutely," Mona said. "I believe she long ago gave them her blessing, but some kind of external circumstance kept them apart."

"Ha." Abigail crossed her arms over her chest. "It was probably a non-believer, another case of stopping someone else's happiness because you didn't believe in the possibility of your own."

"Truly, I don't know." Mona looked around the room at her friends. "All I know is this young woman completely captured Clancy's heart when they were kids. It was no normal summer crush. And when nothing ever came of it, he was terribly hurt. I think on some level, Clancy's always blamed the mermaid for losing her."

"He's never liked the goddess—that's for sure."

"True, Izzy. And while he was busy not liking her, the mermaid had a plan for Clancy. I believe my son has been waiting for the young woman to return, though he would never admit it. And I believe she was meant to return to him."

"So what do we need to do?" Polly asked.

"They are alone together *right now*. We should take advantage of their merging energy to send them clarity, wisdom, and courage. We must thank the Great Mermaid for watching over them through the years and bringing them together again. And we must ask her to protect them in this time of crisis."

The members rose to their fins, formed a perfect circle, and held hands.

"There's one more thing. Clancy came to me yesterday, needing a mermaid costume for this woman, and I gave him my . . ."

"No, you didn't!"

"Yes, I did, Polly. She's been wearing my ceremonial skirt, and it fits her essence perfectly—though it fell a bit low on her hips. She needs the skirt's powers of protection right now."

"But do you know her well enough? The ceremonial skirt shouldn't be worn by a woman whose heart isn't true."

"I trust my son to choose a worthy heart-mate." Mona felt herself smile. "Besides, I got to spend some time with this young woman today, and I sensed a deep goodness in her. She is strong, with sadness threaded through her spirit. But, as it sometimes does, loss has left her open to the mystery."

"You're sure the situation warrants a concurrent intervention?"

"I am. Evelyn is Clancy's heart-mate. I saw it when they were kids, and I see it now, no matter how complicated the situation may be."

"Then let's rock 'n' roll," Polly said.

Chapter Sixteen

Thirty seconds, max. That's how much time it took to close the front door and end up naked in Clancy's bed. Clothes and shells and fins and shoes were thrown everywhere, and now Evelyn had exactly what she'd been craving—the slip of skin on skin, the heat of his body on hers, no distance, rules, or circumstance separating them.

"My God, you are so beautiful."

"I've wanted you so much."

"You feel perfect to me, Evie."

"Kiss me. Please keep kissing me."

He did, and Evelyn felt her edges dissolve in the heat they created. There was nothing about herself or her life that she felt she needed to protect. Nothing to hide. She just *was*—she was the love and lust she'd locked away for so long. It hadn't been reachable before. She hadn't been able to access these feelings—hadn't even wanted to. Could it be she had been waiting? *For him?*

All she knew was she felt freer in the first few minutes with Clancy than she had in the last ten years of her life.

They were about to become lovers. Their lips searched, and their tongues licked. These were wet, hungry kisses intended to consume one another. Clancy put her bottom lip between his teeth and bit down until it stung just a little.

Yes.

Her hands couldn't hold enough of his muscle and flesh. Evelyn wanted all of him, inside her, on her, surrounding her. They rolled. Top, bottom, top . . . legs tangled, arms clutching, hands fisted in hair and wrists pinned to the mattress.

I'm yours. I'm yours. I've always been yours.

Suddenly, Clancy stopped. He supported himself over her, his weight on her wrists.

Evelyn waited.

"I'm not sure where this is coming from." Clancy tried to catch his breath. "I swear . . . I wanted to seduce you slowly . . . and, you know, play with you until you were weak and desperate."

"I kind of pictured it that way, too." Evelyn felt a bead of sweat form on her upper lip. "I fantasized about slowly pulling my clothes off for you, teasing you, making you feel like you'd go crazy if you couldn't have me."

He laughed. "Well, no wonder we attacked each other. I've been feeling like that for days now."

"And I've been weak and desperate since I saw you at the dock."

Clancy dipped his face to hers, licking the sweat off her lip. Their eyes locked for an instant, his dark blue gaze intense, ravenous. Evelyn lay still. She had never felt so naked in a man's presence—flesh and heart. She was on the verge of surrender and happy about it. No danger. No fear. She had already put her life in his hands. At this moment, she was pinned to the sheets under Clancy's weight and the force of his desire. And there was nowhere else she'd rather be.

Evelyn gazed up at him, in awe of how quickly this man's face had become precious to her. She studied his features carefully in the afternoon light, deciding it was the qualities as a whole that tugged her closer. That was the only word she had for it—tug. It was like she was being pulled toward him in a rip current of attraction.

His was a complex face, rugged but approachable. The light in his eyes was often kind but was just as often no-nonsense. The angles and planes of his forehead, cheekbones, and chin were masculine, but when he smiled, everything was transformed to the wild-child boy she'd known. That wide and straight smile cut directly through to Evelyn's heart. She would go anywhere for that smile.

But right at that moment, his lips were made for kissing and being kissed.

He was studying her, too. He dropped his attention to her mouth, neck, and exposed breasts. Clancy swallowed hard, as the muscles in his shoulders and arms strained.

"Are you holding back?" she asked.

He seemed surprised. "I just . . . I might take off like a runaway speedboat—all power and speed and no control."

"What if I don't want you to control yourself?"

"You don't?"

"What if I've had enough of living a controlled life? What if this is my last free day on earth and here I am, a thirty-two-year-old woman who's never been ravaged, never completely surrendered to passion?"

His eyes widened.

"How sad would that be?"

"Prett-tee damn sad."

"So go ahead. Ravage me. Do it, Clancy Flynn. We aren't fourteen anymore. I promise I won't break. And then later, we can play with each other nice and slow."

"Ah, Evie. God, what you do to me."

Clancy pulled her arms up over her head as he used his knees to push open her thighs. He nipped at her breasts, his mouth leaving sucking kisses all around, then on, her nipples, driving her out of her head.

Oh, she wanted to sing and dance and send a thank-you note to fate, because this—*this*—was exactly what she had been missing. The man who fit her. The man who loved her. Not just any man.

This man.

Clancy dropped his lips to hers again, demanding, taking, his tongue claiming her mouth. They crushed themselves together in need. And though the ceiling fan spun and the doors were open to the ocean, it was warm and humid in his bedroom, and their bodies dripped and slipped across each other. She felt the perfection of nature, how the two of them were designed to meld into one. Clancy had become hard and thick, and she was now fully open and swollen, begging for completion. It would only take the smallest flex of his hips and he'd be inside her.

Clancy pulled back, ripped his lips from her nipples and freed her wrists. Oh, God. His mouth dragged down her sternum and ribs, slick with sweat. His tongue flicked and licked, and his teeth scraped, down . . . down. . . .

"Look at you. God, Evie. Thank you. Thank you for coming back to me."

He placed his mouth on the puffy outer lips of her sex. It was magical what he did, nibbling and sucking and caressing the most delicate and sensitive part of her body. Every move he made was for her pleasure. Just for her. His fingers slipped inside of her while his mouth stayed in place, sucking, teasing, nibbling.

The last ten years . . . so much wasted time . . . she had never been anywhere close to this outrageous pleasure. Clancy's mouth pulled her, cut her loose, dragged her under.

She released a cry of bliss that drowned out the roar of the sea. Clancy quickened his fingers and the suction of his mouth, and she felt lost, lost, gone. Every bit of her being continued to crash, on and on, her body rippling as she rode it out.

"Hell, yes," he said. He kissed her everywhere—her sticky inner thighs, knees, arms, throat. In her daze, Evelyn saw Clancy reach across the bed toward his nightstand. Even from her la-la land, the depths of ecstasy, she saw all of him.

He was beautiful, built for speed and pleasure. She wanted to learn him, every inch of him. She lay back in awe of how he moved, contraction and ripple of muscle, strength of bone, length of torso, all that golden skin.

And. Oh. That man's ass. Flawless. He had the body of an athlete and the ass of a distance runner, designed for locomotion, the driving force of a runner's stride. He had big, solid thighs and sculpted calves.

She reached out and touched his forearm. Clancy had a condom wrapper in his hand and a smile on his face.

Evelyn had to laugh. She was the one in a trance of happiness, but he looked like he'd gone there with her. She glanced down at his cock— Oh, holy crap.

"You look really happy," she whispered.

"When you're happy, I'm happy."

"I'm real happy."

"I know. And you're about to get happier."

Clancy rolled with her again, pulling her on top of him. He played with her hard nipples and wet sex for a bit longer. "You are the most beautiful creature I've ever seen."

She let her head loll back as she opened her legs wider.

"Look what you've done to me."

Oh, she saw. Between her spread thighs was an engorged cock. She touched him for the first time. She had made him wait. And talk about male perfection—the brush of silk on her fingertips and unyielding rock in her grip. She gave him a little smile and slid lower on his legs, arching her back like a cat as she let him slip into her mouth. She was intent on bringing him the kind of pleasure she'd just received.

She looked up at him to gauge his reaction, mixing slow and loving caresses with friction and intensity, then back to slow and soft. It was satisfying to hear him moan and cry out, then stare at her like he couldn't quite believe she was real. But eventually, Clancy placed his hand gently on her cheek. She sat up.

Clearly, it was time to be ravished. She was suddenly on her back, Clancy's body wedged between her thighs. She heard the sound of ripping foil and opened her eyes to see him looming over her.

"Give yourself to me, Evie."

She nodded, wordlessly.

His hands lifted her bottom from the bed, and he held her there, fingers pressed into her flesh as he guided himself to the entrance of her body. Evelyn gasped. She was tempted to allow her head to fall back and eyes to close, but she wanted to *be* there with him. She wanted to see it happen.

She was so slick and aroused that the first bit of his cock slipped in her without effort, as if she had pulled him in.

"Ah, God."

Evelyn heard herself whimper. This felt incredible. And it had only just begun.

He pushed. She opened for him. Clancy moved in her, and she moved with him. All the while their eyes were locked on each other's, and they went together into the swirl and rush of energy, desire, and emotion.

She'd asked for ravishment, and she got it. Evelyn had no idea how much time had elapsed, the number of orgasms that had shaken her, or how many ways her body and spirit had been conquered by Clancy's desire. She only knew they clung to each other, urged each other on, and created something that hadn't been there before.

They were lovers.

When he came, she came with him. She might even have blacked out for a few seconds, because she was surprised to find herself lying on her side on the rug, gripped in Clancy's arms, staring directly into four large dog nostrils. She and Clancy had rolled off the bed and were now just inches from the back door screen.

She laughed. Clancy opened one eye.

"Something amusing?"

She nodded. "We have an audience."

He turned his head over his shoulder. "Oh, for crap's sake." Clancy pulled slowly from Evelyn's body and jumped to a stand. "Stay right there, my queen."

Clancy returned a moment later with two towels and a cool washcloth. He spread one towel across the bed, then reached down to pull Evelyn from the floor. He patted the bed, and she stretched out. Clancy swept the cool cloth over every inch of her sweaty body, taking his time, then patted her dry with the second towel.

"God*damm*. You wiped me the hell *out*, Miss Mc-Guinness."

Clancy's cell phone rang, and he staggered like an old man as he tried to locate his shorts. He dug the phone out of a pocket and answered. It was a short conversation. Clancy crawled back into bed

"You have to go into work?"

"Nope. It was Rowan."

Evelyn sat up. "Uh-oh."

"It's all good." Clancy touched her arm. "She said not to bother coming back until the clambake. Turns out Jellybean is the belle of the ball over there. She wants to take a nap on the porch hammock, and Annie wants to adopt her."

Evelyn sighed with relief. She'd assumed the call meant their moment of romance had been just that—a moment. She lay back down, relaxed into his body, and enjoyed the feel of the fan cooling them.

"Your family is going to figure it out, Clancy."

"Probably. But she's completely safe with them."

Evelyn surrendered to the need to close her eyes. Her mind wandered back to that faraway summer. "The sweetest summer of my life."

"Mine, too."

That's when Evelyn realized she had said that out loud. She blinked her eyes at Clancy. She had to know. "Do you remember what we said to each other?"

The corners of his mouth twitched. "Today or when we were fourteen?"

"Back then."

"Sure. I said I loved you."

"And I said I loved you, too. Do you think it was really possible?"

They were still, the sound of the ocean rushing beyond the deck, seabirds crying, their hearts beating—and the dogs breathing.

"Kind of ruins the moment."

Evelyn laughed. "I don't mind. This is life. Life is pretty strange sometimes."

"You got that right." Clancy kissed her cheek stroked the side of her face. "I do think we could have been right all those years ago."

"Why do you say that?"

"Because it's still the same, Evie. For both of us."

The warm night was made tolerable by a steady and gentle breeze along Haven Beach. Evie wore the mermaid getup again and complained that she was hot, but she really had no choice. Clancy looked forward to the day when she could simply be herself, and the world could know they were together.

Christina had been pleased to see Evie when they returned to the Safe Haven in time for the clambake, but there was no indication she'd felt deserted by her. Jellybean chattered on about what she had done that day and how much she loved the mermaid's castle. "She said I can come every day and every night if I want!"

The dinner was fabulous, the way it always was at the clambake. The three of them ate at a small round table on the beach, and Christina snarfed down a mound of shrimp and two large ears of corn. Where she put it, he had no idea. Clancy's family was especially sweet to Evie and were obviously smitten with her niece, but there was an underlying awkwardness in the evening. Especially with Mona.

He suspected Evie had been right, and they had figured out what was going on. And though he had no doubt he could trust them, he anticipated a few questions as soon as they could get him alone.

Clancy made sure that never happened. Evie stayed at his side all night, and both of them always had an eye on Jellybean. As they danced under the fairy lights, they talked about what a strange concept time was. Both of them agreed that it seemed time had folded in on itself, and the years in between their last clambake and this one had never even existed.

The evening's only permitted bonfire was under the watchful eye of Deon and a volunteer firefighter. Clancy gave his buddy a quick hello before he joined the girls around the fire. Since it was getting late, Jellybean crawled into his lap and fell asleep, while Evie sat tucked close to his side.

Yeah, he knew Deon was staring at him, and Clancy knew he would have five hundred questions for him the first time he got him alone, and the first one would be *"Who the hell was that woman you were with last night at the bonfire?"*

He wasn't sure how he would answer him.

They decided it was time to get Christina to bed, and headed up the beach. As they began to climb the Safe Haven's private steps, Rowan and Ash stopped them. Jellybean was flopped over Clancy's shoulder, sound asleep. It felt like she might even be drooling on the back of his shirt.

"You know, she's welcome to stay here tonight." Rowan's voice was kind. Evie thanked her, but took a rain check. When they returned home, Evie got Christina settled and immediately retreated to the bathroom. She came out a few minutes later wrapped in nothing but a towel. She grabbed a T-shirt out of Clancy's dresser and crawled into his bed.

Some men might get freaked out when a new girlfriend made herself at home like that. Not Clancy. He was thrilled. But then again, she wasn't exactly a new girlfriend, was she?

Evie fell asleep on his chest. He held her close, in awe that this already felt normal. He dozed off with a smile stuck on his face.

Chapter Seventeen

Richard couldn't believe someone had the audacity to show up unannounced at his suite, and at this ungodly hour of the morning. He hadn't had his first cup of coffee or even a shower!

"Just a moment." He went to the bedroom to trade the comfort of the hotel robe for trousers and a polo shirt, grumbling to himself. Whoever this was had gotten through the front desk. His cardiologist? No. He was the last guy who would want to startle Richard first thing in the morning.

Walt Henson, his lawyer? Possibly, but Walt always called first.

Maybe it was the FBI again. Special Agent in Charge Teresa Apodaca and her buddies had become like family to him this last week. Hey, maybe he could order breakfast from room service for everyone! They could hold a news conference right here, with Richard in his robe! He could stand off to the side like a fool until it was his cue to say, "I remain hopeful."

Ha! Just more lies. He didn't feel hopeful—he felt panicked. Because if they couldn't find Christina, it meant he had just caused a stupefying amount of collateral damage to his life—campaign contributions, approval ratings, committee assignments, access to the

Derricks' deep-fried pockets, and even his shot at a VP nod.

For nothing.

If Richard were brutally honest with himself, he would have to admit that the only reason he was prepared to walk away from the life he had was because he had another life waiting—life as a father.

If they never found Christiana, he would be left with no life at all.

He would not let that happen.

Now dressed, Richard arrived at the hotel suite door and put his eye to the peephole. *Jesus!*

He opened the door for M.J. and immediately retreated to one of the sofas.

"Got any coffee around here?"

"No."

M.J. curled up on the couch opposite Richard. She stared at him. "Comfy."

Yes, it was. That's why Richard liked the Jefferson: guaranteed discretion and seating that didn't feel like steel girders shoved up his ass.

"What can I do for you, Mary Jane?"

"I've come to tell you a bedtime story."

"I just woke up."

"Well, you might spend the rest of the day in bed after you hear it."

Richard laughed softly. "My sincere apologies, but I have neither the patience nor the energy to deal with your passive-aggressive bullshit this morning."

M.J. swung her legs around and leaned forward. "You don't even remember, do you?"

"Remember what?"

"Sunday morning. Right before you went on-air with Tamara. I told you there was something you really needed to know, and you told me it had to wait. Well, I don't think it can wait any longer."

Richard leaned back into the sofa cushions. "Make it short."

She flashed a perfectly evil smile. "Sure. The title of this story is 'Above and Beyond.' It's about a young girl named Amanda McGuinness and her adventures in the nation's capital. It's a cautionary tale, really. "

Richard lowered his chin and stared at M.J. as dread pressed down on him. "Go on."

M.J. tossed an envelope onto the coffee table. Richard knew it was her letter of resignation. "First, you need to understand the setting for this story. We were eyeballs deep in reelection strategy for your third term. You'd just been appointed chair of the oversight subcommittee. Your approval rating was off the charts. You'd already raised eight-point-five million from Super PACs alone. You were golden."

"What . . . did . . . you . . . do?" Richard sat up straight, his blood pressure mounting.

She laughed. "I did what I've done for you for sixteen years: I cleaned up your mess."

"I'll ask you one more time." Richard crooked his arm and aimed his right pointer finger across the coffee table at her. "What did you do to Amanda?"

M.J. rose from the sofa and hugged herself. She began pacing the room. "You are incredibly dense, Richard, more so than your average congressman. I found the girl cowering in the corner of the ladies' room, sobbing because she was in love with you and had just found out she was pregnant with your baby. She was scared to death, trying to summon the courage to tell you, daring to hope that you'd leave Tamara for her the way you'd promised. She was a lost little kitten. So I made it simple for her."

Richard stood up, suddenly dizzy. His heart began to race and skip. "Dammit, M.J.! You knew about the baby? All these years? For Christ's sake, why didn't you tell me? And what did you do to that poor girl to make her run like she did?"

M.J. looked disgusted with him. "I told her I'd take care of everything and she should just sit tight. I promised to be the go-between, and I would help her in any way I could."

"Where was I during this? Why didn't I know what was going on?"

She laughed. "You were in a caucus meeting all afternoon and then dined at Charlie Palmer's with some of your generous friends from Mass Mutual, but the reason you didn't see she was miserable was because the girl meant nothing to you unless she was naked in your favorite suite at the Jefferson." M.J. looked around. "Oh, my! We're in it right now!"

"Enough."

"Let me finish!" Her eyes turned to dark, hard pebbles. It was obvious she didn't plan to stop until she drew blood. "While you were enjoying your prime rib, I dropped by Amanda's cheap little apartment. I brought her an envelope with six one-hundred-dollar bills and passed on your message: *Get rid of the baby.* I told her you didn't love her and never would. And I broke the news to her that, no, you would not be leaving Tamara."

Richard felt his mouth fall open. It stayed open in complete horror.

"And then I advised her that she needed to leave the city because being a congressional aide who was young, female, and pregnant could be hazardous to her health. I explained that women such as her had been known to disappear in this town."

"No. *You didn't.*" Richard went numb. "M.J., please tell me you didn't threaten her like that. Oh, Jesus."

"And that's how I made sure that no one ever heard about the baby. I did it so we could continue with the plan, Richard. And look how far we've come—we are a stone's throw from getting the VP spot and going to the White House. It's what you promised me. Ring a bell?"

He felt his knees weaken.

"But you've gone and ruined everything, you son of a bitch!"

It was beyond his control. Richard felt hot tears roll

down his face at how wrong this whole thing was, how cruel, and how it had ended with the complete waste of Amanda's life. She'd been smart and beautiful. She should still be alive. What was wrong with him? How could he have been so twisted up in his own ego that he never even checked on Amanda after she left? How could he have not known what his own chief of staff was doing?

Richard landed on the couch, lost in disbelief. Maybe he hadn't exactly loved Amanda, but he had cared for her! She was a good kid. Kind to others. She was funny. When she entered a room, people instinctively smiled.

This town chewed her up and spit her out. It was his fault.

What would have happened if she'd come to him with news of the child? Would he have been tempted by the one thing power and money could never provide? Maybe he would have found the courage to leave Tamara and ride the wave of scandal like a man. Maybe he would have left politics. He would never know, because he hadn't been allowed to make that decision for himself.

M.J. had made it for him.

"You stole my power to choose." He heard his voice shake with fury. "You made decisions you had no right to make."

M.J. snorted. "Oh, for the love of God, Richard, don't be so melodramatic. Now, there is one matter we need to settle before we part ways."

He was stunned.

"I hope you're listening because here's how it's going to work."

Richard was suddenly too tired to think.

"You work for me, now."

He heard himself let go with a slow, weary laugh.

"I know how the old-boy system works. You might be down, but you'll never be all the way out. You'll get another law gig somewhere, maybe even transition into life as a lobbyist. So if I ever need you to smooth the path for me in any way, you'll do it. You owe me that."

"Or what, Mary Jane?"

She gave him a malevolent smile. "The world will learn exactly how you managed the magical custody-by-default ruling in your favor. Think about it. Not only will you go down in history as a dirty old man, but you'll probably be charged with bribing a public official, perjury, influence peddling—a veritable cornucopia of improprieties!"

Richard's face had gone dead. He wasn't sure if he was having a stroke or reacting to a political pistol-whipping courtesy of his most faithful confidante, the person who had done his bidding for the past sixteen years. Yes, the island cop might have had a hunch, but his chief of staff *knew*.

"Is this a threat?"

"No. It's your new reality."

Richard looked at M.J.'s face as if he were seeing her for the first time. All that rage, all those hard lines, all that scheming and grasping for one moment of glory—he understood her perfectly.

Because he'd taught her everything she knew.

The truth was, if it weren't for Christina, Richard wouldn't give a goddamn if he did prison time—as unlikely as that would be for a congressman with a heart condition and the best lawyers money could buy.

"You disappoint me, Mary Jane."

She laughed. "And you failed me."

Richard thought about that for a moment. "You're right. I did. I suppose you should do whatever you believe is right, expose me if you must, and I'll face the consequences. If they don't find Christina, nothing matters anyway."

"What the . . . ?"

"You win." He raised his chin. "Isn't that what you want—to win? Your resignation has been regretfully accepted. Now, get the hell out."

M.J. moved to the door. She placed her hand on the doorknob, then glanced over her shoulder to Richard.

That smile was back. Yet again, he thought of Tamara, and he shivered.

"You know, I'm really going to enjoy watching you crash and burn, Congressman."

He waved her off. "It's an empty threat, and you know it. You'd only incriminate yourself."

Her smile widened. "Perhaps I'll get immunity in exchange for delivering your ass on a platter. You taught me everything I know about making deals, Richard. Remember?"

Charlie knew it was a risky idea, but it was his birthday, and he was so lonely that he craved the comfort memories could provide. Even if he had to settle for memories tainted with sorrow.

He hadn't opened this door in over a month. The last time he'd come in Amanda's room was right after Wahlman's lawyer had shown up. That was the night Evie had told him the whole story. He learned of Amanda's affair with the congressman she worked for, and when he had discovered she was pregnant, the bastard had insisted she terminate the pregnancy and threatened her life if she didn't leave the city immediately. No wonder the country was going to hell in a hay wagon—Congress was nothing but a cesspool of power-hungry, lying degenerates like Richard Wahlman. God help the USA.

Sometimes, Charlie thought it a blessing that his Ginny hadn't lived to see what happened to Amanda—and now Evelyn. It would have been too much for her to bear.

Charlie flipped on the light and crossed the old wood floors to sit on the double bed. Amanda had always been a free spirit, such a bright and creative young woman. The colors in her bedroom reflected her personality perfectly—yellows and oranges and reds everywhere he looked.

The room was just as she had left it. Framed photographs and books and pillows scattered about. The comforter still held her scent. Amanda's computer was on her desk, covered in a thin layer of dust. Wonder of wonders—the FBI hadn't stolen all her personal things the way they had Evelyn's. Maybe search warrants only applied to the living.

Charlie sat on the edge of the bed for a moment, soaking in the presence of his younger child. He missed Amanda down to his bones. He missed Jellybean and Cricket inside every cell of his body. What was he to do with his life now that everyone he loved had gone? It was like all the color had been sucked out of his world.

Charlie didn't fight the waterworks. But eventually he opened his eyes and decided he would keep on somehow. There were animals to feed and water. Maybe now was the time to get another dog for company. Maybe even a border collie like Jordi.

Through his tears, Charlie noticed a small corner of bright blue paper sticking from beneath Amanda's computer keyboard. He found it curious, maybe because it didn't match the rest of the room. He pushed himself from the bed and yanked it loose.

It was a vacation brochure for Bayberry Island's Mermaid Festival. Tucked in its pages was a piece of white memo paper from Amanda's job. In her handwriting he saw this: *"9 months from now. Pop-Pop's 70th b-day, same hotel??? Same rooms? Check ferry schedule, block out vacation, remind Evie. Festival 3rd wk Aug."*

Charlie froze where he stood, the pieces falling into place in his mind. Evie had, in fact, planned to take vacation this week, the third week of August. Today was his seventieth birthday. He and Ginny had taken the girls to the festival once.... What was it, almost twenty years ago now? Had Amanda planned to re-create that happy time for his birthday?

He felt a huge smile break out across his face. So that's how Evie had done it—she had used plans made by Amanda nine months before for her escape. Evie and Chrissy were on Bayberry Island, at least they had been, at one point. Surely, Charlie would have heard if agents had found them, if not a personal phone call, then at least from the news.

No. Evie had likely left before the FBI came looking for them. She was so smart. All that running had made her focused and strong, and Charlie knew if anyone could get through this, it would be his Evelyn.

He suddenly knew in his heart that his girls would be all right. He thanked God for their mystery helper, whoever it might be.

The kitchen phone rang. For fifty years now, Charlie had resisted getting a phone upstairs, but he was too old to keep running up and down the steps like this. Maybe it was time to get with the times.

"Hold yah horses! I'm comin'!"

Evie and Christina spent the later part of the morning on the beach with the dogs. Mr. T and Earl never left their side, even when they waded into the gentle surf and swam around. The dogs paddled out with them, sometimes barking, then swimming away only to come back and bark some more. It felt to Evie as if they had been assigned bodyguard duty, and she appreciated their service.

"Silly dogs!" Christina reached out to touch Mr. T's big head. "Look! He's a seal!"

Evelyn thought back to the events of that morning. Christina had woken up smiling, and her first question of the day was *"Where's Sir Clancy?"* Evie had sat on the edge of the guest bed and explained that he'd had to go to work at the police station and he would be home later.

"Can we go see him there?"

"Not today."

"Is he catching all those bad guys?"

"If there are any bad guys, yes, he will catch them."

"You sure?"

Evie had pulled Christina into her arms and hugged her tight. "I'm sure, Jellybean."

"Did he got Mr. Richard, too?"

Evelyn had done everything in her power not to flinch. This was, officially, the first time Christina had ever mentioned him. She had endured four supervised play sessions with Wahlman in the child protective services agency back home, but she never talked about those visits nor asked any questions about Richard. Evie and Pop-Pop had explained to her that Richard was a new friend who wanted to get to know her. It seemed as if Christina had no reaction to him, one way or the other.

But somewhere in the recesses of her four-year-old brain, she had formed an opinion, and it hadn't been favorable.

Evelyn steadied herself and held Christina away so she could check her expression. "Mr. Richard is a bad guy?"

Christina had nodded.

"Why do you say that?"

Christina looked around the guest room and gave a quick shrug of her shoulders. "We had to leave because of him."

"What?"

"I don't want to talk about him anymore."

Evelyn had watched in amazement as Christina jumped out of bed and went to the bathroom. Then she calmly went out to the dining room table to play with her paper dolls.

Evelyn kept an eye on her niece while she made steel-cut oats and fruit for breakfast, absolutely stunned by the conversation they'd had. Clearly, Chrissy understood more than they had given her credit for.

That's when they heard a knock on the front door, and she had caught Christina before she opened it. Evie peeked out the front window to see it was Annie, and told Christina to go ahead.

"Annie, Annie, Annie, Annie!" Christina had launched herself into Annie's arms.

"How are you guys this morning?" Annie had kissed

Christina on the cheek and sat her down, then handed Evelyn a bag from a store called the Wilbury Drug & Dime. "I did a little shopping for you."

Evelyn had looked inside. Right. Two different shades of hair dye—one a deep copper and the other a dark brown. She raised her eyes to Annie.

"Clancy suggested these. I hope they're okay with you." She was already headed down the front porch steps. "If you need anything at all, call me or Rowan. We're always around."

Evelyn's mouth had hung open.

"Bye, Annie!" Christina said.

"Bye, Jellybean!"

"Thank you," Evelyn had said.

And now they bobbed along with the dogs in the warm, shallow waves, a woman with very short dark hair and a little kid with a red buzz cut.

After they lounged around on their towels for a bit, warming up in the sun, they decided to head back into the house for lunch. The dogs ran ahead of them, barking like fiends, while Evelyn carried their gear and her niece. She cleared the top edge of the pathway and plopped Christina down in the grass.

"Aunt Cricket?"

"Just a second, sweetie." She wrestled with the towels and tried to keep her sun hat out of her eyes while she searched her pockets for Clancy's house key. That's when she saw him—a big no-nonsense-looking guy who was obviously a federal agent. Evelyn dropped everything and grabbed Christina, tearing across the backyard. It was a reflex, but she had no idea where she was headed. The man jogged down the deck steps, then rested his hands on his hips like he was completely baffled.

So much for bodyguards—the dogs seemed thrilled to see the man. Earl had his paws on his chest and Mr. T was rolling around on his back with joy. Both of their tails were wagging uncontrollably.

Evelyn stopped running. Christina buried her face in her shoulder. Wait a minute. . . .

Dark curly hair. Blue eyes. God's gift to women.

"Look, I'm sorry to startle you." He cocked his head and stared at her. "I . . . uh, do we know each other from somewhere?"

It was Duncan! Her answer came out as a hoarse whisper. "We are Clancy's houseguests."

One of his thick dark eyebrows shot high on his forehead. "Oh, *reeeeealy*?"

"Was he expecting you today?"

For some reason, he found that question particularly funny. "Naw. I'm a little earlier than usual."

"Maybe I'd better call him," Evelyn said.

"Maybe you should."

"I know you have a key, but you can't stay at my house right now, dude."

"It does seem pretty crowded with your wife and kid and all. I know it's been a while since we've talked, but holy hopscotching Jesus, you work fast!"

Clancy tilted back in his office chair. "It's good to see you. Welcome home. How are things?"

His brother sighed. "Oh, you know."

"No, I don't."

"I know." Duncan grinned. "But I'm good. Lots of changes now with our withdrawal, but just because the troops leave doesn't mean the problems are gone."

"So you'll be doing another tour?"

"I go wherever and whenever they tell me. It's my job. How's everybody?"

"Good. Mom's health is about the same, but, big news—she's giving up being Grand Poobah of the merms."

Duncan's eyes went wide. "No way! Are you shittin' me?"

Clancy shook his head. "Nope. She's finally letting it go."

"Thank God!" Duncan closed his eyes in relief. Clancy knew if there was anyone who disliked the mermaid more than he did, it was Duncan. "Wait. Does that mean . . . has Rowan . . . ?"

"God, no. I think Ma's finally given up trying to convince Rowan to join, so she got another lady to take her place."

Duncan nodded. "That's a relief. So how's Da? Do our parents still hate each other?"

Clancy held out his hands out. "I have no idea. I think last year's cookout was the last time they spoke, but I try not to get involved."

"Yeah, 'avoid all preexisting Charlie Foxtrots.' That's what my first unit commander always said. How about Rowan and Ash?"

"They're great. You'll get all the deets when you sleep there for the duration of your shore leave."

Duncan burst out laughing. Clancy stared at his brother, mulling it over. He had no idea how much to tell him about Evie.

"Spit it out."

"What?" Clancy took his feet off his desk.

"What's going on?"

"With what?"

Duncan put his elbows on Clancy's desk and lowered his voice. "Dude, they got cable at all major airports, and I didn't get here by rowboat."

Clancy frowned at him.

"It took me a minute, but I eventually put it together. Man, I'll tell you what: she looks better as a brunette. The kid's a cutie, too, despite the Ronald McDonald hair. How about you tell me the part of this I'm missing?"

Clancy said nothing.

"I'm damn sure missing something, right? Because my brother the fucking Eagle Scout is *harboring a fugitive.*"

"The only thing you're missing is the big picture."

"Then hook me up."

At that moment, Clancy decided it wasn't enough that the door was closed—he needed to lock it, too.

Once he did, he stayed standing and dropped his voice to just above a whisper.

"I'm working on it."

"Anything I can do to help?"

Clancy crossed his arms over his chest and smiled at Duncan. His brother could be an ass, but he could count on him when it really mattered. "She hasn't done anything wrong—well, technically, she did take the kid across state lines in violation of a custody ruling, but the congressman is not on the up-and-up."

"That's a shocker."

"I got Mickey Flaherty on it."

Duncan squinted at him. "Whoa. I thought for sure he'd retired from all the Secret Squirrel shit."

"He's only thirty-two."

"Oh, I'm well aware of that. In his line of work, anytime you're still alive is the right time to retire."

"I don't even know exactly what he does."

"Better that way. So how's he helping you?"

Clancy paced the office. "He's working with an IT friend of Evie's. The three of us are in constant contact. We're covering all the bases—the congressman's finances, sex life, physical and mental health, personal enemies. Apparently, Mickey's almost got Wahlman's chief of staff ready to turn on him. He's working on the guy's wife, too."

"Mickey's always had skills with the ladies."

They were quiet for a moment.

"Look, Duncan, the woman at my house—"

"Evelyn from Maine."

Clancy nodded.

"You know, there's something else vaguely familiar about her. I've seen her before the news stories. I can't put my finger on it."

"She was a tourist here eighteen years ago. The summer I was fourteen. I wouldn't think you'd remember her, though."

Duncan blinked a few times in surprise. "Well, whaddya

know?" Then he stood and grabbed his duffel. He gave Clancy a big, hard hug. "You look good, bro. If there's anything you need, I got your back."

"Thanks."

"Does the fam know what's going on with your girl?"

"They figured it out. Both Rowan and Mom called me this morning to talk about Evie. They really like her and have sworn to secrecy, but they're worried about me catching hell for helping her."

Duncan nodded. "And Da?"

"He doesn't know jack. Something like this would freak him out."

Duncan laughed. "The mayor always seems to be the last to know." He headed for the door.

"So, you gonna let Ma know you're here or make her worry until tomorrow night?"

"I'm on my way to see her right now." Duncan's hand touched the doorknob and froze there. "So this Evie . . . she had long, wavy hair back then, didn't she?"

"Yep."

"So she came here for help? You stayed in touch all these years?"

Clancy laughed. "No. She never wrote me after that summer, and I never saw her again, until Friday, when she showed up here, trying to stay under the radar with her niece. We recognized each other, and she confided in me."

Duncan spun around. He had an odd look on his face, but Clancy couldn't pinpoint what was wrong. "What?"

"Nothing." Duncan laughed uncomfortably. "So it was fate, eh? A coincidence that you found each other again?"

"More fate than coincidence, I think."

"Interesting. Catch you later, bro."

With that, Clancy's hard-to-read big brother was gone.

Eighteen years ago ...

Ah, man. This was it. Evie's fingers slid along the inside of Clancy's wrist and brushed down the center of his outstretched palm. She took one step forward — and she was gone. Her scent stayed in the air for an instant before it was washed away by the breeze.

She walked off between her mom and dad and headed up the ferry gangway.

Right then, Clancy felt like a museum specimen or psychology experiment on public display. Even Old John noticed he was bawling. The ferry conductor winked at him and gave him a salute. Maybe other people, even Old John, understood how it felt to be so in love with a girl that your heart couldn't keep beating when she left. Maybe Clancy wasn't the only guy in the world whose bones and guts felt like they were being ripped from his body because *she* had just walked away.

Evie leaned against the outer railing of the ferry for a good five minutes, staring at him, the wind tossing around her long brown hair. She started crying, too. It was too much. She waved good-bye one last time and disappeared into the passenger cabin.

The ferry horn made its racket, and the big, smelly

beast pulled away, bound for Nantucket. Clancy had no idea how long he stood there, stiff on the outside and crumbling on the inside.

Chip suddenly appeared at his shoulder. "I know you really liked her. I don't blame you. She was awesome." He patted Clancy on the back real quick, then pulled his hand away. There was a big difference between being a friend and being completely dweebish, and Clancy was glad Chip knew the difference. "I'll stand here with you if you want."

Clancy couldn't thank him, because trying to talk would make him cry harder. He stayed there until the dark plume of the ferry's diesel smoke disappeared over the horizon. "I'd better go home," he told Chip.

"I'll walk with you."

They were on the boardwalk when he sensed that Mickey Flaherty just snuck up behind them. The stale Marlboro stink traveling upwind was always a dead giveaway. Clancy ignored him. He really wasn't in the mood for whatever Mickey had to contribute.

"So the fish bitch got you after all."

Clancy twisted around, his arm already cocked. Chip held him back, growling at Mickey. "Leave him alone!"

"Ha!" Mickey started dancing around the two of them, doubled over with laughter. "We *told* you the mermaid was gonna pop a cap in your ass for being so disrespectful! And look at you now, the Prince of Bayberry Island just cryin' like a baby."

"He's an asshole. Let's just keep walkin'."

Maybe that was true, but Clancy knew even assholes could be right every once in a while.

By the time he arrived at the Safe Haven, he felt numb. The sadness sat like a big lump in his gut, but the crying had stopped, and now he had no idea what to do with himself. Evie was gone.

He headed across the lawn and down the family's stairs to Haven Beach. It was a cloudy morning. The rest of his family was probably helping his dad set up for the closing ceremonies. He had promised he would be there, too, but right now he just couldn't face anyone.

Clancy shoved his hands in the pockets of his shorts and walked, heading nowhere. He realized he'd never again be able to stroll along this beach without thinking of her—how soft her skin was, how sweet she tasted and smelled, how happy she made him feel.

As soon as Clancy turned back, he saw a figure running toward him. He knew who it was, even from this distance. Perfect form, great speed, effortlessly long strides eating up the beach—it was Duncan.

It took about two minutes for them to meet up.

"Mom sent me to look for you."

"Well, you found me, Sherlock."

"What's your problem, dude?" Duncan leaned down and looked up into Clancy's face like he was a lost kid at Island Day. He made a fake pouty face. "Did Felicity go home?"

"Shut up."

Duncan chuckled, swinging his arm around Clancy's shoulders. "Look, I'm telling you straight up—fourteen is too young to become stuck on one girl. It's not healthy, okay? You're not even a man yet, and men are supposed to spend, like, ten to twenty years checking out all the options before they make a choice."

"Thanks, Dr. Ruth."

"Clancy. Dude. I'm trying to be a helpful and understanding big brother, for real."

"I'm honored to benefit from the vast experience of a sixteen-year-old."

"Hey, it's two more years than you got, suckah."

They walked quietly for a few moments; then Duncan patted him on the back, and not very gently. "You need to get over her, man. Move on. It was a summer fling, and they never amount to anything."

"This one will. She promised to write me."

Duncan shook his head. "They all do."

"Evie is different."

"Whatever you say, champ." Duncan bumped his knuckles against Clancy's biceps. "You're gonna make it. You can't see it now, but one day you won't even remember that girl's name."

Chapter Eighteen

At least she wasn't half naked.

That was the mantra Evelyn repeated to herself as Clancy drove up a small gravel road to his mother's house. Tonight was the annual Flynn family cookout, and Clancy assured her there was no reason the two McGuinness girls needed to hide behind costumes. No one ever attended their cookout except family. That certainly made things smoother with Christina, since she now refused to wear her pirate ensemble. After they had returned from viewing the children's play the previous day, Chrissy insisted she was a mermaid.

Mermaid Jellybean.

But since she didn't have a mermaid ensemble yet, tonight she was dressed as a kid: a light cotton hoodie, shorts, and sport sandals, along with the Boston Red Sox ball cap Clancy had given her.

Evie, on the other hand, was greatly relieved to make her debut as a nonmermaid. She had chosen a simple khaki skirt, a white lace-trimmed fitted T-shirt, and sandals. And, for the first time since arriving on Bayberry, she accessorized. She chose a simple pair of gold dangly earrings that Clancy said looked "chic" with her new hairdo.

Maybe he was right. Now a dark brunette, Evie had played with smoothing down her short pieces of hair instead of spiking them up. The result—she'd gone from Brigitte Nielsen to Audrey Hepburn in a single afternoon.

They parked the Jeep along the road and walked together through the rickety gate and down the walkway, Clancy holding the side dish Evie had prepared. Mona's cedar shingle house was cute—along the lines of Clancy's—with a brightly painted front door and a huge variety of garden flowers. Evie took a deep breath. She was nervous, no doubt, but there would be only one person she didn't know tonight.

Frasier Flynn, the family patriarch.

Clancy whispered into her ear. "Remember what I told you about my parents. If, God forbid, you find yourself trapped in a situation where you're tempted to try to smooth things over between them, just say you have to go to the bathroom."

Christina raced ahead under an old arbor and into the side yard, getting a hardy welcome from everyone. Ash gave her a high five—which was a low five for him. "It's lean, mean Jellybean!"

"Hi, Mr. Ass." The joke never seemed to get old with this crowd.

Suddenly, Christina backed away from Rowan. Oh, crap. No one had even thought about Chrissy's reaction to seeing the mermaid without her tail.

Rowan got on her knees in the grass and motioned for Chrissy to come near. Evie watched, fascinated, as her niece cautiously approached her idol.

"I am sorry, sweetie. I forgot to tell you that sometimes, mermaids who spend a lot of time on land wear regular clothes. See, because I love a human—"

"Flatterer," Ash whispered.

"I have to blend in with life on the island. Do you understand?"

Christina nodded. Rowan gave her a big hug and a kiss on the cheek. "Would you like some lemonade?"

Once that little drama played out, Evie was welcomed

with equal enthusiasm, getting hugs from everyone there, including Ash and Nat this time.

But not Duncan. He shook her hand formally. "Nice to see you again. Sorry to freak you out yesterday."

"Oh, it was nothing." She smiled at him kindly. "Was just a little surprised to see you standing there."

"You look lovely tonight," Rowan said.

"Thank you."

Annie leaned in. "*Love* your hair color."

Evie laughed. "Do you? I had a private consultant choose the shade."

She already felt calmer, thanks to the friendly greeting, and was relieved that Frasier hadn't arrived yet. She was still a little hesitant to meet him, though Clancy had helped her prepare in advance for the encounter. He assured her that the mayor wasn't known for his keen powers of observation, and wouldn't make the connection between the woman standing in front of him in his estranged wife's yard and the whole kidnapping, worldwide manhunt thing. They had agreed that Evie should be as vague as possible with Frasier but not avoid him entirely. If he learned who Evie was, Clancy said Frasier would be torn between his duties as mayor and Clancy's boss, and his role as a dad.

Evie kissed Mona's cheek. "Everything looks lovely."

"Thank you, my dear." She took the casserole dish from Clancy's hands. "Does this need heating or refrigeration?"

"The fridge would be great until we're ready to eat, thanks."

Mona peered through the glass lid. "It looks delicious. May I ask what it is?"

"Sure—a quinoa salad with sautéed kale, pears, and roasted almonds."

Mona's eyes widened. "Well, doesn't that sound interesting? Be right back."

Once her mother was in the house, Rowan draped an

arm over Evie's shoulder. "She has no flippin' idea what you just said." Everyone laughed.

The backyard was set up with a large charcoal grill, horseshoe pit, badminton net, and a fire grate surrounded by a variety of lawn chairs and side tables. The bonfire was ready to light. And under a large sycamore, Mona had created a charming dining area right out of Martha Stewart's magazine. She'd covered a long table with crisp summery white linens and mismatched vintage china and glassware. Chairs of every description and size were pulled alongside. In the middle of everything was a lush centerpiece of wildflowers, sea grass, cattails, and shells. It was simple and unpretentious, yet one of the most beautiful arrangements Evie had ever seen.

Just then, she noticed one chair had been topped with a child's booster seat in preparation for Chrissy.

Clancy put his lips to her ear. "She borrowed it from a neighbor."

"How kind of her."

"This evening is very important to my mom. She does this every Wednesday of festival week, without fail. She wants us to all be together in the same way, year after year. Like a ritual."

Evie allowed her eyes to meet his. She tried to fight it off, but an overwhelming sadness washed over her. Her mother had been the same way. Christmas, Easter, birthdays—all held together with the thread of ceremony, doing things the same way time and time again. It was a big part of why her childhood always made sense.

"I miss this. A lot."

Clancy kissed her cheek. "It's here for you tonight. Right now. I want you to know that my woo-woo family is your woo-woo family."

She was grateful he made her laugh.

A voice bellowed from the side of the house. "By the look of this crowd I'd say there's been a mass escape at the Municipal Lockup!"

"Prepare to be schmoozed," Clancy whispered. "Just be yourself."

The tall and still handsome Frasier Flynn strolled across the lawn like he owned the place, which, according to Clancy, he did not. Mona had rented this house when they separated two years before.

Frasier went around the yard hugging and kissing everyone and slapping his sons on the back. Jellybean had decided to hang on to Evie's leg during the commotion, and she couldn't blame her.

"Clancy? Would you do the honors?"

"Da, this is my old friend Evie. We met back in school."

"A pleasure." Frasier kissed the top of her hand. "I can't imagine why my son waited so long to add you to our festivities, but we are so pleased you're here."

Clancy patted Chris on the ball cap. "And this is Jellybean."

Frasier's manner softened immediately, and it was obvious that he'd had kids of his own. He squatted down. "Hi there. I'm Clancy's dad. It's good you're a Red Sox fan."

"Hi." She peeked around Evie's thigh. "You Rowan's dad, too? I saw her castle. I'm allowed to play there if I want."

Frasier smiled sweetly. "Yes, and I'm Duncan's dad, too. Maybe I'll see you over at the castle someday." He rose up, and winked at Clancy, then helped himself to the beer tap.

Just then, Mona returned from the kitchen. Evie saw her spine stiffen and her lips tighten. Her eyes fixed on her husband's back, and he seemed to turn around instinctively. Their eyes flashed at each other, but no words were exchanged.

The meal was delicious, healthy, and varied. Mona placed a huge tureen of fish soup on the table to start everyone off, and Evie moaned with pleasure at the first chunky spoonful of cod, clams, mussels, and prawns swimming in a rich, seasoned broth.

Though the chatter was loud, Christina's little voice broke through the noise.

> *In Dublin's fair city*
> *Where girls are so pretty . . .*

And before Evie knew what was happening, the whole table erupted in song. Glasses of wine and mugs of beer were raised as they made their way through two verses.

Christina's eyes remained wide with surprise through the whole rendition. When it was done she slapped her palms on the tablecloth. "You *know* the mussel song?"

The rest of dinner was a joyous, loud, fun event. Mona served roasted lamb, grilled salmon, fresh green beans and summer squash, homemade bread, and roasted rosemary potatoes. The quinoa salad was quickly consumed.

Mona reached around Christina and patted Evie's hand. "Now I have to be honest. I wasn't sure about that salad, but it really was very good."

Evie smiled and thanked her.

One thing was obvious—everyone except Frasier had avoided asking Evie questions about her life. For every one of Frasier's inquiries—*where she was from, what she did for a living, how long she planned to stay on the island, and where, exactly, was she staying*—Evie had to come up with a mostly honest and fairly vague answer until Clancy, or someone, could change the subject. At one point, Christina looked like she was gearing up to contribute to the conversation, so Mona rushed her inside to use the facilities.

"But I don't *have* to go!" she said, just as the kitchen screen door closed.

Duncan was as rowdy as anyone else at the table, but he never addressed Evie directly or looked at her when she spoke. She had to admit it bothered her. Obviously,

he didn't like her or approve of Clancy protecting her—
or both.

After cleaning up the main meal, Evie helped Mona,
Annie, and Rowan bring out coffee and dessert—a
freshly baked rice pudding with a salted caramel sauce.
No, it wasn't exactly one of her feed-the-speed recipes,
but it was *unbelievable*. Chrissy shoveled it in, making
humming noises and smacking her lips as she went.

"That's how I feel, Jellybean," Nat told her.

Before the dishes were cleared, Rowan and Ash
fetched glasses and two bottles of champagne. "We
thought we'd make a little toast this evening," Rowan
said, filling everyone's glass. "To celebrate all of us being
together."

"Oh, how perfectly lovely!" Mona smiled, raising her
glass.

Ash cleared his throat. "Oh, and also, Rowan and I
are getting married."

Everyone exploded with surprised laughter and
shouts of joy. Evelyn felt honored to witness the happiness and tears everyone shared. Even Duncan beamed,
appearing more lighthearted than he'd been all evening.

The engagement celebration went on for many long
minutes. Then Christina asked, "Which castle will you
live in? The one under the sea or the one on land?"

The evening wound down and everyone moved to the
fire. Since Clancy could be called away at any time, he
was the only adult not drinking wine or beer. In addition
to the champagne, Evelyn had enjoyed some chilled pi-
not grigio, and she couldn't remember the last time she'd
felt relaxed enough to sip a glass of wine.

Throughout the evening, she'd heard plenty of stories
about life as a Flynn kid, and from what she could tell, it
was a typical family dynamic, filled with rivalries, loyal-
ties, arguments, territories, and a lot of laughter. As
adults, Clancy and Rowan were tight, but Duncan
seemed more detached. It made sense. He'd spent a total
of about six weeks on the island in the last twenty years.

Evie excused herself and took Christina in the house, because this time she really did have to go. They didn't take more than ten minutes, but by the time she and Chrissy returned to the circle of chairs, everything had changed.

Clancy stood on one side of the flames and Duncan the other. Nat and Ash were on the edge of their chairs, as if on alert.

"That's enough, the two of you. Sit down." Frasier glanced at Clancy. "Duncan hasn't even been home two days and you two have to get into it like this?"

Clancy laughed. "*Me*, Da? Are you joking?"

Annie hopped up and went over to Evie, gathering Chrissy. "I'll take Jellybean inside again."

Evie said there was no need, and that they would be leaving.

That's when she felt Clancy's hand grab hers. "Please stay. You need to hear this."

"No, I don't."

Clancy squeezed her hand and locked his gaze with hers. "Please. Trust me. You'll want to hear what he has to say."

She moved closer to Clancy's side, cautiously taking a peek at Duncan's tensed face in the firelight. The brothers were obviously arguing, but she didn't know why it had anything to do with her, unless . . .

Evie went rigid. *Duncan was going to turn her in!*

"Tell her." Clancy's voice was laced with fury. Evie began to shake. *After all this? This was how it would end?*

She whispered to Clancy. "You told me we were safe."

"You are safe."

"So Duncan didn't . . ."

Clancy suddenly realized what she was afraid of. He hugged her tight to his hip. "No, Evie. Not that. No worries." Clancy paused. "Go ahead and tell her, Duncan."

The big man shrugged, the light throwing shadows across his hard face. "I ripped up your letter."

"My . . . what?"

"Your letter. The letter you sent my brother, back

when you were kids. I got it out of the mailbox and I ripped it up and tossed it in the trash. He never knew you'd written."

Evie let go with a laugh of disbelief. This was so strange—impossible. *"Why would you do something like that?"*

"Because I was an ass."

Frasier ran a hand over his eyes. "Oh, Jesus."

Mona let go with a soft cry of disappointment.

"But . . . ?" Evie looked at Clancy again. "I don't understand. Why did he do that? Why would he care if I wrote you?"

"Because he was jealous and angry. He still is."

Duncan relaxed his stance. "Come on, man. I didn't mean anything by it."

"Are you fucking *kidding*?" Clancy let go of Evie and stomped toward the fire. Nat and Ash stood up. "You meant it, you mean son of a bitch. You said Evie didn't care about me and would never contact me, but when she did, you couldn't stand that you were wrong and that I'd really found someone special. You had to squash my happiness like a bug."

Frasier stood up, too. "Boys, this is enough."

Evie put her hand on Clancy's shoulder and felt him tremble as he answered his father. "I am not a boy, Da. And neither is Duncan. He needs to man up here."

Duncan shook his head. "You don't have any idea what it means to man up, dude."

"That's it."

Clancy tore around the circle, slipping through Ash and Nat's body blocks. Duncan was already barreling toward him, fists at his side. He used his chest to shove Clancy back into the center of the lawn.

Evie covered her eyes. She had no interest in watching this kind of primitive caveman display.

Suddenly, she heard all movement stop, and dared to look up. The two brothers were breathing hard, staring into each other's eyes, arms stiff at their sides. It was a standoff. They did have some self-control, after all. Duncan took a step back. He held his arms wide, open palms facing Clancy. "Hit me."

Clancy's nostrils flared.

"You two will never grow up." That was Rowan.

"Please don't do this to each other." That was Mona.

"They need to sort this out once and for all," Frasier said. "Maybe it's time Clancy beat the hell out of Duncan. It's been a long time comin.'"

"Da's right. Go ahead and hit me." Duncan's voice was strangely flat. "I fucked with your life and it wasn't right." His dark eyes flashed toward Mona. "Sorry about the language, Ma."

"You're right. That's *exactly* what you did. You completely—" Clancy glanced at his mother, too. She was shaking her head and crying. Clancy returned his attention to Duncan. "That was not your decision to make, asshole. My feelings for Evie were none of your goddamn business. You changed the course of my *life*."

Slowly, Duncan got right in front of Clancy. "So make me pay."

Evie saw Clancy's right arm twitch and she was about to jump on him when he relaxed. She went to his side again. Everyone closed the circle tighter.

Suddenly, Clancy smiled. "I don't need to hit you. Do you know why?"

Duncan said nothing.

"Because it didn't work, dude. Evie is here with me now. Your jealousy was no match for love. Being strong enough to love someone, strong enough to risk everything by loving someone—*that* is manning up, bro."

"Yes! Yes!" Mona clapped her hands.

Frasier sighed. "Baby Jesus on the B Train."

"I'm sorry to have ruined the cookout, Ma." Clancy turned to Evie. "We'd better go."

"Wait." Duncan came up to Evie and Clancy. "Look, I'm sorry for what I did. It was wrong. I will make it up to you both."

Clancy stared at Duncan, his mouth pulled tight. Evie couldn't tell if he was still angry, or just plain hurt. "Not necessary. Good night, everyone," he said.

"I have nuthin' more to say to you, Mr. Wahlberg. I told you on the phone yesterday that you shouldn't waste your time comin' up here. Good-bye, now."

"There's no one else I can talk to about this, Charlie. Not a soul. You're the person who needs to hear it."

The farmer leaned against the doorframe of the old house and considered him carefully.

"It's about Amanda. Please." Richard approached him carefully. He was a little concerned he'd be punched again.

"Ayuh, take a seat, then. I'll be out with something for us. You like beer?"

"Beer? You told me you don't drink."

"I lied. I love a good pilsner at the end of a hot summer day. But is it safe for you to have it with your heart condition?"

Richard couldn't help but laugh. Not a damn soul but his cardiologist cared enough these days to ask about his health. All his close friends had turned out to be neither close nor friends. As was now apparent, his relationships had been about what he could do for *them*, and when he wasn't in the position to do much at all, they disappeared. And yet here was a man who had every right to hate him, asking him if it was safe for him to have a beer.

Richard figured any ill effects from the brew would be more than offset by a few moments of honest, human conversation.

"Sure, Charlie. That would be wonderful. Thank you."

He took a seat in one of the porch rockers, almost immediately feeling his pulse slow and his blood pressure stabilize. He leaned his head back and enjoyed the view of the early-evening sun on the rolling fields and the peaceful, blue mountain lake beyond. Maybe when all this was over—with or without Christina—he'd find a place like this to live. Silence. Beauty. Something real and alive. Something that had nothing to do with politics or power.

Charlie came out the screen door and placed a frosty mug on a little wooden table.

"What time does the sun set up here?"

"Same as it does down there."

"What are you growing, Charlie?"

"In these pastures?"

"Yes, everything we can see from up here on the porch."

Charlie took a long draw on his beer and smacked his lips. "Hay."

"Oh."

"You don't know what hay looks like?"

"Well, yes, I suppose I do. I've just never thought much about it."

"Ayuh, this year I've got sixty acres of alfalfa, twenty-five of mixed clover, and a hundred of tall fescue."

"And what do you do with it?"

Charlie laughed. "I sow it, fertilize it, maintain it, cut it, bale it, and sell it at auction as animal feed. You know—horses, cattle, sheep, goats, and even llamas."

"I never imagined."

"Ayuh, and what do you do at your job?"

"I fertilize."

Charlie nodded quietly. "So what is it you have to say? I don't think I need to tell you that you're not my favorite person and never will be."

"That's why I'm here." Richard put the mug down. "Charlie, I've come to apologize."

The farmer's rocker ceased creaking. He concentrated on his beer and didn't make eye contact with Richard.

"Just yesterday, I learned something horrible. I found out that when Amanda worked for me, my chief of staff took it upon herself to handle the ... situation ... without consulting me. I only just now learned what she did to Amanda, and I was shocked and sickened."

Charlie swiveled his head. "You're blaming your second-in-command for how you treated my daughter?"

"I'm not blaming. I take full responsibility for having an inappropriate relationship with Amanda."

"But all the rest is someone else's fault?"

"Charlie, I came here to share what I've just learned. For the first time, I know how badly Amanda was treated and how much it must have hurt her. My chief of staff—well, she's now my former chief of staff—gave Amanda money for an abortion and said it came from me. It didn't. If I had known she was pregnant, which I did not, I never would have asked her to do that."

Charlie's lips trembled.

"And then my chief of staff told Amanda that if she didn't leave DC immediately—"

"She might disappear the way young women in trouble sometimes do in Washington. Like the young interns and staffers who are never heard from again."

Richard gripped the armrests.

"After Amanda died, Evelyn told me the whole story, including how you threatened my little girl."

"It was a travesty. My chief of staff was just trying to intimidate her. She was never in any danger." Richard hung his head. "Now that I know the truth about all this, I felt it was only right to apologize from the bottom of my heart."

Charlie was quiet for a long moment before he spoke. "What do you expect from me, Wahlman? You want me to reach out and pat you on the head and say all is forgiven?"

"I . . ."

"If I ever get there, I'll be sure to let you know."

"Fair enough, but I didn't come to win your forgiveness, just to tell you the truth and let you know how much I regret all of it."

Charlie sighed. "You say you're truly sorry?"

"I am."

"Prove it."

Richard reeled back. "How would I do that?"

"Simple. If you feel remorse for what you did to my Amanda, then let Evelyn go. Call off the FBI. Stop this circus. Let my girls come home where they belong."

"I . . . I don't even know that I can do that, Charlie. Now that the federal government has opened a case—"

"Ayuh, more fertilizer." Charlie sipped his beer. "You can do anything you want and you know it. Just make it happen, like you made the custody decision happen. In honor of Amanda, who suffered terribly at your hands."

"Uh . . ."

"Your chief of staff's hands."

"Yes."

"So stop this ludicrous manhunt and then maybe we can come to some kind of civilized agreement about custody. Christina deserves the adults around her to behave like adults. But only if you call off the FBI."

Richard took a deep breath. "All right. I'll see what I can do." He rose, suddenly feeling a little unsteady on his feet. He checked his watch—his flight was scheduled to leave Augusta in an hour and a half. "May I use your bathroom, please, before I hit the road?"

Charlie began snickering. "Knock yourself out, Congressman. Last door on the left just before you enter the kitchen."

A moment later, Richard stood in the half bath, taking a leak while staring at a copy of one of his old campaign posters, a handful of darts stuck between his eyes and a thousand tiny holes poked in his face.

He was still chuckling as he walked toward the front door, when something caught his eye. On an antique hall table was a brochure. For an instant, the words didn't register. But. Wait. Of all the places . . . it was a brochure for the Bayberry Island Mermaid Festival. What the hell?

Bayberry Island?

Since Richard didn't believe in coincidence, the truth was pretty obvious: Evelyn and Christina had to be on Bayberry Island, and that thoroughly unpleasant police chief knew it. Was he protecting Evelyn McGuinness? Suddenly, the police chief's personal dislike for Richard made perfect sense, and he knew if they found that cop, they would find Evelyn and Christina.

Richard collected himself, trying to subdue the big smile on his face. Things were looking up. Maybe he was right back on track to have everything just the way he wanted it—his career *and* his child.

Richard cleared his throat when he returned to the front porch. "Charlie, as much as I've enjoyed our chat and your bathroom artwork, I need to get going."

The old guy narrowed his eyes at him. "So, you'll let me know?"

"Absolutely." *Not.* "Thanks for the beer."

"How soon can you call off the search?"

"We'll just have to wait and see. I'll be in touch."

"I'm Mermaid Jellybean!"

Yes, she certainly was. With Mona's help, Christina had been transformed into a beautiful junior sea goddess. Her hair was long and luxuriously blond, her tail was loose-fitting silvery blue that gave her legs lots of room to move. It was paired with a matching top, modest in its coverage and decorated with tiny shells and faux coconut fringe. Christina twirled in front of the mirror, until her eyes caught Evie's in the reflection.

"You are so pretty, too."

"Thank you, honey." She added the borrowed earrings and evaluated the total effect.

"You are prettier than anyone ever was pretty in the whole world of prettiness!"

"Wow. That's pretty darn pretty."

"It is."

There was a gentle knock on the door. Evie couldn't help but feel bad for Clancy—he was knocking on the door of his own bedroom. The man had been kicked out so that the girls could use it as a Mermaid Ball dressing room.

"Come on in."

Clancy opened the door and stopped in his tracks. He had obviously come to give her news because he held his cell phone in his hand, but he wasn't saying anything.

She wasn't either. All she could do was gawk. This was the first time she had ever seen Clancy in anything but beach attire or a police uniform. And—whoa—the man cleaned up well.

He wore a white linen suit with a soft blue open collar shirt and a pair of newer Docksiders. He was clean-shaven, and the light fabric accentuated his tanned skin and dark eyes. Evie knew she had to have a goofy love-struck expression on her face, but she couldn't stop staring.

Clancy stared, too. He let his gaze travel up and down her body and let out a whistle. "Holy moly." Then he made sure to comment on Christina, who was already posed for his admiration. "And look at you! I'm sorry, but have we met?" He bent at the waist. "What is your name, gorgeous mermaid?"

She giggled. "I love you, silly Sir Clancy." She ran up and hugged his knees tightly. Evie and Clancy caught each other's eyes, surprised. Then they both broke out in a smile.

"I love you right back, Jellybean."

At that instant, Evie's chest filled and her eyes stung. Sometimes her thoughts could get so far ahead of reality, that she'd even imagined the day that the three of them made a little family here on Bayberry Island. Of course that would require a world without Richard Wahlman— or women's prison.

"Can I go over and tell Evie how pretty she is?"

"Yep!"

As Christina bounced down the hall, Clancy moved closer. He let his fingertip brush across her Evie's collar-bone and over the tops of her breasts. "Damn."

"You like?"

"Uh, I'm sure there's something wrong with lusting

for a woman wearing your sister's dress, but I swear to God I've never seen her in it and if I have, she didn't look like this."

Evie gave a twirl much like the one Christina had just executed, and the wide white skirt sailed around her thighs. The sundress was a kind of retro style, with straps going up and tying around the back of her neck. Mona had given her a pair of antique pearl clip-on earrings that had belonged to Frasier's mother, and Annie, who also wore a size nine shoe, came up with a cute pair of tie-on espadrilles.

Clancy's eyes were huge. "You look like a French vanilla ice cream drizzled with sex sauce."

Evie laughed. "You're pretty sweet yourself." She grabbed him around the waist and pulled him in for a kiss. If Christina happened to see, they would just have to deal with it.

"Oh, man. Okay." Clancy gave himself a quick tap on the cheek. "Evie. I have news. I just got a text."

Her face fell.

"No. Good news. Incredible news." He gave her a reassuring kiss, then wrapped his arms low on her hips. "Remember my buddy who was helping Hal?"

"Of course!"

"Well, he arranged a meeting this afternoon between House ethics investigators, the Justice Department, and Wahlman's wife and chief of staff. They're taking him down."

"What?"

"It's ugly. The chief of staff claims there have been repeated instances of sexual misconduct, and the wife tipped them off about possible misuse of campaign contributions. But"—he glanced behind him to make sure they were alone and lowered his voice—"the important thing for you to know is it looks like Wahlman bribed a court clerk in order to win custody of Christina."

Evie slapped a hand over her mouth.

"My buddy says Wahlman promised the clerk a

better-paying job in exchange for helping him cheat the system."

Evie felt herself began to tremble with relief and joy. "You mean . . . ?"

"It's almost over. So tonight, we're just going to relax and enjoy the Mermaid Ball, because tomorrow the shit is going to hit the fan for Wahlman. Ash has already called a good friend of his in Boston—a criminal defense attorney—who's going to help us out. He'll be here tomorrow to walk you through everything. It's going to be okay, Evie."

She squealed with joy and hugged him as hard as she possibly could. *It was over! She didn't have to run anymore!* Clancy lifted her off the floor.

"You're awfully quiet."

Teresa Apodaca pulled her gaze from the window to stare at Richard with annoyance. She replied to him via her microphone. "We're on a Federal Bureau of Investigations helicopter, Congressman, on our way to rescue a child abduction victim. It's not especially conducive to small talk."

This girl had barely tolerated him during this last week, but Richard assumed she would perk up by the prospect of capturing her prey. Guess not.

The helicopter pitched slightly and he put his hand on his chest. There it was again—that faint fluttery feeling. As soon as this ordeal was over he'd check himself into the Cleveland Clinic for a cardiac follow-up. It was probably just the return of harmless atrial fibrillation, but with his history, he couldn't take that chance.

The special agent in charge glowered at him. "Are you feeling all right, Mr. Wahlman? You seem a little pale."

"I'm fine. I'm just looking forward to finally having my daughter by my side."

Four more FBI special agents were on board, occupied on their computers or cell phones, and Richard sat with his own thoughts for several minutes. His whole life was about to change. As soon as this helicopter landed, he would have his child. He would be a father. And then he could go about the business of getting his career back on track. There was nothing stopping him now.

"So what are your plans with Christina? Have you arranged for child care?"

Richard blinked, trying his best to hide his surprise. "Of course. I plan to hire a nanny."

"So you've already gone through the interviewing and screening process and have hired someone?"

There's a process? "I've narrowed it down. I'm quite close to selecting one."

"Where will you be living?"

Richard was beginning to feel uncomfortable with this interrogation. "I have a suite at the Jefferson right now. But that's only temporary, of course. I'm working closely with a real estate team." He made a note to himself to find a real estate agent.

"I see." When Apodaca resumed looking out the window, Richard could see her reflection in the glass—and she'd just rolled her eyes at him! He chuckled. Apodaca, M.J., Tamara—he was fucking surrounded by smug women! Why him?

"Do you have children, Agent?"

She nodded, still looking away. "Three—ages two, seven, and eight."

He couldn't hide his shock. "With this job? Dear God, how do you make something like that work?"

She smiled at him. "Any way you can, Congressman. But I'm very lucky—my husband has flexible hours and doesn't travel for his job anymore, and my mom is right around the corner. How about you? Do you have extended family nearby?"

Richard leaned back into the seat restraints, not sure if this woman was engaging him in a friendly parenting conversation or lecturing him on how hideously unprepared he was to bring Christina into his life. He found that ludicrous. As a member of the U.S. House of Representatives, he was one in a million—literally. Anyone and everyone could have children. How difficult could it be?

"Have you looked into preschools? Pediatricians? Have you gotten all her medical records from her family . . . I mean the McGuinnesses?"

"Do you have a problem with me, Special Agent?"

She turned her head and looked him in the eye. "No, sir, Congressman Wahlman. No problem at all."

Just then, they approached Bayberry Island. It looked like damn Disney World down there. "What the hell is all that?"

"The Mermaid Ball," Apodaca's sidekick said. "It's the last big party of their festival. You know, like their big finale."

Richard smiled to himself. Certainly, it would be the end of Evelyn McGuinness.

What an evening it had been. Though they weren't quite ready to buy billboard space to announce Evie's identity, they didn't worry much about anyone recognizing her. First of all, she bore almost no resemblance to her publicly circulated photos tonight. With that dress, chic haircut, earrings, and a little bit of makeup, she looked more like a movie star than a fugitive. Secondly, her date was the police chief and she'd been one of the mayor's repeat dance partners—which didn't exactly scream *outlaw* to the tourist crowd.

Clancy was in awe of Evie, and of the happiness unfolding inside him. He was grateful for how everything had come together. By tomorrow morning, Richard Wahlman's case against Evie would start to unravel. He would face charges and the manhunt would be called off. Clancy and Evie could then concentrate on untangling whatever legal predicament remained.

The only thing that marred the otherwise perfect evening was Clancy's feud with Duncan. His big brother had been AWOL until about a half hour ago, when he parked Da's powerboat illegally in an emergency-only spot along the public dock. Yet again, the rules didn't seem to apply to his big brother.

Duncan planned to leave in the morning, and like always, they wouldn't get to the heart of their conflict. Clancy didn't hate Duncan—not at all. But he sure as hell didn't understand him.

Clancy had just finished a rumba with Jellybean when the DJ announced the last song of the ball. "This is a special request, ladies and gentlemen. This song is for everyone, young or old, who is in love tonight."

As planned, that was Nat's cue to deliver Evie into Clancy's arms, then sweep Mermaid Jellybean away. The music began to flow over the dance floor.

Evie looked at him with happy confusion.

"You arranged this?"

"I did."

"So, you remember our song?"

"Of course."

Clancy dipped Evie in his arms, snapped her up, and kissed her hard. He whispered in her ear. "But I do have something to confess."

"Please do," she whispered back.

"I've never really loved the song."

Evie giggled. "The sentiment is good, but you're right— those were some bad years for music."

Clancy held her tight, his hand pressed to the small of her back and his cheek to hers, knowing he had the most precious gift he'd ever received right there in his arms.

He felt it before he heard it. A deep vibration rose up through the boards and into the soles of his feet. Clancy backed away from Evie and spun around. He hadn't been paying attention. His focus had been on Evie and the music had blocked out the noise.

And now they were right on top of them.

Chapter Nineteen

A helicopter and a speedboat barreled right toward them from less than a nautical mile offshore while four other copters headed to the airfield.

Clancy turned to Evie and saw the horror in her eyes. "Get Christina. Come right back here to me."

It was chaos. Tourists who had only moments ago been slow dancing to pop music were now scattering like pins in a bowling alley. People were screaming and running in every direction as one of the helicopters hovered directly overhead, whipping the air into a violent vortex.

"Clancy!" Evie had Christina in her arms. The sight of the little girl's sweet face twisted up and red with panic was the most heart-wrenching thing he'd ever seen. He knew he had to make it right for her. And for Evie.

This was some kind of federal raid, obviously. But why now? Why the hell would the Justice Department swoop down on Evie when they were already preparing charges against Richard Wahlman? Was there no communication between FBI headquarters and their field offices?

Clancy called dispatch. Every officer was already headed to the public dock, and private security from the Oceanaire construction site was on their way, too.

Not that it would make much difference. Local law

enforcement couldn't put an end to whatever badly timed blowout the FBI had on its to-do list, but it *was* their responsibility to see that no one got injured in the process.

Duncan and Da arrived at his side. Clancy's brother stood in front of Evie and Christina, blocking them from the wind.

"Feds." Duncan sounded bored, like a helicopter landing on the Mermaid Ball dance floor was an everyday occurrence. "That's a modified UH-60 Black Hawk. Talk about overkill."

"Four more are headed to the airfield," Clancy said.

"Smaller birds. Leased. Probably national media."

"Ah, shit."

The wind whipped and the noise of the large helicopter became deafening. Everyone backed away from the center of the dock.

"For God's sake, what is this?" Frasier was outraged. "This is the Bayberry Island Mermaid Festival, not a *Die Hard* sequel!"

"What should we do?" Evie remained stoic as she stood right next to Clancy, though Christina continued to cry.

"Let's just take this one step at a time, Evie. Obviously, there's been some miscommunication."

Her eyes flashed with worry, so he reached for her hand. "It's going to be okay. We'll cooperate fully until the situation sorts itself out."

She took a deep breath and for an instant, her gaze locked with his. He understood without her having to say the words—she trusted him. She counted on him. Evie took Christina to a bench away from the wind.

The helicopter's rear and front wheels touched down, and once they were stabilized and the rotors powered off, the doors opened. Five agents spilled out, followed by a slow-moving Wahlman.

A voice called from behind Clancy. "Chief!"

Oh for the love of God, it was Heather Hewes and

her freelance video camera. "Stand back, Heather. Da, get her out of here!"

"No!" Heather slammed her foot on the dock. "I demand freedom of the press! I have a constitutional right to cover this story!" She hoisted her camera to her shoulder and began filming.

She'd finally found some sexy.

Clancy was relieved when Deon arrived with Chip and Jake. "Get everyone a block away from here. I have no idea what's about to go down. And please escort the mayor from the dock."

"What?" Frasier looked stunned.

"Shit, Clancy," was all Deon said.

The FBI Special Agent in Charge marched toward Clancy, with four agents behind her. She looked perturbed.

Clancy smiled at her. "Welcome to Bayberry Island, Special Agent Apodaca."

She wasn't amused. "Good evening, Chief Flynn. As you might guess, things just got mighty complicated for you."

Duncan's deep voice cut through the noise. "What's going on here, Agent?"

She glanced his way, then froze. A flash of recognition lit up her eyes. She examined him from head to toe. "Coronado?"

"Little Creek."

Apodaca nodded. "My husband is retired Team 3, BUD/s 242."

Duncan nodded politely, but didn't share his particulars. "I'm on active duty, ma'am. And I'm the chief's brother."

Wahlman finally joined the party. It had taken him several minutes to walk across the dock.

"We meet again, Chief."

The congressman was pasty and sweaty. He didn't look well.

Wahlman sneered at Clancy. "Well, where are they? Let's get this over with. Chop-chop."

Apodaca rolled her eyes before she addressed Clancy.

"We're here to take Evelyn McGuinness into custody and return the child to her court-appointed custodial parent." The tone of her voice made it clear she wasn't thrilled to be Wahlman's champion. "Regretfully, you will need to come along for questioning, Chief Flynn. Hope you got a good lawyer."

Wahlman grew impatient. "Where the hell is my daughter?"

"I'm afraid there's been some confusion, Congressman." Clancy took a step toward him, and noticed a greenish tint to Wahlman's skin. "You won't be raising Christina as your daughter, because you'll be in prison or at least on house arrest awaiting trial."

Wahlman laughed. "Are you insane?"

Apodaca stepped between the men and pulled Clancy aside. "Something you'd like to share, Chief?"

"Yes. This evening, the Justice Department was presented with evidence that Wahlman bribed a court official. He used his political connections to win custody of Christina McGuinness."

Apodaca closed her eyes for a moment.

"And Wahlman's wife and chief of staff were deposed today in Washington. They won immunity and then threw the good congressman under the bus for a whole range of offenses. The case is expected to go to the grand jury."

Apodaca glared at him. "And just how in the hell do you know all this when I don't?"

"I wish I could tell you, but it's classified."

She tipped her head back and laughed, glancing around at the paper lanterns, fairy lights, and decorations. "You know what, Chief? This is a very pretty little island, but it's kind of like a New England *Twilight Zone.* You got naked people, crazy people, naked and crazy people playing tennis, people dressed up like fairies and mermaids and starfish. You've got kidnappers and Navy SEALs and now you've got sources for classified intel? Seriously, this place cracks my ass up."

Duncan chuckled.

"Check it out for yourself," Clancy said. "Make a few calls to your superiors. See if I'm right."

"Dammit!" The agent's eyes flashed over to where Evie and Christina sat. She barked orders as she jogged off toward the helicopter. "Make sure the suspect stays put. Keep the police chief and Evelyn McGuinness separate."

Just then, Clancy noticed that Wahlman had wandered over to the bench. Evie stood when he approached, and though they kept their distance, they began to talk. Clancy saw Evie's face and shoulders tighten as Wahlman reached out for Christina. The little girl turned away and buried her face in Evie's neck.

That's when Clancy saw Heather crouched behind another bench about twenty feet away from Evie and Wahlman, her camera light on. It hardly mattered. It wasn't as if her footage would be seen by millions on *60 Minutes*, right?

Richard felt nauseous and dizzy, but he'd come too far to give up now. His daughter was just inches from his grasp. He pictured the moment of triumph in detail—a father reunited with his abducted child, posing for the cameras. That image alone would turn the polls around. Even party leadership couldn't resist something that touching.

But where was the FBI? Why weren't they arresting Evelyn McGuinness? Richard looked behind him to see agents standing with Chief Flynn, looking useless, weapons not even drawn. Apodaca had gone back to the helicopter and was now slowly making her way back to the police chief. He was baffled. Why wasn't she going completely Amazon on this McGuinness woman and dragging her off in handcuffs like she deserved?

The kid started crying.

"Give her to me, you crazy bitch."

Evelyn McGuinness stood stiffly and the girl cried

louder. "She belongs with us, Wahlman. She belongs with her family."

"Well, the court says she belongs *to* me!" Oh, Jesus, he wished someone would shut this kid up. She was howling now, the skin of her face and neck getting all splotchy and red and she thrashed in her aunt's arms. She looked like a Tasmanian devil.

"It doesn't work like that. You can't own someone — all you can do is love them, and I don't think you have the slightest idea how to do that."

Richard put his hand on his chest. His heartbeat was erratic. "Shut the hell up and give her to me."

"You cheated us in court. You stole Christina from us by bribing a court official."

He laughed. "So what if I did? You'll never be able to prove any of it!"

Just then, the girl beat her fists on her aunt's chest and kicked her legs, pummeling the woman in the stomach. Richard was horrified. Was this child mentally ill? Or was she simply a product of a poor upbringing? Well, he would change all that soon enough.

He grabbed the girl. For God's sake — she *bit* him! She just chomped down on the flesh between his thumb and forefinger, drawing blood. Richard lost his grip on her and she ran off.

FBI agents suddenly surrounded them.

"Chrissy!" Evelyn McGuinness was restrained by agents as the girl ran down the dock. She screamed at Richard. "What have you *done*?"

Richard yelled at Apodaca, his chest tightening. "Get my kid! Do your fucking job!"

That's when everything went black.

Clancy saw Jellybean hike up her mermaid skirt, yank off her wig, and run barefoot under the lights, heading toward the marina. Evie was already removing her party shoes, itching to run after her niece.

Apodaca grabbed his arm. "We will handle this, Chief. Do you understand?"

"No." Clancy clutched Evie's hand and pulled her to his side. "Please let us get her. She is scared to death. Please. She's just a terrified little girl. Once she's safe we'll go wherever you want us to go."

Apodaca shook her head. "God I hate this assignment." She sighed deeply. "All right." She looked at her agents. "Help them out if need be, but don't crowd the little girl." Just then, Richard collapsed to the dock. "And somebody call the EMTs!"

Clancy and Evie were off. They rounded the corner toward the marina.

"She could be anywhere!" Evie sounded panicked.

"She can't go far. When she sees it's just us, she'll show herself. Besides, I know every hiding place on this marina."

They raced down the dock, peering behind every trash can and piling and bench. She was nowhere. They headed toward the boat slips, where a crowd of vacationers were gathered.

"Anyone seen a little girl?"

"She just ran over there!" A woman gestured with her cocktail toward the shack otherwise known as Sully's Marine Repair..

Clancy heard Evie mumbling to herself. *"Why did I stay here? Oh, God, what have I done?"*

Suddenly, two helicopters hovered overhead, news cameras and blinding spotlights trained on their every move. Duncan was suddenly at his side.

"She went toward Sully's," Clancy told him.

"That's where the FBI left their speedboat."

As soon as Evie heard that, she raced away so fast that Clancy and Duncan remained a good three seconds behind her. They slowed down when they saw the shine of Evic's white dress at the edge of the dock. She was leaning over the railing, calling out to Christina.

Oh, God, no. Jellybean was in the water again?

Suddenly, a speedboat sputtered away from the boatyard, dragging its lines behind. It looked like no one was on board.

"What the hell?" They arrived at Evie's side just in time to see the boat increase its speed in a sudden jerk and head out toward open water. But it wasn't empty. A little mermaid with a red buzz cut was in the captain's chair, staring up at the dock as she moved away, then shielding her eyes from the searchlights.

"Dad's boat," Duncan said.

The brothers and Evie turned back, nearly running over the FBI agents still following them. They raced toward the emergency-only docking area, and Clancy thanked God the rules didn't apply to his brother. He kept glancing out to sea, seeing the speedboat's running lights get farther and farther away. Duncan jumped into the boat first and immediately flipped on the engine. Evie boarded next, while Clancy pulled up the fenders. As soon as he got inside, Evie yelled, "Go!"

Duncan turned on the boat's nighttime running lights and its single searchlight. They picked up speed, heading in the direction they'd last seen Christina.

With the helicopters and engine noise, all conversation on the boat had to be done with shouting.

"The FBI must have left the keys in the boat. They didn't even know how to tie a cleat hitch! How stupid can you get?" Duncan kept his eyes forward.

"What does she know about boats, Evie?"

She scanned the black water, her face frozen in concentration. "Pop-Pop has a power boat on Moose Lake. He's let her drive on his lap a couple times, turn it on and off, and steer."

"Great."

"Well, this ain't Moose Lake," Duncan said.

The news helicopters decided to follow along, making it even harder to see and whipping the water into a frenzy all around them. The sea spray drenched them.

"Can you get those fucking things out of here?"

Clancy grabbed his police radio and reached Chip.

"Tell Agent Apodaca to order all media back. *Order media helicopters back!* They're endangering the child!"

"10-4, Chief! Be safe!"

"We have to have a plan," Duncan said. "Clancy? You want to captain or board?"

"I'll board. She knows me well and won't be as afraid."

Water sprayed. Lights blinded. Duncan went faster.

"Where the hell is she? Where did she go?" Evie was trying her best to keep it together, but Clancy could see she was battling back panic.

Suddenly, Duncan changed direction, heading southeast. "I think I see her!"

"Hold on!" Clancy yelled to Evie.

Duncan pushed Da's boat past its limits, hitting fifteen knots at one point, even though the sea was choppy. Clancy was concerned that Evie would be tossed into the water, but saw how her hands clutched the side of the boat, determination in her eyes. She wasn't going anywhere.

"Got her!" Duncan called out. "Two points off the bow!"

"Oh my God. Is she still in the boat?"

"Can't see yet," Clancy said. "Does she know to put on a life jacket?"

Evelyn raked her hands through her hair. "I don't know! I don't know!"

"Binocs."

Duncan handed a pair of binoculars over his right shoulder and Clancy focused them. Oh, no. He couldn't see her. There was no little head anywhere.

"Is she there? Oh, God, tell me! Is she still in the boat? Please, please be in the boat!"

Just then, he saw movement in the FBI powerboat, a head poking up along the side. "Got her! Got her! She's there!"

Evie gasped in relief.

"Hold on. I estimate two minutes to target." Duncan

pulled back a little on the throttle and kept on a straight course. "Goddamn! Why are these birds still here?"

The helicopters hadn't backed off. They'd moved closer, now probably hovering only thirty feet overhead, their searchlights sweeping everywhere. Thanks to them, this little maneuver would be a hundred times harder than it had to be.

Clancy put his head down, seawater smacking him in the face, limiting his line of sight. "Duncan! Reach under the seat! See if Da's got a bullhorn!"

"Not here!"

"Evie. Hop up."

She reached under her seat and handed him the small megaphone. Clancy turned the power switch, hoping to God the batteries weren't dead.

"Jellybean. Can you slow the boat down?"

"She's looking right at us." Duncan was in perfect alignment to pull alongside.

"Make it go slower if you can," Clancy called out to Chrissy.

The boat jerked, and went faster.

Duncan shouted, "Almost there. This is going to go quick. Are you ready, Clancy?"

"Hold on tight, Jellybean! I'm going to come help you. Grab tight onto anything you can reach and hold on!"

He removed his jacket and shoes and pulled his service weapon from the waistband of his trousers, handing it to Duncan.

They approached the FBI vessel. He stood. Clancy caught Duncan's eye to ensure his brother was ready.

"On my mark!" Duncan pulled up alongside, but they were still going way too fast to attempt something like this. Not that they had any choice.

Duncan edged slightly ahead of the other boat so the instant Clancy spent in midair wouldn't cause him to land in the water—or on the boat's propeller.

"Three!"

He balanced.

"Two!"

Evie shouted, "I love you, Clancy!"

"One!"

Clancy jumped.

Below him was a three-foot-wide band of black sea, and he barely made it. He hit the deck hard and the boat lurched. Christina flew out the other side and hit the water.

Everything he had ever known, seen, and experienced raced through Clancy's mind. He heard Evie's scream somewhere off in the distance and he knew this was it. He would only get one chance.

As the lights swirled and the water sprayed, Clancy dove in after Jellybean, her point of entry into the water firm in his mind's eye.

Freezing cold. Black. Silent. He pushed away any hint of doubt and pushed on. She might rise to the surface. She might not. She might be stunned by the cold. How many seconds did he have before she ran out of air? Before hypothermia set in? The water temperature had to be in the fifties this far from shore.

The searchlights penetrated the water, providing a dim wash of light. What a mysterious and otherworldly place this was, the cold undersea at night.

No Jellybean. She was nowhere. Nowhere.

He kept swimming, eyes open in the gray-green floating nighttime, his brain calling out to her.

Nothing. Nothing.

His lungs ached and his head felt full, like his skull was about to crack. He knew he had to surface to get more air, and started to push himself up.

Just then, he saw something. A mermaid tail. Her costume! She was there! Clancy pressed on, knowing he had one shot at reaching her. Closer, closer.

Something happened. The little girl began moving through the water as if she were powered by jet fuel. He would never be able to catch her. How could she move that fast?

Clancy startled. That hadn't been Jellybean, because the little girl was right in front of him, suspended in the water, unmoving. He reached a hand out for her and missed. She began to float away.

He was down to his last seconds. He couldn't resist the urge—he had to gasp for air in a place he knew he would never find it. His mouth opened. And that's when he witnessed the impossible—a bevy of ethereal sea goddesses gathered around him, curiosity in their eyes and soft, sad smiles on their exquisite faces. So much beauty . . .

Funny how he had spent his whole life denying the possibility of mermaids, and here in the last flash of life he discovered he'd been wrong.

Suddenly he felt the water churn around him. A mermaid tail beat with force directly before him, silken hair cascading behind, the creature catching Jellybean's lifeless body in her outstretched arms. Together, they shot toward the surface.

Clancy let himself go. He felt something solid against his chest and he embraced it, as he rushed up, up, to his death.

Oh, how he had loved Evelyn. He hoped she would remember him. Always . . .

In the next instant, everything exploded—air, life, noise, light, cold—he was slammed with it. Clancy realized that he was in the ocean and it was night and over the roar of boat engines and helicopters he heard a soft whimper. He looked down. A person was tucked under his arm. A child. Jellybean. And she was crying. *She was alive! He was alive, too!*

Wait.

What?

He and Christina were suddenly lifted from the cold water. When he next opened his eyes he had no idea how much time had passed. All he knew was that Evie was there, holding Jellybean and kissing Clancy all over his face.

He tried to concentrate so he could get the words out. "Is she—?"

"Yes! You saved her life! You saved her!"

He didn't have the strength to keep his eyes open. Such strange thoughts . . .

"Clancy, can you hear me? I knew the second you went in the water . . . if you didn't come up, all the joy would disappear from my life. You and Christina are the most important things in the world to me. I love you. I love you! Do you understand what I'm saying? You are the only man I've ever loved and the only man I ever will."

He tried to wrap his mind around what had happened. Down there, down in that watery world below the surface, what had been real and what had been illusion? Which was worse—a brain without oxygen or a bowl of 'shroomer chili? Maybe the psychedelic result was much the same.

But some of it was real—the searchlights, jumping from one boat to the other, the shock of the freezing water against his flesh, the pain in his lungs, the graceful propulsion of the . . .

Uh-oh.

His eyes popped open. Clancy clutched Evie's hand and pulled her closer. He had to tell her. She needed to know. It was important that she understood they were real. He had really, truly seen the beautiful creatures, he had touched them! And if he and Christina were alive, it was because of them.

He pulled on Evie's sleeve.

"What is it, Clancy? Are you all right? Tell me."

"Mermaids," he whispered. *"Beautiful mermaids everywhere."*

Epilogue

Mr. T made his move while the flower girl wasn't paying attention, and the vanilla soft serve with rainbow sprinkles was suddenly gone. All that remained was the point of sugar cone and a sticky drip down her thumb.

"Hey! You silly dog!"

"Not again," Clancy sighed.

"Earl?"

"Mr. T this time. Do you think they meet in advance to decide whose turn it is?"

"Oh, I'm certain they do," Evie said. "I bet they have a five-year business plan, too."

"Yeah, they're brilliant like that, aren't they?"

Clancy and Evie were enjoying their stroll into town, an outing that would kill the gap between the wedding ceremony and the reception. When Rowan married Ash today she became the first Flynn of her generation to get hitched. Clancy had a hard time deciding who was more excited about that—the bride or her mother. The reception may prove to be a different story, though. His parents had agreed to sit at the same table for the catered affair, but now Frasier was running around trying to swap out seating cards.

True, Clancy and Evie could have stayed at the Safe Haven or hung out at home for an hour, but it was so beautiful outside—approaching record-breaking warm temperatures for October—that they decided to make the most of it. Winter would be coming soon enough. And besides, Charlie was visiting for the weekend and the little house was awfully cramped with three adults, two dogs, and a preschooler.

Of course, there was another reason for this stroll. Evie just didn't know it yet. If all went well, she was about to make Clancy the luckiest man on Earth.

So much had happened in the last couple months. The last time Clancy Skyped with Duncan, his brother joked that no one would have believed the events of that night on the dock if Heather Hewes hadn't sold her freelance news footage to *60 Minutes*.

Richard Wahlman had suffered another heart attack the night of the Mermaid Ball. He was fine now—well, at least his heart was fine. He left Congress and quit politics altogether, and his wife, who had filled in for him during his illness, was now a shoo-in for the midterm elections just a week away. Wahlman's former chief of staff, the one who stuck it to him, worked for the wife now. Most of the criminal charges against him had been dropped, though he was set to go to trial for influence peddling next year.

When he was still hospitalized, Richard signed over his parental rights and backed away from any custody or visitation action. He said that night on the dock taught him he didn't have what it took to be a father—the health or the mind-set. He said it was clear that Christina belonged where she was, but he wanted to create a trust fund for her education and be nearby should she ever want to get to know her biological father. So he bought a house on Martha's Vineyard.

Perhaps the oddest turn of events in Wahlman's life was his claim that his heart attack led to a near-death experience and an encounter with God. In an effort to set things right with Her, he joined an online Goddess worship community and applied for membership to the Bayberry Island Mermaid Society. They denied him by a unanimous vote, saying he was "simply too out there." They referred him to the Fairy Brigade.

Richard paid every cent in attorney fees that Clancy and Evelyn accrued in their efforts to untangle their legal issues. It had taken nearly two frustrating months, but everything was behind them now.

Or maybe everything was ahead of them.

They approached Fountain Square to enjoy the last bit of the mermaid's glory. Tomorrow, the fountain would be shut off for the winter, and her pipes drained to ward off winter damage. It was nice that Earl, Mr. T, and Christina got one last day to chase one another around the fountain.

"Are you happy, Evie?"

She stopped walking. Those sea glass green eyes of hers were puzzled. "You know I am. I tell you every day."

The dogs and the flower girl went around again.

"Do you love me?"

Evie laughed and grabbed both his cheeks. "Of course I love you. You are my first and will be my last."

Dogs and girl zoomed by again.

"I'm glad, but I have to be honest. I think something's missing."

Evie took a step back and frowned. Clancy got down on one knee and pulled two small velvet boxes out of his pocket.

"Oh, my God."

He opened the smaller of the two and held it up as an offering. "Evelyn McGuinness, will you do me the honor of being my wife? I want to share the rest of this strange and beautiful life with you."

"Yes." She laughed. "Yes! Yes! Yes!"

Clancy slipped the ring on her finger, jumped up, and took her into his arms. He kissed her hard.

They heard heavy breathing, and pulled their lips apart. Two dogs and a little girl stared up at them.

Christina put her hands on her hips. "Do you love her and want to marry her?"

"With all my heart. And I love you, too."

Clancy gave the larger box to Christina. She ran to a bench near the fountain, and pulled out the delicate silver chain and mermaid pendant. Her eyes widened as she stared at Clancy.

"This is for me?"

"Absolutely." Clancy and Evie went to sit on either side of Christina.

"Can you help me put it on?"

Clancy kissed her vanilla cheek and reached around her sticky neck, fiddling with the clasp. All of a sudden, he had the oddest feeling that someone had joined them, and he raised his head to see who it was. No one was there. Except . . . his eyes traveled upward.

She towered over them. The Great Mermaid gazed out to sea in unmoving silence, the way she'd always done and always would do.

In his own thoughts, Clancy thanked her for everything. Just in case.

Read on for a look at the first book
in Susan Donovan's Bayberry Island series,

SEA OF LOVE

Available from Signet Select.

"Is it true what they say about the mermaid statue?"

"Yeah, like, can she really hook us up with some hot guys while we're here?"

Rowan Flynn's eyelid began to twitch. She gently closed the cash drawer and smiled at her latest arrivals, grateful they couldn't read her thoughts. But holy hell—this had to be the hundredth mermaid question of the day! At this rate she'd never make it through festival week without completely losing her mind.

"And, like, where's the nearest liquor store?"

But wait . . . what if this were the opportunity she'd been waiting for, the perfect time to knock some sense into the tourists? Maybe these girls—two typical, clueless, party-hungry twentysomethings checking into her family's godforsaken, falling-down bed-and-breakfast—would be better off knowing the awful, horrible truth about the Bayberry Island mermaid legend. And love in general.

The thought made her giddy.

Rowan was prepared for this opportunity. She'd rehearsed her mermaid smackdown a thousand times. The words were locked, loaded, and ready to *zing!* from her mouth and slap these chicks right on their empty, tanned foreheads, perhaps saving them from years of heartache and delusion.

Yo! Wake up! she could say. *Of course there's no truth to the legend. Trust me—the mermaid can't bring you true love. It's a frickin' fountain carved from a lifeless, soulless hunk of bronze, sitting in a town square in the middle of a useless island stuck between Nantucket and Martha's Vineyard, where . . .*

"Uh, like, hell-*oh*-oh?"

The girls stared at Rowan. They waited for her answer with optimistic, wide eyes. She just couldn't do it. What right did she have to stomp all over their fantasies? How could she crush the romantic tendencies nature had hardwired into their feminine souls? How could she jack up their weeklong vacation?

Besides, her mother would kill her if she flipped out in front of paying guests. The Flynns relied on the B and B to keep them afloat—a predicament that was 100 percent Rowan's fault.

So she handed her guests the keys to the Tea Rose Room, put on her happy-hotelier face, and offered up the standard line of crap. "Well, as we locals like to say, there's no limit to the mermaid's magical powers—but only if you *believe.*"

"Awesome." The dark-haired woman snatched the keys from Rowan and glanced at her friend. "Because I *believe* we need to get laid this week!"

The girls laughed so hard they practically tripped over themselves getting to the grand staircase. Rowan cocked her head and watched them guffaw their way to the landing, banging their rolling suitcases against the already banged-up oak steps. For about the tenth time that day, she imagined how horrified her loony great-great-grandfather would be at the state of this place. Rutherford Flynn's mansion was once considered an architectural wonder, a symbol of the family patriarch's huge ego, legendary business acumen, enormous wallet, and enduring passion for his wife—a woman he swore was a mermaid.

"Oh! Like, ma'am, we forgot to ask. Where's our room?"

Ma'am? Rowan was only thirty, just a few years older than these girls! Since when was she a damn *ma'am*?

Oh. That's right. She'd become a *ma'am* the day she'd left the real world to become the spinster innkeeper of Bayberry Island.

"Turn right at the top of the stairs." Rowan heard the forced cheerfulness disappear from her voice. "It's the second room on the left. Enjoy your stay, ladies."

"We are so going to try!"

As the giggling and suitcase dragging continued directly overhead, Rowan propped her elbows on the old wood of the front desk and let her face fall into her hands. So she was a ma'am now, a ma'am with three check-ins arriving on the evening ferry. She was a ma'am with one clogged toilet on the third floor, twenty-two guests for breakfast tomorrow, four temporary maids who spoke as many languages, and eight hellish days until the island's annual Mermaid Festival had run its course. Oh, and one more detail: the business was twenty-seven thousand dollars in the hole for the year, losses that absolutely *had* to be made up in the coming week or bankruptcy was a distinct possibility. Which also was this ma'am's fault, thank you very much.

And every second Rowan stayed on the island playing pimp to the mermaid legend was a reminder of the lethal error she'd made while visiting her family exactly three years before. She'd dropped her guard with that fish bitch just long enough to leave her vulnerable to heartbreak, betrayal, and the theft of what little remained of the Flynn family fortune. It was hard to believe, but Rowan had been happy before then. She'd studied organizational psychology and had a career she loved, working as an executive recruiter in the higher-education field. She had a great apartment in Boston and a busy social life. So what if she hadn't found her true love? She'd been in no rush.

But she'd returned for the Mermaid Festival that year and met a B and B guest named Frederick Theissen. He was so charming, handsome, and witty that before she could say, "Hold on a jiff while I check your references," Rowan had fallen insanely in love with a complete stranger determined to whisk her away to New York. Her mother and her cronies insisted it was the legend at work and that Frederick was her destiny.

As it turned out, her charming, handsome, and witty stranger might have loved her, but he also happened to be a Wall Street con man who used her to steal what remained of her family's money. Destiny sucked.

Of course, her mother wasn't entirely to blame for her downfall. Rowan should have known better. But she still had the right to despise anything and everything related to the frickin' mermaid until the day she died.

The familiar *putt-putt* of a car engine caught her attention, and Rowan raised her head to look out the beveled glass of the heavily carved front doors. She watched the VW Bug plastered with iridescent fish scales come to a stop in the semicircle driveway. Since it was festival week, the car was decked out for maximum gawking effect, with its headlights covered in huge plastic seashells and a giant-assed mermaid tail sticking out from the trunk. Her mother got out of the car and strolled through the door.

"Hi, honey! Everything going smoothly? How many more are due on the last ferry?"

Rowan gave Mona the once-over and smiled. Like the car, her mother was in her festival finery, in her case the formal costume of the president of the Bayberry Island Mermaid Society. Mona's flowing blond wig was parted in the center and fell down her back. She wore shells on her boobs, sea glass drop earrings, and a spandex skirt of mother-of-pearl scales that hugged her hips, thighs, and legs. The skirt's hem fanned out into a mermaid flipper that provided just enough ankle room for her to walk around like Morticia Addams. Unlike Morticia, however,

Rowan's mother wore a pair of coral-embellished flip-flops.

"Hi, Ma." Rowan checked the B and B reservation list. "Two doubles and a quad—parents and two kids."

"Will you put the family in the Seahorse Suite?"

"No. I've already got a family in there. I'm putting the new arrivals in the Dolphin Suite."

Her mother approached the front desk, leaned in close, and whispered, "What's the status of the commode?"

"I'm hoping it'll get fixed before they check in."

One of Mona's eyebrows arched high, and she tapped a finger on the front desk. "You'd better do more than hope, my dear. The Safe Haven Bed-and-Breakfast has a reputation to uphold."

Rowan held her tongue. Some might argue the establishment's only reputation was that it had seen better days and was owned by the island's first family of cray-cray.

"But why worry?" Mona waved an arm around dramatically, a move that caused one of her shells to shift slightly north of decent. "The evening ferry might not even make it here. Did you hear the forecast?"

This was a rhetorical question, Rowan suspected, but she could tell by the tone of her mother's voice that the news wasn't good. "Last I heard, it was just some rain."

Mona shook her head, her blond tresses swinging. "Ten-foot swells. Wind gusts up to forty-five knots. Lightning. The coast guard's already issued a small-craft advisory. And the island council is meeting with Clancy right now to decide if they should take down the outdoor festival decorations—a public safety concern, you know. We wouldn't want that giant starfish flying around the boardwalk like back in 1995. Nearly killed that poor man from Arkansas."

"Absolutely." Rowan pretended to tidy some papers on the desk as she forced her chuckle into submission. They both knew the real public safety risk was that council members could come to blows deciding whether to undecorate for what might be just a quick-moving summer squall. She didn't pity her older brother Clancy. Tempers were known to flare up during festival week, a make-or-break seven days for anyone trying to eke out a living on this island, which was nearly everyone. And that didn't count the latest twist. A Boston developer's plans to build a swanky marina, golf course, and casino hotel had split the locals into two warring factions. About half of the island's residents preferred to keep Bayberry's quaint New England vibe. The other half wanted increased tourism revenue, even if it meant crowds, traffic, noise, and pollution. And the Flynns were at the center of the dispute, since their land sat smack dab in the middle of the mile-long cove and was essential to the development plans. Much to the dismay of every other property owner on the cove, both Mona and Frasier were listed as owners, and Mona forbade Rowan's father to sell the land. This meant that one little, middle-aged, spandex-clad mermaid was holding a major real estate developer, every other cove landowner, and half the population of the island hostage.

Rowan had come to view the conflict as a kind of civil war, and like the more historically significant one, the conflict had pitted family member against family member, neighbor against neighbor. The weapon of choice around here wasn't cannon or musket, though. It was endless squabbling, ruthless name-calling, and an occasional episode of hair pulling or tire slashing.

Rowan might not be thrilled about running from Manhattan with her life in shambles, but one thing could be said for her place of birth. It wasn't dull.

"Well, Ma, I'm sure Clancy will handle the situation with tact and diplomacy. He always does."

"That is so true." As Mona's gaze wandered off past the French doors and into the parlor, a faint smile settled on her lips. Rowan was well aware that her mother was enamored with her two grown sons—Clancy, a former Boston patrol officer who was now the island's chief of police, and Duncan, a Navy SEAL deployed somewhere in the Middle East. As the baby of the family, Rowan had grown up accepting that her mother was unabashedly proud of her two smart, handsome, and capable boys. Of course Mona had always loved Rowan, too—but *enamored*? Not so much. Exasperated was more like it, especially starting in about fifth grade, when Rowan began talking about how she couldn't wait to escape the island and start her real life.

"This *is* your real life," her mother would say. "Every day you're alive is real. And if you can't be really alive here on Bayberry Island, you'll never be really alive, no matter where you go."

God, how that used to piss Rowan off. It still did.

Mona adjusted her shell bra and returned her attention to her daughter. "I told Clancy to come over here after the meeting and help you with the storm shutters. God knows your father is useless when it comes to that sort of thing, if he cared enough to check on the house in the first place."

Rowan ignored the jab. She'd adopted a hands-off policy when it came to her parents' ongoing power struggles, including their opposing positions on the development plans. "Only a few shutters are in good enough condition to make a difference, and besides, Clancy's got more important things to do right now."

Mona didn't like that response, apparently. Her brow crinkled up. "Who's going to help you, then? Has a handsome and single handyman managed to check in without me noticing?"

"Not possible, Ma."

"It's not possible that such a man would want to visit Bayberry Island?"

"No—it's not possible you wouldn't have noticed."

"True enough." Mona giggled. "It *is* my job, you know."

Rowan's eyes got big, and all she could think was, *Dear God, not this again.* Her mother was the retired principal of the island's only school, but she'd just alluded to her other "job"—that of Mermaid Society president and keeper of all things legend related. It was a wide net that Mona and her posse used to fish around in other people's love lives.

Her mother glanced down at Rowan and put her hands on her scale-covered hips. "You look like you have something facetious to say."

"Nope. Not me, Ma. I'm totally cool with the legend. Love is a many-splendored thing . . . all you need is love . . . back that ass up and all that shit."

Mona gasped. "*Rowan Moira Flynn!*"

Just then, the *tap-tap* of quick footsteps moved through the huge formal dining room and headed toward the foyer, which was enough to divert Mona's attention.

"Imelda!"

The petite older woman clutched her chest in surprise, then cut loose with a long string of Portuguese-laced obscenities. "You're gonna give me a heart attack one day, Mona."

"I was just happy to see you."

Imelda Silva, who had once been the family's private housekeeper and was now the B and B's cook, shook her head and marched through the foyer on her way to the staircase. "I've been working for your family for twenty-five years. You and I both know you're not happy to see me. You just want me to do something for that fruity mermaid group of yours and the answer is still *não*! I'd rather fix the toilet in the Dolphin Suite! And you, Rowan." Imelda pointed an accusatory finger in her direction. "Stay out of the butter pecan ice cream. It's the topping for tomorrow's waffles."

Mona looked hurt as she watched Imelda trudge up the grand staircase. "What is *wrong* with everybody this year?" She sighed loudly. "Everywhere I turn, it's just one bad attitude after another! What happened to the joy and delight of the biggest week of the whole summer season? Why aren't people filled with excitement?"

"We're tired."

"Ha!" Mona narrowed her eyes at Rowan. "We are

the people of Bayberry Island, my dear, caretakers of the mermaid, the sea goddess of love. This week is nothing short of sacred to us, to our way of life. We have no time to be tired." She paused for dramatic effect. "Mark my words, honey. If we don't perk the hell up around here, we're completely screwed."

Also available from
USA Today bestselling author

Susan Donovan

SEA OF LOVE
A B

For years Rowa   ayberry
Island and its   ter her
investor fiancé   fortune,
Rowan reluctant   Bed-and-
Breakfast, deterr   idiculous
fanta

But when a handsome stranger arrives at the B and B the
night before the annual Mermaid Festival, Rowan's life
takes a turn for the interesting. Could it be the divine
hand of the town's patroness? Or is Rowan being set up
for another disappointment?

Available wherever books are sold or at
penguin.com

facebook.com/LoveAlwaysBooks